Aspiring Women

ASPIRING WOMEN
Short Stories by
Canadian Women
1880–1900

CANADIAN
SHORT
STORY
LIBRARY
No. 16

Lorraine McMullen
and Sandra Campbell

University of Ottawa Press

Canadian Short Story Library, Series 2
John Moss, General Editor

© University of Ottawa Press, 1993
Printed and bound in Canada
ISBN 0-7766-0367-1

Canadian Cataloguing in Publication Data
Main entry under title:
Aspiring Women: Short Stories by Canadian
Women, 1880–1900

(Canadian short story library; 16)
Includes bibliographical references.
ISBN 0-7766-0367-1

1. Short stories, Canadian (English)—Women
authors. 2. Canadian fiction (English)—Women
authors. 3. Canadian fiction (English)—19th century.
I. McMullen, Lorraine, 1926–   . II. Campbell,
Sandra. III. Series.

PS8325.A86 1993   C813'.01089287   C93-090472-9
PR9197.33W65A86 1993

 UNIVERSITÉ D'OTTAWA
UNIVERSITY OF OTTAWA

Series design concept: Miriam Bloom
Book design: Marie Tappin
Cover photo courtesy of Queen's University Archives
Kingston Photo Collection (PG-K 187A-15)

For
Barbara Van Orden Campbell
and
Anna Foley McMullen

CONTENTS

Acknowledgments

Introduction 1

Ethelwyn Wetherald 15
"How the Modern Eve Entered Eden" (1882) 19

Sara Jeannette Duncan 47
"Up the Sittee in a Pitpan" (1885) 50

Isabella Valancy Crawford 59
"Extradited" (1886) 62

Susan Frances Harrison ("Seranus") 75
"Crowded Out!" (1886) 78
"The Story of Delle Josephine Boulanger" (1886) 85

Agnes Maule Machar ("Fidelis") 99
"Parted Ways" (1891) 103

Louisa Murray 123
"Mr. Gray's Strange Story" (1892) 127

E. Pauline Johnson ("Tekahionwake") 143
"A Red Girl's Reasoning" (1893) 146

Annie Fowler Rothwell 165
"How It Looked at Home: A Story of '85" (1893) 168

Lily Dougall 185
"Thrift" (1895) 188

Maud Ogilvy 199
"A Dangerous Experiment" (1895) 201

Catherine E. Simpson Hayes 207
"An Episode at Clarke's Crossing" (1895) 210

Sarah Anne Curzon 229
"The Ill Effects of a Morning Walk" (1896) 232

Joanna Wood 241
"A Mother" (1896) 244

Margaret Marshall Saunders   253
"Poor Jersey City" (1896)   256
Ella S. Atkinson ("Madge Merton")   277
"The Widowed Stranger" (1897)   279

Jessie Kerr Lawson   287
"Love Me, Love My Dog" (1898)   290

Agnes Laut   305
"Koot and the Bob-Cat" (1903)   309

Frances Elizabeth Herring   321
"Nan: A Tale of Crossing the Plains to California
in the Rush of '49" (1913)   324

ACKNOWLEDGMENTS

The editors are grateful to the following for their advice and assistance: Paul Banfield, Phebe Chartrand, Gwen Davies, Klay Dyer, Carole Gerson, George Henderson, Duncan McDowall, Carrie MacMillan, Susan Office, Jeremy Palin, Stewart Renfrew, Shirley Spragge, David Staines, Frank Tierney, Tom Vincent, Elizabeth Waterston and Jane Watt. Marie Tremblay-Chenier, Joanne Kloeble, and Julie Sévigny-Roy efficiently assisted with administration and word processing.

Research for *Aspiring Women* was made possible by a grant from the Faculty of Arts, University of Ottawa. We wish to express our gratitude to Marcel Hamelin, Rector and former Dean of Arts; Carlos Bazan, Dean of Arts; and Jean-Louis Major, Associate Dean of Arts. Lorraine McMullen's research on Canadian women's fiction is also supported by the Social Sciences and Humanities Research Council of Canada.

We wish to thank Mrs. C.E. Humphrey, grand-niece of Isabella Valancy Crawford, for her kind co-operation in the publication of "Extradited."

Attempts have been made to trace copyright ownership of Catherine E. Simpson Hayes' and Margaret Marshall Saunders' stories.

INTRODUCTION

" Fidelis," "Garth Grafton," "Canadensis," "Hugh Airlie," "Gilbert King." The pseudonyms frequently employed by late nineteenth-century Canadian women as they penned short fiction often presented shields of masculinity or fervent patriotism that veiled the complex women behind them. Yet no nom de plume can mask the creativity of these Canadian women writers. As is the case with novels by women in nineteenth-century Canada, short fiction by women needs to be recovered and reappraised; hence, this anthology. The collection forms a companion volume to *Pioneering Women*, which covers short fiction of the early nineteenth century, and *New Women*, which anthologizes women's fiction written in the first two decades of the twentieth century.

All of the writers in this volume were aspiring women in that their careers saw them enter the world of work outside the home, whether as short story writers, editors, journalists, poets, or several or all of these. Female autonomy was a personal experience for women writers as well as something "in the air" in the latter half of the nineteenth century.

The research for *Pioneering Women* and *Aspiring Women* has clarified the extent to which the short story form evolved; stylistically, its possibilities broadened in the course of the nineteenth century. Canadian women writers used the form in artistically varied and socially subversive ways. Frequently, it was employed to express some of the realities and tensions of female gender. For example, one has only to contrast the genteel, pastoral setting and "angel in the house" ethic of many of the stories found in the Montreal periodical *Literary Garland* in the 1840s with the realistic small-town Ontario setting and the antiheroine (a larcenous, church-defrauding widow) of Ella Atkinson's 1897 story "The Widowed Stranger," to understand that both the female writer and the form itself evolved in significant ways in the course of the century.

Women writers have long been associated with the development of the country's literature. As in other literary genres, their early and continuing record of accomplishment in the short story form bears examination. Female achievements in the novel antedated those in short fiction. Frances Brooke wrote the first novel set in Canada—*The History of Emily Montague* (1769), and Julia Beckwith Hart wrote the first Canadian novel published in this country—*St. Ursula's Convent; or, The Nun of Canada* (1824). During Hart's lifetime (1796–1867), the development of the short story from the essay and the sketch was underway in the English-speaking world. Hart does not appear to have published any short fiction, although late in her career she did publish an excerpt from a novel in a New Brunswick newspaper.[1]

By the 1840s and 1850s, however, Canadian women writers in Atlantic and central Canada were taking an important role in the creation and publication of short fiction. The development of short fiction in British North America, as in England and the United States, was linked with the development of newspapers, gift books, periodicals, and story papers. With the extension of education and the expansion of literacy and leisure time came an increasing demand for reading material. Before mid-century the dime novel made its appearance in the first major development of paperback publishing: by the 1860s scores of dime novels were being imported by British North American bookstores from United States publishers.[2] As well, story papers came into being and proved immensely popular, with readerships of some American papers in the hundreds of thousands. Most were published weekly and included in each issue excerpts from novels in varying stages of serialization and three or four short stories.

Along with the explosion of popular reading material that provided an escape for middle and working classes, was an increase in the number of literary papers and periodicals. Among the most prestigious of periodicals in British North America was the *Literary Garland* (1838–1851), published in Montreal, to which Louisa Murray contributed at the beginning of her career. And later in the century, *The Week* (1883–1896), perhaps the most successful periodical, provided an outlet for the poetry and prose of Susan Frances Harrison, Ethelwyn Wetherald, and Sara Jeannette Duncan, among others. At the same time Canadian women also took advantage of the opportunities afforded by the proliferation of American papers, magazines, and literary journals.

Despite the short lives and financial travails of early Canadian periodicals, Canadian women occupied an important place as editors and writers—and as readers. As well as appearing in Canadian periodicals such as *Rose-Belford's Canadian Monthly and National Review, Dominion Illustrated,* and *The Week,* the short fiction of Lily Dougall, Ethelwyn Wetherald and Sara Jeannette Duncan can be found in the columns of prestigious and popular American magazines such as *Godey's Ladies' Book, Harper's, New England Magazine* and *Atlantic Monthly,* and British periodicals such as *Longman's, Pall Mall, Temple Bar,* and *Chambers Journal.*[3]

Many of Canada's well-known female writers had first been pioneers in another literary field—journalism. As they won legitimacy for themselves as journalists, such women established reputations that made their short fiction more marketable. Sara Jeannette Duncan won her spurs in journalism before turning to fiction with novels and stories. For pioneering journalists like Ella Atkinson, Ethelwyn Wetherald, and Duncan, short fiction offered an imaginative counterpoint to their more factual and workmanlike essays and articles. As Barbara Freeman and Marjory Lang have discussed, female journalists, although often underpaid in relation to males, could make a living in full-time positions by the late nineteenth century.[4] Poems and stories were a more perilous financial proposition. In the case of writers like Ethelwyn Wetherald and Susan Frances Harrison, one suspects that if poetry and fiction had offered financially viable careers in nineteenth-century Canada, they might have devoted themselves almost exclusively to belles-lettres. Reporting one of the most poignant moments in the history of nineteenth-century women's writing in Canada,

Susan Frances Harrison tells of Isabella Valancy Crawford's chagrin at being told by Harrison, then editor of *The Week*, that that periodical paid nothing for poetry. Fiction, however, offered more possibilities. Jessie Kerr Lawson did achieve economic independence through her fiction by writing for popular and recreational magazines and papers, including, of course, American and British periodicals.

If women like Duncan, Atkinson and Wetherald were pioneering writers of journalism in the nineteenth century, establishing a new occupational niche for their sex as they wrote society pages, penned book columns or covered the Parliament of Canada, there is also a strong documentary element to their short stories. From the earlier Susanna Moodie to Frances Elizabeth Herring at the century's end, women writers also continued to record the physical and imaginative settlement of a new country, a process begun in the sketches of Susanna Moodie and Catherine Parr Traill in the *Literary Garland* in the 1830s and 1840s.

The sketch, a forerunner of the modern short story, was a significant genre in Canada throughout the nineteenth century. Carole Gerson and Kathy Mezei describe it as "more descriptive and episodic than the essay, but less bound by plot and character development than the short story."[5] The informal, anecdotal style of the early sketch can be seen in Sara Jeannette Duncan's early journalistic writing, including her 1885 story "Up the Sittee in a Pitpan," which appears in this volume. The documentary quality of the sketch continues to the present day to characterize much Canadian writing, as Gerson and Mezei point out;[6] it is evident here in the later stories of the prairies by Kate Simpson Hayes and of early British Columbia life by Frances Elizabeth Herring—both written on the basis of first-hand experience in a frontier landscape.

Nineteenth-century historical events provide a backdrop to some of these stories. For example, in "How it Looked at Home: A Story of '85," Annie Rothwell depicts the Riel Rebellion of 1885 from the perspective of women relegated to the margins—waiting for their soldier–lovers. Also late in the century, Ella Atkinson wrote local-colour fiction redolent of the more settled life of small-town Ontario in that era. Atkinson's fiction looks back to the earlier sketch and forward to Stephen Leacock's story cycle of small-town life, *Sunshine Sketches of a Little Town* (1912). Pauline Johnson's short fiction, from a perspective of a writer marginalized by both gender and race, recounts a clash of native and white culture that played itself out in her own life. The encounter between white and aboriginal cultures underlies several of the stories in the anthology, and writers like Hayes, Herring and Johnson seem aware that both aboriginal and female cultures were subjected to the power of a white patriarchy.

One can clearly trace the gender norms and tensions of nineteenth-century British North American society in many of these women's stories. Women's economic dependence and lack of autonomy is a frequent subtext. In Frances Herring's "Nan," the female protagonist is victimized by both husband and parents. The maternal role, so valorized in Victorian society, is in some of these stories portrayed ironically. While Herring's Nan is cast off by a ruthless mother, in Joanna Wood's "The Mother," a mother's devotion to her deviant son is so profound that it results in her own death—and for no good result. In fact, women writers of the 1880s and 1890s often portrayed the complexities of women's lives in plots that saw them as under the yoke rather than on a pedestal. The dark side of women's lives as daughters, wives, and mothers is evident in stories by Herring, Harrison, Hayes and Dougall, which have as subtext sexual, social and occupational subjugation and victimization, realities in the lives of many women, be they wives, daughters, mothers, female domestics or aboriginal women.

With the advent of the concept of the "New Woman" in the Western world in the 1880s and 1890s, the interest in social, intellectual and economic autonomy found its way into Canadian short stories as well as Canadian novels. Women's burgeoning aspirations for self-expression, economic autonomy, and even the vote, were accompanied by shifts in the portrayal of female protagonists. Late nineteenth-century Canadian women writers like Sara Jeannette Duncan, Ethelwyn Wetherald, and Ella Atkinson treated traditional female stereotypes playfully or ironically. Duncan's "Up the Sittee in a Pitpan" (1885) portrays with both affection and irony the new woman on the prowl in the exotic tropics. Duncan used the name Garth Grafton to publish the piece but the male pseudonym has become an ironic wink at convention: the narrator is unmistakably female. Ethelwyn Wetherald undermines romantic female stereotypes in "How the Modern Eve Entered Eden." The widow in Atkinson's "The Widowed Stranger" subverts the stereotype of the devout widow through her very emancipated career as a confidence woman. By the 1880s, then, women writers themselves were consciously altering the women characters of literature in keeping with the changing social and political status of women.

In 1886, tongue firmly in cheek, Sara Jeannette Duncan bid adieu to the passive "heroine of old-time [fiction], drifting fast and far into oblivion" with her "golden hair, the rosebud mouth, the faintly-flushed, ethereal cheek, and the pink sea-shell that was privileged to do auricular duty in catching the never-ceasing murmur of adoration that beat about the feet of the blonde maiden." Instead she asserted that women were being presented in fiction as "intelligent agents" on "the same plane of thought and action" as male characters, and not "as a false ideal."[7] In her fiction, Duncan created women characters who functioned as "intelligent agents": witness her subtle and shrewd female narrator in "Up the Sittee in a Pitpan." Even a patriarchal male editor suspected that women writers had much of value to say about the female sex and its status. In 1893, Hector Charlesworth wrote in the *Canadian Magazine* of the "temperamental force" characteristic of Canadian womanhood. His "Canadian girl" did, however, sound suspiciously like one of Duncan's saccharine old-time heroines:

6

The Canadian girl is making sacrifices, dreaming
dreams, breaking hearts, throbbing with passion,
just as girls have been since the world began; and
when the supreme simplifier springs up—Stevenson
says that the great novelist is not he who depicts
'life as it is,' but rather one who makes a beautiful
and simple exposition of one phase of life—on the
advent of the simplifier, he will find a maidenhood
glorious enough to tempt the brush of any artist.
Perhaps the supreme simplifier whom Canada is to
produce will be a woman.[8]

As discussed in the introduction to *New Women*,
the exploration in women's writing of social issues such as
feminism, prohibition and labour activism is prominent in
the early years of the twentieth century. In *Aspiring Women*,
which takes us back to the last two decades of the nineteenth
century, we see that such concerns are already evident, if not
so conspicuous. In the late nineteenth century women were
coming to public attention as temperance activists, and the
evils of drink are evident in the plots of stories by Lily
Dougall and Frances Herring, among others. In "Nan," the
final story in this anthology, Herring interpolates into her
tale of a battered wife and a drunken husband a *cri de coeur*:

Women's rights outside that [of motherhood] are
only a need created by fallen manhood, which is
apt to run to sensuality, and so to abuse the 'weaker
vessel.' When manhood has learned self-control,
there will be no necessity for any 'protection' for
women; but, when that time arrives, the millenium
will be at our door.

Several of the writers in this volume were also
known for their contributions to the debate about women's
rights and duties. Even before Confederation, the consciousness of "the woman question" had been so current in the
country that in 1863 the *Canadian Illustrated News* published
in its humour column a satirical "List of Women's Rights
Which Have Been Sadly Overlooked." The list began: "It is

woman's right to stay at home. For what other reason did her husband marry her?" The list concluded:

> It is women's right to be content with her own garments, without encroaching on those of her husband.
> And, finally, it is woman's right to remain a woman, without endeavouring to be a man.[9]

In the face of tensions like these, many women writers addressed women's right to education and financial autonomy. In 1891, for example, Maud Ogilvy, in an article on the "Progress of Women in Montreal," called for McGill to admit women to all of its courses and suggested that working women such as teachers might do well to organize into trade unions:

> . . . I do maintain, and that most emphatically, that no hindrance should be put in the path of women who desire education in any branch whatsoever to enable them to learn a livelihood for themselves. 'Knowledge is power.' The axiom may be a hackneyed one, yet nevertheless it is true, and especially nowadays when all fields of labour are so crowded; when women, strong or weak, are perforce obliged to compete in the terrible struggle for their daily bread, it is the duty of everyone to facilitate their efforts to help themselves.
> . . . If women who teach would only form trades unions and keep together in the business-like manner in which workingmen do, much might be effected.[10]

Sarah Anne Curzon, for her part, espoused maternal feminism in journalism and in fiction. As Secretary of the Women's Enfranchisement Association of Canada, she crisply told readers of the *Dominion Illustrated* in an 1890 letter, "I trust that the time is not far distant when our men, laying aside their selfishness, jealousy and prejudice, may say to woman, 'Come over and help us, not only in making pure and righteous homes, but in making our nation.'"[11] Curzon's witty play for the satirical magazine Grip, "The Sweet Girl Graduate" (1882), made it clear that she believed any notion of inherent female intellectual inferiority to be laughable. In "The Ill Effects of a Morning Walk," Curzon examines some of the stifling socialization within the world of women, setting her story in a fashionable girls' school whose regimen foreshortens the horizon of young girls. Mrs. Grundy wins a short-term victory, but the adventurous young schoolmistress wins a moral victory and the hearts of her former charges. Of course there were women writers who tended to be more conservative on women's issues. Nevertheless, in late nineteenth-century women's fiction, as in the era itself, currents of social change were evident and many women aspired to influence in a wider sphere than the domestic.

Research for this volume has also brought to light the importance of sorority and collegiality to female writers in Canada, links particularly important to writers marginalized by both gender and market. Ethelwyn Wetherald published supportive and analytical appraisals of Louisa Murray, Agnes Maule Machar, Annie Rothwell and Susan Frances Harrison in *The Week* in the 1890s. As a journalist, Ella Atkinson was praised for her supportiveness to other women journalists in the profession. Louisa Murray, despite her relative isolation on Wolfe Island, became acquainted with Agnes Maule Machar in nearby Kingston. Undoubtedly such links were crucial at a time and place where female gender and literary occupation were each so restrictive in their possibilities.

Some interesting correspondences emerge in these stories. For example, women's writing in the nineteenth century often uses the prima donna as an image of women's creativity and autonomy. Sometimes the image of the woman singer—of woman and song—is fascinatingly multiedged. The musical woman in Maud Ogilvy's "A Dangerous Experiment" is a domestic murderer, whereas the image of the bird singing over the frozen body of a dead mother in Joanna Wood's "The Mother" is an ironic emblem of the debasement of the maternal ideal by poverty, crime and ignorance.

If the women writers in this anthology wrote from a distinctively female perspective, they also shared some of the fictional and social concerns of their male contemporaries. Nature and the opening of the West preoccupied Agnes Laut and Frances Herring as much as Gilbert Parker or Ralph Connor. Ella Atkinson and Adeline Teskey (see *New Women*) were as fascinated with the small town as was Stephen Leacock. The later nineteenth century's increasing interest in spiritual phenomena such as clairvoyance, automatic writing, telepathy, and apparitions, found expression in fiction by both men and women. For those who had lost their faith in traditional Christianity such phenomena offered a hope for immortality, the possibility of convincing themselves of human survival after death. For others, séances attempting to communicate with the dead were motivated by the search for consolation through communication with lost loved ones. Lily Dougall, long a member of the Society for Psychical Research, gives an original twist to the question of materialization of spirits in a story of a young woman who is prevented from attachment to another man by a lover who was struck down by a stroke years earlier at her rejection of him and has remained in a vegetative state since that time; since then he materializes beside her whenever a man displays affection for her.[12] In this volume Maud Ogilvy's "A Dangerous Experiment" reveals a concern with spiritualism and hypnotism, and the dangers inherent in experimenting with the unknown.

The richness of this female short story world is striking. Working on *Aspiring Women* made us aware of a various and little-examined body of women's work, just as research for *New Women* made us aware that the literary world of 1900 to 1920 was not the interregnum in women's writings that some literary historians have declared it to be, solely on the basis of the seeming paucity or mediocrity of the work by the male writers of the period.[13]

While much of the short fiction by women anthologized here has been unretrieved for decades, some had originally reached a large audience, much of it female. Women often published in the leading popular periodicals of the day. For example Lily Dougall published "Thrift" in the leading American magazine *Atlantic Monthly* and Pauline Johnson's "A Red Girl's Reasoning" won the *Dominion Illustrated* (Montreal) fiction prize in 1892. Yet the publication history and the ephemeral reputations of most of these writers mirrors the restrictions of gender experienced by many of the women in their own lives in nineteenth-century Canada. In the two decades covered by the stories of *Aspiring Women*, women were just winning acceptance at the universities as students, but women had not yet joined professorial ranks. Agnes Maule Machar, the acknowledged equal of intellectuals William Douw Lighthall and William Dawson Le Sueur, never joined these male confreres in the Royal Society of Canada, barred from that honour by her sex. Kate Simpson Hayes, unlike her journalist colleague and lover Nicholas Flood Davin, is largely forgotten today. Agnes Laut's wilderness stories have never received the attention given to those of Charles G.D. Roberts or Ernest Thompson Seton, though their themes are similar, and Laut enjoyed a large North American following for her writings at the turn of the century. Ethelwyn Wetherald is arguably one of the most underrated writers of the turn of the century, given her skilled and socially conscious short fiction as well as her fine poetry. To recover the short fiction of Canadian women of the later nineteenth century is to discover an intrepid and impressive group of pioneers—pioneers in gender, in genre, and in time, who were aspirants to wider fictional and worldly horizons.

Notes

1 Julia Beckwith Hart, "The Three Courtships of Chas. McDonald," in *New Brunswick Reporter and Fredericton Advertiser*, 29 December 1847 to 26 January 1848.

2 For a discussion of the dime novel and Canadian book publishing, see George Parker, *The Beginnings of the Book Trade in Canada* (Toronto: University of Toronto Press, 1985), 131.

3 See James Doyle, "Canadian Women Writers and the American Literary Milieu of the 1890s," in *Re(Dis)covering Our Foremothers: Nineteenth-Century Canadian Women Writers*, ed. Lorraine McMullen (Ottawa: University of Ottawa Press, 1990), 30–36.

4 See Barbara Freeman, *Kit's Kingdom: The Journalism of Kathleen Blake Coleman* (Ottawa: Carleton, 1989) and Marjory Lang, "Separate Entrances: The First Generation of Canadian Women Journalists," in *Re(Dis)covering Our Foremothers: Nineteenth-Century Canadian Women Writers*, ed. Lorraine McMullen (Ottawa: University of Ottawa Press, 1989), 77–90.

5 Carole Gerson and Kathy Mezei, *The Prose of Life: Sketches from Victorian Canada* (Toronto: ECW Press, 1981), 1.

6 See the excellent introduction to Gerson and Mezei, *The Prose of Life*, 1–15.

7 Sara Jeannette Duncan, "Saunterings," in *The Week*, 28 October 1886, 771–772.

8 Hector Charlesworth, "The Canadian Girl: An Appreciative Medley," in *Canadian Magazine* I, 1893, 186–193.

9 "List of 'Woman's Rights' Which Have Been Sadly Overlooked," in *Canadian Illustrated News* (Hamilton), 25 July 1863, 128.

10 Maud Ogilvy, "Progress of Women in Montreal," in *Wives and Daughters* (London, Ontario), January 1891, 7.

11 Sarah Anne Curzon, "Woman's Domain" [Letter to the Editor], in *Dominion Illustrated*, 21 June 1890, 398.

12 Lily Dougall, "The Soul of a Man," in *A Dozen Ways of Love* (London: Adam and Charles Black, 1897), 251–292.

13 By 1899 a number of women writers were winning some journalistic attention, as, for example, in Thomas O'Hagan's "Some Canadian Women Writers" in *Catholic World*, vol. 63, 1899, 779.

Ethelyn Wetherald (1857–1940)

HOW THE MODERN EVE ENTERED EDEN (1882)

A major figure in the Canadian journalistic and literary
scene of the late nineteenth century, Ethelwyn Wetherald
was known for the acuity and wit of her newspaper columns,
her astute critical judgment, her editorial skills, and most
of all, her poetry. Less known was her short fiction, which
appeared in American and Canadian publications, including
New England Magazine, *Rose-Belford's Canadian Monthly and
National Review*, *The Week*, the *Globe* (Toronto), *Wives and
Daughters*, *Outlook* (New York), *Smart Set*, *Puck*, and the
Free Press (Detroit).

  The sixth of eleven children of Quaker parents
Jemima Harris Balls and William Wetherald, Agnes
Ethelwyn was born on 26 April 1857 at Rockwood, near
Guelph, Ontario, where her father operated a boarding
school. She was seven when, in September 1864, her father
left Rockwood to become superintendent of Haverford
College, a Quaker institution near Philadelphia. William
Wetherald stayed at Haverford only a few years before
resigning to return to Ontario, where he bought and ran a
fruit and dairy farm at Fenwick in the Niagara peninsula. He
became an ordained minister of the Society of Friends and
travelled extensively in his ministry. Ethelwyn was first
educated at home, then attended the Friends' Boarding
School at Union Springs, New York, and later Pickering
College, Ontario.

  Like other Canadian women writers of the nineteenth century (such as the earlier Rosanna Leprohon and
May Agnes Fleming), Wetherald began her writing career
while still a schoolgirl. She was seventeen when her first
poem was accepted by *St. Nicholas*, a New York children's
magazine. By the early 1880s she was publishing in a variety
of American and Canadian publications. In 1886, she began

to write a regular column, choosing as pen name her paternal grandmother's name, Isabel Thistlethwaite, which she shortened to "Bel Thistlethwaite." She continued to live at her Fenwick home and submitted her columns from there. She also still wrote for other periodicals. Wetherald moved a few years later to London, Ontario, as chief editorial writer for the London *Advertiser* and assistant editor of the new monthly *Wives and Daughters*, a paper directed to a female audience. Three years later, when in 1893 *Wives and Daughters* ceased publication, Wetherald returned to Fenwick and to free-lance writing from her home, as she had done earlier.

In 1895–96 Wetherald once again left Fenwick, this time to spend most of the winter in Philadelphia as assistant to Francis Bellamy, literary editor of the *Ladies' Home Journal*. Then she received an offer from Forrest Morgan in Philadelphia, an editor of *The World's Best Literature*, who was working on the thirtieth and final volume, to act as his assistant. On completion of this project, Morgan offered her a job as "a first-class proof reader at a larger salary." Wetherald refused and once again returned to the family home to continue her writing from there. To poet Wilfred Campbell, she wrote on 10 February 1896, "I shall be rather glad to go back to Fenwick and the sweet realities of life away from the bubbles and baubles of journalism." Wetherald continued to publish poems, articles, reviews, and sketches in a wide range of publications. Editor and writer E.W. Thomson appears to have been her closest friend as well as her mentor.

Wetherald's writing career continued until a few years before her death in 1940. According to Clara Bernhardt, she maintained her interest in Canada's literary scene, writing to Clara Bernhardt only a week before her death, "Tell me about the younger poets with whom you feel in closest affinity. I am always interested." Only a few weeks earlier she had hosted a garden party for the Canadian Authors' Association.

Wetherald's short fiction is scattered throughout a variety of journals and papers. "How the Modern Eve Entered Eden" is an earlier story, published before she left Fenwick for the Toronto *Globe*. Wetherald's title somewhat belies its focus, since the main character is male and Eva enters only in the latter half of the story. The story begins rather slowly, but increases tempo half way through, and the introduction of Eva adds wit and humour. Far from the usual romantic heroine, Eva first appears awkwardly attempting to ride a heavy farm horse: "She herself, attired in a blue calico dress and wide straw hat, was rather round faced and chubby. Philip found nothing romantic, but a good deal that was comical, in the scene, as the young girl, swaying and clinging in a frightened manner to the saddle, came along." As the narrator remarks, "If she had been a stately and beautiful damsel, as lithe and supple as the whip she bore, and enthroned on a fleet and graceful steed, Philip Kale, as a young man who knew much more of novels than of real life, would easily have supposed that that was just what might have been expected." The autobiographical elements are obvious. Like Eva, Wetherald had first learned to ride while visiting cousins on a farm in the west, and one can imagine her experiences being similar to young Eva's. The view of the ameliorating effects of country life expressed in the story was heartfelt and remained throughout Wetherald's life. Although her career led her to accept positions in Toronto and London, Ontario, and later in Philadelphia and New York, and she lived for a period in St. Paul, Minnesota, Wetherald always returned to the family farm at Fenwick, Ontario. Her Quaker upbringing and education remained very much a part of her, influencing her ideology and her writing, although not generally as overtly as in this story, where the Quaker philosophy is so strongly endorsed through the gentle and sweet Ruth Pinkney and her effect on her misanthropic nephew.

~

Suggested Reading:

Bernhardt, Clara. "Ethelwyn Wetherald." In *Saturday Night* (13 April 1940):11.

Moyles, R.G. "Ethelwyn Wetherald: An Early, Popular, and Prolific Poet." In *Canadian Children's Literature* 59 (1990):6–16.

Wetherald, Ethelwyn. "A Modern Lear." In *New England Magazine* (6 July 1892):603–606.

_____. "A Bit of Country Life." In *The Week* (1 February 1889):138.

_____. *Lyrics and Sonnets.* Toronto: Thomas Nelson and Sons, 1931.

HOW THE MODERN EVE ENTERED EDEN

Ethelwyn Wetherald

P hilip Kale's occupation was that of a clerk in a city drug store; his appearance was dark, slight and prepossessing; his age twenty-three; his manner reserved to the verge of taciturnity; his views of religion and life alike tinged with unhealthy morbidness, the consequence of an hereditary predisposition to dyspepsia. He believed devoutly in the theory that it was a most unfortunate thing to be alive, but that being alive nothing remained but to make the best of it; and he strove to adhere strictly to his idea of the highest plane of duty, which consisted, chiefly, in never complaining—that was a weakness; never mingling in society—that was a folly; and in throwing his whole heart into his work—that was a necessity if life was to be made endurable. Negative rules of conduct are comparatively easy to follow, but the positive decree that one shall throw one's heart into one's work—and keep it there—is difficult to enforce. Philip found it so, at any rate, and he was struck with the added and melancholy fact that his occupation was one in which enthusiasm was not required, and absorbing interest little needed. It wanted a certain kind and amount of knowledge, with carefulness and despatch, but in return it refused to absorb his empty fears and perplexities, his ever-deepening depression of spirit. He began to think very little of himself and a great deal *about* himself, and to feel sorry for every one else. If they were unfortunate or miserable, he pitied them, because, poor fellows, they were as badly off as he was; and if they were light-hearted and gay, because they were unconscious of the misery that was really their portion. With the first heats of summer came a time when he lost his appetite, and when the familiar sights and sounds of the city became exquisitely painful to him. His dogged resolution kept him up, but it could not prevent him from turning weak and pallid, nor keep his hands from trembling. His employer noticed it.

'Why, Kale!' he exclaimed, one morning, taking the young man by the shoulder, 'you're sick.'

'A little that way,' said Philip, with a wan smile; 'It's the warm weather, I suppose.'

'Better take a holiday of a week or two. A run up in the country will do you good.'

Philip's first feeling was one of blankness. His home and friends were in the city. He knew no one outside of it. But stay—there was his Aunt Ruth, a widowed sister of his father's, whom he had once visited long years before; he could go and see her. He sent a telegram announcing his coming without delay, and prepared for departure with pleasanter emotions than he had ever expected to experience again. He reproached himself for not having yet outgrown the boyishness of being elated at the idea of change.

Mrs. Ruth Pinkney lived in solitary contentment, on a small place of two or three acres, several miles from the nearest railway station. Her estate was not large enough to be considered a farm, but it might properly be called a garden, as within its borders grew almost every variety of vegetable and fruit with which its owner was acquainted. She was also blest with a faithful man-servant and hand-maiden, who performed the heaviest of the outdoor and household labour. A row of stately trees near the fence screened the quaint, old-fashioned house from the gaze of passers-by, without depriving it of its daily portion of sunshine. The square, grassy front yard was cut into halves by a straight

ETHELYN WETHERALD

gravel walk, on either side of which bloomed flowers as sweet and odd and unworldly as their mistress.

When the stage containing her nephew stopped at the gate, Mrs. Pinkney, or rather Ruth Pinkney, as she would best like to be called—for she is a Quakeress—smoothed her thin locks of grey hair and the voluminous folds of her grey dress, neither of which required smoothing in the slightest degree, and, clasping her hands in a delicate, old-fashioned way at her waist, went down to meet her young kinsman with a sweet smile of welcome. She spoke little until the stage had rattled away again, and then, reaching up her two hands to his shoulders, she softly said:

'Dear boy, I am rejoiced to see thee once more. It was very good of thee to think of paying thy old aunt a visit.'

It is pleasant to be praised for doing what we please, so Philip Kale thought as he kissed the lovely old face uplifted to his, and expressed his pleasure at seeing it again.

'But how poorly thee is looking,' continued his aunt, glancing at him keenly over her spectacles. 'Thee has done wisely to come into the pure country air. We shall see what fresh eggs and new milk will do for thee; we have them both in abundance.'

'Oh, dear Aunt,' said Philip, seating himself on the pleasant porch beside her, 'you have a very squeamish guest on your hands. I'm afraid I can't digest your nice eggs and milk. I'd like to, but my stomach is very weak.'

'Just like thy father,' murmured Ruth Pinkney. 'I see thee favours him in many ways. But he used to say that no one could cook for him but sister Ruth; so if it is thy stomach that is disordered, I'll engage to send thee back in improved health at the end of thy stay.'

Philip gave a trustful sigh of relief, and his hostess rose to show him to his room. It was not very large, but it had three windows; the walls were white-washed, and the floor covered with a sober-hued rag carpet. There were a great many green and climbing plants growing near the light. A single picture relieved the wall, representing broad-hipped maidens with their rustic swains attendant upon a flock of fine looking sheep. As a work of art it was not satisfactory, but it was in sweet and peaceful 'unity,' as Ruth Pinkney would have expressed it, with the general effect of the room. Beneath Philip's armour of defence, his hard and worldly exterior, there beat a sensitive heart, easily impressed by outside influences; and it yielded readily to the brooding spirit of peace that hovered almost in visible form over his aunt's abode. It gladdened him to think that, sick and unrestful and life-weary as he was, he could yet enter into blessed communion with the deep unworldliness of his surroundings. Looking from his western window he could see the same gnarled old pear trees and rows of gooseberry bushes that had delighted his boyish heart years before. The familiar scene made him almost willing to believe that he was a boy again, instead of a man, grown old, not with years, but with cares and doubts, and a deepening despondency. All his old troubles seemed to resolve themselves into a dark, distant cloud, and to float away out of sight, leaving his sky blue and serenely beautiful. The veriest trifles afforded him pleasure. He was even grateful that his slippers were not gaudy carpet ones, and that they did not squeak.

Philip spent the days of his vacation in the way that best suited him. He went to bed and rose early; he dug in the garden till his strength gave out, and then read Whittier to his aunt in the shady front porch, while she shelled peas for dinner; he picked berries in the same little tin pail in which he had picked them on his previous visit, and ran to empty it in the big pan under the apple tree, with almost the same light step. His out-door labours, combined with Ruth Pinkney's unapproachable cookery, gave him a slight but increasing appetite. He learned how to 'can' fruit, to make the best soups, and the lightest Graham gems, and he envied women their inalienable right to practise and perfect the culinary art. As a housemaid he was not beyond reproach. On one occasion, when he had been entrusted with the delicate task of brushing off the pantry shelves, he whisked down and broke a china mug, with the words, 'A Gift,' on it in gilt letters. He carried the fragments with a rueful countenance to his hostess, and she surveyed them with an air of mock severity and with a deeply-drawn sigh.

'Thee is a reckless youth, nephew Philip,' said she, 'I fear I shall have to give thee an eldering.'

'An eldering, Aunt Ruth? Do you mean to chastise me with a branch of elder bush?'

'No, no, foolish boy! Whenever the giddy young people of our society misbehave themselves, the elders in the meeting are constrained to admonish them. That is what some among us call an 'eldering.'

Philip saw small signs of giddiness among the Quaker youth of the neighbourhood when he and his aunt went to 'Fourth day' meeting; yet neither young nor old had an air of dispirited solemnity. It appeared an odd thing to him to meet for worship on a weekday morning, and the deep hush that fell upon the assembly seemed to offer him special opportunities for studying the quaint physiognomies of some of the Friends who sat facing the meeting, and to meditate upon this peculiar form of religious service.

'I don't like this method of dividing off the men and women into separate companies,' he said to himself. 'It is too forcibly a reminder of that text about the sheep being on one side and the goats on the other. How still every one is! Silence is golden, and I should think it might easily become as heavy and chilling and blunt as *any* kind of metal. I wonder what being 'moved to speak' really means. Aunt Ruth talks of it as if it were some heavenly injunction laid upon the soul of the speaker, which must be instantly obeyed; but I suspect it is oftener the prompting of duty which must come into the heart of every practised preacher to do his part toward keeping up the interest of the meeting. Yet nobody looks in the least anxious or responsible, and that does not accord with my theory.' Then his mind wandered to the dress of the women. 'I like those soft, grey patternless shawls, with the three folds at the back of the neck, but I can't admire the bonnets. Those silk crinkles in the crown are very unseemly, to say the least. What a grand face and figure that woman sitting at the head of the meeting has!

She is immeasurably more striking and impressive than a score of stylish girls, with their fashionable gew gaws and gibberish.'

At this moment the woman who had won his admiration untied her bonnet with trembling fingers, and, falling upon her knees, gave utterance to strong and fervent supplication. The high intense voice praying that 'our hearts may be purified from every vain and wayward thought, and made fit for the indwelling of the Holy Spirit,' smote upon Philip as if it had been a personal rebuke. He had risen with rest of the congregation, and when he sat down again, he felt as if her prayer had been answered. The service made a more forcible impression upon his mind from the fact that sounds reached them through the open door of mowers sharpening their scythes, and occasionally of a passing lumber waggon. The deep religiousness of everyday life came over him as it had never done before.

He talked this over with Ruth Pinkney on their way home. It was so easy to talk with her; and the sympathetic old lady—who, like most old people, liked to be confided in by her youngers, just as most young people liked to be asked for opinions by their elders—felt more drawn towards him than ever. When they reached home he lay down on the chintz-covered lounge, and Ruth Pinkney brought a pillow for him as downy and white as a summer cloud, and arranged the shutters, with a view to letting in the most air with the least light. Philip thought his Aunt Ruth almost an ideal of womanhood, and felt that it would be forever impossible for him to admire a dress on any female form whatever that was not grey in colour, and whose skirt was not of generous amplitude, and made precisely the same behind that it was before. She came and sat down beside him, and he twitched a fold of her gown between his nervous fingers.

'Oh, dear Aunt,' he said, 'I wish I could be still, and happy, and good, like you.'

The Quakeress mused much upon this saying, and the young man who had made it, as she laid the table for dinner.

'I feel a call to do something for him,' she murmured to herself, 'but I can't see my way clear yet. Dear boy! my heart feels greatly tendered towards him.'

Not many days after, Philip went back to his work, strengthened and refreshed by the visit, but more discontented with his city life than ever. His Aunt mourned for him, and Thos. Shaw, the serving man, and Charlotte Acres, the serving woman, saw him depart with real regret. He seemed to belong to them, and to the place, yet doomed to perpetual exile. Early in the succeeding winter Ruth Pinkney was stricken down with a sickness from which she never recovered. Philip was deeply grieved by the tidings, and begged her to let him know should she become worse. She continued in much the same condition until spring, when she suddenly and peacefully died. Her nephew had abundant proof that she had not forgotten him, for in her will, along with numerous bequests to surviving relatives, and her faithful servants, she bequeathed to him her house, with all that it contained, and the land surrounding it. Ruth Pinkney had 'seen her way clear' at the last.

It was not a dazzling fortune, but if anything could have consoled Philip Kale for the loss of his best friend, it was the fact of his new possessions. He threw up his situation—it was hardly a position—in the city, and came down to it at once. His sorrow was temporarily quenched by the joy and pride of ownership. He would live for himself, and by himself, and in precisely the way that best suited himself. He said, with an exultant throb of satisfaction, that he could not afford to keep help, and that the out-door and in-door work he would do would be light labour enough, even for a sick man. Thomas and Charlotte had long contemplated a matrimonial union, and, in accordance with their misstress's wishes, were united shortly after her death. They were to be Philip's nearest neighbours, and Charlotte was to come over once a week and do his washing and ironing and give the house a thorough sweeping. The young man felt perfectly equal to every other department of household labour, and his brain teemed with new experiments in hygienic cookery, and plans for living in luxury and gaining health and strength at the nominal expense of five cents per meal. It was late in March when he took possession of his new property—a time of year when the pleasantest of country places looks forlorn; but he gloried in the fact that it was all his own, and walked untiringly over almost every foot of it, making mental arrangements for Spring work. When he entered the house he walked slower and felt graver. Everything was eloquent of the loving and lovely woman who had departed from the place forever. His eyes grew moist, and he hung his head at thought of his joyous forgetfulness of the great loss which had brought him this great gain. As he opened the door into what had been his Aunt's room, he saw the dear old grey dress hanging up on the wall, and an uncontrollable impulse made him lay his face in the folds for a moment. Then he came softly out and closed the door behind him.

The next month was a very busy one for the young master of, what was known in the neighbourhood as, the Pinkney place. He did not work much, but he thought and planned a great deal. He had a passion for flowers as great as his ignorance concerning their cultivation; hence the long hours he spent in the study of horticultural monthlies and floral guides. He made a map of the house and grounds, with the exact location and name of every vegetable bed, every berry bush, every climbing plant, and every different flower that had been, or should be, marked thereon. Thomas had already made the hot beds, and promised his aid and experience at transplanting time. He puzzled long over an empty lot at the back of the house, which his Aunt had been in the habit of loaning to a neighbour every summer for the pasturage of his cow, for which she received a small money consideration. It was out of the question for the young farmer to allow any portion of his property to be let out to a stranger, and he finally resolved to plant it with fruit trees. To be sure, there was a prospect of more apples and pears on the trees now standing than he could possibly use, but there were plenty of ways—remunerative ones, too,—in which to dispose of surplus fruit. Besides, he wanted to do something on a grand scale by way of celebrating his release from the drudgery he despised, and the consecration of his powers to what he was fond of calling, with little expense of originality, the noblest employment of man. He forgot his dyspeptic fears and his once ever-present dread of the morrow—forgot, or laughed at them. The sunshine and the soft airs that visited his abode seemed a part of his good fortune, and he never wearied of meditating upon and rejoicing in his riches. How delightful it was to leave his books and his papers scattered over the table at night, with the consciousness that they would remain in precisely the same position till the next evening, without the interference of some vain housemaid, who would most probably indulge the horrible propensity of her class in doing what she imagined was 'putting things to rights.' He had little time or need for cooking. There were vegetables and a great deal of canned fruit in the cellar; tea, butter and sugar he never used; sometimes he purchased a few scraps of meat from a passing butcher and made an appetizing stew; but the supply of bread never troubled him; his first batch turned out so hard that it bid fair to last him his natural life.

With the improvement in his health there came a sturdy happiness to the mind of Philip Kale. He had no longing for society; he had had over much of it of an uncongenial sort all his life. To cut loose from the meaningless and artificial restrictions of the multitude, to come close to the heart of nature, and live for her improvement and for his own— this was liberty, this was freedom, this was the elixir of life! Here was his world, his garden of Eden; and he was the first man. He had not yet dreamed of the possibility of an Eve, though sometimes the remembrance of the grey gown led him to imagine that his life was not quite rounded, not yet complete. This fancy, however, did not intrude itself very often, as he had no time to indulge fancies of any kind. He was such a very busy young man. Thomas was hired, of course, to do most of the work, but then it was always necessary for Philip to stand near and see exactly how it was done, and why it was done so, and what would be the results if it were done otherwise. He laughed over his own mistakes as he had never laughed at anything in his life before. He ceased to walk, at least out of doors, and fell into a habit of light-hearted and light-footed running. It was a truthful and rhythmic remark of Mrs. Kale's that her sickly son, if he was able to walk, would want to run or fly, and if he was not able to walk, would be ready to lay down and die. He had been resigned to the thought of death most of the time that he could remember, but now he was more than resigned to life. He sported—no other word will express the vanity he felt in his strange attire—a suit of coarse clothes much too large for him, and a broad straw hat, neither of which could conceal the handsome lines of his comely face and slight figure. When the novelty of his situation failed a little, and all his plans were in good working order, he lapsed into a quieter contentment. Then it was that he re-arranged all the books in the tall old bookcase, and read, just before he retired, some passages that Ruth Pinkney had marked in her favourite authors. He felt very grateful, very glad. He longed at intervals to do good to others, but he still took pleasure in saying to himself that he was doing more good to others by keeping away from them than he could do in any other way. This was selfish, but he seemed to be continually steeped in an ecstatic consciousness of self. He revelled in the growing and greening grass, in the lengthening and brightening days, in the blissful chorus of the birds, singing the return of Spring to this earthly paradise. He spent balmy May afternoons in the hammock under one of the trees near the road, watching a pair of birds build their nest on a branch near by.

One day his attention was arrested by an object which proved ever more interesting than nest-building. This was a young lady on horseback, riding by. If she had been a stately and beautiful damsel, as lithe and supple as the whip she bore, and enthroned on a fleet and graceful steed, Philip Kale, as a young man who knew much more of novels than of real life, would easily have supposed that that was just what might have been expected. But this youthful *equestrienne*

Ethelyn Wetherald

was of an entirely different type. She was evidently unaccustomed to the saddle; the animal she rode was a heavy farm horse, and she herself, attired in a blue calico dress and wide straw hat, was rather round faced and chubby. Philip found nothing romantic, but a good deal that was comical, in the scene, as the young girl, swaying and clinging in a frightened manner to the saddle, came along, accompanied by a sturdy boy, presumably her brother, who rode beside her, barebacked. Philip was glad that the thick intermingling branches of the trees allowed him to see and hear without danger of detection. At a few yards from his gate the young lady slipped to the ground, saying, in a despairing tone—

'It's no use trying any more. I never *can* learn to ride!'

'That's a pity,' said the boy, hopefully.

She buried her face in the horse's mane. The sympathetic brute immediately lapsed upon three legs, and hung his head lower than ever. Then a sudden infusion of resolution came over her.

'But I *will* learn!' she cried.

'That's the right way to talk,' said her companion. 'It must be mighty mean, the first time you're on a horse. I can't remember when I was.'

'I know I'm old and stiff,' continued the courageous voice, 'but if my ambition is not greater than my stupidity, then I'll give up!' She thought over what she said a moment, and, laughingly, added, 'Highly probable.'

'I've heard it said that people ought to learn without a saddle—nothing but a strap and a blanket—but you'd turn a sideways somerset right away.' Then, encouragingly: 'I believe you'd do first rate if you weren't scared.'

'But I can't help being scared,' said the girl. 'All the horse's muscles and sinews, and fibres and things, keep moving in such an awful way.'

'And his legs, too!' added the youth, soberly, and then he burst into a roar of laughter.

'Oh, don't laugh, Joe; someone will hear you, and fancy what a picture we make. Who lives in that house since Mrs. Pinkney died?'

'Nobody worth mentioning,' returned Joe, with a boy's outspoken contempt for one whose acquaintance he found it impossible to make. 'Some mighty stuck-up acting fellow from the city. Well, shall we get on?'

'I suppose so; but you'll have to help *me* to mount first.'

This was rather a difficult task, but with a great many 'Yo heaves,' and strenuous efforts on the part of Joe, the young lady was fairly mounted at last.

'Good gracious, girl,' he muttered, as he arranged the blue drapery, 'you *are* a lift! I should think you must weigh as much as seventy-five stone.'

'Do you know the weight of a stone?' inquired his sister, severely.

'N—no, not exactly; but, of course, I don't mean very big stones. Just middling-sized ones.'

They rode off, and the eavesdropper rose up, feeling much refreshed. He was interested in the pretty country girl who had candour enough to confess her fright, and pluck enough to resolve upon overcoming it. He had no one to talk with or question about her, as Mr. and Mrs. Shaw had departed, leaving with him minute directions for the care of a house and garden. He walked up and down the veranda a few times, laughing at the recollection of her comical way of riding, and then he went in and picked up a favourite book, and forgot all about her.

But the next afternoon she passed again, this time alone, and on succeeding days she did not fail to make her appearance. Philip soon knew what hour to expect her, and he was generally in his hammock at that time. Naturally he wished to see if she made any improvement in the equestrian art, and the results of his daily observation were, that she did not so much gain in skill as lose in fear, and that her peculiar style of horsemanship, though seemingly capable of promoting her health and pleasure, was not of a kind to win, even under the most favourable circumstances, the plaudits of the crowd. Yet, with all her imperfections, he did not cease to watch her. The drooping hat brim nearly concealed

ETHELYN WETHERALD

her face, but on one occasion it was clearly revealed to him. This was when her hat, loosely tied with a blue ribbon, was blown from her head. Philip longed to rush after it, but he restrained himself, and she dismounted and went after it herself. She had pale brown hair, and her face was fresh and blonde, and pretty. He wished many times during the remainder of the day that he had gone and picked up her hat; then, next day, she would be sure to favour him with a slight glance of recognition, and he might be emboldened to make a bow. In the present monotony of his life, such an incident would assume the proportions of an adventure. Her preference for riding past his house was easily explained; the road near which it stood was little more than a lane, and scarcely ever used save by pedestrians. She was the only lady he had seen since coming into the country, and he grew, unconsciously, to look forward to his brief daily glimpses of her. In the character of Adam in Paradise, he felt a peculiar fitness in calling her Eve; and he appreciated the interested glances which she occasionally threw over into the garden of Eden, and her probable wondering at the non-appearance of its master. Philip was unwilling to take fate in his own hands, but how he wished that some favouring wind of fortune would—blow her hat off again. He felt assured that she had never seen him. Once he had not started for the hammock until she was in sight, but her head was turned the other way. One Saturday it rained, so he did not see her, and on Sunday he could not expect to, but she was continually present in his thoughts. The youthful hermit, who had gloried in his solitude, was ashamed of himself for longing to see the one strange face that had invaded it.

Early the next morning Charlotte Shaw came to wash, and Philip Kale sat out on the back porch and talked with her. He found it very pleasant to be able to talk once a week—even if it were solely upon trivial topics. He began to realize that the true aim of conversation was not to gain or impart knowledge, but for sympathy, inspiration, the sense of companionship, and the exercise of one's mental and vocal powers. He blushed to think that he, who had fallen to sleep the night before over a favourite volume of poems, was now absorbing with eager interest the empty gossip of the neighbourhood. With assumed indifference he inquired the name of the heavy young lady who so frequently rode on horseback.

'You must mean Miss Harding. They call her Eve (Philip started), but I believe her right name is Eva. I don't think she is heavy, Mr. Kale; leastways, she walks across a room just like a kitten, and carries herself so prettily. She used to think the world and all of your Aunt, and she was over here a few days before she died. My! but didn't Mrs. Pinkney sound your praises to her, though.' Philip blushed. 'On her way out she stopped in at the kitchen, and says she, "Is the young Mr. Kale at all like his Aunt?" "Law, Miss," says I, "they're as like as two peaches; one of them ripe and ready to fall, and the other rather hardish yet." Then she praises up your Aunt, and praises up the place, and finally says, just as she's going: "There's no portrait of Mrs. Pinkney's nephew lying about, is there?" "No, Miss Harding," says I, "there beant."'

If Mrs. Shaw had any particular design in view in thus dwelling upon the details of Miss Harding's knowledge of Philip, she did not reveal it in her face, which looked stolid and sensible as before. Philip felt alternate heats and chills; but he led the conversation to a more impersonal ground. After that revelation he felt that there was a subtle sympathy established between the spirit of his unknown Eve and himself, and wondered how he could have found so much joy in life before it was illuminated by the daily vision of a sweet-faced girl, riding by on a farm-horse.

About this time he received a letter from his mother, reproaching him in half-playful terms for so abruptly cutting himself loose from family and friends to live in the woods, as she could not doubt he did, in a half barbaric state, and commanding him, if he had any remains of filial or paternal affection left, to make it manifest by an immediate visit to his father's house. Philip felt, as his Aunt Ruth would probably have expressed it, a distinct 'call' to go. He had a great deal of repressed affection for his parents and brothers and sister. He wished to show them that his 'half-barbaric' life was making a new man of him, physically and mentally. He wanted to contrast the satisfying pleasure of solitude with the empty delights of society. Perhaps he had an unacknowledged feeling that the former needed all the advantages of a strong contrast to brighten the dull colours that had glowed so warmly for him at first. Whatever may have been the number or nature of his motives, he was fully determined to go. Thomas would have an eye to his garden, and Charlotte would improve his absence in prosecuting the necessary and unpleasant labour of house cleaning. When he arrived in the city he felt rather jaded, but the abrupt change from his solitary nook to the thronged and bustling streets brought him a factitious excitement, an exhilaration of spirit, and a quickened expression, which, in conjunction with his tanned complexion, his frequent bursts of laughter, and brilliant flow of conversation, transformed him entirely in the eyes of his own family. He was the hero of the hour; and the enthusiastic way in which he related his rural experiences gave them something of the thrill and strangeness of adventures on sea or foreign shores to his interested group of listeners. He sat on the sofa beside his sister Fanny, and trifled with the long braid of hair that fell down her back.

'And I suppose you never miss going to Quaker meeting?' said this young lady.

'Oh, yes; I miss it every time,' said her brother, with a little frown and a slight shade of embarrassment. 'But I guess my loss is their gain, and *vice versa*. The trouble is, if I go once I shall feel a kind of obligation to go again—and again; and I don't want to be inveigled into getting mixed up with even the best kind of other people.'

'The usual exception with regard to present company, I suppose. Flattered, I'm sure!'

'Well, I thought,' remarked Mrs. Kale, 'that Friends considered themselves apart from the world.'

'That is the way I consider myself,' said her son, significantly.

'You should attend Divine service somewhere,' said Mr. Kale, gravely.

'Yes, sir,' said Philip; but he mentally decided to meditate upon his father's statement for several months, at least, before he ventured to put it into practice.

'Don't you long, sometimes, for the sight of a woman's dress?' asked Fanny. Philip had carefully omitted making any mention of Eve.

'Oh, I can appreciate them all the more when I do see them. This is a pretty muslin you have on. Just the colour of peach blossoms, isn't it? I believe I like blue better. Very odd that peach blossoms should come out before the leaves.'

His sister laughed. 'Oh, I dare say,' said she, 'but there are some things that strike me as odder even than that. How long are you going to keep it up, Philly?'

The young man sprang with a quick, nervous motion to his feet, so as to face his sister. 'I'm not keeping it up at all,' he said, 'it's keeping *me* up! my health and spirits, and everything! Do you think I'm the least bit tired of it?'

Everyone looked at him, and every one was constrained to admit, 'No.' Then he crossed the room to his mother's side, and had a little talk with her concerning some domestic matters, which had proved in his experience rather unmanageable. Mrs. Kale had never been more interested in her son than now. From the days of his sickly childhood, when he alternated from excited joyousness to fretful morbidness, she had always considered him a queer boy; and she was glad now that his queerness had found vent for itself. How brown and earnest, and wide awake he was. Though she had never been neglectful of him, she felt a motherly pang that he had gone so completely out of her life before becoming what he was; that it was in scenes remote from her presence and influence that he had risen to a higher plane of life. She was a handsome, worldly-faced woman, with a smile and manner rather too hard to be agreeable. When they went up stairs together, she stood on the landing, saying good night, with a strange, wistful expression, to Philip, a few steps beneath her. He laid his hand on her

ETHELYN WETHERALD

shoulder a moment. She caught her breath, and then bent over him. 'You are a good fellow, Phil.!' she cried, the tears coming into her eyes. 'I am sure you will never forget your mother.'

In a week or two Philip returned to the country. It was impossible, he said, for a farmer to be long absent from his crops during the growing season, and his mother saw him depart with more regret than she had ever imagined his absence would cause her. If Philip was not glad to leave his old home, he was not sorry to return to his new one. He wanted to see if his strawberries were ripe, and if Miss Harding still rode daily past his gate. Her importance in his thoughts had dwindled considerably since he had seen and talked with other charming young ladies, friends of his sister, who were quite as pretty as the unskilled young *equestrienne*. He could not help feeling glad, for the sake of the world, that there were so many sweet and good women in it; but that one of them could be immeasurably fairer, and more to be desired, than her sisters,—this was the empty fancy of lovers, or of idle and romantic young men who spent a certain part of every afternoon in a hammock. He had outgrown all that now.

With these practical and prudent reflections in his mind, it was rather strange that Philip Kale, on stepping out of the car into the presence of Miss Harding and a number of other people, should have experienced a suddenly increasing beating of the heart. He could not understand it at all. It was unreasonable, it was abominable, but it was so. The boy, Joe, was apparently going on a journey, and his sister had accompanied him to the depot. Philip stood not far from her, as he could easily do in the crowd without being noticed. She was laughing, and he told himself angrily that he couldn't bear girls that laughed in public. She had evidently been teasing Joe unmercifully, for on the youth's face were exhibited mingled emotions of rage, mirth, and despair.

'You're real mean,' he blurted out.

'And the boy's honest,' thought Philip, his mind reverting to 'nobody worth mentioning.'

'Well, Joe,' said his sister, sobered at once, 'it's better for you to think so, than for me to be so! You know I don't mean anything.'

'And I didn't mean to say that, either, Eva.'

'Then there's no meanness about either of us,' said Eva, laughing again.

Philip told himself that he had never heard a young lady make puns before, and he never wanted to again.

'But now,' exclaimed Miss Harding, 'you must go! Good by, my dear fellow. Be sure you write.'

Philip said that 'my dear fellow' was simply disgusting. But he knew that his angry thoughts amounted to nothing at all. They were merely the last effort of nature to preserve him in his boasted independence. It was too late. His heart was irrevocably in the possession of Miss Eva Harding.

He decided to walk out to his home. It was healthful exercise, and would do him good. A long walk in the country on a June day is a beautiful thing in theory, but Philip found that in practice it had several drawbacks. The sun was hot, the scenery was dull, and he himself was not in the full glow of health and vigour. Every carriage that swept past left a cloud of dust for him to travel through. He was feeling very much incensed by this fact, when a fresh sound of wheels from behind caused him to turn a vengeful glance in that direction. There he saw Miss Harding, looking very cool and contented, sitting in a buggy, and drawn by a horse much better looking than the one with which she usually appeared. She drove in a very leisurely fashion, looking hard at Philip's back, and wondering if it would be very improper for a young lady of acknowledged social position, driving in her own conveyance, to offer a ride to a stranger who was so evidently respectable, weak, and weary. She was very kind hearted, had a habit of acting quickly upon her generous impulses, and was, moreover, an original young lady, with a liking for doing original things. All of these forces combined to stop the horse just as he reached Philip's side.

'If you care to ride, I can readily accommodate you,' she remarked.

ETHELYN WETHERALD

There was mingled embarrassment, defiance, and kindness in the tones; but the young man chose to recognise the latter quality alone, as he said, with a bright glance at her—

'Oh, thank you, I would indeed. It makes my head ache badly, walking in the sun. You are very kind.'

He got in at the left side, allowing her to retain the reins. She was evidently quite reassured by his words and manner.

Philip's heart beat quick. He observed with pleasure that his companion looked incomparably better in a buggy than she did on horseback; that her hat, which had a blue feather in it, displayed a forehead, milk white and boldly rounded, with a single thick lock, not fringe, of fair hair falling across it, that her eyes were not penetrating nor searching, but deep and placid; that her pretty shoulders were femininely narrow, and that she had those easy, restful ways of leaning back and looking around so delightful to a nervous man. He forgot all the harsh things he had thought about her, and was sure that nowhere upon earth existed the girl so wonderfully sweet and wholesome looking as the one beside him. As a dyspeptic, he knew the worth and rarity of this combination of two of the best qualities in nature.

'How far do you go?' she asked.

Philip hesitated. It would sound rather queer to say, 'to my house,' besides, that would necessitate all kinds of explanations, which he had no desire to make. He had not dissembled before, but it is never too late to learn bad as well as good practices. 'To Mr. Kale's,' he replied, 'I believe it is some distance from here.'

'It's a little way this side of our place,' she said, 'up a green lane. You have never been in this part of the country before?'

'Oh, yes; I was here a long time ago, when Mrs. Pinkney was living. Her nephew is a sort of connection of mine. I don't know whether you could call it a relationship or not. Did you know Mrs. Pinkney?'

'Very well, indeed. She was a dear friend of mine. Our neighbourhood felt its loss deeply when she died last winter.

I never knew any one to live so entirely for others.'

'Living for others sounds very fine,' said Philip, argumentatively. 'Can you tell me precisely what it means?'

The young girl looked at him a little doubtfully, as if she half liked and was half afraid of this turn in the conversation. 'I think I can tell you what it meant in Mrs. Pinkney's case,' she said. 'She continually blessed and gladdened the lives of those around her by her words, her actions, and, perhaps, most of all, by the sweet peacefulness of her presence. To every one that came in contact with her, she seemed to supply a special need, and to those who were satisfied with themselves and the world she brought something of the beauty of heavenly things. Why,' with a little blush for the enthusiasm with which she had spoken of her dead friend to a stranger, 'she did the noblest thing that any one can do— she made the world better because of her living in it.'

'Is that a very uncommon thing to do?'

'Oh, I'm afraid it is; and I hate to think so, too! So few people seem to understand that that is the real meaning and object of life; and even when they do understand it, they are apt to act upon it in such a poor, grudging, discontented sort of way. It is as if they felt it a miserable responsibility instead of a marvellous privilege. I hope you don't think I'm gushing. I am a good deal too much in earnest for that.'

'I can easily believe you,' said Philip, warmly; 'and I know Mrs. Pinkney to have been all that you represent her. Does the nephew to whom she left her property inherit any of her virtues?'

'Why, as to that,' replied Miss Harding, with a short laugh, 'it's difficult to say. He has scarcely been seen by any one since he took possession. I should say that he was entirely different from his Aunt. But it is very rude for me to discuss his character with you.'

Philip thought so, too, but, instead of saying that, he immediately exclaimed:

'It would be a positive kindness to me. I am very little acquainted with him, I assure you, and understand him still less, though our habits and tastes are identical. I was at college the same time that he was, and thought him a terribly reserved fellow. He is, really, the last person in the world from whom I should have expected an invitation to visit.' Philip drew a long breath at the end of his speech.

'I should think so,' said his companion, thoughtfully. 'Why, he appears to be the most unsocial man you could possibly imagine. He lives for himself quite as completely as his Aunt lived for others, and in same house and garden, too! It seems too bad! He is not known to go to any church, or to the village, or anywhere. He is no more to the people among whom he lives than a snail in its shell, and when he dies I suppose will be missed about as much.'

'Well,' said the young man, feeling a little shocked, 'at least he does no harm.'

'Not to others perhaps, but a great deal to himself. It is thought a very terrible thing to be narrow-minded; but to my thinking it is worse to be narrow-hearted. What can you think of a person who digs out all the roots of affection, leaving one central plant to twine around, and beautify, and perfume his own best-beloved self?'

She smiled as she spoke, and Philip noticed how strong and white her teeth were. He was stung into self-defence.

'But it is in solitude that mental riches are acquired, genuine personal improvement made. Surely one must be of some benefit to the world who so thoroughly benefits one person in it.'

'But don't you see that, by concentrating his efforts upon one person, he not only fails to benefit the rest of the world, but himself as well? It is a good thing to gain mental and material riches, but that does not justify any one in turning miser. Wisdom in a single brain, and gold in a single box, are worse than useless, because they engender selfishness and conceit in their owner. It is circulation that makes them both useful.'

The young lady did not snap out her utterances. She spoke in smooth gentle tones, as one who had thought long and felt deeply on the subject. Philip tried to find some of his old arguments in favour of a life of solitude, but they slunk shame-faced away from him.

'Really,' continued Mentor, 'I should apologise for speaking of your friend in this plain way.'

'Oh,' said Philip, 'I am sufficiently acquainted with Kale to know that your words are not strictly applicable to his case. He has always been in poor health, and perhaps that has tended to give him rather sickly views of life and society. He finds it impossible to adapt himself with the slightest degree of pleasure to the conditions and requirements of the world.'

'Probably he thinks there is nothing in common between him and ordinary people.'

'No, I'll do him the justice to say I can't believe that of him. I remember hearing him say once, that he had a great affection for the world in the abstract; that in certain heroic moods he felt that he could gladly lay down his life for the sake of doing it some lasting good, but that he could not mingle, useless and unappreciated, with its frivolities and frigidities, merely because most people did so. At another time he said, he fancied that each member of society was like one of those noise producers in use at an old-fashioned *charivari*,—all discordant and each trying to make itself loudest heard; and that solitude was like a great musician playing by himself on a sweet instrument.'

Miss Harding actually laughed, 'Ah, yes; very pretty, very fine!' then she stopped short. Philip's brown eyes, burning with reproach, were full upon her. 'I beg your pardon,' she said, looking distressed; 'I *am* rude. But,' with strenuous earnestness, 'I wish that Mr. Kale could understand that his fancies, or those of any one else on this subject, are, and must always be, of secondary importance. The great fact remains that society is organized that its members may help one another; and no one has any right to shirk his part. If in any place society is frivolous and frigid, it shows that the earnest minded and warm-hearted people of that place hold themselves aloof from it. Do you think,' abruptly, 'that it is very unjust for me to lecture you on account of Mr. Kale?'

ETHELYN WETHERALD

'No,' replied Philip; 'if I were not in sympathy with him I could not uphold his views. Do you think he is very selfish and shallow?'

'No, only greatly mistaken. I hope you will be able to convert him to my—our views.'

The young man smiled. 'Of course you are in the right,' he said. 'You place it so on a moral ground.'

'Oh, no, excuse me, but I don't. It is on a moral ground already. It has always been firmly rooted there.'

He pressed his hand over his eyes.

'I have made your head worse,' said the young girl regretfully. She herself from experience had no very clear idea of what a headache was, but she felt a great deal of pity for the handsome, suffering young stranger, whom she had been talking at so forcibly. She wished from her heart that she could do something for him, and presently she saw her opportunity. Not far off, on the road side, was a group of girl acquaintances, coming towards them, and casting interested glances at the gentleman beside her. Leaning a little toward Philip, and turning her full face toward him, Miss Harding, with bewitching little smiles and gestures of the head, poured out a stream of steady commonplace which lasted till the girls had passed, breaking off only to give them a bow. Philip was amazed by her look, manner, and especially by what she said, but he must have been blind not to see that this young lady wished to give her girl friends to understand that she was in company with a gentleman whom she highly appreciated, and whose favour she was determined to win. There was something decidedly flattering in this, and Philip felt cheered by it a little. Still he thought that Miss Harding was a very self-assured young person, and he found it inconceivable that a country girl whom he had so often laughed at, should be lording it over him in this way. He wondered if he should reveal himself to her when they reached his gate. That would certainly bring a blush for her rudeness to her fair cool cheek, if anything would. But, perhaps, with her dreadful lack of sensibility, she would laugh at him. No, he decided it would be wiser not to make a revelation. Miss Harding was very attentive.

She audibly regretted his indisposition, handed him her parasol, for the sunshine was now in their faces, and seemed so much interested in him that he shivered in fear that she would ask his name. It was just such a thing as this frank matter-of-fact girl would do. Nevertheless she did not do it.

As they went up the grassy lane, and neared the Pinkney place, its owner felt a glad thrill of pride and joy. How heavenly fair it looked. He was sure that Charlotte had finished cleaning house, for the old porch had such a clean scrubbed look. The grass had grown thick and rank, the flowers were blooming, the birds were singing; there must be young ones in that nest near the hammock by this time. And it was all his own! He looked at it with increasing delight. The young lady asked him if it was not strange that Mr. Kale did not come out to meet him, but he did not answer, except to thank her cordially for the ride she had given him. When he got out of the buggy he was surprised to see his companion get out also.

'I have no intention to leave a sickly stranger alone in this desolate place,' said she, with quite unnecessary kindness, as she tied her horse to the fence. 'We'll have good fun hunting up the misanthrope. Very likely he's hiding somewhere. I've heard he has a habit of hiding.'

She preceded him merrily through the gate. Philip followed her mechanically. Every man's house is his castle, and his was peculiarly so, but when a beautiful young woman opens the castle gate, no man, or at least no gentleman, can turn her out again. The modern Eve seemed to be in the best of spirits. She made a rush for the hammock, and shook it as though in the expectation of seeing a man slip through the interstices. 'Not here!' she cried. Then she walked along the whole line of trees, glancing up into their tops, and calling out frequent reports of her lack of success to her stunned companion on the gravel walk.

'Where shall we look now?' she asked, coming up with a face brimful of fun.

'I don't know,' replied Philip, despairingly.

'Perhaps I'd best go over to Mrs. Shaw's. I know she has a key to the house, and then you could hunt round inside.'

'Oh, I don't think that is necessary,' said Philip, uneasily. 'If he never goes away from home he must be here somewhere.'

'Why, yes!' said the girl, stooping to pick a flower; 'but he seems to have odd ideas of hospitality. This is very unpleasant for you.'

'It is, indeed!' groaned the sufferer. 'You are very good, but I cannot allow myself to trespass further upon your kindness.'

'Don't mention it. I hope you didn't think me capable of leaving you in this strait after the way I talked to you this afternoon.'

They walked around the house; the lady on the alert, leading the way, the gentleman stupidly following; and came back to the front porch again.

'Well,' said Miss Harding, 'I have a strong impression that Mr. Kale is *somewhere* in this place.'

'So have I,' said Philip, languidly.

'Furthermore, I think he is in sight.' Involuntarily, Philip glanced around.

'I believe I am speaking to Mr. Kale.'

Philip made an exaggerated bow. 'That is my name, and I have the pleasure of addressing Miss Harding. To what am I indebted for the hon—that is, I am pleased to make your acquaintance.'

'Oh, Mr. Kale!' said the young girl, struggling between mirth and penitence, 'you need not look so aggrieved. You behaved nearly as bad as I did all the time.'

'Did I?' asked Philip, in honest doubt.

'Indeed you did! You tried to deceive me the whole time.'

'But I didn't succeed.'

'No, but your efforts were none the less interesting on that account. And then you thought—Oh, you must have thought all kinds of horrible things about my behaviour.'

'That's true!' emphatically.

'Well, you see I don't deserve them. If you had been an entire stranger, I wouldn't have asked you to ride, and talked to you the way I did for worlds. Why I *couldn't*! Not if you had been ten times as sick and fifty times as respectable-looking as you are. But why, you see, Mrs. Pinkney told me all about you, and Mr. and Mrs. Shaw told me and all the rest of the neighbourhood about you. So I am quite well acquainted—besides, seeing you every day for a long time past. I hope you don't think *now* that I am coarse and rude and ill-bred.'

Philip looked at the sweet pleading face and delicate blonde hands, playing with their tiny gloves, of the maiden before him. How beautiful his Eve looked in his Eden! 'Some other time,' he said softly, 'I will tell you what I think of you.'

She turned quickly away. 'Now that I have found your host for you, I believe I had better go. But first may I trouble you for a drink of water?'

'Oh, yes! I will get a glass in a moment.'

He rushed to the door and fumbled in his pocket for the key, but it could not at once be found. The young lady smiled archly.

'Your key has been listening to your afternoon's talk,' she said. 'No wonder it refuses to acknowledge you as its owner.'

Philip fairly beamed at her. He thought he had never heard such a delicious witticism. The door was opened at last.

'Come in and inspect bachelor's hall!' he cried.

He waited only to see how much the room was improved by her presence, and then ran to the pantry. Through the window he could see the strawberry bed, which reminded him to take a saucer out too. Presently he returned, bearing a glass of water in one hand, and a saucer of immense berries in the other.

'You see I am not only host and guest, but obedient servant too.'

'And gardener also. Why those *are* strawberries! How did you make them so fine? I thought you did hardly anything but lie on the hammock.'

'Oh, that was only when you——a little while in the afternoon. How ever did you see me through those branches? I never thought for an instant this afternoon that you knew me from Adam.'

The young lady laughed.

'But, then,' he continued, 'I am Adam.'

She looked at him inquiringly.

'This is the garden of Eden, you know.'

'Why, how odd!' she cried, between two bites of an especially large strawberry; 'and I am E——. Well, then, you see I didn't know you from Adam after all!'

Philip made no reply. She rose suddenly, looking a little embarrassed, and said she believed she had better go. 'I don't know why it is,' she cried, turning round at the door, 'but I feel *contemptible*—just such a feeling as that I experienced at boarding school, the night I stole the water-melon. I have been stealing your privacy, your right to solitariness, your—what shall I call it—?'

Philip's eyes told her that she might call it his heart, but he dared not trust himself to speak.

She walked away with a rapid step and closed the gate behind her, but it was not alone.

'May I call upon you?' asked the world-weary misanthrope, as he handed her the reins.

'Certainly not,' was the almost angry response. 'Who ever heard of Adam leaving Eden until—'

'Until an angel obliged him to leave,' said her ingenious tormentor, with a smile. 'I shall certainly call.'

The modern Eve departed with unnecessary speed, but she remained away only a few months, and when she returned it was to make the life of Adam a paradise indeed.

✑

Rose-Belford's Canadian Monthly and National Review
(February 1882), 131–146.

Sara Jeannette Duncan (1861–1922)

UP THE SITTEE IN A PITPAN (1885)

Sara Jeannette Duncan forged a major reputation as both fiction writer and pioneering female journalist in the last two decades of the nineteenth century. "Kit" Coleman, the Toronto *Mail*'s women's columnist in the 1890s, was perhaps more of a household word, but Duncan shone in the weighty and patriarchal world of Canadian political journalism.

Christened Sarah Janet, she was the eldest of ten children of New Brunswicker Janet Bell and Charles Duncan, a Scottish-born merchant established in Brantford. She was educated at Brantford Collegiate, the Ladies' College and the County Model School for Teachers, as well as at Toronto Normal School, where she earned a teaching certificate in 1882. She taught briefly in her home town. As early as 1880, a childhood desire to become a writer prompted her to publish short pieces in magazines and journals. She began her journalism career on a local paper, then wrote for the Toronto *Globe*, the London (Ontario) *Advertiser* and the Washington *Post*. In 1886 at the *Globe*, she became Canada's first full-time female editorial writer. In 1887, she moved to the Montreal *Star*, becoming one of two women members of the Parliamentary Press Gallery; she also contributed to *The Week*, where she published "Up the Sittee in a Pitpan" as "Garth Grafton," a favorite pseudonym. "Careers, if possible," this pioneering newswoman wrote in the *Globe* on 12 November 1886, "and independence anyway, we must all have, as musicians, artists, writers, teachers, lawyers, doctors, ministers, or something."

The Central American setting of "Up the Sittee in a Pitpan" anticipates the exotic settings of her later Indian fiction and of Duncan's first book, *A Social Departure; How Orthodocia and I Went Round the World by Ourselves* (1890), a lively account of her round-the-world trip with fellow journalist Lily Lewis. The latter was based on articles sent to the *Star*. Duncan spent her second year abroad in London, where her novel was published. In the fall of 1890, she returned to Calcutta to marry English-born Everard Cotes, then a museum official, whom she had met on her travels.

She lived in India for twenty-five years, working in journalism with her husband and travelling frequently to Canada and to England where she spent her last years. Duncan published twenty-two books, set variously in Canada, England, India, and the United States. Best known today is her Canadian novel *The Imperialist* (1904) about religious and political small-town Canada. The theme of the new woman animates *A Daughter of Today* (1903). Duncan later became interested in theatre, and though none of her plays was really successful, some had brief runs, several in London's West End. She died in Ashton, Surrey, in 1922, where her tombstone reads "This leaf was blown far. . . ."

"Up the Sittee in a Pitpan," one of Duncan's early works, already embodies her sophisticated control of narrative voice and her ability to paint the intricacies of the British colonial order as she was to do so superbly in her Indian fiction. This dramatic narrative was in fact one of the pieces that helped to establish her reputation as a journalist and writer. Little known in 1884, she had travelled to the New Orleans Cotton Exposition, and convinced prestigious publications like the Washington *Post* and Goldwin Smith's *The Week* to accept her pieces. In New Orleans, she met Robert Tuckfield Goldsworthy, Governor-General of British Honduras, at whose invitation she visited there in March 1885.

The story is proof of the belief she expressed in an 1888 piece called "Women in Journalism" that "special articles of a light sort are . . . in great demand, for the vast newspaper-reading public that does not care one jot to be edified, but requires unceasingly to be amused. These [pieces] can be . . . written readily by women." One of its delights is Duncan's deft and subtle skewering of colonial

48   SARA JEANNETTE DUNCAN

pomposity and pretension in the personae of the Dignitary and his lady. (One wonders what her host made of the story.) For all her satirical lightness of touch, her rendering of the Honduran potpourri of races and classes makes the visiting narrator's final question "Who are you?" refract back throughout the story to pose questions about identity, place, race and power.

"Up the Sittee in a Pitpan" is a bravura prelude to what was to become a characteristic Duncan theme, particularly in her Indian novels: the face of Empire in the tropics as seen and experienced by a shrewd female narrator.

&

Suggested Reading:

Dean, Misao. *A Different Point of View: Sara Jeannette Duncan*. Montreal: McGill-Queen's University Press, 1991.

Duncan, Sara Jeannette. *A Daughter of Today*. 1894. Ottawa: Tecumseh, 1988.

_____. *A Social Departure: How Orthodocia and I Went Around the World by Ourselves*. London: Chatto, 1890.

_____. *The Imperialist*. 1904. Ottawa: Tecumseh, 1988.

Fowler, Marian. *Redney*. Toronto: Anansi, 1983.

Tausky, Thomas, ed. *Sara Jeannette Duncan: Selected Journalism*. Ottawa: Tecumseh, 1978.

_____. *Sara Jeannette Duncan: Novelist of Empire*. Port Credit: P.D. Meany, 1980.

UP THE SITTEE IN A PITPAN

Sara Jeannette Duncan

It was the Dignitary's plan. Out of his august inner
consciousness the Dignitary always evolved pleasant plans;
therefore, when one hot morning, under the musical
pattering of the cocoa-nut leaves, he delivered himself of a
proposal to "pitpan" up the Sittee, we arose in joyful con-
currence and said we would. The Dignitary lives in Belize,
which is the capital, as you are probably not aware, of
British Honduras. British Honduras is not an island nor an
extinct volcano, as is popularly supposed, but a colonial
dependency of Great Britain, occupying about 75,000
square miles, between Mexico and Guatemala, on the
Atlantic slope of Central America. I am thus explicit,
because when I arrayed myself in my linen duster and stated
my intention of visiting the colony, I observed a certain
blankness upon people's countenances that led me to the not
unreasonable supposition that it must be situated in some
other planet. The Dignitary, to revert from popular geo-
graphical depravity to a more agreeable theme, is a Briton,
of course, with a ruddy complexion and a rising inflection,
as is also the private secretary, without the complexion. The
private secretary, however, has many characteristics less calculated to minister to his vanity which make his acquaintance valuable.

A quaint old town is Belize. The jalousied frame-
houses throw long shadows across the unpaved dusty brown
streets that wander hither and thither past the flaming

garden growths and out to the desolate black-pooled mangrove swamp. A wide-roofed market stands in the middle, around which smiling Caribs squat in the sun and dispose of the yams and plantains and salt fish that constitute Honduranian diet. Spanish Indians are there too, gracefully lounging against the posts in bright loose garments, sashes and broad hats. Sauntering through the town are to be seen the magnificently-physiqued men of the West India Detachment stationed here, in their short red jackets, white turbans, and loose blue trousers gathered at the ankle. Almost all the colonial officials and their wives are white, and most of the tradespeople; beyond that the population is chiefly composed of Creole negroes of every imaginable shade. A church spire here and there, and lying out toward the sunset the lonely graveyard, where the dead people are housed as in Louisiana. Very desolate and still is this grassy place, with its straggling rows of these moss-grown final habitations of all the Honduranians. "*Super terrene*"[1] is the orthodox expression, which the Dignitary, who ought to know better, has corrupted into "soup tureens," thereby adding a new and culinary horror to death in Belize.

The waves plashed foaming among the great conch shells along the shore, rolled back in a crystalline hurry, and stretched away blue and shimmering among the coral cays that tossed their graceful palm fronds against the sky, on the morning that witnessed the maturity of the Dignitary's plan. A ten-minutes' pull from the shore lay the mail steamer *Dallas*, by which we were to make the thirty-mile run to the river bar. Her broad upper deck was crowded with olive-skinned Spaniards; grizzled old men, long-nosed and meditative over the invariable cigarette; young matrons of twenty, wan and worn, smiling down upon a numerous and energetic progeny that kicked its dusky legs on the deck, and was a constant source of embarrassment to the private secretary, who invariably stepped on it. By-and-by, when the yellow flame began to burn lower in the west, and a vast flood

---

1. *Super terrene*: Latin for "above ground."

of purple light fell softly over the sea, there came up from somewhere the exquisite melody of the *flautin*[2]; and, as the sudden darkness fell, some golden throated donna took up the strain, and even the stars listened. Presently the ship stopped and a boat shot out from the denser shadow of a group of feathery palms; and in a few minutes we were surveying our lodging-place for the night. It was a deserted plank house, the former residence of a sugar-planter of more ambition than capital. Inside, the walls stopped two feet from the rafters, with jalousies that rather united than divided the rooms. By that magic, of which dignitaries are special necromancers, hammocks had been swung; the indispensable mosquito-net hung over couches dilapidated but downy, and a feast of fat things spread upon a table, whereof the legs were three and a-quarter, and the accompanying chairs unreliable exceedingly. A ramble along the shore in the mystic light of the low hung stars was experience enough for one evening. Within a few feet of the water stretched a long avenue or "walk" of tall cocoa-nuts leaning this way and that after the fashion of that erratic tree, and always murmuring far up in the darkness the secrets of the old tragical pirate days. At our feet the waves threw strange forms of sea-weed and tiny pink shells and scraps of coral, and went curling away again; and away behind the house the jungle reflected itself darkly in a still lagoon. True the sandflies made merry at our individual expense; the "bottle" flies also and the yellow-backed "doctors," compared with which the familiar hornet is an unaggressive insect with limited ability to protect itself. The bottle-flies, exactly the shape of a soda-water bottle, attack the hands chiefly, and leave a tiny black spot, giving the victim the appearance of having been well peppered.

Owing to the peculiar interior architecture aforesaid, nobody slept well that night. Every snore, every infuriated slap, every anathema hurled into the midnight air, resounded from room to room with maddening effect, and

---

2. *Flautin*: A "flautino" is a small flute.

SARA JEANNETTE DUNCAN

in the morning the ablutions of the earliest riser splashed metaphorically in every ear. I arose betimes, and so did her Grace. Her Grace, be it understood, sustains the marital relation toward the Dignitary. You should have been introduced before, only, of course, I had to ask her permission. We descended the crazy steps and wandered around the premises together. The short dry grass was spangled with tiny white flowers that grew close to the ground and perished speedily in the sun. The tiny horses of Central America that were to carry the party, and the mule of sad countenance that was to convey our effects and Ganymede and such fluids as he had special charge of, stood about and whisked their tails with melancholy patience. After breakfast we mounted our diminutive steeds and rode away along a narrow road past the lagoons, through the sugarcane fields to the estate of Regalia. Here and there the hut of a labourer peeped through the luxuriant cane growth, always well ventilated, if not very scientifically, and thatched with dried palm fronds in the most raggedly picturesque fashion. Strange purple flowers grew among the canes, and everywhere the small yellow blossom of the ipecac, much the colour and shape of a cowslip. Our first glimpse of the Sittee was an exquisite bit of scenery. Ridge beyond ridge the Coxcomb mountains rose into the purple distance, then the riotous dark masses of the tropical forest and the pale green of hundreds of acres of canes, twisting through it all the "silver ribbon" of the river, and in the foreground half-a-dozen of the huts aforesaid, a huge sugar-mill, and scores of brightly-clad coolies. These odd little black creatures, with their bright eyes, expressive features, and yellow bandanas, were imported from the East Indies by Jamaicans originally, and thence here. The Honduranian planters value their services highly and look anxiously for further relays. They work reasonably and respectfully, while the Creoles of the colony are indolent and impudent. We dined at Regalia, and the fact is worth chronicling, for the turtle of gastronomic fame is a staple in British Honduras, and we had the aldermanic delicacy in soup, in steak, in croquette. And how shall

I dilate upon the attractions of the yam, which is a corpulent potato brought to the table pinned up in a napkin, with one end cut off to admit the entrance of a spoon? Okra also, a vegetable of a savour much like asparagus, the homely plantain roasted and fried, the soft-shelled crab, the bird of the land, which is the turkey—truly one may live royally in Central America! But the Briton who is planting cacao in a lonely spot thirty miles from Belize, and whose diet is limited to pork and "dough-boys," reminds me that ours was a dinner extraordinary. To horse again for Kendal, the next estate, just five miles further on. The road led into the forest, and presently we were riding in the dense shade of tall cohoon palms, mango, wild fig and bread-fruit trees. The cohoon palm is especially graceful, its great fronds shooting up twenty or thirty feet into the air and curving outward in a lovely arch. The tree bears a great grape-like cluster of nuts, from which is extracted the valuable cohoon of commerce. Here and there we saw the glossy leafing of the noble mahogany, and the lighter bark and foliage of the logwood tree. Cacao grew wild, pineapples, and the vanilla vine. The pod of cacao, from the seeds of which we obtain our morning chocolate, grows at intervals out of the trunk and branches of the tree. Lady Brassey, who describes it in her last book, must have a peculiar taste in ice-cream. I found nothing even remotely suggestive of that confection in the sticky pulp that surrounds the seeds. "Tie-ties," or jungle rope, hung thickly from the trees, and swung before us like a bamboo screen. A long avenue of arching palms suddenly opened before us; we spurred our willing ponies, and with a mad short gallop of a quarter of a mile, that set the red and yellow macaws chattering overhead, and caused great perturbation to two or three small brown monkeys who stood not on the order of their going, we dashed into Kendal. Two hundred acres of broad-leaved, bowing bananas spread out before us. They bear constantly, the flower, if one may call it such, resembling a great red tulip about to open. Cacao is often planted with the bananas, for the shade of the latter; the banana profits, moreover, being particularly

SARA JEANNETTE DUNCAN

acceptable to the lonely planter during the four years which the more valuable product requires to mature.

For the second of our memorable dinners, our Jamaican host and the Dignitary concocted a curry of inestimable East Indian quality. It was a beef curry, and over the compounding of it much anxious discussion took place. For an instant the Dignitary's spoon poised in mid-air as he partook of the dish so dear to the colonial British palate, then over his features stole a look of unutterable anguish. Investigation proved that Ganymede, influenced by Rocquet and responsibility, had added to the mixture two cans of preserved peaches!

Then we all sat out in the luminous darkness under the verandah, and listened to the sounds that fill a tropical night. Suddenly, above the hoarse cries of the tree-crickets and the melancholy howlings of distant monkeys, there came a clear, low bird-whistle, "Who are you?" The query was as impudent and inquisitive as possible, and the effect was startling. Presently, from another tree across the river, came the answer, clearly and melodiously, a trifle higher, "Who are *you?*" All night long we heard the snobbish interrogation and reply. Next morning a scorpion, a tarantula, a Tommy Geff and an iguana enlivened proceedings, brought in by a couple of Caribs bent upon our edification and accustomed to the British tip. The Tommy Geff is a small light-green snake with a fatal bite. The iguana is a sort of lizard, varying in length from three to five feet: a hideous, grayish-green animal, with a short, square head, green eyes and webbed feet. It is harmless, however, and the flesh is much sought after as food. It is said to resemble chicken, but your informant deponeth not as to the fact, having lacked experimental courage. The Caribs brought it in the usual cruel manner, with the feet crossed upon the back, the claws of one foot caught in the bleeding sinews of the other. In this way they keep the unfortunate creatures lying for days upon the market place, waiting for customers. The particular iguana of our entertainment, however, found a pitying champion in her Grace, who indignantly demanded its release. With difficulty they unfastened the claws, and, like a swift green flash, the creature made for the river and was gone.

Down upon the banks sat our Carib boatmen sunning themselves. A dory and a pitpan rocked in the shade, and in them we cautiously established ourselves. A dory is hollowed out of a single log, usually cedar; a pitpan is a craft from thirty to forty feet in length, and from two to three in width. Both are paddled, and are used exclusively for transporting freight and supplies in the Colony. The boatmen stand at either end, the passengers and load being stationed in the middle.

Off we went. In some places the river banks were high and rocky; in others, fifty feet of dense vegetation rose straight up in every shade and shape. Underneath alligators might be creeping, and snakes uncoiling in the slime, but overhead the sun shone and the tall tree-ferns waved, and brilliant birds with strange cries flashed among the green. The water was crystalline purity itself, sparkling and dashing over moss-covered stones, here in pale shallows, there in dark, mysterious pools, but always green and cool and enticing. Rapids were frequent where the river foamed and lashed itself in its furious and often steep descent. There our boatmen sprang over and hauled the pitpan with their sturdy arms, the water dashing often over the sides to the serious detriment of her Grace's skirts and equanimity. Weeds and mosses of the daintiest green and gray and pink and brown swayed under the transparent water, or floated in lovely patches in the shallows. Here and there, from the upper branches of a tall dead tree, hung like long bags the ingenious nests of the yellow-tail, the clever little architects constantly darting in and out of them. On we went. The river widened and narrowed, twisted and turned. Great branches met over our heads, and the sunlight filtered softly down through the fluttering green roof. Two or three fruit-laden native dories passed us on their rapid way down stream, in each a Carib woman or two in wide straw hat and scanty attire lying lazily back, puffing a short pipe. To the chaffing of the private secretary, they responded shrilly and

SARA JEANNETTE DUNCAN

sharply, their black eyes twinkling and their mahogany countenances illuminated by an ecstatic grin. Occasionally we passed a "bank," or clearing, teeming with dark-skinned life. Nine miles of this brought us to a spot where the river rushed between two immense boulders at a width of about five feet—Hell Gate. Beyond, the water eddied and foamed about innumerable rocks; one could see the pebbly bottom everywhere, and the banks rose steep and jagged. Half-a-mile further on we disembarked and lunched. Only a horror of giving my article too gastronomic a colouring restrains me from describing that picnic. Worse than the caterpillar is the centipede; worse than the mosquito the inexpressible bottle-fly; but never, I fancy, was marmaladed bread-and-butter discussed more enjoyably than there in the shade of the mangoes overhanging that high-spirited little Central American river.

By-and-by we stepped again into our rocking craft for the return journey. Little or no paddling was necessary, the chief responsibility being the steersman's, who stood in the stern with watchful eye and paddle alert, as the pitpan shot along in her mad course. Through Hell Gate with marvellous speed, some agitation and a great deal of water, from rapid to rapid in foaming succession, we sped along. The sun sank lower and lower till the last ray glorified the cedar tops; through the wonderful palms the golden afterglow floated mysteriously for a little space, and the broadening river gave back the shadows in magical silence. Then darkness fell, and as we swung around a bend and drew swiftly near the friendly light at the landing-place, there came musically from the shadows on the other side the not irrelevant inquiry, "Who are you?"

༄

The Week (1 October 1885), 697–698.

Isabella Valancy Crawford (1850–1887)

Extradited (1886)

Arguably the most talented woman poet of nineteenth-century Canada, Isabella Valancy Crawford had an even more impecunious and difficult career than a male contemporary such as Archibald Lampman, and the details of her life are more obscure than those of her male peers.

According to the research work of Dorothy Livesay, Penny Petrone, Katherine Hale and others, Isabella Valancy Crawford was born in Dublin, Ireland on Christmas Day, 1850, the daughter of Dr. Stephen Dennis Crawford and Sydney Scott. She was the sixth of twelve children, only three of whom survived beyond childhood. Around 1854, the family appears to have emigrated to Wisconsin, where Crawford's sister Emma Naomi was born, and by 1858, the family had settled in Paisley, Bruce County, then "just struggling out of the embrace of the forest," where Dr. Crawford pursued an unsuccessful medical practice, his career blighted by alcoholism. Here Valancy (as Livesay tells us she was called by her family) spent a girlhood close both to pioneer nature and the educated sensibilities of her parents, for she was schooled mostly at home. By 1864 the family had relocated to North Douro (Lakefield), thanks to the help of the Strickland and Traill families, where the young girl became friendly with both Catherine Parr Traill and her daughter Katie, and developed a love of literature and music. In 1869, the Crawfords, still dogged by poverty, moved to the larger town of Peterborough, where Dr. Crawford died in July 1875, leaving Mrs. Crawford and her three children in financial straits. By 1876, Crawford's invalid sister Emma Naomi had died, and her brother Stephen had left to work in Algoma, from where he was able to offer only sporadic monetary support.

Valancy Crawford early directed her talent for poetry and fiction to attempts to support her family. Much of her prose in particular was written to appeal to the conventions of the day and to find publication in the more lucrative American periodicals such as *Frank Leslie's Magazine* and *Fireside Monthly*. In 1883, the poet and her mother moved to Toronto, where they lived in a succession of downtown rooming houses. Mrs. Crawford was supportive of her daughter's work, as Maud Miller Wilson tells in a 1905 sketch now at Queen's University Archives, and adversity strengthened the bond:

> Never had author more responsive listener than Mrs. Crawford proved to be to her daughter, laughing over her wit, entering into her moods and fancies, and like the Mother of old, hoarding up in her heart all the sayings of her child. . . . [In Toronto, the two were] almost completely by themselves. . . . They were deeply interested in English and European literature, and could speak together constantly.

Susan Frances Harrison (see page 75), then music and literary editor of *The Week*, tells of a visit from Crawford, to whom she had to announce the disappointing news that the magazine did not pay for poetry. She left a vignette of Crawford describing her as "a tall, dark young woman, whom most people would feel was difficult, almost repellant in manner," although her Toronto neighbours of the time also remembered her wit, and her love of music and cooking.

Isabella Valancy Crawford died on 12 February 1887. Despite privation, she left behind a remarkable body of poetry and prose, and even published a volume of her verse at her own expense, *Old Spookses' Pass, Malcolm's Katie and Other Poems* (1884). Fifty of its one thousand copies found buyers, although the reviews were largely favourable; later critics have appreciated the richness and complexity of her themes and symbols, which include nature, the Indian, and the emerging country.

"Extradited" draws on Crawford's memories of the Ontario pioneer landscape. Written at the end of her life, the story portrays the dark side of "angel in the house" maternal feeling in its portrayal of the smug and selfish Bess, who actually loves her son less selflessly than the hired man she betrays. The first image associated with Bess is that of the serpent, and like the biblical serpent, she is subtle and treacherous. In this story, Crawford moves away from the more sentimental fairy and society love stories of her early career to a more subtle portrayal of character.

"Extradited" was published in the Toronto *Globe* in September 1886. In February 1887, Crawford wrote, in a letter now at Queen's University Archives, to another writer: "I have contributed to the *Mail* and *Globe*, and won some very kind words from eminent critics, but have been quietly 'sat upon' by the High Priests of Canadian periodical literature."

∽

Suggested Reading:

Crawford, Isabella Valancy. *Selected Stories of Isabella Valancy Crawford*, ed. Penny Petrone. Ottawa: University of Ottawa Press, 1977.

Farmiloe, Dorothy. *Isabella Valancy Crawford: The Life and the Legends*. Ottawa: Tecumseh, 1983.

Hale, Katherine. *Isabella Valancy Crawford*. Toronto: Ryerson, 1923.

Ross, Catherine Sheldrick. "I.V. Crawford's Prose Fiction." In *Canadian Literature* 81 (Summer 1979), 47–58.

Tierney, Frank, ed. *The Crawford Symposium*. Ottawa: University of Ottawa Press, 1979.

Extradited

Isabella Valancy Crawford

"Oh, Sam! back so soon? Well, I'm glad."

She had her arms round his neck, she curved serpentwise in his clasp to get her eyes on his face.

"How's mammy?" she asked, in a slight panic, "not worse, is she?"

"Better," returned Sam; he pushed her away mechanically, and glanced round the rude room with its touches of refinement: the stop organ against the wall of unplastered logs, the primitive hearth, its floor of hewn planks.

"Oh yes! Baby!" she exclaimed, "you missed him; he's asleep on our bed; I'll fetch him."

He caught her apron string; still staring round the apartment.

"Where's Joe, Bess? I don't see him round."

Bessie crimsoned petulantly.

"You can think of the hired man first before me and Baby!"

"Baby's a sort of fixed fact. A hired man, ain't," said Sam, slowly. "Mebbe Joe's at the barn!"

"Maybe he is, and maybe he isn't," retorted Bessie sharply. "I didn't marry Samuel O'Dwyer to have a hired man set before me and my child, and I won't stand it—so there!"

"You needn't to," said Sam, smiling. He was an Irish Canadian; a rich smack of brogue adorned his tongue; a kindly graciousness of eye made a plain face almost captivating, while the proud and melancholy Celtic fire and intentness of his glance gave dignity to his expression. The lips were curved in a humorous smile, but round them were deeply graven heroic and Spartan lines.

"Sure, darlin', isn't it you an' the boy are the pulses of my heart?" he said, smiling. "Sure Joe can wait. I was sort of wonderin' at not seein' him—that's all. Say, I'll unhitch the horses. They've done fifteen miles o'mud holes an' corduroy since noon, an' then we'll have supper. I could most eat my boots, so hurry up, woman darlin', or maybe it's the boy I'll be aitin', or the bit of a dog your daddy sent to him. Hear the baste howlin' like a banshee out yonder."

"It's one of Cricket's last year's pups," cried Bessie, running to the waggon. "Wonder Father spared him; he thinks a sight of her pups. My! ain't he a beauty; won't baby just love him!"

She carried the yelping youngster into the house, while Sam took the horses to the barn, a primitive edifice of rough logs, standing in a bleak chaos of burned stumps, for "O'Dwyer's Clearing" was but two years old, and had the rage of its clearing fires on it yet. The uncouth eaves were fine crimson on one side, from the sunset; on the other a delicate, spiritual silver, from the moon hanging above the cedar swamp; the rude doors stood open, a vigorous purple haze, shot with heavy bars of crimson light, filled the interior; a "Whip-Poor-Will" chanted from a distant tree, like a muezzin from a minaret; the tired horses whinnied at a whiff of fresh clover, and rubbed noses in sedate congratulation. Sam looked at the ground a moment, reflectively, and then shouted:

"Hullo, Joe!"

"Hullo, Sam!"

By this time Sam was stooping over the waggon-tongue, his rugged face in the shadow, too intent on straps and buckles to glance up.

"Back all right, you see, Joe," he remarked. "How's things gettin' along?"

"Sublimely," said Joe, coming to his assistance. "I got the south corner cut—we've only to draw it tomorrow."

"I never seen the beat of you at hard work," remarked Sam. "A slight young chap like you, too. It's just the spirit of you! But you mustn't outdo the strength that is in you for all that. I'm no slave-driver; I don't want your heart's blood. Sure, I've had your sweat two long years an' the place shows it—it's had your sense an' your sinews, so it had. I'll never forget it to you, Joe."

Joe's tanned, nervous face was shaded by the flap of his limp straw hat. He looked piercingly at Sam, as the released horses walked decorously into the barn.

"Go to your supper, Sam," he said. "I'll bed them. I venture to say you're pretty sharp-set; go in."

"I'll lend a hand first," returned Sam. He followed the other into the barn.

"It's got dark in here suddenly," remarked Joe. "I'll get the lantern."

"Don't," said Sam, Slowly. "There's something to be spoke about betwixt you an' me, Joe, an' I'd as lieve say it in the dark; let the lantern be. I'd as lieve say it in the dark."

⌒

"A thousand dollars!"

Bessie rose on her elbow and looked at her sleeping husband. Slumber brought the iron to the surface instead of melting it, and his face became sterner and more resolute in its repose. Its owner was not a man to be trifled with, she admitted as she gazed, and watching him she shivered slightly in the mournful moonlight. Many of her exceedingly respectable virtues were composed mainly of two or three minor vices: her conjugal love was a compound of vanity and jealousy; her maternal affection an agreement of rapacity and animal instinct. In giving her a child, nature had developed the she eagle in her breast. She was full of impotent, unrecognized impulses to prey on all things in her child's behalf. By training and habit she was honest, but her mind was becoming active with the ingenuity of self-cheatry. She held a quiet contempt for her husband, the unlearned man who had won the pretty schoolmistress; and, hedged in by the prim fence of routine knowledge and imperfect education, she despised the large crude movements of the untrained intellect, and the primitive power of the strong and lofty soul. He muttered uneasily as she slipped out of bed. The electric chill of moonlight did not affect her spirit—she was not vulnerable to these hints and petitions of nature. She crept carefully into the great rude room, which was hall, parlor, and kitchen. The back log, which never died out, smouldered on the hearth. A block of moonlight fell like a slab of marble on the floor of loose planks which rattled faintly under her firm, bare feet. The wooden benches, the coarse table, the log walls, started through the gloom like bleak sentinels of the great Army of Privation. She looked at them without disgust, as she stole to the corner where her organ stood. She sang a silent little hymn of self-laudation.

"Some women would spend it on fine fallals for their backs or houses." She thought, "I won't. I'll bank every cent of it for baby. Money doubles in ten years. A thousand dollars will grow nicely in twenty—or I'll get Daddy to loan it out on farm mortgages. I guess Sam will stare twenty years hence when he finds out how rich I've got to be. I'm glad I know my duty as a parent—Sam would never see things as I do—and a thousand dollars is a sight of money."

She groped on the organ for her paper portefolio, an elegant trifle Joe had sent to the city for, to delicately grace her last birthday; its scent of violets guided her. She took from it a paper and pencil, and standing in the moonlight scribbled a few lines. She dotted her "i's" and crossed her "t's" with particularity, and was finnickin in her nice folding of the written sheet. Her cool cheeks kept their steady pink; her round eyes their untroubled calm; her chin bridled a little with spiritual pride, as she cautiously opened the outer door.

"It's my clear duty as a parent and a citizen," she thought, with self-approval, "the thousand dollars would not tempt me if my duty were not so plainly set before me; and the money will be in good hands. I'm not one to spend it in vain show. Money's a great evil to a weak and worldly mind, but I'm not one for vain show."

She looked up at the sky from under the morning glories Joe had thoughtfully planted to make cool shadows for her rocker in the porch.

"It will rain to-morrow. So I'll not wash till Friday; I wonder will that pink print Sam fetched home turn out a fast color; I'll make it up for Baby; he'll look too cunning for anything in it, with those coral sleeve links Joe gave him. I hope he won't cry, and wake Sam before I get back."

He did not. As she had left him she found him on her return, a little snowy ball, curled up against his father's massive shoulder, the beautiful, black, baby head, thrust against the starting sinews of the man's bare and massive throat. When choice was possible Baby scramble into the aura of the father—not of the mother. Sam stirred, started, and yawned.

"What's up, Bess?" he asked sleepily.

"I went to the well to draw fresh water," she replied, folding her shawl neatly on the back of a chair. "I was wakeful and thirsty—the night is so hot."

"Guess that consarned pup worried you with his howlen'," he said, "I don't hear him now—hope he won't get out of the barn—but that ain't probable—Joe shut him in, right enough; you should have sent me to the well, girl darlin', so you should."

Bessie picked out a burr which she felt in the fringes of her shawl, and said nothing. She was strictly truthful, so far as the letter of truth went; she had gone to the well and had drawn a bucket of cool water from that shaft of solid shadow. What else she had accomplished she decidedly had no intention of confiding to Sam. She slipped into bed, took the baby on her arm, and kissed his pouting lips.

"God bless the darling," she said with her pretty smile.

"Amen," said Sam earnestly. "God come betwixt every man's child an' harm." Bessie dozed off placidly, the child on her arm. Sam lay staring at the moonlight, listening, thinking, and grandly sorrowing.

Isabella Valancy Crawford

There was the unceasing sound of someone tossing feverishly on a creaking bedstead, the eternal sound of heavy sighs resolutely smothered.

"He ain't sleepin' well, ain't Joe," thought Sam. "Not even though he knows Bessie an' me is his friends, true as the day. Guess he ain't sleepin' at all, poor chap!"

"The consarned pup is gone," remarked Sam, disgustedly, as he came in to breakfast. "Guess he scrambled up to the hay gap and jumped out. Too bad!"

"He's safe enough," said Joe. "He probably ran for home. You will find him at your father's on your next visit, Mrs. O'Dwyer. Dogs have the 'homing' instinct as well as pigeons.

"Yes, I guess he went back to pa," said Bessie. Her color rose, her eyes flashed. "Do put baby down, Joe," she said sharply, I don't want—that is, you are mussing his clean frock."

Joe looked keenly at her.

"I understand," he said, gently. He placed the child tenderly on the rude lounge, which yet was pretty like all Bessie's belongings, and walked to the open door.

"I think I'll straighten things a bit at the landing," he said. "Piner's booms burst yesterday and before the drive reaches here it's as well to see to the boats—those river drivers help themselves to canoes wherever they come across them."

"Just as you say, Joe," said Sam, gravely. "I've never known your head or your heart at fault yet."

Joe gave a long, wistful look of gratitude, and went out. He did not glance at Bessie, nor she at him.

"Bess, woman," said Sam, "what ails you at Joe?"

"You know well enough," she said placidly. "He's free to stay here; I don't deny he's worked well; though that was his duty, and he was paid for it, but he shan't touch my child again. No parent who understood her duty would permit; I know mine, I'm thankful to say."

Her small rancors and spites were the "Judas' doors" through which she most frequently betrayed herself. She had always faintly disliked Joe, before whom her shabby little school routine, her small affectations of intellectual superiority had shrivelled into siccous leaves. She would assert herself now against Sam's dearly-loved friend, she thought, jealously and with an approving conscience, and it was her plain duty to tear him out of that large and constant heart, she was pleased to feel.

Sam's face changed, in a breath, to a passionate pallor of skin; a proud and piercing gloom of anger darkened his blue eyes to black; he looked at her in wonder.

"What's all this, woman?" he demanded, slowly. "But it's never your heart that's said it! Him that gave the sweat of his body and the work of his mind to help me make this home for you! Him that's saved my life more nor once at risk of his own young days! Him that's as close to my heart as my own brother! Tut, woman! It's never you would press the thorn in the breast of him into his heart's core. I won't demane myself with leavin' the thought to you, Bessie O'Dwyer!"

He struck his fist on the table; he stared levelly at her, defying her to lower herself in his eyes.

She smoothly repaired her error.

"I spoke in a hurry," she said, lifting the baby's palm, and covering Sam's lips with its daintiness. "I feel hurt he had so little confidence in me. I wish him well; you know that."

Sam smiled under the fluttering of the child's palm upon his lips; he gave a sigh of relief. "Be kind to him, Bessie darlin'," he said, "Shure our own boy is born—but he isn't dead yet: the Lord stand betwixt the child an' harm! An' there is no tellin' when he, too, may need the kind word and the tender heart. Shure I'm sorry I took you up in arnest just now."

"I spoke in a pet," said Bessie gently. "I remember, of course, all we owe to Joe—how could I forget it?"

"Forgettin's about the aisiest job in life," said Sam, rising. "Guess I'll help Joe at the landin', he's downhearted, an' I won't lave him alone to his trouble."

ISABELLA VALANCY CRAWFORD

Bessie looked after his disapprovingly.

"Trouble indeed! I thought Sam had clearer ideas on such points. The notion of confounding trouble with right-down sin and wickedness! Well, it's a good thing I know my duty. I wonder if Pa has any mortgage in his mind ready for that money? It must be a first mortgage; I won't risk any other—I know my responsibility as a mother better than that."

∽

"Why, man alive!"

Sam was astonished; for the first time in his experience of Joe, the latter was idle. He sat on a fallen tree, looking vacantly into the strong current below him.

"I'm floored, Sam," he answered, without looking up, "I've no grit left in me—not a grain."

"Then it's the first time since I've known you," said Sam, regarding him with wistful gravity. "Don't let the sorrow master you, Joe."

"You call it sorrow, Sam?"

"That's the blessed an' holy name for it now," said Sam, with his lofty, simple seriousness, "what ever it may have been afore. Hearten up, Joe! Shure you're as safe at O'Dwyer's Clearin', as if you were hid unther a hill. Rouse your heart, man alive! What's to fear?"

"Not much to fear, but a great deal to feel," said Joe. "Am I not stripped of my cloak to you—that's bitter."

"The only differ is that I'm dead sure now of what I suspicioned right along," said Sam. "It's not in reason that a schollard an' a gentleman should busy himself on O'Dwyer's Clearin' for more nor two years, unless to sconce shame an' danger. Rouse your sowl, Joe! don't I owe half of all I have to your arm an' your larnin'? When this danger blows past I'll divide with you, an' you can make a fresh start in some sthrange counthry. South Americay's a grond place, they tell me; shure, I'll take Bessie an' the boy an' go with you. I've no kin nor kith of my own, an' next to her an' the child it is yourself is in the core of my heart. Kape the sorrow, Joe; it's the pardon of God on you, but lave the shame an' the fear go; you'll do the world's wonder yet, boy."

Joe was about three-and-twenty, Sam in middle age. He placed his massive hand on the other's bare and throbbing head, and both looked silently at the dark and rapid river: Joe with a faint pulse of hope in his bruised and broken soul.

"Piner's logs'll get here about to-morrow," said Sam at last, 'shure it's Bessie'll be in the twitteration, watchin' the hens an' geese from them mauraudtherin river drivers. I wish the pup hadn't got away; it's a good watch dog his mother is, an' likely he'd show her blood in him—the villain that he was to run away with himself, like that, but liberty's a swate toothful, so it is, to man or brute."

The following day, Bessie having finished her ironing and baking with triumphant exactness, stood looking from the lovely vines of the porch, down the wild farm road. She was crystal-clean and fresh, and the child in her arms was like a damask rose in his turkey-red frock and white bib. A model young matron was Mrs. O'Dwyer and looked it to the fine point of perfection, Sam thought, as he glanced back at her, pride and tenderness in his eyes. She was not looking after his retreating figure, but eagerly down the farm road, and, it seemed to Sam, she was listening intently. "Mebbe she thinks the shouting of them river drivers is folks comin' up the road," he thought, as he turned the clump of cedar bushes by the landing, and found Joe at work, patching a bark canoe. As usual he was laboring fiercely as men rush in battle, the sweat on his brow, his teeth set, his eyes fixed. Sam smiled reprovingly.

"Shure it's all smashed up' you'll have her, Joe, again she's mended," he remarked, "more power to your elbow; but take it easy, man! You'll wear out soon enough."

"I must work like the devil, or, think," said Joe, feverishly. "Some day, Sam, I'll tell you all the treasures of life I threw from me, then you'll understand."

"When a man understands by the road of the heart, where's the good of larnin' by the road of the ears?" said Sam, with the tenderest compassion; "but I'll listen when it's your will to tell, never fear. Hark, now! don't I hear them rollickin' divvils of pike pole men shoutin' beyant the bend there?"

"Yes; Piner's logs must be pretty close," answered Joe, looking up at the river.

"They'll come down the rapids in style," said Sam, throwing a chip on the current, "the sthrame's swift as a swallow and strong as a giant with the rains."

They worked in silence for a while, then Joe began to whistle softly. Sam smiled.

"That's right, Joe," he said, "there's nothing so bad that it mightn't be worse—there's hope ahead for you yet, never fear."

A glimmer of some old joyous spirit sparkled in the young man's melancholy eyes, to fade instantly. "It's past all that, dear old friend," he said. As he spoke he glanced towards the cedar scrub between them and the house.

"Here comes Mrs. O'Dwyer with the boy," he said, "and Sam, there are three men, strangers, with her."

"Shanty bosses come to buy farm stuff," said Sam. He turned on Joe with an air of sudden mastery.

"Away with you down the bank," he said. "Into the bush with you, and don't come out until you hear me fire five shots in a string. Away with you!"

"Too late, Sam," said the other, "they have seen me."

"What's all this, Bessie?"

Bessie wiped the baby's wet lips with her apron.

"These gentlemen asked to see you, Sam. I guess they want some farm stuff off us for Piner's Camp. So I brought them along."

She looked placidly at her husband; the baby sprang in her arms eager to get to his friend Joe, whose red flannel shirt he found very attractive.

"Potatoes or flour?" asked Sam curtly, turning on the strangers.

"Well, it ain't neither," said one of them—he laid his hand on Joe's wrist. "It's this young gentleman we're after; he robbed his employer two years back, and he's wanted back by Uncle Sam. That's about the size of it."

There was nothing brutal in his look or speech; he knew he was not dealing with a hardened criminal. He even felt compassion for the wretched quarry he had in his talons.

"He's in Canada—on British soil; I dare you to touch him!" said Sam fiercely.

"We have his extradition papers right enough," said one of the other detectives. "Don't be so foolish as to resist the law, Mr. O'Dwyer."

"He shan't for me," said Joe, quietly. He stood motionless while the detective snapped one manacle of the handcuffs on his wrist; the steel glittered like a band of fire in the sun.

The child leaped strongly in Bessie's arms, crowing with delight at the pretty brightness. She was a little off her guard, somewhat faint as she watched the deathly shame on the young man's face which had never turned on her or hers but with tenderness and goodwill. Her brain reeled a little, her hands felt weak.

Suddenly there was a shriek, a flash of red, a soft plunge in the water. Joe threw his arms open, dashing aside the detectives like straws.

"Don't hold me—let me save him!" he cried.

Sam could not swim; he stood on the bank holding Bessie, who screamed and struggled in convulsions of fright as she saw her child drowning. Joe rose in the current, fighting his way superbly towards the little red bundle whirling before him. One of the detectives covered him with a revolver.

"Try to escape and I'll shoot," he called out, "understand?"

Joe smiled. Escape to the opposite shore and leave Sam's child to drown? No; he had no idea of it. It was a terrible fight between the man and the river—and the man subdued it unto him. He turned back to shore, the child in his teeth, both arms—one with the shining handcuff on it— beating the hostile current with fine, steady strokes.

Another moment and he would be safe on shore, a captive and ashamed.

He spurned the yellow fringes of the current; he felt ground under his feet; he half rose to step on the bank.

ISABELLA VALANCY CRAWFORD

Then there rose a bewildering cry from Sam and the men watching him; he turned and saw his danger.

With one sublime effort he flung the child on the bank, and then with the force of a battering-ram the first of Piner's logs crashed upon him. It reared against him like a living thing instinct with rage, and wallowing monster-like led its barky hordes down the rushing stream, rolling triumphantly over a bruised and shattered pigmy of creation, a man.

"Extradited, by ginger," said one of the detectives, as the groaning logs rolled compactly together over the spot where Joe had gone down.

Before the men departed, Bessie, with the baby on her arm, in a nice clean frock, found opportunity to ask one of them a momentous question. "Do you think, he being dead, that I shall get any of the reward promised for his arrest? Only for me sending that note to Pa tied round the pup's neck, you would never have found him away back here, you know."

"I guess not," replied the detective, eyeing her thoughtfully. "You're a smart woman, you are, but you won't get no reward all the same; pity, ain't it?"

"It's a shame," she said, bursting into a passion of tears. "It don't seem that there's any reward for doing one's duty; oh, it's a downright shame."

"Best keep all this tol'ble shady from that man of yours," said the detective, meditatively. "He ain't got no idee of dooty to speak of, he ain't, and seein' he was powerful fond of that poor, brave, young chap as saved that remarkably fine infant in your arms, he might cut up rough. Some folks ain't got no notion of dooty, they ain't. You best keep dark, ma'am, on the inspiritin' subject of havin' done your dooty an' lost a thousand dollars reward."

And Bessie followed his advice very carefully indeed, though she always had the private luxury of regarding herself as an unrewarded and unrecognized heroine of duty.

꙳

The Globe (Toronto: 4 September 1886), 10.

Susan Frances Harrison "Seranus" (1859–1935)

CROWDED OUT! (1886)

THE STORY OF DELLE JOSEPHINE BOULANGER (1886)

Like Rosanna Leprohon and May Agnes Fleming, Susan Frances Harrison began publishing in her teens. A woman of many talents, she published poetry, essays, reviews, stories, and novels, composed an opera, edited the Toronto *Conservatory Monthly*, and was for twenty years principal of the Rosedale Branch of the Toronto Conservatory of Music.

Born in Toronto on 24 February 1859, Susan Riley was the daughter of John Byron Riley; her mother's name was Drought. Both her parents were Irish. She was educated at private schools, first in Toronto, then in Montreal. In 1879 she married musician John W.F. Harrison and moved with him to Ottawa, and in 1886, to Toronto, where John Harrison taught at the Toronto Conservatory of Music. She died in Toronto in 1935.

Marriage and motherhood did not slow Harrison's production of poetry, journalism, and fiction. Her works appeared in the United States and Great Britain, as well as Canada, in *Pall Mall Magazine*, *Temple Bar*, *The Strand*, *New England Magazine*, *Cosmopolitan*, Detroit *Free Press*, Montreal *Canadian Illustrated News*, *Stewart's Quarterly*, Toronto *Globe*, *The Week*, *Canadian Monthly*, and *Saturday Night*, under various pseudonyms, including "Medusa," "Gilbert King," and most often, "Seranus." The latter pseudonym came from a misreading of her signature of her given name name, Frances.

Throughout her career, Harrison maintained an interest in French Canada. Her novels *The Forest of Bourg-Marie* (1898) and *Ringfield* (1914) are set in rural and small-town Quebec. Most of the stories in *Crowded Out! and Other Sketches* (1886), are also set in Quebec. Harrison's writing evinces her awareness of the 1880s and 1890s aesthetic movement in England, especially in the decadent element evident in her novels and some of her stories, and in her interest in the villanelle and other French fixed forms then undergoing a revival in English poetry. Some of her fiction reflects the influence of Edgar Allen Poe.

Harrison's stories are those of a poet, characterized by intensity, compression, complexity, symbolism, and effective creation of atmosphere through setting. Both "Crowded Out!" and "The Story of Delle Josephine Boulanger" are claustrophobic in setting and atmosphere.

"Crowded Out!," the first story in the volume, is reportedly based on Harrison's personal experience during a visit to England in an attempt to interest English publishers in her work. Apparently, the little attic room of the protagonist is similar to Harrison's own room in London at that time. The story is experimental in its use of internal monologue, which has affinities with twentieth-century stream of consciousness technique as well as with Tennyson's monodramas, notably "Locksley Hall" and "Locksley Hall Forty Years Later." The male narrator expresses the desperation and heartbreak of the unrequited lover and rejected artist, his emotional intensity conveyed through cadenced repetition and abrupt shifts in thought, and amplified by his description of London and his attic room. His failure to find artistic recognition in England parallels his failure to win back his aristocratic French Canadian lover.

In "The Story of Josephine Boulanger," Harrison uses setting and colour effectively, from the desolate first impression of the little village and the claustrophobic effect of the snow which traps the narrator in the house, to the milliner's dramatic red hat, "a nightmare red, a kind of mute scarlet 'Raven,'" the latter an obvious reference to Poe's poem. The male anglophone observer–narrator is common to most of Harrison's stories of French Canadian life. The snow, which keeps falling until it obliterates the door and residents who must wait for someone to come and dig them out, is not only claustrophobic but also linked with death: "The whole world seemed smothered in the soft thick pillows of snow." Ultimately the snow provides a tomb for Mademoiselle Josephine Boulanger. But it also allows the narrator to learn Josephine's story, to learn of the incident from twenty years past for which she spends the rest of her life doing penance—self-imprisoned in virtual solitary confinement in her tiny house—and to achieve an understanding of the extent to which she has been haunted throughout her life by the incident.

∽

Suggested Reading:
Harrison, Susan Frances. *Crowded Out! and Other Sketches*. Ottawa: *Evening Journal*, 1886.
_____. *Ringfield*. Toronto: Musson, 1914.
MacMillan, Carrie, "Susan Frances Harrison: Paths through the Ancient Forest." In *Silenced Sextet*. Montreal: McGill-Queen's University Press, 1992.

CROWDED OUT!

Susan Frances Harrison ("Seranus")

I am nobody. I am living in a London lodging-house. My room is up three pair of stairs. I have come to London to sell or to part with in some manner an opera, a comedy, a volume of verse, songs, sketches, stories. I compose as well as write. I am ambitious. For the sake of another, one other, I am ambitious. For myself it does not matter. If nobody will discover me I must discover myself. I must demand recognition, I must wrest attention, they are my due. I look from my window over the smoky roofs of London, What will it do for me, this great cold city? It shall hear me, it shall pause for a moment, for a day, for a year. I will make it to listen to me, to look at me. I have left a continent behind, I have crossed a great water; I have incurred dangers, trials of all kinds; I have grown pale and thin with labor and the midnight oil; I have starved, and watched the dawn break starving; I have prayed on my stubborn knees for death and I have prayed on my stubborn knees for life—all that I might reach London, London that has killed so many of my brothers, London the cold, London the blind, London the cruel! I am here at last. I am here to be tested, to be proved, to be worn proudly, as a favorite and costly jewel is worn, or to be flung aside scornfully or dropped stealthily to—the devil! And I love it so this great London! I am ready to swear no one ever loved it so before! The smokier it is, the dirtier, the dingier, the better. The oftener it rains the better. The more whimsical it is, the more fickle, the more credulous, the more self-sufficient, the more self-existent, the better. Nothing that it can do, nothing that it can be, can change my love for it, great cruel London!

But to be cruel to *me*, to be fickle to *me*, to be deaf to *me*, to be blind to *me*! Would I change then? I might. As yet it does not know me. I pass through its streets, touching here a bit of old black wall, picking there an ivy leaf, and it knows me not. It is holy ground to me. It is the mistress whose hand alone I as yet dare to kiss. Some day I shall possess the whole, and I shall walk with the firm and buoyant tread of the accepted, delighted lover. Only to-day I am nobody. I am crowded out. Yet there are moments when the mere joy of being in England, of being in London, satisfies me. I have seen the sunbeam strike the glory along the green. I know it is an English sky above me, all change, all mutability. No steady cloudless sphere of blue but ever-varying glories of white piled cloud against the gray. Listen to this. I saw a primrose—the first I had ever seen—in the hedge. They said "Pick it." But I did not. I, who had written three years ago,—

> I never pulled a primrose, I,
> But could I know that there may lie
> E'en now some small or hidden seed,
> Within, below, an English mead,
> Waiting for sun and rain to make
> A flower of it for my poor sake,
> I then could wait till winds should tell,
> For me there swayed or swung a bell,
> Or reared a banner, peered a star,
> Or curved a cup in woods afar.

I who had written that, I had found my first primrose and I could not pluck it. I found it fair be sure. I find all England fair. The shimmering mist and the tender rain, the red wall-flower and the ivy green, the singing birds and the shallow streams—all the country; the blackened churches, the grass-grown churchyards, the hum of streets the crowded omnibus, the gorgeous shops,—all the town. God!

do I not love it, my England? Yet not my England yet. Till she proclaim it herself, I am not hers. I will make her mine. I will write as no man has ever written about her, for very love of her. I look out to-night from my narrow window and think how the moonlight falls on Tintern, on Glastonbury, on Furness. How it falls on the primrose I would not pluck. How it would like to fall on the tall blue-bells in the wood. I see the lights of Oxford St. the omnibuses rattle by, the people are going to see Irving, Wilson Barrett, Ellen Terry. What line of mine, what bar, what thought or phrase will turn the silence into song, the copper into gold? * * * * I come back from the window and sit at the square centre table. It is rickety and uncomfortable, useless to write on. I kick it. I would kick anything that came in my way to-night. I am savage. Outside, a French piano is playing that infernal waltz. A fair subject for kicking if you will. But, though I would I cannot. What a room! The fire-place is filled with orange peel and brown paper, cigar stumps and matches. One blind I pulled down this morning, the other is crooked. The lamp glass is cracked, my work too. I dare not look at the wall paper nor the pictures. The carpet I have kicked into holes. I can see it though I can't feel it, it is so thin. My clothes are lying all about. The soot of London begrimes every object in the room. I would buy a pot of musk or a silken scarf if I dared, but how can I?

I must get my bread first and live for beauty after. Everything is refused though, everything sent back or else dropped as it were into some bottomless pit or gulf.

Here is my opera. This is my *magnum opus*, very dear, very clear, very well preserved. For it is three years old. I scored it nearly altogether, by *her* side, Hortense, my dear love, my northern bird! You could flush under my gaze, you could kindle at my touch, but you were not for me, you were not for me! * * * * My head droops down, I could go to sleep. But I must not waste the time in sleep. I will write another story. No; I had four returned to-day. Ah! cruel London! To love you so, only that I may be spurned and thrust aside, ignored, forgotten. But to-morrow I will try again. I will take the opera to the theatres, I will see the managers, I will even tell them about myself and about Hortense—but it will be hard. They do not know me, they do not know Hortense. They will laugh, they will say "You fool." And I shall be helpless, I shall let them say it. They will never listen to me, though I play my most beautiful phrase, for I am nobody. And Hortense, the child with the royal air, Hortense, with her imperial brow and her hair rolled over its cushion, Hortense, the *Châtelaine* of *Beau Séjour*, the delicate, haughty, pale and impassioned daughter of a noble house, that Hortense, my Hortense, is nobody!

Who in this great London will believe in me, who will care to know about Hortense or about *Beau Séjour*? If they ask me, I shall say—oh! proudly—not in Normandy nor in Alsace, but far away across a great water dwells such a maiden in such a *château*. There by the side of a northern river, ever rippling, ever sparkling in Summer, hard, hard frozen in winter, stretches a vast estate. I remember its impenetrable pinewood, its deep ravine; I see the *château*, long and white and straggling, with the red tiled towers and the tall French windows; I see the terrace where the hound must still sleep; I see the square side tower with the black iron shutters; I see the very window where Hortense has set her light; I see the floating cribs on the river, I hear the boatmen singing—

> Descendez à l'ombre,
> Ma Jolie blonde.

And now I am dreaming surely! This is London, not *Beau Séjour*, and Hortense is far away, and it is that cursed fellow in the street I hear! The morrow comes on quickly. If I were to draw up that crooked blind now I should see the first streaks of daylight. Who pinned those other curtains together? That was well done, for I don't want to see the daylight; and it comes in, you know, Hortense, when you think it is shut out. Somebody calls it *fingers*, and that is just what it is, long fingers of dawn, always pale, always gray and white, stealing in and around my pillow for me. Never pink, never rosy, mind that; always faint and shadowy and gray. * * * *

It was all caste. Caste in London, caste in *Le Bas Canada*, all the same. Because she was a *St. Hilaire*. Her full name—*Hortense Angelique De Repentigny de St. Hilaire*—how it grates on me afresh with its aristocratic plentitude. She is well-born, certainly; better born than most of these girls I have seen here in London, driving, walking, riding in the Parks. They wear their hair over cushions too. Freckled skins, high cheek-bones, square foreheads, spreading eyebrows—they shouldn't wear it so. It suits Hortense—with her pale patrician outline and her dark pencilled eyebrows, and her little black ribbon and amulet around her neck. *O, Marie, priez pour nous qui avons recours à vous!* Once I walked out to *Beau Séjour*. She did not expect me and I crept through the leafy ravine to the pinewood, then on to the steps, and so up to the terrace. Through the French window I could see her seated at the long table opposite Father Couture. She lives alone with the good Père. She is the last of the noble line, and he guards her well and guards her money too.

"I do remember that it vill be all for ze Church," she has said to me. And the priest has taught her all she knows, how to sew and embroider, and cook and read, though he never lets her read anything but works on religion. Religion, always religion! He has brought her up like a nun, crushed the life out of her. Until I found her out, found my jewel out. It is Tennyson who says that. But his "Maud" was freer to woo than Hortense, freer to love and kiss and hold—my God! that night while I watched them studying and bending over those cursed works on the Martyrs and the Saints and the Mission houses—I saw him—him—that old priest—take her in his arms and caress her, drink her breath, feast on her eyes, her hair, her delicate skin, and I burst in like a young madman and told Father Couture what I thought. Oh! I was mad! I should have won her first. I should have worked quietly, cautiously, waiting, waiting, biding my time. But I could never bide my time. And now she hates me, Hortense hates me, though she so nearly learned to love me. There where we used to listen to the magical river songs, we nearly loved, did we not Hortense? But she was a *St. Hilaire*, and I—I was nobody, and I had insulted *le bon Père*. Yet if I can go back to her rich, prosperous, independent—What if that happen? But I begin to fancy it will never happen. My resolutions, where are they, what comes of them? Nothing. I have tried everything except the opera. Everything else has been rejected. For a week I have not gone to bed at all. I wait and see those ghastly gray fingers smoothing my pillow. I am not wanted. I am crowded out. My hands tremble and I cannot write. My eyes fail and I cannot see. To the window! * * * * The lights of Oxford St. once more; the glare and the rattle without, the fever and the ruin, the nerves and the heart within. Poor nerves, poor heart; it is food you want and wine and rest, and I cannot give them to you. * * * *

Sing, Hortense, will you? sit by my side, by our dear river St. Maurice, the clear, the sparkling. See how the floating cribs sail by, each with its gleaming lights! It is like Venice I suppose. Shall we see Venice ever, Hortense, you and I? Sing now for me,

Descendez à l'ombre,
Ma Jolie blonde.

Only you are *petite brune*, there is nothing *blonde* about you, *mignonne*, my dear mademoiselle, I should say if I were with you of course as I used to do. But surely I *am* with you and those lights are the floating cribs I see, and your voice it is that sings, and presently the boatmen hear and they turn and move their hands and join in—Now all together,

Descendez à l'ombre,
   *   *   *   *   *   *   *

It was like you, Hortense, to come all this way. How did you manage it, manage to cross that great water all alone? My poor girl did you grow tired of *Le bon Père* at last and of the Martyrs and the Saints and the Jesuit Fathers? But you have got your amulet on still I hope. That is right, for there is a chance—there is a chance of these things proving blessings after all to good girls, and you were a good girl Hortense. You will not mind my calling you Hortense, will you? When we are in *Le Bas Canada* again, in your own seignieury, it will be "Madamoiselle," I promise you. You say it is a strange pillow, Hortense? Books, my girl, and manuscripts; hard but not so hard as London stones and London hearts. Do you know I think I am dying, or else going mad? And no one will listen even if I cry out. There is too much to listen to already in England. Think of all the growing green, Hortense, if you can, where you are, so far away from it all. Where you are it is cold and the snow is still on the ground and only the little bloodroot is up in the woods. Here where I am Hortense, where I am going to die, it is warm and green full of color—oh! such color! Before I came here, to London you know London that is going to do so much for me, for us both, I had one day—one day in the country. There I saw—No! they will not let me tell you, I knew they would try to prevent me, those long gray fingers stealing in, stealing in! But I *will* tell you. Listen, Hortense, please. I saw the hawthorne, pink and white, the laburnum—yellow—not fire-color, I shall correct the Laureate there, Hortense, when I am better, when I * * publish! * * * It is dreadful to be alone in London. Don't come, Hortense. Stay where you are, even if it is cold and gray and there is no color. Keep your amulet round your neck, dear! * * * * I count my pulse beats. It is a bad thing to do. It is broad daylight now and the fingers have gone. I can write again perhaps. * * The pen * * * The paper * * * * The ink * * * * God. Hortense! There is no ink left! And my heart—My heart—Hortense!!!

> Descendez à l'ombre
> Ma Jolie blonde.

∾

Crowded Out! and Other Sketches (Ottawa: *Evening Journal*, 1886), 5–10.

SUSAN FRANCES HARRISON

THE STORY OF
DELLE JOSEPHINE BOULANGER
Susan Frances Harrison ("Seranus")

CHAPTER I

Delle Josephine Boulanger, Miss Josephine Baker; Miss Josephine Baker, Delle Josephine Boulanger. What a difference it makes, the language! What a transformation! I thought this to myself as I stood on the opposite side of the street looking at the sign. To be sure, it was only printed in French and sad little letters they were that composed the name, but my mind quickly translated them into the more prosaic English as I stood and gazed. Delle Josephine was a milliner and I had been recommended to try and get a little room "*sous les toits*" that she sometimes had to let, during my stay in the dismal Canadian village with the grand and inappropriate name of *Bonheur du Roi*. Bonneroi, or Bonneroy, it was usually called. Such a dismal place it seemed to be; one long street of whitewashed or dirty wooden houses, two raw red brick "stores," and the inevitable Roman Catholic Church, Convent and offices, still and orderly and gray, with the quiet priests walking about and the occasional sound of the unmistakeable convent bell. I arrived on a sleety winter's day early in December. Everything was gray, or colorless or white; the people's faces were pinched and pale, the sky was a leaden gray in hue, and I thought as I stood opposite to my future abode under Delle Josephine's roof that the only bit of "local color" so far was to be found in her window. I could distinctly see from where I stood the most extraordinary *hat* I had ever seen. I immediately crossed the road to examine it. It was a triumph in lobster-color. In shape like a very large Gainsborough, it was made of shirred scarlet satin with large bows of satin ribbon of the same intense color and adorned with a bird of paradise. I can see it now and can recall the images it suggested to my mind at the time. These were of cardinals and kings, of sealing-wax and wafers, of tropic moons and tangled marshes, of hell and judgment and the conventional Zamiel. It looked fit to be worn by a Mrs. Zamiel, if there be such a person. I looked so long and earnestly that I evidently attracted the notice of the mistress of the shop, for I saw a hand push back the faded red curtain that veiled the interior and a queer little visage appeared regarding me with something I thought of distrust. Did I look as if I might break the glass and run off with the hat? Perhaps I did, so I entered the shop immediately and said in a reasoning tone,

"I am looking for rooms in the village, Mademoiselle, and hear you have one to let. Can I see it now, if not too much trouble?"

"You come from Morréall?"

This I learnt was meant for Montreal.

"Yes," I returned.

"You are by yourself, Monsieur, you are sure? No ladees, eh?"

"O dear! no" said I laughing. "I am making some studies—sketches in this locality and am entirely alone. Do you find ladies a trouble?"

"Oh, perhaps not always. But there was one Mees I had. I did not like her, and so I said—we will have no more Mees, but again and always Messieurs." She was frank enough but not unpleasant in her manner. A little bit of a woman, thin and shrivelled, with one shoulder slightly higher than the other, black beads for eyes, and the ugliest mouthful of teeth that I had ever seen on any one. Had it

SUSAN FRANCES HARRISON

not been that her expression was honest and good natured and her manner bright and intelligent, I should have recoiled before the yellow tusks of eye-teeth, and the blackened stumps and shrunken gums revealed to me everytime she spoke. She wore a print dress made neatly enough which was very clean, and a black crape ruff round her sallow neck. The shop was small but clean and at the back I saw a kind of little sitting room. Into this I went while she ran up-stairs to prepare the room for my inspection. The carpet was the usual horribly ingenious affair of red squares inside green octagons, and green squares inside red octagons, varied by lengthwise stripes of bright purple. The walls were plain white, covered with many prints in vivid colors of the Crucifixion, the Annunciaton and the Holy Family; also three pictures of three wonderful white kittens which adorn so many nurseries and kitchens. There were no ornaments, but there was a large looking-glass framed in walnut, and over it a dismal wreath of roses and their leaves done in human gray hair. The glass was opposite the door and I saw Delle Josephine descending to meet me just as I was turning away from this suggestive "in memoriam." A crooked little stairway brought me to a small landing, and three more steps to my room. I may call it that for I took it on the spot. It was large enough for my wants and seemed clean and when the paper blinds, yellow, with a black landscape on them, were raised, rather cheerful. We were opposite the chief "*épicerie*," the only "*marchandise sèches*," and a blacksmith, whose jolly red fire I could sometimes catch a glimpse of.

Now, this is a really a true story of French Canadian life, or rather let me say, a true story of one of my own French Canadian experiences, and so I must confess that once installed in my little room *chez* Delle Josephine Boulanger, nothing whatever of any interest took place until I had been there quite a week. I lived most regularly and monotonously; rising at eight I partook of coffee made by my landlady, accompanied by tinned fruit for which I formed a great taste. Then I went out, getting my mid-day meal where I could, eggs and bacon at a farmhouse, or tough steak at the hotel, and sometimes not getting anything at all until I returned ravenously hungry to my lodging. On these occasions the little Frenchwoman showed herself equal to the extent of cooking a chicken or liver and bacon very creditably and then I would write and read in my own room till eleven. I must not forget to say that I never failed to look at the wonderful scarlet hat in the window every time I went out or came in. Purchasers for it would be rare I thought; I half formed the idea of buying it myself when I went away as a "Souvenir."

One day I came home very tired. After walking about, vainly waiting for a terrific snowstorm to pass over that I might go on with my work—the frozen fall of Montmorenci, framed in the dark pines and sombre rocks that made such a back ground for its glittering thread of ice, I gave it up, chilled in every limb, and began to consider whether I was not a fool for pains. Although I started quite early in the afternoon on my homeward walk, the snow, piled in great masses everywhere along the route, impeded my progress to such an extent that it was nearly seven o'clock and pitch-dark when I got into the village. Bonneroy was very quiet. Shutters were up to every shop, nobody was out except a dog or two and the snow kept falling, falling, still in as persistent a fashion as if it had not been doing the same thing for six hours already. I found the shop shut up and the door locked. I looked everywhere for a bell or knocker of some description. There was neither, so I began to thump as hard as I could with my feet against the door. In a minute or two I heard Delle Josephine coming. Perhaps I had alarmed the poor soul. She did look troubled on opening the door and admitted me hurriedly, even suspiciously, I thought. The door of the little sitting-room was closed, so fancying that perhaps she had a visitor I refrained from much talking and asking her to cook me some eggs presently and bring them up, I went to my room.

These cold days I had to keep a fire in the small open "Franklin" stove going almost constantly. She had not

Susan Frances Harrison

forgotten to supply it with coals during my absence, and lighting my two lamps I was soon fairly comfortable. How it did snow! Lifting the blind I could actually look down on an ever-increasing drift below my window and dimly wonder if I should get out at all on the morrow. If not, I proposed to return to Montreal at once. I should gain nothing by being confined in the house at Bonneroy. Delle Josephine appeared with eggs and tea—green tea, alas for that village shortcoming—there was no black tea to be found in it, and I looked narrowly at her as she set it down, wondering if anything was amiss with her. But she seemed all right again and I conjectured that I had simply interrupted a *tête-à-tête* with some visitor in the sitting-room at the time of my return. When I had finished my tea I sat back and watched my fire. Those little open "Franklin" stoves are almost equal to a fireplace; they show a great deal of fire and you can fancy your flame on an English hearth very easily—if you have any imagination. As I sat there, it suddenly came home to me what a curious life this was for me; living quite alone over a tiny village shop in *Le Bas Canada*, with a queer little spinster like Delle Josephine. Snowed up with her too! To-morrow I would certainly have to go and shovel that snow away from the front door and take down the shutters and discover again to the world the contents of the one window, particularly that frightful hat! I would—here I started it must be confessed almost out of my seat, as turning my head suddenly I saw on a chair behind the door the identical hat I was thinking about! I sat up and looked at it. It must have been there all the time I was eating my tea. I still sat and looked. I felt vaguely uncomfortable for a moment, then my common sense asserted itself and told me that Delle Josephine must have been altering it or something of that kind and had forgotten to take it away. I wondered if she sat in my room when I was away. I had rather she did not. Just as I was about to rise and look at it more closely, a tap came at my door. I rose and admitted Delle Josephine. She took the tea-things away in her usual placid manner, but came back the next moment as if she had forgotten something, clearly the hat. With a slight deprecatory laugh she removed it and went hurriedly down the stair. Whatever had she been doing with it, I thought, and settled with a sigh of satisfaction once more to my work, now that the nightmare in red, a kind of mute scarlet "Raven," was gone from my room. How very quiet it was. Not a single sleigh passed, no sounds came from the houses opposite or from next door, the whole world seemed smothered in the soft thick pillows of snow quietly gathering upon it. After a while, however, I could distinctly hear the sound of voices downstairs. Delle Josephine had a visitor, undoubtedly. Was it a man or a woman? Not a large company I gathered; it seemed like one person besides herself. I opened my door, it sounded so comfortably in my lonely bachelor ear to catch in that strange little house anything so cheerful as the murmur of voices. My curiosity once aroused, did not stop here. I went outside the door, not exactly to listen, but as one does sometimes in a lazy yet inquisitive mood, when anything is going on at all unusual. This was an unusual occurrence. If Delle Josephine had visitors often, I was not aware of it. Never before had I noticed the slightest sound proceed from her sitting-room after dusk. So I waited a bit listening. Yes there was talking going on, but in French. As I did not understand her *patois* very clearly, I thought there would be no harm in overhearing, and further I thought I should like to have a peep at her and her companion. I could see that the door was partly open. Taking off my slippers, I ran softly down and found it wide enough open to admit of my seeing the entire room and the occupants in the looking-glass, that being opposite. It was quite dark in the little hall and I should be unobserved. So I crept—most rudely I am willing to say—into the furthest shadow of this hall and looked straight before me.

I saw none but Delle Josephine herself. But she was a sight for the gods. Seated on a kind of ottoman, directly in front of the looking-glass, she was holding an animated conversation with *herself*, wearing a large white antimacassar—one of those crocheted things all in wheels—pinned under

SUSAN FRANCES HARRISON

her chin and falling away at the back like a cloak, and upon her head—the wonderful scarlet hat! I was amazed, startled, dismayed. To see that shrivelled little old woman so travestying her hideous charms, smiling at and bowing to herself, her yellow skin forming a frightful contrast to the intense red of her immense hat and her bright black eyes, was a pitiful and unique spectacle. I had intended but to take a peep at the supposed visitor and then go back to my room, but the present sight was one which fascinated me to such an extent that I could only look and wonder. She spoke softly to herself in French, appearing to be carrying on a conversation with her image in the glass. The feathers of the bird of paradise swept her shoulder—the one that was higher than the other—and mingled with the wheels of the white antimacassar. I looked as long as I dared and then, fearing from her movements that the strange scene would soon be over I went softly up again to my room. But I thought about it all evening, all night in fact. The natural inquiry was—was the poor girl a maniac? Even if only a harmless one, it would be well to know. As I sat down again by my fire I considered the matter in every light. It was a queer prospect. Outside the snow still fell. Inside, the fire languished and the time wore on till at half-past ten I really was compelled to call on my landlady for more coal. I could hear the muttered French still going on, but I did not know where the coal was and could not fetch it myself. I must break in upon her rhapsodizing.

"Delle Boulanger!" I called from my open door. "Delle Boulanger!"

The talking stopped. In a few moments Delle Josephine appeared, calm and smiling, *minus* the hat and the antimacassar. "Coming, *monsieur*."

"I shall want some more coal," said I, "It is getting colder, I think, every minute!"

Mais oui, monsieur; il fait fret, il fait bien fret ce soir, and de snow—oh! it is *comme*—de old winter years ago, dat I remember, *monsieur*, but not you. *Eh! bien*, the coal!"

I discovered nothing morbid about her manner; she was amiable and respectful as usual, if a little more garrulous. The French will talk at all times about anything, but our conversation always came to a sudden stop the moment one of us relapsed into the mother tongue. As long as a sort of common maccaronic was kept to we managed to understand one another. After I made up my fire I sat up till long past twelve. I heard no more talking downstairs but I could fancy her still arrayed in those festive yet ghastly things, seated opposite her own reflection, intent as a mummy and not unlike one restored in modern costume. Pulling the blind aside before going to bed, I could see with awe the arching snowdrifts outside my window. If it went on snowing, I should not be able to open it on the morrow.

CHAPTER II

My prediction was verified in the morning. The snow had ceased falling, but lay piled up against the lower half of my window. On the level there appeared to be about three feet, while the drifts showed from six to twenty feet. I had never seen anything like it, and was for sometime lost in admiration. Across the road the children of the *epicier* and the good man himself were already busy trying to shovel some of it away from the door. It seemed at first sight a hopeless task and I, looking down at Delle Josephine's door, wondered how on earth we were ever to get out of it when not a particle of it was to be seen. Not all that day did I get out of the house, and but for the absorbing interest I suddenly found centred in Delle Josephine I would have chafed terribly at being so shut up. Trains were blockaded of course, it was the great fall of '81, and interrupted travel for half of a week. All that day I waited so to speak for the evening. Snow-boys there were many; customers none. The little Frenchwoman brought me some dinner at one o'clock, pork, tinned tomatoes, and a cup of coffee. About five o'clock I strolled down into the shop. It was lighted very meagrely with three oil lamps. Delle Josephine was seated on a high chair behind the one counter at work on some ribbon, white ribbon. She was quilling it, and looked up with some astonishment as I walked up to her.

"Do you object to a visitor Miss Josephine?" said I with the most amiable manner I could muster. Poor soul! I should have thought she would have welcomed one.

"*Mais non Monsieur*, but I speak so little English."

"And I so little French. But we can manage to understand each other a little, I think. What do you say to the weather? When shall I be able to go out?"

Delle Josephine laughed. She went on quilling the ribbon that looked so white against her yellow hands.

"O *Monsieur* could go out dis day if he like, but de snow ver bad, very thick."

"Do you ever go out, Miss Josephine?"

"*Non Monsieur*. I have not been out for what you call a valk—it will be five years that I have not been."

"But you go to church, I suppose? "

"*Mais oui Monsieur*, but that is so near. And the good *Père Le Jeune*—he come to see me. He is all the frien Delle Josephine has, ah! *oui Monsieur*."

"Ah! Bonneroi is'nt much of a place, is it? Have you ever been to Quebec or Montreal?"

"Ah! *Quebec—oui*, I live there once, many years ago. I was taken when I was ver young by *Madame de la Corne de la Colombière pour une bonne; vous comprenez?*"

"Oh! *bonne*, yes, we use that word too. It means a nurse-maid, eh! Were there children in the family?"

Delle Josephine dropped her ribbon and threw up her hands.

"*Mon Dieu! les enfants! Mais oui, Monsieur*, they were nine children! There was *Maamselle Louise* and *Maamselle Angelique* with the tempaire of the *diable* himself *oui Monsieur*, and François and Réné and *l'ptite Catherine*, and the rest I forget *Monsieur*. And dey live in a fine *château*, with horse and carridge and everything as it would be if they were in their own France. *Monsieur* has been in France?"

Only in Paris, I told her; a spasmodic run across the Channel—Paris in eight hours. Two days there then return—"that does not give one much idea of France."

"*Non, non, Monsieur*. But there is no countree like France dey say dat familee—and that is true, eh, *Monsieur*?"

"I am afraid I cannot agree with you, Delle Josephine," said I. "To me there is no country like England, but that may be because I am an Englishman. Tell me how long did you live in Quebec with this family?" "I was there ten year *Monsieur*. Then one day, I had a great accidence—oh! a ver sad ting, ver sad!" The Frenchwoman laid down the ribbon and went on. "A ver sad ting happen to me and the *bébé Catherine*. We were out *l'ptite* and me, for a valk, and we come to a part of the town ver slant, ver hilly. *L'ptite Catherine* was in her carridge and I let go, and she go all down, *Monsieur*, and I too over the hill—the cleef, you call it—but the *bébé* was killed and I *Monsieur*, I was alive, but like this!" showing her shoulder. "And what did hey do?"

"At the *château*? Ah, *figure-toi, monsieur*, the agony of dat *pauvre dame*! I was sent away, she would not see me, and I left *Québec* at once. I was no more *bonne*, monsieur; Delle Josephine was enough dat. I could make de hats and de bonnets for de ladees, so I come away out to Bonneroi, and I haf made de hats and de bonnets for the ladees of Bonneroi for twenty year."

"Is it possible?" I said, much touched by the little story. "And the ladies of Bonneroi, are they hard to please?"

Delle Josephine, who had spoken with the customary vim and gesture of the French while telling her tale, resumed her quilling and said, with a shrug of one shoulder,

"They do not know much, and dat is true." I laughed at the ironical tone.

"And you—you provide the *modes*?"

"I haf been to *Québec*," she said quietly.

"Twenty years ago," I thought, but had too much respect for the queer little soul to say it aloud.

"I see amongst other things," I went on, "a most—remarkable—a very pretty, I should say—hat in your window. The red one, you know, with the bird of paradise."

Delle Josephine looked up quickly. "Dat is not for sale, *monsieur*."

"No? Why, I had some idea of perhaps purchasing it for a friend of mine. Did you make that hat yourself?"

She nodded with a sort of conscious pride. Yet it was not for sale! I wondered why. The strange scene of the foregoing evening came into my mind, and I began to understand this singular case of monomania. It must be that having lived so many years in almost solitary confinement, one might say, her mind had slightly given away, and she found her only excitement and relaxation in posing before the glass in that extraordinary manner. I hardly knew whether it would be an act of kindness to remove the hat; she talked quite rationally and cheerfully, and remembering the innate vanity of the French as a nation, I concluded to let the matter rest. That night I heard no talking in the sitting-room. I slept profoundly, and woke up later than usual. We were not dug out yet, though two snow-boys with their shovels were doing their best to unearth us. I waited some time for Delle Josephine to appear with the tray; but she too was late, evidently, for at ten o'clock she had not come. I dressed and went down stairs. As I passed the sitting-room I saw her tricked out as before in the hat and the antimacassar seated on the ottoman in front of the looking-glass. Heavens, she looked more frightful than ever! I made up my mind to speak to her at once, and see if I could not stop such hideous mummery. But when I advanced I perceived that indeed I had come too late. The figure on the ottoman was rigid in death. How it ever held itself up at all I could never think, for I gave a loud cry, and rushing from the room knocked against the open door and fell down senseless.

Outside, I suppose, the snow-boys shovelled away as hard as ever. When I came to myself I did not need to look around; I knew in a flash where I was, and remembered what had happened. I ran to the shop door and hammered with all my might.

"Let me out!" I cried. "Open the door! open the door! for Heaven's sake!" Then I ran upstairs, and did the same at my window. It seemed years upon years of time till they were enabled to open the door and let me out. I rushed out bare-headed, forgetful of the intense cold, thinking first of all of the priest *Père Le Jeune*, so strong is habit, so potent are traditions. I knew where he lived, up the first turning in a small red brick house next the church of St. Jean Baptiste. I told him the facts of the case as well as I could and he came back at once with me. There was nothing to be done. Visitation of God or whatever the cause of death Delle Josephine Boulanger was dead. The priest lifted his hands in horror when he saw the ghostly hat. I asked him what he knew about her, but he seemed ignorant of everything concerning the poor thing, except the *aves* she repeated and the number of times she came to confession. But when we came to look over her personal effects in the drawers and boxes of the shop, there could be no doubt but that she had been thoroughly though harmlessly insane. We found I should think about one hundred and fifty boxes: from tiny little ones of pasteboard to large squares ones of deal, full of rows and rows of white quilled ribbon, similar to the piece I had seen her working at on that last night of her life on earth. Some of the ribbon was yellow with age, others fresher looking, but in each box was a folded bit of paper with these words written inside,

Pour l'ptite Catherine.

What money there was, *Père Le Jeune* must have appropriated for I saw nothing of any. After the dismal funeral, to which I went, I gathered my effects and went to the hotel. The first day I could proceed, I returned to Montreal and have not visited Bonneroi since. The family of *de la Corne de La Colombière* still reside somewhere near Quebec, I believe. The *château* is called by the charming name of Port Joli, and perhaps some day I may feel called upon to tell them of the strange fate which befell their poor Josephine. Whether the melancholy accident which partly bereft her of her reason was the result of carelessness I cannot say but I shall be able, I think, to prove to them that she never forgot the circumstance, and was to the day of her death occupied in making ready for the little coffin and shroud of her "*ptite Catherine*." My sketch of the frost bound Montmorenci was never finished, and indeed my winter sketching fell through altogether after that unhappy visit to Bonneroy. I was for weeks haunted by that terrible sight, half ludicrous, half awful, and I have, now that I am married, a strong dislike to scarlet in the gowns or head-gear of my wife and daughter.

Crowded Out! and Other Sketches (Ottawa: *Evening Journal*, 1886), 49–60.

Agnes Maule Machar ("Fidelis") (1837–1927)

Parted Ways (1891)

Agnes Maule Machar, essayist, poet and novelist, was one of the foremost social commentators of her time, and an ardent advocate of the Social Gospel and of maternal feminism. Her many articles were read and respected in such leading periodicals as the *Canadian Monthly and National Review* and *The Week* as well as leading American journals of opinion. Descended from ministers on both sides of her family, she was a fervent, liberal Christian. "Canadensis," another of her pseudonyms, expresses her ardent nationalism.

Agnes Maule Machar was born to an influential Kingston family. She was the daughter of Scottish immigrants Margaret Maule, an active local philanthropist, and Reverend John Machar, a Presbyterian minister who became the second principal of Queen's University. The Machar household was one of weighty intellectual, religious and political concerns, giving young Agnes exposure to such visitors as John A. Macdonald, George Monro Grant, and the novelist Grant Allen, a relative by marriage. Machar was given an exceptional classical education, chiefly at home. She spent one year at a boarding school in Montreal, headed by Harriet Lyman, later principal of Vassar. The experience sowed the seeds of her lifelong interest in French Canadian history.

Machar's first major publication was her prize-winning juvenile work *Katie Johnson's Cross: A Canadian Novel* (1870), whose purpose is proclaimed in its preface: "to illustrate how great a blessing may flow from an affliction, if met and borne in a spirit of faith and Christian cheerfulness." A flood of poems, articles and novels followed, often written under the pseudonym "Fidelis." The pseudonym honoured both her mother's wish that, as a woman, Agnes conceal her identity (a convention of the time) and her own desire that her ideas should be judged on their merits rather than according to gender stereotypes. Moreover, she told Ethelwyn Wetherald in an interview for *The Week* that faithfulness was the quality she most valued and cared most to possess. Ironically, Machar's achievements went beyond those posited for her by her family; Nancy Miller Chenier, in a 1977 Carleton University M.A. thesis, makes clear that she "was not urged by her family to develop her talents beyond the role of a well-informed but discreet gentlewoman."

By the 1890s, the decade in which "Parted Ways" appeared, Agnes Maule Machar was at the peak of her career, active as a religious and social critic. She was a maternal feminist who took a leading role in the National Council of Women, advocating higher education for women, as well as espousing wider, Social Gospel-allied causes such as temperance, and labour and educational reform. Her poetry and fiction were driven by her moral and social commitments to an exceptional degree: she was a didactic artist par excellence. For example, the hero of her best novel, *Roland Graeme, Knight: A Novel of Our Time* (1894), becomes a radical journalist fighting for labour reform in the face of exploitative industrial practices. Novels like *For King and Country: A Story of 1812* (1874) and *Marjorie's Canadian Winter: A Story of the Northern Lights* (1892) breathe her nationalism and pride in the history of both New France and British North America. Her Canadian nationalism embraced both linguistic groups, so much so that she published a poem pleading for Riel's life after the Northwest Rebellion of 1885, a sympathy for things French that also animates her *Stories of New France* (1890). Machar's patriotism and charity continued beyond her death at the age of ninety: she willed the bulk of her estate to the League of Nations and the Kingston General Hospital, and to the establishment in Kingston of the Agnes Maule Machar Home for elderly women.

"Parted Ways," published in Canada's leading periodical *The Week*, is typical of what Ruth Brouwer has called the "high minded conversation" of Machar's love stories, and bespeaks her interest in the cultivation of women's sense of intellectual, moral and social responsibility. In Machar's own life—at Kingston, and at "Ferncliffe," her summer home in the Thousand Islands—Machar played friend and mentor to such female literary colleagues as Ethelwyn Wetherald, Pauline Johnson and Marjorie Pickthall. This is a story of ideas, where conscience and intellect rule emotion, and where the female protagonist is the male's moral and intellectual superior. The heroine spurns the male's worldly focus and lack of faith: "Better the pain of parting now, than to be tortured by the perpetual sense of separation of soul!" Even the landscape is congruent with Machar's theme: a love such as Harold's is like that of a fickle, transient "Indian summer." Helen finds succour in a helping profession until her former lover painfully comes to see the light. The plot is congruent with Machar's own beliefs about women:

> Who can doubt that if our Canadian young women, *as a class*, should become truly cultivated, earnest, high-toned, full of the noble ambition to devote life to noble work for noble ends, a very few years would strikingly demonstrate their influence in raising our young men, as a class, to a very much higher plane than that which they at present now occupy? The question of higher female education, then, . . . is simply that of the development of woman to the highest possible point of intellectual and moral excellence . . . surely well worthy the attention of every thoughtful man and enlightened patriot.

〜

Suggested Reading:
Brouwer, Ruth Compton. "Moral Nationalism in Victorian Canada: The Case of Agnes Machar." In *Journal of Canadian Studies* 20 (Spring 1985), 90–108.

Machar, Agnes Maule. "Higher Education for Women."
    In *Canadian Monthly and National Review* 7 (February
    1875), 144–157.
————. *Stories of New France*. First Series. Boston:
    Lathrop, 1890.
Wetherald, Ethelwyn. "Fidelis." In *The Week* (5 April 1888),
    300–301.

PARTED WAYS
Agnes Maule Machar ("Fidelis")

I.

" I am afraid it has all been a mistake, Harold," she said, slowly and sadly, without turning to look at him, gazing straight before her at the glowing October landscape that lay spread around them.

"What a mistake!" he exclaimed in a startled tone, turning to look at the speaker's half-averted face, paler than its wont; at the delicate profile, with the broad brow arched with soft dark-brown hair, that stood out relieved against a back-ground of iron-grey rock. But the large, soft, thoughtful eyes did not meet the keen dark ones that looked into them. They were seemingly absorbed in contemplation of the dreamy radiance of the lovely Indian summer day, that flooded with its mellow light the glancing gold and crimson of the palm-like sumachs about them, the sparkling tide of the river that wound at their feet, the rich mosaic of autumn foliage on the opposite shore, even the grey-green lichens that crusted the granite rock on which they sat, and the brown pine needles that filled in all its crevices, seeming like a soft mantle thrown over the tiny ferns and delicate vegetation that nestled so confidingly therein.

She kept silence for a few moments, as if gathering her strength, while he repeated his question with a mingling of tenderness and impatience in his tone, and on the dark eager intellectual countenance in which a close observer might have traced a good deal of latent ambition, blended with a strong suggestion of suppressed passion and of a self-will that tended to obstinacy. "What is a mistake? Helen darling?" he repeated.

"Our engagement, dear," she said, at last, very gently, yet as if the words had been forced out, almost against her will.

"Helen, are you dreaming? What nonsense is this! It isn't like you to say such unkind things! What if we do see some things differently? Don't we know and love each other, and isn't that enough? Haven't we a thousand thoughts and feelings in common? What are a few points of difference in comparison with a love like ours—like mine, at least," he added, a little reproachfully, "and what I supposed yours to be!"

"Ah, Harold, don't doubt my love," she exclaimed. "It is its very strength that makes me feel as I do! What are a few thoughts and feelings in common, if there is hopeless separation at the very core of it all; of all that makes the real beauty and meaning of life? It is like the 'little rift within the lute!' Look at that tiny seam in this great rock. Don't you know how it will widen and widen, winter after winter, till at last the whole mass drops apart forever!"

"Mere poetical fancies, Helen! You are trifling with yourself and me! It isn't a question of lutes and rocks, but of hearts that love and will love on, I hope—"

"Forever?" she asked, for the first time turning and looking full in his face.

"What have we to do with 'forever' just now, Helen? Now is enough for me! Life is so sweet and beautiful, and we love each other! Isn't that enough? It is in the present we have to live, not in the future. And where there is love, it can stand a great deal of difference of opinion."

"A great deal—yes! But not that which goes to the very heart and root of things—that on which the very essence of life and love seem to me to depend."

"All sentiment, my dear children! Can't you let dreaming alone, and be your own sensible self? What can we really

AGNES MAULE MACHAR

know about the future, or what you call the 'spiritual world?' No! I don't want to distress you. Keep your dreams and fancies about them if they make you happy." He had almost said, "if they amuse you." "But this unknown quantity need never come between us two. We have enough to fill our united life with, in what we do know! I can quote poetry, too, and from an unexceptionable source:—

> Trust no future, howe'er pleasant,
>   Let the dead past bury its dead,
> Act, act in the *living present*!"

He stopped, and she finished the stanza:—

Heart within and God o'erhead.

His face hardened perceptibly, "Keep the last, if you think you need it, the first is enough for me!"

"But, dear, you don't understand, you can't understand the constant torture of living the best half of my life totally apart from you, utterly out of sympathy with you! It is the constant impulse to share with you what I love and value so dearly, the constant sense of the blank wall of separation between us, that makes this pain greater than I can bear! It seems like a nightmare, as if I were always struggling to get to you, across it, and were always thrown back again, do what I would."

"Then why not be philosophical, and school yourself to the inevitable? What is the use of crying for the moon, when you might be happy without it? Of course it would be delightful, if we could see all things just alike—'like two eyes on one face,' though even they don't see just alike; but mightn't it be a little dull? And what does it all matter, in the end? Surely you agree with me that the main thing is to be true to oneself, and that 'conduct is three-fourths of life.' He can't be wrong whose life is in the right!"

"Ah, Harold dear, but that is what troubles me most! It seems so clear to me that life can't be right apart from its true foundation! And I do feel that your ideals and aims are changing, with your view of life! You haven't any longer the old aspirations, the old enthusiasms."

"Boyish fancies!" he exclaimed contemptuously. "A man soon finds his level as he grows older. If one does his own little bit of work fairly well, that is his contribution to the general result, without his taking the universe on one's back! What are we all but just bits of machinery in the great mill?"

Helen sighed with a sense of the hopelessness of argument. But she braced herself anew for what she had to say.

"But you can never do the good you might, with such a narrow ideal as that, dear! You could be so much more than a mere bit of machinery; you were meant to be!"

"Meant!" he echoed, with a bitter smile.

"Yes, I know," she said, wearily; "I forgot that word had no meaning for you! But there, you see, we always come back to the blank wall! The things dearest to me are nothing to you! Indeed, you often seem to hate them! I can't love you as I do, and think of this life, beautiful as it is, being all there is; of love itself as at the mercy of the beating of these hearts of ours, which at any moment might be stopped by some sudden accident and all be ended forever! To me, the very sacredness of love lies in its immortality; while you—you—"

She could not go on. Her face quivered, and she turned away to hide the tears she could no longer keep back.

Harold caught her at once in his strong encircling arms, and pressed her closely to his heart, trying to kiss away the fast-flowing tears. This strange mood would soon be over now, he thought.

But she struggled hard for composure, and presently freed herself from his embrace, while he exclaimed tenderly: "My darling, don't torture yourself and me any more!— You've been brooding over things till you have unnerved yourself."

"If I have," she replied,—"it is because the thought will not let me rest, it haunts me so,—the consciousness of that horrible idea of yours, that there is nothing in the universe but blind force, and our frail human love. It is the very strength of my love for you that troubles me. I want so much to be at one with you—that we should see things with the same eyes, that I often feel as if I were losing hold of the only thing that is fixed and stable—as if a black chasm of nothingness were opening at my feet. Ah, you don't know how many wakeful nights, and how many bitter tears it has cost me! Your death, dear, I could bear, with the 'sore and certain hope' of reunion, but the blackness of desolation, the death in life that seems to loom up before me when my faith seems drifting from my hold, is more than I could bear! Don't you see, I am afraid—afraid lest, under the constant influence of your questioning, incredulous spirit, I might lose the light altogether, and, for me, that would be the most terrible loss of all!"

There could be no question of the intensity of her feeling. It impressed Harold in spite of himself, and indeed it touched some chords in his own breast which still vibrated painfully. Presently he said, gloomily: "I suppose Harvey has been meddling! Do you think I can't see through that? And I suppose, if he manages to separate us, he will hope to console you himself, by and by!—Fanatical bigots, all of them!" he muttered.

"Harold, dearest," she said, with a look of unutterable pain, "Do you think I should allow him or any one to talk to me on such a subject? or that any one else could influence me, when you cannot? This is solely and entirely my own deliberate judgment."

"Yet I thought you believed in the sacredness of love and betrothal!"

"But what if you do not? And, with your philosophy, how can anything be 'sacred?' Love is simply 'a product,' you say. Why should it be more sacred than any other product? I did believe that love's claims were supreme, that where two people loved each other, nothing, not even this, should come between them. And if I were stronger, myself, I might decide differently; I might feel able to go on, unchanged myself, always hoping, what you have told me I need not hope for! But as it is—oh Harold, darling—I feel I dare not!"

"And do you really mean that for this shadowy reason, we must part, after all our close intimacy, our dear friendship, our dear love, our plighted troth?"

"Harold," she replied, "I am not thinking of myself alone. I shall never cease to love you—never forget you! But I honestly believe it is best for you, too. Don't you think I have seen how your present distasteful work and narrow sphere fret and gall you? Can I help knowing that but for me and our engagement, you would not think of staying here—that you would gladly avail yourself of the opening your uncle has offered you, to enter the profession that has always been your own choice? And if I let you make the sacrifice, for I know it is one, how will it be by and by? Might you not come to feel you had made a mistake? No, dear, I have not come to this conclusion hastily. It has been a long, hard struggle, but I do see it now."

"Well, Helen," he rejoined, in a colder tone, "I should, of course, never hold you to an engagement you wish to break. If this is really your decision, the sooner we part, the better! I had another letter from my uncle last evening, again urging me to come to him, and begging for an immediate reply. I did not tell you of it, as I knew it would give you pain. But if you are serious in this madness, as I regard it, I had better reply that I will avail myself of his offer as soon as I can get a substitute for my work here, which I know I can do at once." His voice sounded hard and metallic. His face had quite lost the tender pleading look it had worn. Helen knew that he was very angry, and felt keenly wounded by his tone. She made no reply, and as he unconsciously rose, she rose, too, and he instinctively offered his hand to help her down the path that led to the shore, where their boat lay waiting. As they descended, she looked up, and their eyes met. The wistful pleading look in her sad eyes was too much for him. Instantly his mood changed. Once more he clasped her in his arms, strained her passionately to his breast, and held her as if he could not let her go. Her beauty and her love were so sweet to him, the old habit of loving was so strong. "My darling! my darling! I cannot give you up!" he murmured, as he kissed again and again the soft cheek, wet with tears. But she did not answer, and silently took her seat in the stern of the skiff. There was no sign of yielding in the pale thoughtful face, or in the curves of the slightly compressed lips. Nor did Harold—the burst of passionate emotion over—care to renew the contest. The homeward row was very silent. Now and then a lovely bit of colour, glowing out in the sunset light, called forth a few admiring comments, but, for the most part, the hearts of both were too heavy for the effort of conversation, while Helen was often fain to turn away her head to hide the tears that would rise to her eyes under the foreboding feeling that this was, in all probability, their last row. As Harold helped her to land at the foot of her father's grounds, he held her tightly for a moment, with a few earnest words:—

"I am not going to take what you have said for final, Helen, darling! I can't think it could really be your deliberate decision. I should never hold you or any woman to an irksome pledge; but I know you love me, and I know how good and true you are! and I think, if you send me away, it will be as hard for you as for me. For both our sakes, reconsider it, dear. I will come in to-morrow evening, and I hope you will tell me that it has all been a bad dream. Good bye, my own darling!"

He let her go, sprang into the boat, and with a few rapid strokes had disappeared round a bend of the stream. Helen stood still till he was out of sight, then, sinking down on the grass, she buried her face in her hands and gave way to the burst of weeping she had with such difficulty restrained. "Oh, if things could only be different!" she murmured. "If I only could keep him and my faith, too! But, as things are, how could we ever be happy together? Better the pain of parting now, than to be tortured by the perpetual sense of separation of soul!"

While Harold's thoughts, as he rowed on with gloomy brow and set lips, ran thus: "What a hold these illusions must have, after all, on a soul like hers! I believe she loves me intensely—perhaps more intensely than I love her—and yet she can give me up sooner than these shadows! Poor girl! I don't want to rob her of them if they give her any satisfaction! But why can't she be reasonable, and not insist on tearing our hearts asunder? It seems as if women never can be reasonable!"

Then for a moment the thought occurred to him how it would be if he should profess for the time being to be at least partially convinced of what she clung to so tenaciously. But it was only for a moment. Honour and manliness rose to repel any such subterfuge. Harold Vaughan was too much a man to attempt to deceive the true woman he so truly loved.

II.

Life is so complex that we never find it stand still to serve as a background for our own griefs, however absorbing they may be to ourselves. When Helen—her overburdened heart somewhat relieved by the burst of tears—had regained her usual composure and returned to the house, she found the little household in commotion. Dr. Musgrave's well-worn "buggy" was standing at the gate, while the brown spaniel Rover was leaping up on the patient horse, eager for the start. The doctor himself—his overcoat and gloves on—was standing by the table, swallowing a cup of tea which the thoughtful old servant had hastily prepared for her master.

"Glad you've come in, my dear," he said. "I am just off to the Sinclairs'. They have had a bad accident there with the threshing-machine. Poor Jem! I am afraid it's all over with him."

"Oh, father, how dreadful!" she exclaimed, the slight flush on her cheek disappearing and leaving it paler than before. Presently she continued, eagerly: "Oh, father dear, let me go too. Jem's wife, you know, poor Maggie! Perhaps I could do something for her, at least. Do let me go at all events."

"Indeed, my dear child, I'll be only too glad if you will. Only you must eat something, or at least take some tea. You'll need all your strength."

Helen forced herself to drink a cup of tea, and in a few minutes they were driving rapidly out of the little town and along the quiet country road that led to the Sinclair homestead—a place associated in Helen's memory with many pleasant visits. The rich rose and purple tones of the afterglow were rapidly fading into the more sombre ones of moonlight with its clear cold lights and intense shadows. As they approached their destination, it seemed to Helen—whose own personal pain seemed for the time numbed by her intense sympathy with this crushing sorrow—as if the calm beauty and repose of the scene, the fair sloping fields, the dark line of forest behind, the little group of farm buildings standing out in the whiteness of moonlight, made too painful a contrast to the suffering and suspense within. "Jem" Sinclair had been only a few months married, and his young wife had been one of Helen's special favourites. She still had vividly in her mind the pretty picture they made coming into church together, on the first Sunday after their marriage.

It was even as Dr. Musgrave had said. It was "all over" with the poor fellow, whose injuries were too severe to admit of any treatment save the administering of stimulants to keep up his sinking strength. Mr. Harvey was also there, ministering such consolation as the dying man was able to take in, while the poor young wife seemed utterly stunned by the sudden blow. Before dawn, poor "Jem" had quietly breathed his last, with a faint smile of hope and of loving farewell to his stricken wife, and the murmured words on his lips: "Don't fret, Maggie—please God, we'll meet again!"

"He was always such a good boy!" said Helen to Mr. Harvey, when all was over, and she could command her voice to speak.

"Yes, he was one of my steadiest and most hopeful young men," said the clergyman, who was himself deeply moved. "Thank God for lives and deaths like his! They make one take heart and hope for the rest."

The words seemed to go to Helen's heart, and woke again the pain that had seemed partially asleep. She could not let herself think yet, however. She had to care for poor Maggie, now utterly prostrated by her grief, and with her she spent the greater part of the day, walking home alone in the late afternoon, after she had seen the poor little widow, at last, sink into an exhausted slumber. It was a grey day, very different from the glowing one that had preceded it. The rich tones of the woodland appeared already dulled and sobered, and there was a suggestion of winter in the penetrating chill of the air, while its strange stillness seemed like nature holding her breath in anticipation of the storms to come. Helen was glad that it was so, for she felt she could hardly have borne a repetition of the exquisite, dreamy beauty of the day before. It seemed as if nature had no right to be bright and beautiful, as if in mockery of human pain. Her mind was busy with the coming interview with Harold. The scenes she had been passing through had tended to strengthen her previous resolve. She knew instinctively that, in her lover, she could look for no sympathy with the feelings called forth by the experience of the past twenty-four hours—feelings penetrating to the very roots of her being. He would not even comprehend them. She knew she should not even be able to speak of them to him with whom she would fain have shared her whole life. How could she bear a seeming union in which she should have to live a life apart as regarded the deeper half of her being, her inmost, truest life, unshared—nay, she knew well—antagonized by the whole force of her lover's mind? How could she bear to feel that what was to her but a symbol of the inner undying union of heart and soul, was to him a thing of a few years or months or days, as the "chances and changes of this mortal life" might determine? Would it not seem like a dark shadow, ever deepening around her, till perhaps it had blotted out the very light of life and left her in darkness? No! whatever weakness of possible yielding there might have been before, she felt there could be none now. After coming thus face to face with the slight tenure of "this mortal coil," to her, under the influence of that sorrowful night, had come the subtle and mysterious call, stronger than all others,

AGNES MAULE MACHAR

which, when it is once heard, natures finely touched like hers cannot choose but obey.

Harold could read her face well enough to know that further pleading would be of little avail. He was shocked at her pale and worn look, but somewhat reassured when she briefly explained the cause. He had heard of the accident, but in his own preoccupation had thought little about it.

"It is not good for you, dear, to go into such scenes; they take too deep a hold on you and make you morbid," he said, tenderly.

"I could not have stayed away; I was needed there," she said simply.

"Well, try not to think of it any more. I need you now, Helen. I can't give you up. It's no use to think of it."

"I don't give you up, Harold. I shall always love you and hope for you! But to live a divided life—apart from you in all I care for most—I cannot, Harold, I dare not! I should be miserable myself; and being so, I could not make you happy."

"We could agree to differ!" he replied.

"Ah, Harold, we cannot! Whatever happens—wherever we begin—we find ourselves always tending to the one issue—it is so interwoven with all our life. And even if we never approached it in speech, do you think I should not always feel your pronounced, even bitter, antagonism of feeling?"

"But if you are sure that you are right, and believe that everything will come out all right, after all, why should you distress yourself! You don't think that I am going to suffer eternally, because I can't see as you do?"

"Ah, Harold, dear, I am not strong enough, and my love for you is too strong. If my faith were only stronger, I might; as it is, I could not bear it."

"Helen," he exclaimed, "do be worthy of yourself! You are an intellectual woman, nobly gifted. How can you be so fettered by an effete superstition?"

The last word called up all her resolution. "You see, dear," she said, sadly, "you cannot help speaking from your point of view. Our positions are so hopelessly at issue! And yours would tell on me in time, more than mine would on you. For it isn't with such things as with mere intellectual conclusions. To realize my faith, I have to live it out, not argue it out. Believe me, dear, it is best for us both to part now. Perhaps a better time may come. I shall hope so, oh, how dearly! You are, and always will be, my one love. But now, as things are, it is best to part."

"Well, if that is really your deliberate opinion, I suppose it is best so," he said gloomily. "But I never expected it of you, Helen."

It was a sad relief to Helen when that interview was over, and Harold left her to write that decisive letter. His post in the Ashurst High School, which he had retained only because it gave him an earlier prospect of marriage, for Helen would not hear of leaving her father alone, could, he said, be supplied at a few days' notice by a college friend of his, who was anxiously looking out for such an appointment, so that there was no need for delay, of which Harold was always impatient.

When Helen briefly told her father of her decision, Dr. Musgrave looked at her with his keen professional glance, then drew her to him and kissed her affectionately.

"My child," he said, "I am glad you have decided so! Harold Vaughan is a nice fellow, in many ways, but you and he were not made for each other! And I'm glad you've found it out in time, for you would'nt have believed me if I had told you so. He is one of the people who must be left to fight it out with life and his own soul. God grant you a better mate, my daughter!"

"I don't want one, father, dear! I am never going to leave you!"

"But I shall have to leave you some day, my child; however, let the morrow take care of itself!" And after that the wise old doctor never again alluded to Harold Vaughan.

No one but Helen herself ever knew how hard were the weeks and months that followed the painful, passionate farewell, when Harold, giving way to all the tenderness of his nature, held her in a long embrace, and at last tore himself away with the promise that, at least, she should hear from him often: "I can't let you go out of my life, my darling! and I believe you will be mine yet."

Helen could only murmur a broken "God bless you, my darling," but the memory of that parting embrace haunted her through many lonely days that followed. They were not dreary ones, for she had plenty of occupation, indoors and out; her housekeeping, her ready help to her father in many ways, her visits to his poor patients, her correspondence with scattered brothers and sisters, and visits from nephews and nieces, devoted to "Aunt Helen." Her welcome presence brought many a ray of sunshine into dark and sorrowful lives. And she found so much to do in relieving hardships and enlightening sorrows heavier than her own, that it would have been impossible for her to have grown absorbed in that. But there were many times, unknown to any save herself, when some chance word, a line of poetry, a book opened at a particular page, would start again in all its intensity that aching pain which poor Heine's epithet of "toothache in the heart" so well expresses. Yet, withal, she was not without her compensations. Removed from the disturbing, paralyzing influence of Harold's perpetually questioning, analyzing spirit, she was conscious of relief from long tension and struggle, of a peaceful calm, in contrast to the feverish conflict of the past months, which made her feel more sure of the wisdom of her decision. She felt the too-heavy burden lifted off her mind, satisfied now to "labour and to wait." And indeed the few who had known or suspected the little romance thought that Miss Musgrave was "getting over it" very well, and even began to construct a new engagement with Mr. Harvey, who, indeed, would have been only too glad if the report had been true.

But Harold's letters were the one special pleasure of her life. How dearly she prized them she would have told to no one. Yet she thought she could soon see, with a natural pang, that ambition was getting the better of love, that, with a congenial career and a wider sphere opening before him, he was already happier than he had been in the contracted life of Ashurst. He was working very hard, but that he keenly enjoyed. He was evidently impressing others with his powers and capabilities. Politics, which had always interested him, were attracting him more and more, for he was an enthusiastic Canadian, and the stimulating atmosphere of the city stirred all his pulses and quickened his intellectual life. He soon gained the reputation of being a good and ready speaker, who could do good service in a political campaign. Sometimes he would say in his letters: "I feel you were right, dear Helen, in sending me here. In two or three years now I shall have my profession—and then!" But Helen resolutely put future possibilities out of her mind. She had always felt that his love for her was very different from hers for him, and she would not let herself trust it too much. She was glad that they could, at least, be friends, friends always—she said to herself, and never allowed herself to write a word warmer than friendship. Nor, after the first six months, did Harold himself.

III.

Five years later Helen stood again on the old familiar granite rock, on a fair October day, much like the one she still so vividly remembered. Things round her seemed exactly the same. The orange and crimson flames of the sumachs, the rich maroon and purple of the oak, the gleaming gold of birch and maple, even the green glossy wintergreen leaves at her feet seemed just as they had done then; but other things were changed indeed! Helen's black dress told of recent bereavement; the good old doctor had gone to his rest, and Helen's work in Ashurst was done. She was too young and vigorous not to need some definite occupation, though brothers and sisters had urged her to make her home with them; but she felt that her past life and experience had peculiarly fitted her for the profession of a nurse, to which also her inherited impulses strongly attracted her. She had decided, therefore, to go to a New York "Women's

Hospital" for a few years' training—partly on account of the wider experience she would thereby gain—partly because the city in which her sister resided, and to which she might otherwise have gone, was Harold's home as well, and as he had recently married, she felt it best to avoid the chance of a painful meeting. It was quite natural, she felt, that it should have ended so; Harold's letters had grown gradually fewer, shorter, and more apologetic, and during the year preceding her father's death, had finally ceased altogether. Helen's heart foreboded too surely the real cause; she was not surprised when her sister wrote to tell her of his approaching marriage to a young and very pretty girl, a belle, and something of an heiress. "It is thought a very good match for him," she wrote, "as it will help him on in his political career. She is very sweet and fascinating, though rather a flirt, and devoted to society, but they seem very much in love; and as her idea of religion seems to consist in belonging to the right church, and going through certain observances decorously, his very pronounced scepticism will not trouble her much. Perhaps it is just as well?"

Helen felt almost, if not quite, as much pained by the allusion to his "pronounced scepticism," as by the news of his engagement, though in that she felt a certain natural shock. But the thorough unselfishness of her love came to her relief; surely it must be good for him at least to have the sweet softening influences of home life. She had been afraid that he was growing hard and self-absorbed. Now he would have that which would draw him out of himself, deepen his sense of responsibility, and touch new chords in his being— and then it settled the future for her. And certainty, she felt, was better than even a mingling of suspense. As for Harold, he was greatly surprised when he found himself again in love, the result of a summer holiday, and thought somewhat remorsefully of Helen. But, if she had chosen to reject him for a fantastic scruple, he could not be expected to devote his life to the memory of a dream! Then it was very pleasant to feel himself the object of an almost adoring devotion, and if he sometimes could not help feeling the shallowness of his *fiancée's* mind and character, and comparing them with Helen's rare qualities, the charm of her presence soon drove away the momentary disquiet and he gave himself up to all the sweetness of his new passion. To her cross-questioning, however, he confessed his previous engagement and the cause of its termination.

"And she really gave you up for that!" she exclaimed. "Oh, Harold! she couldn't have loved you as I do! And I don't really believe you are such a pagan! You'll go to church sometimes with me, like a dear?"

"Oh, yes, if you want me to," he said, indifferently, and was duly rewarded. But even at that moment there rose the vision of Helen, with the look of unutterable love he had seen in her eyes when they parted; and with it the old familiar lines they had both loved:—

> I could not love thee dear, so much,
> Loved I not honour more!

But it was only for a moment. The present was too engrossing for such memories; and, for a time, it was satisfaction enough for him. After the "fashionable wedding," duly chronicled in all its details, came the pleasant holiday travel of the honey-moon, and the pleasure of seeing his little wife admired wherever they went, with all the proud sense of proprietorship. For a time he broke away from his habits of absorption in his work, and went into society to please her and himself. But after a time the inanity of the "society" life wearied him, and it was a relief to avail himself of the good excuse furnished by his growing engagements, and to bury himself in his office-work and his politics, while his wife, passionately fond of gaiety, gradually acquiesced in going out alone, especially as lonely days and evenings were not at all to her taste. After a time came a new interest, in the birth of a little daughter, a source of inexpressible delight to Harold who learned to look forward to her baby smiles and caresses, as the sweet recreation of his busy life; but just as she had reached her third year and had entwined herself into every fibre of her father's heart, a cold, brought on through the carelessness of her nurse, suddenly took a serious turn. As it happened, her mother was out that evening, and Harold came home from his office to find the child in a most critical condition; he rushed off for the doctor, sending a cab for his wife, but, by the time she returned, the little one was past help. Harold's grief was terrible; he had no comfort for himself—none for his wife. Indeed in his heart he blamed her, who had been really a fond mother, for her absence at a crisis when timely care might have saved the child. He brooded over this till his manner to her became cold and moody, though of the sorrow itself he never spoke. From that time he was a saddened man, though he threw himself more than ever into professional and public life, to soothe the pain he could not cure. He was soon marked out as a candidate for Parliament, and at the next election, after an energetic canvass, was duly returned. He was even regarded as a future Cabinet Minister when his party, then in Opposition, should come into power. His highest ambition seemed likely to be fully gratified, but this could not still the heartlongings so deeply stirred, or cure the gnawing "tooth-ache in the heart." Between his wife and himself the chilling process had gone on; he was no longer in love, and so could see too clearly her limitations. She had gone back to society for solace, after the conventional period of mourning was over, and by and by people began to talk of Mrs. Vaughan's flirtations, in particular of one which had become rather pronounced, with a young Englishman, who had become an open worshipper at her shrine. At last the gossip reached even Harold's ears; he spoke of it to his wife with stern indignation, hardening every line of his now sombre face. She met him with counter complaints—of his moodiness—his almost constant absence—his neglect. It was a new sensation to feel himself accused, he who had stood so high in his own estimation.

"I thought you liked your own way best," he said. "And you have had it without restraint. But if our ways do run separate that is no excuse for making yourself a subject for remark—remark that desecrates the sacredness of married life."

She laughed satirically. "I thought you didn't believe anything sacred," she said, "and I've got to feel so too."

Like an electric flash, memory brought back the memory of the time when Helen had made a somewhat similar reply. But he would not condescend to argue, only parried his wife's remark with a few words of stern warning, which made the tender flatteries of her new admirer by contrast seem all the sweeter and more beguiling.

～

Helen Musgrave had had a very busy winter. An unusual press of anxious work had absorbed all her time and energies, though Harold Vaughan and his desolated life—of which she had heard with deep sorrow and sympathy—were often in her thoughts. One of the invalids who claimed a share of her attention was a young and lovely woman, who attracted her the more for bearing the name of Vaughan. She was evidently a stranger, and Helen, seeing her evident loneliness and great depression of spirits, decided that she must be a stranded governess, and pitied her accordingly. She was in a rapid decline, and one day the attending physician told Helen that if the patient had any relatives she wished to see they should be summoned at once. Helen cautiously approached the subject, but the invalid shook her head, saying there was no one she desired to summon.

"But perhaps there might be some who would be sorry if you did not let them know," persisted the nurse.

"No! No!" she said sadly. "No one who would care to see me now."

"Then your husband is dead, I suppose?" she half asked.

"Dead to me, at any rate. But you can send a notice of my death to this address"—and she pencilled a few words on a card.

"Harold Vaughan!" exclaimed Helen as she read it. Then the truth flashed on her mind, and she wondered it had never occurred to her before.

"You know him?" the invalid exclaimed. "And you are a Canadian, too. Ah! I know you are the 'Helen' he once told me about. I know it, you are so good." And as Helen's honest eyes did not contradict her, she added: "Ah! why did you not marry him? You were far fitter for him than I!"

Helen gently drew from the poor girl the story of a brief madness, followed by sure retribution; how the unscrupulous young man who had decoyed her from her home—an adventurer and a gambler—had finally tired of her, and had gladly taken advantage of her illness to send her to the hospital and then desert her. Without asking her permission, Helen wrote briefly to Harold, urging him to come without delay. But his absence from home, just then, caused so much loss of time in receiving the letter, that before his arrival the invalid had passed beyond the reach of human forgiveness; not, however, before Helen had helped her to seek that other which is never asked in vain.

"Ask him to forgive me," she said to Helen. "Not for God's sake—he doesn't believe in God, you see—but for the sake of our dead baby!"

When Harold arrived, a prematurely worn-looking man, whose dark hair had become nearly grey during the past year, Helen was so filled with tender pity for the lover of her youth, that she forgot herself altogether as she stood with him by the cold, dead form, and gave him that dying message. And then she turned away, with eyes filled with tears and an unspoken prayer in her heart, as this man—so successful outwardly, so desolate inwardly—overcome by the crushing sense of the tragedy of life, sank on his knees beside the still white face, and wept bitterly.

❧

It was a Christmas morning in the —— Hospital, and the sweetest of all sacred bells were carrying their message of good cheer even thither. The nurses had given all their spare time to prepare some decorations which might make the Christmas day a little brighter, even in the hospital wards. Helen, tired with this work, added to her night duty, was preparing to seek a little rest, when a letter was brought to her—a letter in a once familiar handwriting, yet strangely weak and altered in its character. She opened it hurriedly. As her experienced eye foreboded, Harold Vaughan was very ill. His malady was a serious one, brought on by over-work and nervous prostration. "The doctors do not give me much hope of recovery," he wrote, "though they say it is not impossible with perfect rest of mind and heart. But how to secure that? Otherwise it may be a matter of years or months, or even only weeks. Helen, will you come and nurse me as my wife? It is my only hope. If I did not feel that you loved me still, I could not ask it. Helen, I am no longer the self-sufficient man I was. How indeed could I be? And I have seen God in your eyes, my Helen, and in your enduring, unselfish, forgiving love; and I want you to help me to find Him, for I need Him now! Do not refuse me, but come and be with me till the end, which, who knows, may after all be but a better beginning! I have in my room a little picture of Dante's Beatrice, which has often reminded me of you. Come then and be my guide to that Paradise of peace which I know abides in your heart, for I have seen it in your eyes and on your brow. Come then, dear Helen, and come soon."

Helen's answer was—herself. And so the long parted ways met at last.

⌒

The Week (19 June 1891), 461–463.

AGNES MAULE MACHAR

Louisa Murray (1818–1894)

MR. GRAY'S STRANGE STORY (1892)

Much admired in her own time, Louisa Murray is virtually
unknown today. Her novels were published in serial form,
but none appeared in book form. She also published short
fiction, essays, and reviews, and occasionally poetry, in a
variety of publications including the *Literary Garland*, the
Canadian Monthly and National Review, *The Week*, *Once a
Week* (London, England), the *British American Magazine*,
and *The Nation* (Toronto).

Louisa Murray was the eldest of nine children of
Louisa Rose Lyons and Edward Murray. Her Irish father
was a lieutenant in the 100th Regiment of the British Army
who served in Canada during the War of 1812. Her mother,
daughter of Major Charles Lyons, was born when her father
was stationed at Halifax. Louisa was born at Carisbrooke on
the Isle of Wight on 23 May 1818, and brought up in County
Wicklow, Ireland. In 1841 she emigrated with her family to
Wolfe Island, near Kingston. There she made the acquaintance of Reverend J. Antisel Allen, a poet as well as a clergyman, who encouraged her in her writing. The Allens' son,
Grant, who left Canada with his parents in 1861 and
became a popular and prolific novelist (best known for the
controversial *The Woman Who Did* [1895]), a novel about
the New Woman and sexual freedom), recalls the cultured
backwoods home of the Murrays. Another genteel family
that the Murrays met at this time was the Fowlers. Water-
colourist Daniel Fowler and his family had emigrated to
nearby Amherst Island just two years after the Murrays'
arrival on Wolfe Island. Their daughter Annie Fowler
Rothwell (see page 165) also became a writer. This locale
provided the background for Murray's first two novels,
although she later used Ireland and other European settings.
Throughout her life, Murray continued to publish articles

and essays on literary figures, as well as poetry and fiction. She moved with her family to less remote areas of western Ontario, near Tilsonburg, and later settled near Niagara Falls, where she died on 28 September 1894.

Too often Murray had the misfortune of sending her stories to publications that were about to collapse. She sent her first novel, *Fauna; or, The Red Flower of Leafy Hollow*, to Susanna Moodie's short-lived *Victoria Magazine* (Belleville), which ceased publication before Murray's story could appear. On Moodie's recommendation, she then sent it to John Lovell's *Literary Garland*. It had scarcely appeared in that journal (April–October 1851) when the *Garland*, too, ceased publication. Lovell wrote to Murray, enclosing the proofs of *Fauna*: "Indeed it would be a pleasure to be able to say that I would accept of your contributions in future at a fair remuneration; for I am convinced that they would add much to the merits of the *Garland*, but I regret to say that the miserable support that the *Garland* receives from the Canadian public will compel me to discontinue its publication at the end of this year." Nevertheless, when *Fauna* appeared, it received much attention, and was reprinted in several newspapers, including a New York paper and a Belfast, Ireland journal.

"The Cited Curate," published in the first volume of *The British American Magazine* (June 1863–January 1864), and "Marguerite Kneller, Artist and Woman" in *Canadian Monthly* (January–June 1872) were perhaps her best novels. In "The Cited Curate" a talented young clergyman's overweening ambition has tragic results which belie the Edenic setting. Unfortunately, *The British American Magazine*, in which this novel appeared, lasted only one year. The difficulties inherent in a woman's artistic life are developed fictionally in "Marguerite Kneller, Artist and Woman." The story portrays a young woman painter devoted to her art. She is talented but not beautiful. Her appearance is balanced, however, by an attractive personality. The young artist loses her lover, also a painter, to her more beautiful younger sister. The ending of the novel without

124   LOUISA MURRAY

closure—with the protagonist unmarried—is uncommon for the time, as Rachel Blau Du Plessis's *Writing Beyond the Ending* makes clear. In narrative line and language, the story, which is shorter and simpler than Murray's earlier serials, is realistic.

Murray's essays include several on women writers. "Suppression of Genius in Women," a two-part essay on the lack of opportunity or encouragement for women writers, anticipates Virginia Woolf's *Room of One's Own*. Murray uses Charlotte and Emily Brontë as examples of talented women whose development was limited by their restricted lives, and Dorothy Wordsworth and Jane Carlyle as examples of women who devoted their own genius to supporting and encouraging men. Dorothy Wordsworth contributed her insights and imagination to her brother's poetry. Jane Carlyle, respected for her intellect and wit, led a limited and lonely life, allowed to share very little in her husband's intellectual concerns.

"Mr. Gray's Strange Story," which appeared in *The Week* (26 February 1892), evinces the interest in spiritualism current at the time. It is set in the area of southern Ontario familiar to Murray, and in the type of quiet rural area which she knew and loved. The oblique narrative allows the story of love, and of revenge that reaches beyond the grave, to be told without the necessity of explanation, and without the emotional intensity of a directly involved narrator. The story's tragedy is all the more effective for the peaceful, idyllic setting with which it begins.

✎

Suggested Reading:
Murray, Louisa. "The Cited Curate." In *The British American Magazine* 1 (June 1863), 2 (January 1864).
_____. "Marguerite Kneller, Artist and Woman." In *The Canadian Monthly and National Review* (January–June 1872).

_____. "Suppression of Genius in Women." In
The Week I. Charlotte and Emily Brontë (5 April
1889), 280; II. Dorothy Wordsworth and Jane Carlyle
(12 April 1889), 295–296.

Wetherald, Ethelwyn. "Some Canadian Literary Women."
In *The Week*. III. "Louisa Murray." (19 April 1888), 335.

Zelmanovits, Judith. "Louisa Murray, Writing Woman."
In *Canadian Woman Studies/ Les cahiers de la femme*. 7,
3 (Fall 1986), 39–42.

MR. GRAY'S STRANGE STORY

Louisa Murray

> *What may this mean . . . .*
> *So terribly to shake our dispositions*
> *With thoughts beyond the reaches of our souls.*
> —*Hamlet, Act 1, Scene IV.*

I am a minister of the Presbyterian Church of Canada, fifty years old, in sound health of body and mind. I have never had any belief in spiritualism, clairvoyance or any similar psychical delusions. My favourite studies at college were logic and mathematics, and no one who knew me could suspect me of belonging to that class of enthusiasts in which ghosts and other preternatural manifestations have their origin. Yet I have had one strange experience in my life which apparently contradicts all my theories of the universe and its laws, nor have I ever been able to explain it on any rational hypothesis. That there is some reasonable explanation I believe, and as there is no one living now, except myself, whom the facts concern, I have determined to give them to the world for the benefit of those who are interested in abnormal phenomena.

Twenty-five years ago I was minister of a newly built church, in a village on the shore of Lake Erie. The village had sprung up round the saw mills of Mason and Company, lately erected to turn the giant pines that grew on the sandy borders of the lake into lumber. When the pines were all worked up, the great saw mills and lumber yards sought another locality, and the village which had never had any individuality of its own dropped out of existence.

There was no manse, and I boarded in the house of the chief member of my congregation, Mr. Michael Forrest, who owned a fine farm of four hundred acres close to the village.

The Red House Farm, as it was called from the colour of the paint Michael Forrest liberally bestowed on his buildings and fences, was in those days a pleasant place. There peace and plenty reigned, and everything within and without testified to good management, order and comfort.

My story opens in the parlour of the Red House, where, in the early afternoon of a splendid Indian summer day, a young man was writing at a desk placed under an open window that looked into a spacious verandah enclosed by cedar posts round which climbing plants were twined in picturesque profusion. This "best room" was never used by the family except on Sundays and festal occasions, and at other times was given up to the minister, the Rev. Gilbert Gray, who writes this narrative.

The hurry and bustle of dinner were over, the dinner things cleared away and the kitchen and dining-room made tidy. Mrs. Forrest was sitting in her rocking chair by the sunny kitchen window, and, her knitting in her lap, was taking her afternoon nap, her cat curled up at her feet. All was quiet in the house till light steps came tripping down stairs, and two pretty girls entered the verandah, sitting down on the high-backed bench of rustic work, each holding some bit of light needle-work in her hands. One was the only child of Farmer Forrest and his wife; the other a niece, brought up by Mrs. Forrest from infancy, and filling the place of a second daughter.

I have said they were two pretty girls, but Marjory Forrest was beautiful. She was a tall, graceful blonde, fair and pale, with rose-red lips, violet eyes, and hair the very colour of sun-light. She looked like the heroine of some happy love poem—happy, I say, for there was no hint of tragedy in her pure, serene face. Celia Morris had a

LOUISA MURRAY

Hebe-like face and form, with bright chestnut hair, merry brown eyes and a laughing mouth, showing two rows of pearly teeth. She was just eighteen; two years younger than Marjory.

They made a charming picture in their pretty print dresses, fresh and spotless, their bright heads bending over their work, and catching the changing lights and shades coming in through the autumn-tinted leaves. But the picture darkened and dissolved as a handsome young man stood in the open arch of the doorway. The girls smiled a welcome, and, taking off his hat, he stepped in and threw himself down on a pile of mats made of the husks of Indian corn. He was the son of the head of the great lumber firm of Mason and Company. His father was a hard-working, self-made man, but he prided himself on bringing up his son to be a gentleman. Not an idle gentleman, however, and he had lately sent the young man to the mills to gain some practical knowledge of business before admitting him to a junior partnership. As there had been many satisfactory dealings between Mr. Mason and Farmer Forrest, Leonard Mason was made welcome at the Red House, and speedily established himself on a friendly footing. His frank, unaffected manner, and freedom from what Mrs. Forrest called "city airs," pleased the farmer and his wife; his knowledge of music and light literature charmed Marjory and Celia. The young people were on the most familiar and friendly terms, but Leonard's attentions were so equally divided between them that if he had a preference only a very close observer could have discerned it.

To-day he did not respond as readily as usual to Celia's lively chatter, and he soon got up from his seat on the mats, and, placing himself against one of the posts, from which point of vantage he could better see Marjory's face, said, "I am going to Hamilton."

Marjory looked up with a startled glance. Celia laughed a quick little laugh as she asked, "not this very minute, are you?"

"I am going to-morrow; my father wants me."

"Well, I suppose you mean to come back again," said Celia lightly.

"Yes, but not for a week. Shall you miss me very much while I am away?"

"Why, of course; there won't be any one to sing 'Come into the garden, Maud.' Will there Marjory?"

"No, indeed," said Marjory.

"I wonder which of you will miss me most. If I knew, I would ask her to give me a lock of her hair to wear round my wrist as a keepsake."

Celia's eyes were fixed on Leonard with an eager questioning expression, but he was looking at Marjory, who kept her eyes steadily on her work, though a faint blush was stealing over her face.

"I'll tell you what we must do," said Leonard. "I'll get two long and two short lots, and you must both draw. Whoever draws two long lots loses a lock of her hair to me." "I know you won't refuse me," he continued pleadingly, "because there may be an accident to the train I am going on, and I may be killed, and then you'd be sorry for having been so unkind."

"What nonsense," cried Celia.

"Not at all," said Leonard, "wise men of old believed in the judgment of lots." And breaking off a slender vine-tendril he divided it into two long and two short lots, arranging them with some mysterious manipulations between his fingers. Then, kneeling on one knee, he held them to Marjory.

Slowly, with tremulous fingers and blushing cheeks, Marjory drew a long lot. Leonard seemed going to say something, but checking himself held out the lots to Celia. Celia did not blush; she grew deathly pale as she drew out her lot. It was a short one.

"I see you don't intend to lose, Miss Celia," said Leonard.

I think I hear now the wild, hysterical laugh with which she answered him. Then, I did not heed it.

"If you draw a short one this time," said Leonard, as he again held the lots to Marjory, "we shall have to try again," but as he spoke the second long lot was in her hand.

"Oh, kind fortune!" cried Leonard.

He tried to make Marjory look at him, but she would not meet his eyes. Still, those subtle signs that lovers learn to read—the flickering flame on her cheek, the quivering of her lips and eyelids, who can say what—gave him courage. Snatching up her scissors, he held them over her head. "May I?" he asked beseechingly. With shy, timid grace she bent her fair head still lower; he felt the mute consent, and the next moment one long braid was severed from the rest and lying in his hand.

"Fasten it round my wrist with a true lover's knot," he whispered, softly touching her fingers with the braid. She took it at once, and as he pushed up his sleeve she wound it round his wrist, Leonard helping her to tie the mystic knot. Holding her hand, which did not try to escape, he drew her gently towards him and kissed the virgin lips that confidingly met his.

At that moment a shadow, as if from the wild flight of a bird, passed before the window at which I sat, and swift as an arrow from a bow Celia darted out of the verandah. Till then I had seen and heard all that passed in a sort of stupor, like that which sometimes takes possession of one who listens to his death sentence, though every word is indelibly written on the tablets of his memory. Unwittingly I had been playing the part of an eavesdropper. Now consciousness returned, and, like a man coming out of a trance, I got up and left the room and the house.

∽

I had walked fast and far before I returned to the Red House, and the moon, a brilliant hunter's moon, was flooding earth and heaven with light as I came in sight of the verandah. The inmates seemed all standing outside, among them a tall, finely-made young man, whom I at once recognized as Archie Jonson, farmer Forrest's nephew, generally supposed to be the heir to the Red House Farm. A marriage between him and Celia had been planned by the farmer and his wife while the cousins were children. Archie had always been devoted to Celia, and she had been fond of him till he tried to win her for his wife. Then, either from coyness or coquetry, she became cold and unresponsive. His entreaties for an immediate marriage were indignantly refused, and the utmost concession she would make was that after she was one and twenty she might think about it. A quarrel ensued, and, deeply wounded, Archie left his home. He was passionately fond of the water, and being known as a brave and skilful sailor he found no difficulty in obtaining the place of mate on one of the best schooners on the lakes.

I was surprised at seeing him, as he was not expected home until after the close of navigation, but still more astonished when he came to meet me before I reached the house.

"Where's Celia?" he called out as he came near.

"Celia?" I exclaimed, with a sudden feeling of alarm, "Isn't she at home?"

"No; Marjory thought she went with you to the village."

"She hasn't been with me. I haven't seen her."

"My God!" he burst out passionately; "where can she be?"

"Perhaps she's hiding from you, for fun," I said.

"No; they had missed her before I got here."

The farmer was calling us to come on, and, as soon as we were near enough, he told us that shortly after dinner he had seen Celia running down the road to the bush. "But you see," he said, "I was so taken aback by Leonard coming to ask me for Marjory, that I forgot I had seen her till this minute."

"She must have gone to get maple leaves for her Christmas wreath," said Marjory.

"But what keeps her so late?" said Mrs. Forrest.

"Why, you needn't be scared about her," said the farmer; "there's nothing to harm her. There hasn't been a bear or a wolf, or even a rattlesnake, seen in these woods for forty years; nor no such vermin as tramps, neither."

"There's that swamp," rejoined his wife; "she's always hunting for some sort of weeds in it, and I often think she'll fall in and get drowned."

"She couldn't be drowned if she didn't walk into the middle of it on purpose," said the farmer. "But where's Archie going?"

"To bring home Celia," Archie called back, as he walked off at a pace that soon took him out of sight.

"I'm sure I'm glad he's gone after her," said Mrs. Forrest. "She might have hurt her foot on a stub or a stone, and not be able to walk."

I suggested that Leonard and I had better follow Archie, and Leonard said he was going to make the same proposal.

"Archie won't want you," said the farmer. "If Celia has hurt herself, he can carry her home as easy as a baby; and like the job, too, I guess."

"Oh, let them go, father!" said Marjory. "You see how anxious mother is, and so am I."

"All right, let them go if they like," said the farmer; adding in an irritable tone, that showed he was himself getting uneasy, "woman are always making a fuss about nothing."

The moon was at the full, and the sky without a cloud. Every cluster of golden rod and purple aster along the fences, every stick and stone on the road were as clearly seen as at noonday. Leonard and I hurried on filled with an unspoken dread. The road was at first in a straight line, but on coming to a piece of marshy land it turned away to the bush; a path from this turning led to the swamp, a few yards distant.

These swamps are often places of surpassing beauty. There every species of wild fowl make their nests and rear their young broods, and the brilliant flowers and luxuriant leaves of all kinds of water plants form lovely aquatic gardens, richly coloured with ever-varying tints from April to

December, and always the delight of an artist's eye. Round the edges of the swamp the water is usually shallow enough for the hunters to wade through in pursuit of their game, but in the centre it is often dangerously deep, and only to be crossed in a skiff or canoe.

Where the road divided, Leonard would have kept a straight course to the bush, but a terrible fear dragged me in the other direction. "No; come this way!" I cried, and he turned and followed me in silence. Faster and faster we hurried on till we reached the swamp. There a heart-rending sight met our eyes. Archie Jonson was struggling through the beds of water-lilies, reeds and rushes that obstructed his way, clasping Celia in his arms. Her long hair fell down dank and dripping, her arms hung stiff and lifeless, her face gleamed ghastly white under the strong moonlight. She was dead! "Drowned! drowned!"

As he ran towards him, Archie laid her on a grassy mound. Her limbs were not distorted and her face was composed, except that her eyes were wide open as if in startled surprise. "You are a doctor as well as a minister," Archie said to me, hoarsely; "see if there is any life left."

There was none. She had been dead for hours. As I said so, Archie sprung up from his kneeling attitude beside Celia, and turned to Leonard with a deadly rage and hatred in his eyes.

"This is your doing," he said.

"Mine!" exclaimed Leonard. "Are you mad?"

"I am not mad. There is Celia, the girl I loved better than my life, lying dead before my eyes, and you are her murderer!"

"Good Heavens!" cried Leonard, "What do you mean?"

"The shock has been too much for him," I said. "Archie, my poor fellow, you don't know what you are saying."

"I know very well what I am saying. He—that man there—fooled Celia, poor little innocent child, with his fine flattering manners till she thought he was making love to her, and when she found out he had only been play-acting with her, she couldn't bear it. It made her crazy, and she came down to the swamp and drowned herself. Oh, my God, she drowned herself! But it was he made her do it."

"I never made love to Celia in my life," said Leonard. "I loved Marjory from the first hour I saw her."

"Oh, I dare say. You were only playing with Celia, but she thought you were in earnest. Listen to me, minister," he continued, controlling his passion with wonderful self-command; "I had a warning, but I was a blind idiot and did not take it. Three nights ago, I dreamed that I saw Celia standing on a bank sloping down to a big piece of water, and a man was standing beside her, and while I was looking on in a stupid kind of wonder, I saw she was slipping down towards the water and not able to stop herself, and she held out her hand to the man and cried to him to help her, but he turned right round and went up the bank. Then I woke, and the dream seemed so real it made me feel queer; but I never had any belief in dreams, and when I got up and went out into the daylight, I laughed at myself for being frightened at a nightmare and thought no more about it. But the next night the dream came again; and this time I saw Celia throw herself into the water; and the man stood on the bank and looked on. Then I knew the dream was sent to warn me of some danger to Celia, though I couldn't tell what it meant, and I came home as quick as I could. And the first person I saw was the man I had seen in my dream—the man I am looking at now, and I heard he was going to marry Marjory; and Celia could not be found. Then when aunt Forrest mentioned the swamp, the meaning of the dream came to me like a flash, and I made for the swamp, but I had come too late—too late to save her, but not too late to revenge her wrongs."

I attempted to reason with him as well as I could, and tried to show him how wicked and absurd it was to let a dream—a nightmare, as he had himself called it—put much wild fancies into his head.

"And you cannot know that she drowned herself; it may have been an accident," I said.

"It was no accident; she drowned herself in her madness. When I got to the swamp I saw a bit of ribbon hanging on the reeds, and I went on till I came to the deep water; there I found her. She had not sunk very far down because her skirt had caught on a stake that stood up there, and I got her out easily enough. But she was dead; and you, Leonard Mason, will have to answer to me for her death."

"I tell you I am innocent of her death as you are!"

"Can you swear it?" cried Archie. "Can you swear it while she lies there before your eyes?"

"I can, I never had any love for Celia, and I never tried to make her think I had. I swear it before the God that hears me!"

As Leonard uttered this oath, Archie kept his eyes fixed on him with piercing intensity; but Leonard met the searching gaze without flinching.

"If you have sworn to a lie," Archie said, "your sin will find you out, and you will have to answer to me for what you have done when you least expect it."

Then he wheeled round, and going to his dead sweetheart, took her in his arms. "Go before me, minister," he said—"go before me, and tell them *what* is coming."

He would not allow me to help him, so Leonard and I walked on before, and Archie followed with his piteous burden. He was a tall powerful young man, besides being under such a strong excitement as gives threefold strength to every nerve, and he carried poor Celia's death-weight, as if she had been a living child.

But I can write no more of that night of grief and anguish. When the dismal morning came, Archie had gone.

◡

Three days after her death Celia was laid in the village graveyard; a peaceful spot away from all noise or traffic, on the side of a gentle hill within site of the Red House. No one but Archie Jonson, Leonard Mason and myself ever suspected the manner of her death. It was naturally supposed that while gathering flowers in the swamp she had fallen into some hidden pool from which the water plants that covered it would prevent her escape.

Archie was not at her funeral, nor had he returned to the farm, but, two days after she was buried, he wrote to Mrs. Forrest telling her that he had rejoined his vessel, the *White Bird*, which was going up Lake Superior with a cargo, the last trip she intended to make that season. The letter made no mention of Celia and was very brief, but it was calmly and coherently written, and the Forrests hoped he intended to come home when the schooner was laid up. But this gleam of light was soon lost in deeper darkness. In the middle of November a letter from the owners of the *White Bird* came to Michael Forrest, informing him that the vessel with all her crew had been lost on Lake Superior in one of those sudden storms which, after a long period of fine weather in the fall, sometimes break over the lakes. Her figure head, on which her name and that of the firm to which she belonged were carved, had been found floating, and recognized by another vessel, confirming the fears for her fate that had been felt. The bodies of the crew were never found, for the ice-cold depths of Lake Superior never give up their dead.

The winter passed slowly and sadly at the Red House, but with the spring came the promise of new hope and joy. Mr. Mason had built a pretty house for Leonard and his bride near the Mills, of which Leonard was to be chief manager. They were to be married in May, and the month famous for its caprice wore its fairest aspect that year. The sorrows which Marjory had gone through seemed only to have deepened the tender sweetness of her delicate beauty, and purified the happiness that illumined her lovely eyes. Leonard, as handsome and charming as ever, had grown more manly and thoughtful, and, if possible, was more in love with Marjory than ever. The old people gained new life from Marjory's happy prospects, and if I had not known what depths of regret sad remembrance can lie silent and secret in the human heart I might have thought that Celia and Archie were forgotten.

The wedding day came in warm and bright, and as full of opening buds and blossoms as if it had been expressly made for the occasion. The ceremony was to take place in the Red House parlour at six o'clock in the evening. The supper was to follow immediately. The bride and bridegroom were then to be driven to the nearest station to meet the train for Hamilton where they were to stay a few days and then go on to Niagara Falls to spend the remainder of their honeymoon there.

It was a busy day at the Red House. Two or three young girls from the village came to help in the pleasant task of putting all the rooms in festal array, and in preparing the dainties liberally provided for the wedding feast.

As the time for the ceremony drew near, the day's excitement rose higher and higher. The bridesmaids were dressing the bride, Mrs. Forrest and two favourite assistants were setting out the supper table. The farmer had taken most of the guests to see his new peach orchard. Two young men, one a cousin of Leonard's who had come from Hamilton to be the best man, were chatting and laughing through an open window with two pretty girls who were decorating the wedding cake with dainty little flags bearing embroidered mottos placed among loves and doves and other appropriate devices in sugar. Leonard and I were standing in the doorway of the verandah, and the eager bridegroom was looking at his watch.

"It only wants twelve minutes to six," he said, "I hope Marjory is ready."

"Your watch is too fast," I said, laughing. "Mine wants fully a quarter."

As I spoke a boy employed to do "chores" came round the barnyard and said, "There's a man wants to see Mr. Leonard Mason."

"A man—what man?" asked Leonard impatiently.

"Dun know. He says he must see you for a minute."

"Oh, hang it!" said Leonard. "Well, I suppose I can give him a minute," and he stepped out of the verandah.

Then, looking back at me, he exclaimed, "I hope the day is not going to change."

It was already changing. Grey clouds coming up from the lake were creeping over the sun. An icy wind followed them, chilling me to the bone, and I heard a distant peal of thunder. Farmer Forrest came hurrying his guests into the verandah. "Is all ready, minister?" he enquired. "Where's Leonard?"

"He went to the yard to speak to a man that wanted to see him," I answered.

"Well, we'd best go into the parlour now, and receive the bride and bridegroom in state," said the farmer leading the way.

As Leonard did not come at once, I went to meet him, wondering at his delay. The clouds were growing darker; there was a sharp gleam of lightning, and the thunder that followed showed it was nearer. The storm was certainly coming up, but it might be only a shower.

I looked all round the horizon, and while I was noting the darkening clouds, two men going up the road to the graveyard came into my view; a gleam of the fading sunlight making them distinctly visible. The one in front was more than commonly tall, and led the way with swift, vigorous strides. He was dressed in what seemed a sailor's rough jacket and trousers, and a sailor's glazed hat with floating ribbons. His companion followed him with curiously unequal steps, as if dragged by some invisible chain. It was easy to recognize in this last Leonard in his new wedding suit; and as I gazed the conviction flashed upon me that the man in front was Archie Jonson. After all, then, Archie had not been drowned when the *White Bird* was lost. But by what strange power had he compelled Leonard to leave his waiting bride and follow him to the graveyard?

Such an extraordinary proceeding was both mysterious and alarming, and might be dangerous for Leonard; and on the impulse of the moment I followed them as fast as I could. I was a rapid walker, but they had a start of some minutes, and I could not overtake them.

When I entered the graveyard the whole sky was wrapped in a black pall except a little space above the plot of ground, bordered with periwinkles, in which Celia's grave lay. The white stone at the head of the grave and the figures of two men beside it stood vividly out under that clear space, while the black cloud came swiftly on as if to swallow them up. The tall man had his hand on the gravestone, his face was turned towards me and I could see every feature. It was Archie Jonson's face, lividly pale; or it might have been the shadow of the thunder cloud that made it appear so. Leonard's back was towards me, and he confronted Archie— if Archie it was—in a fixed and moveless attitude. I saw them distinctly for a moment; the next the black cloud that seemed almost to touch the ground covered them, and all was hidden from eyes. Then a bolt of blue flame with a red light in its centre shot from the cloud, and an awful crash seemed to rend the heavens. A blinding torrent of rain suc-ceeded, but it ceased in a minute or two; the cloud passed on, and the sun, now near its setting, shone clear in the western sky. Anxiously I looked round for Leonard and his mysterious companion. Leonard was lying stretched on Celia's grave; Archie, or his avenging ghost, or whatever had assumed his likeness, had disappeared.

Going up to Leonard, I found him dead; killed by the lightning I supposed, though I saw no sign of its having touched him. As I was still stooping over, half stunned by the shock, his cousin and two or three other young men came round me. They had heard a confused account of our having gone to the graveyard, and while others were looking for us in the barns and out-houses, they had come to see if it could be true. We made a rough litter of pine boughs on which we laid poor Leonard, the young men carrying the bier while I walked before, wondering how it would be pos-sible for me to tell the awful tidings it was my hard fate to bring.

But it was not left to me. Marjory, who had been wait-ing and watching in an agony of terror at Leonard's absence, had seen the ominous procession coming down the hill, and before anyone could prevent her she was flying madly to meet it. Desperately I tried to stop her, but she broke away from me, saw her lover's dead body lying on the bier, and fell at the feet of the bearers in a death-like swoon; her dainty wedding dress and fair hair wreathed with flowers, lying in the muddy pools the thunder-rain had made.

It was long before she could be brought back to life, and then her mind was gone. She remembered nothing of the past, she had no recognition of the present; she knew no more, not even her mother; she never spoke, and did not seem conscious of anything said to her. She lingered a few days in this state, and then died so quietly that the watchers did not know when she passed away.

The poor old people did not long survive the wreck of all their earthly hopes. The Red House farm was sold, and Michael Forrest's property was divided among relations he had never known.

Leonard Mason's death was, of course, attributed to lightning. The "chore" boy's description of the man with whom Leonard had gone to the grave was so fanciful, and so mixed with improbable incidents, that his tale was not credited by anyone. From some dreamy, incoherent utterances of Mrs. Forrest's, it was afterwards believed that Leonard had gone to the graveyard at Marjory's desire to lay a wreath of flowers on Celia's grave; and when the conjecture was added that the unknown man must have been an express messenger from Hamilton, bringing the wreath that had delayed by some mistake, the mystery was supposed to be explained. As for the strange things connected with this tragedy that had come to my knowledge, I kept them hidden in my breast.

I have never seen or heard anything of Archie Jonson since his inexplicable appearance on that fatal day; and I have been informed that it was absolutely impossible the best sailor that ever lived could have escaped in such a storm as that in which the *White Bird*, with her crew, foundered.

⌒

The Week (26 February 1892), 198–200.

E. Pauline Johnson ("Tekahionwake") (1861–1913)

A Red Girl's Reasoning (1893)

At the turn of the century, Pauline Johnson's writings and recitals made her one of the best-known native persons in the Canada of the day. In her art, Johnson sought to project a positive, aristocratic image of her own Mohawk lineage and to portray native people as autonomous and worthy of respect. In 1900, for example, she contributed a section dealing with the lives of native women to the report *Women of Canada: Their Life and Work*, the first major study of the status of Canadian women.

Emily Pauline Johnson was born in 1861 on the Six Nations Indian Reserve near Brantford, Ontario. As a status Indian, she was the younger daughter of Emily Susanna Howells, an Englishwoman and sister-in-law of an Anglican minister on the reserve, and George Henry Martin Johnson, a Mohawk chief of historic antecedents. Her heritage shaped her life and her art. Pauline Johnson was educated at home, in the imposing "Chiefswood" built by her father for his bride, now a heritage site. She later attended a native day school and Brantford Collegiate (1877–79). After the death in 1884 of her father, an activist in Indian social issues of the day, the twenty-two-year-old Pauline, her mother and her older sister were compelled to move to cheaper lodgings in Brantford.

In 1885, Pauline, whose literary interests had been quickened in her parents' extensive library, published her first poem, in *Gems of Poetry* (New York). She became a frequent contributor of lyrics to *The Week*. She also wrote sketches for the London *Express* at this time. In 1892, she participated in a poetry reading in Toronto, the point of departure for a successful—but gruelling and financially uncertain—life as "The Mohawk Princess" on recital tours between 1892 and 1909. During performances in Canada,

London and the United States, she was a striking and dramatic figure in ceremonial dress; her native poetry won the praise of English critic Theodore Watts-Dunton.

Johnson's first book of poetry, *White Wampum*, appeared in 1895 as the result of an introduction by Canadian novelist Sir Gilbert Parker to the London publisher John Lane during her first visit to London. When ill health forced her to give up touring in 1909, she moved to Vancouver. There, through a friendship with the Squamish chief Joe Capilano, she absorbed and transcribed versions of traditional Indian legends, an expression of her concern that even the aboriginal peoples themselves were losing touch with traditional lore. The result was *Legends of Vancouver* (1911). Pauline usually added the signature "Tekahionwake" ("Double Wampum") to her name on literary works in order to underline her native heritage. The name had been that of her famous ancestor, Chief Smoke Johnson, a hero of the War of 1812. She saw herself as a voice of her people and told Ernest Thompson Seton: "There are those who think they pay me a compliment in saying I am just like a white woman. My aim, my joy, my pride is to sing the glories of my own people." She died of cancer in Vancouver in 1913, and her ashes are buried in Stanley Park.

"A Red Girl's Reasoning" is a story central to Pauline Johnson's themes and reputation. The story won the *Dominion Illustrated* magazine's fiction prize for 1892 and was published there the following year; Pauline adapted it for use as a playlet in her live performances. The story asserts the pride and self-esteem of a Métis girl in the face of her white spouse's racism and condescension. The theme is intensified by a contrast between the attitudes of the husband and his brother to the other culture—a device by which Johnson avoids reverse stereotyping—and a stinging portrayal of the "high society" Pauline Johnson had seen at first hand. The theme cut prophetically close to Johnson's own life: her engagement to a younger, upper-middle class white man, Charles Drayton, was broken off in 1899, probably in part because of his family's objections to her native blood as well as to her recital career. (Actresses, like natives, were marginalized in Victorian Canada.) Pauline Johnson knew the vicissitudes of her native heritage in late nineteenth-century white Canada, and much of the critical writing about Pauline Johnson has too long sentimentalized or trivialized her efforts to portray her race in her poems, stories and stage appearances. Johnson's native stories sturdily depict her native characters as self-sufficient, acting rather than acted upon, and determined to assert the value of self and of difference. Not for Johnson the archetypal Indian maiden—a staple of nineteenth-century Canadian literature—a fawn-like chief's daughter who at story's end dies saving her white lover (conveniently ending the possibility of miscegenation), or who self-effacingly melts into the forest leaving the field to a lily-white maiden.

◡◠

Suggested Reading:
Johnson, E. Pauline. *Legends of Vancouver*. Toronto: McClelland and Stewart, 1911.

_____. *The Moccasin Maker*. Toronto: Ryerson, 1913.
Keller, Betty. *Pauline*. Vancouver: Douglas and McIntyre, 1981.
Lyon, George P. "Pauline Johnson: A Reconsideration." In *Studies in Canadian Literature* 15.2 (1990), 136–59.
Petrone, Penny. *Native Literature in Canada*. Toronto: Oxford, 1990.

A Red Girl's Reasoning

E. Pauline Johnson ("Tekahionwake")

"Be pretty good to her, Charlie, my boy, or she'll balk sure as shooting."

That was what old Jimmy Robinson said to his brand new son-in-law, while they waited for the bride to reappear.

"Oh! you bet, there's no danger of much else. I'll be good to her, help me Heaven," replied Charlie McDonald, brightly.

"Yes, of course you will," answered the old man, "but don't you forget, there's a good big bit of her mother in her, and," closing his left eye significantly, "you don't understand these Indians as I do."

"But I'm just as fond of them, Mr. Robinson," Charlie said assertively, "and get on with them too, now, don't I?"

"Yes, pretty well for a town boy; but when you have lived forty years among these people, as I have done; when you have had your wife as long as I have had mine—for there's no getting over it, Christine's disposition is as native as her mother's, every bit—and perhaps when you've owned for eighteen years a daughter as dutiful, as loving, as fearless, and alas! as obstinate as that little piece you are stealing away from me to-day—I tell you, youngster, you'll know more than you know now. It is kindness for kindness, bullet for bullet, blood for blood. Remember, what you are, she will be," and the old Hudson Bay trader scrutinized Charlie McDonald's face like a detective.

It was a happy, fair face, good to look at, with a certain ripple of dimples somewhere about the mouth, and eyes that laughed out the very sunniness of their owner's soul. There was not a severe nor yet a weak line anywhere. He was a well-meaning young fellow, happily dispositioned, and a great favorite with the tribe at Robinson's Post, whither he had gone in the service of the Department of Agriculture, to assist the local agent through the tedium of a long census-taking.

As a boy he had had the Indian relic-hunting craze, as a youth he had studied Indian archæology and folk-lore, as a man he consummated his predilections for Indianology by loving, winning and marrying the quiet little daughter of the English trader, who himself had married a native woman some twenty years ago. The country was all backwoods, and the Post miles and miles from even the semblance of civilization, and the lonely young Englishman's heart had gone out to the girl who, apart from speaking a very few words of English, was utterly uncivilized and uncultured, but had withal that marvellously innate refinement so universally possessed by the higher tribes of North American Indians.

Like all her race, observant, intuitive, having a horror of ridicule, consequently quick at acquirement and teachable in mental and social habits, she had developed from absolute pagan indifference into a sweet, elderly Christian woman, whose broken English, quiet manner, and still handsome copper-colored face, were the joy of old Robinson's declining years.

He had given their daughter Christine all the advantages of his own learning—which, if truthfully told, was not universal; but the girl had a fair common education, and the native adaptability to progress.

She belonged to neither and still to both types of the cultured Indian. The solemn, silent, almost heavy manner of the one so commingled with the gesticulating Frenchiness and vivacity of the other, that one unfamiliar with native Canadian life would find it difficult to determine her nationality.

She looked very pretty to Charles McDonald's loving eyes, as she reappeared in the doorway, holding her mother's hand and saying some happy words of farewell. Personally she looked much the same as her sisters, all Canada through, who are the offspring of red and white parentage—olive-complexioned, grey-eyed, black-haired, with figure slight and delicate, and the wistful, unfathomable expression in her whole face that turns one so heartsick as they glance at the young Indians of to-day—it is the forerunner too frequently of "the white man's disease," consumption—but McDonald was pathetically in love, and thought her the most beautiful woman he had ever seen in his life.

There had not been much of a wedding ceremony. The priest had cantered through the service in Latin, pronounced the benediction in English, and congratulated the "happy couple" in Indian, as a compliment to the assembled tribe in the little amateur structure that did service at the post as a sanctuary.

But the knot was tied as firmly and indissolubly as if all Charlie McDonald's swell city friends had crushed themselves up against the chancel to congratulate him, and in his heart he was deeply thankful to escape the flower-pelting, white gloves, rice-throwing, and ponderous stupidity of a breakfast, and indeed all the regulation gimcracks of the usual marriage celebrations, and it was with a hand trembling with absolute happiness that he assisted his little Indian wife into the old muddy buckboard that, hitched to an underbred-looking pony, was to convey them over the first stages of their journey. Then came more adieus, some hand-clasping, old Jimmy Robinson looking very serious just at the last, Mrs. Jimmy, stout, stolid, betraying nothing of visible emotion, and then the pony, roughshod and shaggy, trudged on, while mutual hand-waves were kept up until the old Hudson's Bay Post dropped out of sight, and the buckboard with its lightsome load of hearts, deliriously happy, jogged on over the uneven trail.

E. Pauline Johnson

She was "all the rage" that winter at the provincial capital. The men called her a "deuced fine little woman." The ladies said she was "just the sweetest wildflower." Whereas she was really but an ordinary, pale, dark girl who spoke slowly and with a strong accent, who danced fairly well, sang acceptably, and never stirred outside the door without her husband.

Charlie was proud of her; he was proud that she had "taken" so well among his friends, proud that she bore herself so complacently in the drawing-rooms of the wives of pompous Government officials, but doubly proud of her almost abject devotion to him. If ever human being was worshipped that being was Charlie McDonald; it could scarcely have been otherwise, for the almost godlike strength of his passion for that little wife of his would have mastered and melted a far more invincible citadel than an already affectionate woman's heart.

Favorites socially, McDonald and his wife went everywhere. In fashionable circles she was "new"—a potent charm to acquire popularity, and the little velvet-clad figure was always the center of interest among all the women in the room. She always dressed in velvet. No woman in Canada, has she but the faintest dash of native blood in her veins, but loves velvets and silks. As beef to the Englishman, wine to the Frenchman, fads to the Yankee, so are velvet and silk to the Indian girl, be she wild as a prairie grass, be she on the borders of civilization, or, having stepped within its boundary, mounted the steps of culture even under its superficial heights.

"Such a dolling little appil blossom," said the wife of a local M.P., who brushed up her etiquette and English once a year at Ottawa. "Does she always laugh so sweetly, and gobble you up with those great big grey eyes of hers, when you are togetheah at home, Mr. McDonald? If so, I should think youah pooah brothah would feel himself terribly *de trop*."

He laughed lightly. "Yes, Mrs. Stuart, there are not two of Christie; she is the same at home and abroad, and as for Joe, he doesn't mind us a bit; he's no end fond of her."

"I'm very glad he is. I always fancied he did not care for her, d'you know."

If ever a blunt woman existed it was Mrs. Stuart. She really meant nothing, but her remark bothered Charlie. He was fond of his brother, and jealous for Christie's popularity. So that night when he and Joe were having a pipe he said:

"I've never asked you yet what you thought of her, Joe." A brief pause, then Joe spoke. "I'm glad she loves you."

"Why?"

"Because that girl has but two possibilities regarding humanity—love or hate."

"Humph! Does she love or hate *you*?"

"Ask her."

"You talk bosh. If she hated you, you'd get out. If she loved you I'd *make* you get out."

Joe McDonald whistled a little, then laughed.

"Now that we are on the subject, I might as well ask—honestly, old man, wouldn't you and Christie prefer keeping house alone to having me always around?"

"Nonsense, sheer nonsense. Why, thunder, man, Christie's no end fond of you, and as for me—you surely don't want assurances from me?"

"No, but I often think a young couple—"

"Young couple be blowed! After a while when they want you and your old surveying chains, and spindle-legged tripod telescope kickshaws, farther west, I venture to say the little woman will cry her eyes out—won't you, Christie?" This last in a higher tone, as through clouds of tobacco smoke he caught sight of his wife passing the doorway.

She entered. "Oh, no, I would not cry; I never do cry, but I would be heart-sore to lose you, Joe, and apart from that"—a little wickedly—"you may come in handy for an exchange some day, as Charlie does always say when he hoards up duplicate relics."

"Are Charlie and I duplicates?"

"Well—not exactly"—her head a little to one side, and eyeing them both merrily, while she slipped softly on to the arm of her husband's chair—"but, in the event of Charlie's failing me"—everyone laughed then. The "some day" that she spoke of was nearer than they thought. It came about in this wise.

There was a dance at the Lieutenant-Governor's, and the world and his wife were there. The nobs were in great feather that night, particularly the women, who flaunted about in new gowns and much splendor. Christie McDonald had a new gown also, but wore it with the utmost uncon- cern, and if she heard any of the flattering remarks made about her she at least appeared to disregard them.

"I never dreamed you could wear blue so splendidly," said Captain Logan, as they sat out a dance together.

"Indeed she can, though," interposed Mrs. Stuart, halting in one of her gracious sweeps down the room with her husband's private secretary.

"Don't shout so, captain. I can hear every sentence you uttah—of course Mrs. McDonald can wear blue—she has a morning gown of cadet blue that she is a picture in."

"You are both very kind," said Christie. "I like blue; it is the color of all the Hudson's Bay posts, and the factor's residence is always decorated in blue."

"Is it really? How interesting—do tell us some more of your old home, Mrs. McDonald; you so seldom speak of your life at the post, and we fellows so often wish to hear of it all," said Logan eagerly.

"Why do you not ask me of it, then?"

"Well—er, I'm sure I don't know; I'm fully interested in the Ind—in your people—your mother's people, I mean, but it always seems so personal, I suppose; and—a—a—"

"Perhaps you are, like all other white people, afraid to mention my nationality to me."

The captain winced, and Mrs. Stuart laughed uneasily. Joe McDonald was not far off, and he was listening, and chuckling, and saying to himself, "That's you, Christie, lay 'em out; it won't hurt 'em to know how they appear once in a while."

"Well, Captain Logan," she was saying, "what is it you would like to hear—of my people, or my parents, or myself?"

"All, all, my dear," cried Mrs. Stuart clamorously. "I'll speak for him—tell us of yourself and your mother—your father is delightful, I am sure—but then he is only an ordinary Englishman, not half as interesting as a foreigner, or—or perhaps I should say, a native."

Christie laughed. "Yes," she said, "my father often teases my mother now about how *very* native she was when he married her; then, how could she have been otherwise? She did not know a word of English, and there was not another English-speaking person besides my father and his two companions within sixty miles."

"Two companions, eh? one a Catholic priest and the other a wine merchant, I suppose, and with your father in the Hudson's Bay, they were good representatives of the pioneers in the New World," remarked Logan, waggishly.

"Oh, no, they were all Hudson's Bay men. There were no rumsellers and no missionaries in that part of the country then."

Mrs. Stuart looked puzzled. "No *missionaries?*" she repeated with an odd intonation.

Christie's insight was quick. There was a peculiar expression of interrogation in the eyes of her listeners, and the girl's blood leapt angrily up into her temples as she said hurriedly, "I know what you mean; I know what you are thinking. You are wondering how my parents were married—"

"Well—er, my dear, it seems peculiar—if there was no priest, and no magistrate, why—a—" Mrs. Stuart paused awkwardly.

"The marriage was performed by Indian rites," said Christie.

"Oh, do tell me about it; is the ceremony very interesting and quaint—are your chieftains anything like Buddhist priests?" It was Logan who spoke.

"Why, no," said the girl in amazement at that gentleman's ignorance. "There is no ceremony at all, save a feast. The two people just agree to live only with and for each other, and the man takes his wife to his home, just as you do. There is no ritual to bind them; they need none; an Indian's word was his law in those days, you know."

Mrs. Stuart stepped backwards. "Ah!" was all she said. Logan removed his eye-glass and stared blankly at Christie. "And did McDonald marry you in this singular fashion?" he questioned.

"Oh, no, we were married by Father O'Leary. Why do you ask?"

"Because if he had, I'd have blown his brains out tomorrow."

Mrs. Stuart's partner, who had hitherto been silent, coughed and began to twirl his cuff stud nervously, but nobody took any notice of him. Christie had risen, slowly, ominously—risen, with the dignity and pride of an empress.

"Captain Logan," she said, "what do you dare to say to me? What do you dare to mean? Do you presume to think it would not have been lawful for Charlie to marry me according to my people's rites? Do you for one instant dare to question that my parents were not as legally—"

"Don't, dear, don't," interrupted Mrs. Stuart hurriedly; "it is bad enough now, goodness knows; don't make—" Then she broke off blindly. Christie's eyes glared at the mumbling woman, at her uneasy partner, at the horrified captain. Then they rested on the McDonald brothers, who stood within earshot, Joe's face scarlet, her husband's white as ashes, with something in his eyes she had never seen before. It was Joe who saved the situation. Stepping quickly across towards his sister-in-law, he offered her his arm, saying, "The next dance is ours, I think, Christie."

Then Logan pulled himself together, and attempted to carry Mrs. Stuart off for the waltz, but for once in her life that lady had lost her head. "It is shocking!" she said, "outrageously shocking! I wonder if they told Mr. McDonald before he married her!" Then looking hurriedly round, she too saw the young husband's face—and knew that they had not.

"Humph! deuced nice kettle of fish—poor old Charlie has always thought so much of honorable birth."

Logan thought he spoke in an undertone, but "poor old Charlie" heard him. He followed his wife and brother across the room. "Joe," he said, "will you see that a trap is called?" Then to Christie, "Joe will see that you get home all right." He wheeled on his heel then and left the ball-room.

Joe *did* see.

He tucked a poor, shivering, pallid little woman into a cab, and wound her bare throat up in the scarlet velvet cloak that was hanging uselessly over her arm. She crouched down beside him, saying, "I am so cold, Joe; I am so cold," but she did not seem to know enough to wrap herself up. Joe felt all through this long drive that nothing this side of Heaven would be so good as to die, and he was glad when the poor little voice at his elbow said, "What is he so angry at, Joe?"

"I don't know exactly, dear," he said gently, "but I think it was what you said about this Indian marriage."

"But why should I not have said it? Is there anything wrong about it?" she asked pitifully.

"Nothing, that I can see—there was no other way; but Charlie is very angry, and you must be brave and forgiving with him, Christie, dear."

"But I did never see him like that before, did you?"

"Once."

"When?"

"Oh, at college, one day, a boy tore his prayer-book in half, and threw it into the grate, just to be mean, you know. Our mother had given it to him at his confirmation."

"And did he look so?"

"About, but it all blew over in a day—Charlie's tempers are short and brisk. Just don't take any notice of him; run off to bed, and he'll have forgotten it by the morning."

They reached home at last. Christie said good-night quietly, going directly to her room. Joe went to his room also, filled a pipe and smoked for an hour. Across the passage he could hear her slippered feet pacing up and down, up and down the length of her apartment. There was something panther-like in those restless footfalls, a meaning velvetyness that made him shiver, and again he wished he were dead—or elsewhere.

After a time the hall door opened, and someone came upstairs, along the passage, and to the little woman's room. As he entered, she turned and faced him.

"Christie," he said harshly, "do you know what you have done?"

"Yes," taking a step nearer him, her whole soul springing up into her eyes, "I have angered you, Charlie, and—"

"Angered me? You have disgraced me; and, moreover, you have disgraced yourself and both your parents."

"*Disgraced?*"

"Yes, *disgraced*; you have literally declared to the whole city that your father and mother were never married, and that you are the child of—what shall we call it—love? certainly not legality."

Across the hallway sat Joe McDonald, his blood freezing; but it leapt into every vein like fire at the awful anguish in the little voice that cried simply, "Oh! Charlie!"

"How could you do it, how could you do it, Christie, without shame either for yourself or for me, let alone your parents?"

The voice was like an angry demon's—not a trace was there in it of the yellow-haired, blue-eyed, laughing-lipped boy who had driven away so gaily to the dance five hours before.

"Shame? Why should I be ashamed of the rites of my people any more than you should be ashamed of the customs of yours—of a marriage more sacred and holy than half of your white man's mockeries?"

It was the voice of another nature in the girl—the love and the pleading were dead in it.

"Do you mean to tell me, Charlie—you who have studied my race and their laws for years—do you mean to tell me that, because there was no priest and no magistrate, my mother was not married? Do you mean to say that all my forefathers, for hundreds of years back, have been illegally born? If so, you blacken my ancestry beyond—beyond—beyond all reason."

"No, Christie, I would not be so brutal as that; but your father and mother live in more civilized times. Father O'Leary has been at the post for nearly twenty years. Why was not your father straight enough to have the ceremony performed when he *did* get the chance?"

The girl turned upon him with the face of a fury. "Do you suppose," she almost hissed, "that my mother would be married according to your *white* rites after she had been five years a wife, and I had been born in the meantime? *No*, a thousand times I say, *no*. When the priest came with his notions of Christianizing, and talked to them of re-marriage by the Church, my mother arose and said, "Never—never—I have never had but this one husband; he has had none but me for wife, and to have you re-marry us would be to say as much to the whole world as that we had never been married before. You go away; I do not ask that *your* people be re-married; talk not so to me. I *am* married, and you or the Church cannot do or undo it."[1]

"Your father was a fool not to insist upon the law, and so was the priest."

"Law? *My* people have *no* priest, and my nation cringes not to law. Our priest is purity, and our law is honor. Priest? Was there a *priest* at the most holy marriage known to humanity—that stainless marriage whose offspring is the God you white men told my pagan mother of?"

"Christie—you are *worse* than blasphemous; such a profane remark shows how little you understand the sanctity of the Christian faith—"

"I know what I *do* understand; it is that you are hating me because I told some of the beautiful customs of my people to Mrs. Stuart and those men."

---

1. Fact. [Author's note]

"Pooh! who cares for them? It is not them; the trouble is they won't keep their mouths shut. Logan's a cad and will toss the whole tale about at the club before to-morrow night; and as for the Stuart woman, I'd like to know how I'm going to take you to Ottawa for presentation and the opening, while she is blabbing the whole miserable scandal in every drawing-room, and I'll be pointed out as a romantic fool, and you—as worse; I *can't* understand why your father didn't tell me before we were married; I at least might have warned you to never mention it." Something of recklessness rang up through his voice, just as the panther-likeness crept up from her footsteps and couched itself in hers. She spoke in tones quiet, soft, deadly.

"Before we were married! Oh! Charlie, would it have—made—any—difference?"

"God knows," he said, throwing himself into a chair, his blonde hair rumpled and wet. It was the only boyish thing about him now.

She walked towards him, then halted in the centre of the room. "Charlie McDonald," she said, and it was as if a stone had spoken, "look up." He raised his head, startled by her tone. There was a threat in her eyes that, had his rage been less courageous, his pride less bitterly wounded, would have cowed him.

"There was no such time as that before our marriage, for we *are not married now*. Stop," she said, outstretching her palms against him as he sprang to his feet, "I tell you we are not married. Why should I recognize the rites of your nation when you do not acknowledge the rites of mine? According to your own words, my parents should have gone through your church ceremony as well as through an Indian contract; according to *my* words, *we* should go through an Indian contract as well as through a church marriage. If their union is illegal, so is ours. If you think my father is living in dishonor with my mother, my people will think I am living in dishonor with you. How do I know when another nation will come and conquer you as you white men conquered us? And they will have another marriage rite to perform, and they will tell us another truth, that you are not my husband, that you are but disgracing and dishonoring me, that you are keeping me here, not as your wife, but as your—your *squaw*."

The terrible word had never passed her lips before, and the blood stained her face to her very temples. She snatched off her wedding ring and tossed it across the room, saying scornfully, "That thing is as empty to me as the Indian rites to you."

He caught her by the wrists; his small white teeth were locked tightly, his blue eyes blazed into hers.

"Christine, do you dare to doubt my honor towards you? *you*, whom I should have died for; do you *dare* to think I have kept you here, not as my wife, but—"

"Oh, God! You are hurting me; you are breaking my arm," she gasped.

The door was flung open, and Joe McDonald's sinewy hands clinched like vices on his brother's shoulder.

"Charlie, you're mad, mad as the devil. Let go of her this minute."

The girl staggered backwards as the iron fingers loosed her wrists. "Oh, Joe," she cried, "I am not his wife, and he says I am born—nameless."

"Here," said Joe, shoving his brother towards the door. "Go downstairs till you can collect your senses. If ever a being acted like an infernal fool, you're the man."

The young husband looked from one to the other, dazed by his wife's insult, abandoned to a fit of ridiculously childish temper. Blind as he was with passion, he remembered long afterwards seeing them standing there, his brother's face darkened with a scowl of anger—his wife, clad in the mockery of her ball dress, her scarlet velvet cloak half covering her bare brown neck and arms, her eyes like flames of fire, her face like a piece of sculptured greystone.

Without a word he flung himself furiously from the room, and immediately afterwards they heard the heavy hall door bang behind him.

"Can I do anything for you, Christie?" asked her brother-in-law calmly.

"No, thank you—unless—I think I would like a drink of water, please."

He brought her up a goblet filled with wine; her hand did not even tremble as she took it. As for Joe, a demon arose in his soul as he noticed she kept her wrists covered.

"Do you think he will come back?" she said.

"Oh, yes, of course; he'll be all right in the morning. Now go to bed like a good little girl, and—and, I say, Christie, you can call me if you want anything; I'll be right here, you know."

"Thank you, Joe; you are kind—and good."

He returned then to his apartment. His pipe was out, but he picked up a newspaper instead, threw himself into an armchair, and in a half-hour was in the land of dreams.

When Charlie came home in the morning, after a six-mile walk into the country and back again, his foolish anger was dead and buried. Logan's "Poor old Charlie" did not ring so distinctly in his ears. Mrs. Stuart's horrified expression had faded considerably form his recollection. He thought only of that surprisingly tall, dark girl, whose eyes looked like coals, whose voice pierced him like a flint-tipped arrow. Ah, well, they would never quarrel again like that, he told himself. She loved him so, and would forgive him after he had talked quietly to her, and told her what an ass he was. She was simple-minded and awfully ignorant to pitch those old Indian laws at him in her fury, but he could not blame her; oh, no, he could not for one moment blame her. He had been terribly severe and unreasonable, and the horrid McDonald temper had got the better of him; and he loved her so. Oh! he loved her so! She would surely feel that, and forgive him, and— He went straight to his wife's room. The blue velvet evening dress lay on the chair into which he had thrown himself when he doomed his life's happiness by those two words, "God knows." A bunch of dead daffodils and her slippers were on the floor, everything—but Christie.

He went to his brother's bedroom door.

"Joe," he called, rapping nervously thereon; "Joe, wake up; where's Christie, d'you know?"

"Good Lord, no," gasped that youth, springing out of his armchair and opening the door. As he did so a note fell from off the handle. Charlie's face blanched to his very hair while Joe read aloud, his voice weakening at every word:

"DEAR OLD JOE—I went into your room at daylight to get that picture of the Post on your bookshelves. I hope you do not mind, but I kissed your hair while you slept; it was so curly, and yellow, and soft, just like his. Good-bye, Joe.
"Christie."

And when Joe looked into his brother's face and saw the anguish settle in those laughing blue eyes, the despair that drove the dimples away from that almost girlish mouth; when he realized that this boy was but four-and-twenty years old, and that all his future was perhaps darkened and shadowed for ever, a great, deep sorrow arose in his heart, and he forgot all things, all but the agony that rang up through the voice of the fair, handsome lad as he staggered forward, crying, "Oh! Joe—what shall I do—what shall I do?"

∽

It was months and months before he found her, but during all that time he had never known a hopeless moment; discouraged he often was, but despondent, never. The sunniness of his ever-boyish heart radiated with a warmth that would have flooded a much deeper gloom than that which settled within his eager young life. Suffer? ah! yes, he suffered, not with locked teeth and stony stoicism, not with the masterful self-command, the reserve, the conquered bitterness of the still-water sort of nature, that is supposed to run to such depths. He tried to be bright, and his sweet old boyish self. He would laugh sometimes in a pitiful, pathetic fashion. He took to petting dogs, looking into their large, solemn eyes with his wistful, questioning blue ones; he would kiss them, as women sometimes do, and call them "dear old fellow," in tones that had tears; and once in the course of his travels, while at a little way-station, he discovered a huge St. Bernard imprisoned by some mischance in an empty freight car; the animal was nearly dead from starvation, and it seemed to salve his own sick heart to rescue back the dog's life. Nobody claimed the big starving creature, the train hands knew nothing of its owner, and gladly handed it over to its deliverer. "Hudson," he called it, and afterwards when Joe McDonald would relate the story of his brother's life he invariably terminated it with, "And I really believe that big lumbering brute saved him." From what, he was never known to say.

But all things end, and he heard of her at last. She had never returned to the Post, as he at first thought she would, but had gone to the little town of B———, in Ontario, where she was making her living at embroidery and plain sewing.

The September sun had set redly when at last he reached the outskirts of the town, opened up the wicket gate, and walked up the weedy, unkept path leading to the cottage where she lodged.

Even through the twilight, he could see her there, leaning on the rail of the verandah—oddly enough she had about her shoulders the scarlet velvet cloak she wore when he had flung himself so madly from the room that night.

The moment the lad saw her his heart swelled with a sudden heat, burning moisture leapt into his eyes, and clogged his long, boyish lashes. He bounded up the steps—"Christie," he said, and the word scorched his lips like audible flame.

She turned to him, and for a second stood magnetized by his passionately wistful face; her peculiar greyish eyes seemed to drink the very life of his unquenchable love, though the tears that suddenly sprang into his seemed to absorb every pulse in his body through those hungry, pleading eyes of his that had, oh! so often, been blinded by her kisses when once her whole world lay in their blue depths.

"You will come back to me, Christie, my wife? My wife, you will let me love you again?"

She gave a singular little gasp, and shook her head. "Don't, oh! don't," he cried piteously. "You will come to me, dear? it is all such a bitter mistake—I did not understand. Oh! Christie, I did not understand, and you'll forgive me, and love me again, won't you—won't you?"

"No," said the girl with quick, indrawn breath.

He dashed the back of his hand across his wet eyelids. His lips were growing numb, and he bungled over the monosyllable "Why?"

"I do not like you," she answered quietly.

"God! Oh! God, what is there left?"

She did not appear to hear the heart-break in his voice; she stood like one wrapped in sombre thought; no blaze, no tear, nothing in her eyes; no hardness, no tenderness about her mouth. The wind was blowing her cloak aside, and the only visible human life in her whole body was once when he spoke the muscles of her brown arm seemed to contract.

"But, darling, you are mine—*mine*—we are husband and wife! Oh, heaven, you *must* love me, you *must* come to me again."

"You cannot *make* me come," said the icy voice, "neither church, nor law, nor even"—and the voice softened—"nor even love can make a slave of a red girl."

"Heaven forbid it," he faltered. "No, Christie, I will never claim you without your love. What reunion would that be? But, oh, Christie, you are lying to me, you are lying to yourself, you are lying to heaven."

She did not move. If only he could touch her he felt as sure of her yielding as he felt sure there was a hereafter. The memory of times when he had but to lay his hand on her hair to call a most passionate response from her filled his heart with a torture that choked all words before they reached his lips; at the thought of those days he forgot she was unapproachable, forgot how forbidding were her eyes, how stony her lips. Flinging himself forward, his knee on the chair at her side, his face pressed hardly in the folds of the cloak on her shoulder, he clasped his arms about her

E. PAULINE JOHNSON

with a boyish petulance, saying, "Christie, Christie, my little girl wife, I love you, I love you, and you are killing me."

She quivered from head to foot as his fair, wavy hair brushed her neck, his despairing face sank lower until his cheek, hot as fire, rested on the cool, olive flesh of her arms. A warm moisture oozed up through her skin, and as he felt its glow he looked up. Her teeth, white and cold, were locked over her under lip, and her eyes were as grey stones.

Not murderers alone know the agony of a death sentence.

"Is it all useless? all useless, dear?" he said, with lips starving for hers.

"All useless," she repeated. "I have no love for you now. You forfeited me and my heart months ago, when you said *those two words*."

His arms fell away from her wearily, he arose mechanically, he placed his little grey checked cap on the back of his yellow curls, the old-time laughter was dead in the blue eyes that now looked scared and haunted, the boyishness and the dimples crept away for ever from the lips that quivered like a child's; he turned from her, but she had looked once into his face as the Law Giver must have looked at the land of Canaan outspread at his feet. She watched him go down the long path and through the picket gate, she watched the big yellowish dog that had waited for him lumber up to its feet—stretch—then follow him. She was conscious of but two things, the vengeful lie in her soul, and a little space on her arm that his wet lashes had brushed.

ᔕ

It was hours afterwards when he reached his room. He had said nothing, done nothing—what use were words or deeds? Old Jimmy Robinson was right; she had "balked" sure enough.

What a bare, hotelish room it was! He tossed off his coat and sat for ten minutes looking blankly at the sputtering gas jet. Then his whole life, desolate as a desert, loomed up before him with appalling distinctness. Throwing himself on the floor beside his bed, with clasped hands and arms outstretched on the white counterpane, he sobbed. "Oh! God, dear God, I thought you loved me; I thought you'd let me have her again, but you must be tired of me, tired of loving me, too. I've nothing left now, nothing! it doesn't seem that I even have you to-night."

He lifted his face then, for his dog, big and clumsy and yellow, was licking at his sleeve.

∽

Dominion Illustrated (February 1893); reprinted in *The Moccasin Maker* (Toronto: Briggs, 1913), 102–126.

E. PAULINE JOHNSON

Annie Fowler Rothwell (1837–1927)

HOW IT LOOKED AT HOME: A STORY OF '85 (1893)

Because Annie Rothwell Christie was the daughter of the
important early watercolour artist Daniel Fowler (1810–1894),
one of the few articles about her muses whether it is better
to be the distinguished father of a daughter or the father of
a distinguished daughter. One thing is certain: as is so often
the case with women, posterity has been much more mindful of the life and works of the painter/father than of the
artist/daughter. Daniel Fowler's memoirs say much about
his life, his painting and his love of the outdoor life, but little
about his family. The career of Annie Rothwell, like that of
other Canadian women writers like Faith Fenton and J.G.
Sime, makes us mindful of the obscurity in which women
often worked or into which their reputations so often lapsed
in the nineteenth and early twentieth century, the causes a
blend of convention, patriarchy and culturally conditioned
self-effacement.

Marianne Bessie Fowler was born in London,
England on 31 March 1837. In 1843, she was brought to
Canada by her parents, Elizabeth Gale and Daniel Fowler.
Fowler, an artist and teacher from an upper-middle class
English family, emigrated to British North America partly
for health reasons, and settled on Amherst Island, near
Kingston, where there were a few genteel families, among
whom was his brother-in-law. One of five children, Annie
Fowler grew up on this lovely island in the St. Lawrence,
stimulated by the family interest in art and literature,
educated by her mother and father (who used issues of
the *Illustrated London News* as a teaching tool) and by a
governess. The Fowlers were friendly with writer Louisa
Murray (see page 123), who lived for a time on nearby Wolfe
Island. After a three-year visit to England, Annie Fowler
married in 1862 a Kingston man, John Rothwell, brother

of the longtime Anglican clergyman on Amherst Island. She was widowed twelve years later and in 1895 married Reverend Isaac Christie, an Anglican clergyman, who died in 1905. She moved to Ottawa, where she was active in the Women's Canadian Historical Society. She died in New Liskeard, Ontario, on 2 July 1927.

Annie Rothwell, as her readers knew her, published stories and poems in such periodicals as *Dominion Illustrated*, *British North American Magazine*, and *Appleton's Journal* (New York). Her long fiction included "Requital," a serial for the Toronto *Globe*, and, most accessible today, *Loved I Not Honour More!* (1887), a short novel considered by Ethelwyn Wetherald to be her best work. The novel, set in the little town of Fairport, which bears similarities to Kingston, tells the story of a quarry owner, the love entanglements of his extended family and the fortunes of his business. The story presents one activist character in the social gospel mode, and the novel has affinities with the work of Agnes Maule Machar, whom Rothwell certainly knew.

"How It Looked at Home" deals with the Northwest Rebellion of 1885 from the perspective of the home front, a perspective suited to a woman writer with Annie Rothwell's political interests. Wetherald described her thus:

> . . . she takes the deepest interest in Canadian politics . . . she would prefer to hear good speeches at an election meeting to reading most of the new novels, and would rather witness the movements of a battalion in the drill shed than go to the opera. Love of her adopted country is perhaps her ruling passion, which was fanned to fever height at the North-West Rebellion. From this epoch all her poems are dated. Into the cause of the volunteer she threw herself with an enthusiasm rewarded by a most gratifying recognition from persons and places far apart.

Women of course did not have the vote at this time and their political influence was negligible.

The Northwest Rebellion, encompassing as it did the death of Ontario Orangeman Thomas Scott and the subsequent execution of Métis leader Louis Riel, aroused virulent passions and divisions in the country. In the story, published eight years after the fact, Miss Thorpe and Rexborough—a name which suggests Kingston—view the rebellion from a perspective similar to that of Annie Rothwell, offspring of a conservative, privileged family of English origin. Rothwell chooses to focus mainly on the effect of war on the women waiting at home, and documents the effect of the skirmishes at Duck Lake and Batoche on a conservative Ontario barracks town. The rebellion exacts two casualties—a fighting man and a waiting woman.

☙

Suggested Reading:
A Standard Dictionary of Canadian Biography, 1934, vol. 2, s.v. "Marianne Bessie Fowler."
Canadian Who Was Who, vol. 2, s.v. "Fowler, Marianne Bessie (1837–1927) Mrs. Isaac Christie."
Rothwell, Annie. *Loved I Not Honour More!* Toronto: Rose, 1887.
Smith, F.K. *Daniel Fowler of Amherst Island, 1810–1894.* Kingston, 1979.
Wetherald, Ethelwyn. "Some Canadian Literary Women—IV. Annie Rothwell. In *The Week* (28 June 1888), 494–95.

HOW IT LOOKED AT HOME: A STORY OF '85

Annie Fowler Rothwell

I.

The place is the city of Rexborough. The time is the first of April, 1885.

It was a bright fair day of a late spring. Snow lay on the ground, but the warmth of the sun and the feet of passengers had transformed its purity into slush and mire. Of passers there were many, for the fine old city wore an aspect very different from its normal quiet; streams of people, with anxious and excited faces, tended all one way; there was gloom on some men's brows, there were grave, stern words on some men's tongues; here and there a woman was in tears; at the corners watching listening groups were gathered; the oft-repeated names of certain men and places were even in the children's mouths; there was a breath of expectation in the very air.

Among the passengers who alighted from the stage that made the daily trip from the village of Woodburn was a young woman, who looked about her in some wonder at the unusual stir. She had a grave and sweet, if not a beautiful face, wearing now a slight expression of anxiety foreign to its accustomed calm. She asked no questions, but, avoiding the throngs that filled the thoroughfares, proceeded without delay to a quiet house in a quiet part of the town.

She was expected, for the woman who opened the door expressed no surprise, but broke at once into exclamation.

"Oh, Miss Thorpe! What a day for you to come! And why? I hope there's no trouble with the doctor, as well as the trouble that's come on us all."

"I hope not," said the girl quietly. "But what do you mean? What is the stir in town for?"

"Why, don't you know? Haven't you heard, or read the papers? There's extras out—"

"We only get a weekly paper," said Miss Thorpe. "What is the matter?"

"You've not heard? Why, there's more trouble in the North West. There was a fight last Thursday, and nine men killed."

"Never!" exclaimed Miss Thorpe, in no slightest degree realizing the meaning of the words.

"Yes: the same man has raised it that was at the bottom of the '70 trouble, when my son was out; but they say this is worse. Anyway the soldiers are on their way to the West; they're to be here today, and there's great excitement over it. My boys are down to the station now to see them come in."

"But I can't believe it!" said Miss Thorpe, incredulously. "How is it we had no warning—that we've heard nothing about it before?"

"Ah, that's the wonder!" said her hostess, shaking her head. "Some people must have known, of course, but folks like you and me have been left in the dark. Why, even last week the papers said there was no fear. But now tell me about yourself—you expect the doctor?"

"Yes; I got a card from him to be here to-day."

"And I got one to say that you'd come. Anything up?" she added, with a significant smile.

"No, Mrs. Gould, I don't know why I'm here, any more than you do."

"Well, if the doctor fixed it, it's all right; he never does anything without a reason, and a good one, doesn't Mr. Thorold. Of all the students I ever boarded he was the most reliable. You're a lucky girl, Miss Thorpe, even if you do have to wait a while."

Miss Thorpe did not answer, and a thought seemed to occur to her hostess. "Why, you must be tired! sit down while I make you a cup of tea. Here's all the papers, and you can study up the rebellion while you wait for the doctor. Likely he'll come on the train with the soldiers—the express is in long ago."

So Miss Thorpe sat down to "study up the rebellion," a study in which she had many fellow-scholars that spring. The word had startled her. She had read some history and knew what it had sometimes meant, what, wherever it is breathed, it may mean. At first in her reading she was perplexed; events of which she had never heard were spoken of as being of deep significance—places whose names were unknown to her (as indeed they were unknown to many of us Canadians until a fierce necessity compelled a new study of geography) were referred to as being centres of vital interest; but as her attention became more fixed, as she by degrees disentangled facts from its wrappings of heated discussion, she learned what is now history—in our history, alas! a black-bordered page. She learned that the country was threatened—no, not threatened—but quivering under the shock of an insurrection of which no one at that time knew the extent or could foresee the end; she learned that battle, murder, and sudden death had startled the land like a lightning flash from a summer sky; that sedition had lifted its serpent head and that patriotism had arisen to crush the reptile under its heel; that the menaced nation had appealed to her children to sustain her majesty and her authority; and that throughout her length and breadth they had responded to the call.

It had not entered her mind that events of such importance could concern so humble a person as herself; her interest was entirely impersonal, but as she read, something woke in her breast that had never before stirred there; and her pulse quickened at the story how a few days before the Queen City had poured forth her sons on that loyal errand

ANNIE FOWLER ROTHWELL

from which alas!—alas? yes, but also to their eternal honor—some of them were never to return.

She was of course, incapable, as were many others, of judging of the merits of the case; the oft-repeated phrases "Half-breed claims," "Bill of Rights," "Misgovernment avenged" etc., were to her but words; but accurate knowledge is seldom necessary to strength of feeling, and Miss Thorpe threw all the strength of hers on the side of existing law. The very name rebellion presupposed a system of order against which to rebel, and which, however far from perfect, must be preferable to the chaos resulting from its rash and violent overthrow. Time has taught us that then, as on other occasions, there was right, as there were faults, on both sides; but it needed time to teach the lesson, and to Miss Thorpe the fact that five days before the northern snow had been stained with the blood of nine brave and loyal men who had laid down their lives in obedience to, and in defence of, law and country, was sufficient to rouse a passion which left little room for discussion as to where the greater share of the blame might lie.

While she studied and pondered the day waned and the dusk fell. She was in a gloomy reverie, her thoughts far away with the dead at Duck Lake and the living who wept them, when one of the children of the house came and said to her in an awe-struck whisper, "There's a soldier here that says he's Dr. Thorold."

She could hear the beating of her heart as she went to meet him, and paused a moment with her hand upon the door. The opaque lamp left the room partly in shadow, and she hesitated as the unfamiliar figure advanced to greet her.

"Grace, darling—" and in an instant she was in his arms.

"Forgive me, dear, for having left you waiting so. As you see—my time is no longer my own."

She looked up quickly; there was no need of questions. The dress he wore told her all.

"Oh, Paul—I did not think—I did not know—"

"You did not know, dear, because there was never need to tell you; but the need has come."

Again she could say nothing but, "Oh, Paul!"

On their further words let us not intrude for a while. There were many such spoken in those days.

"So you see," he said, after an interval, "the country doctor is no more exempt from the call of duty than the business man or the workman. And I hope he is no less willing to obey."

As she looked at him the expression on his face caused her to exclaim: "Oh, Paul, do you think it so serious?" She spoke imploringly, as if his opinion must with her outweigh all others.

"I fear so," he returned. "There are those, I know, who profess to make light of it, and I hope they may be right; but I am afraid it will be no play."

She drew a long sigh.

"Therefore—I could not go without seeing you again. You know—sometimes—people—when those men went out from Prince Albert last week they did not come back, Gracie, dear."

"But, Paul—you don't seem sorry—I believe you are glad to go!"

"Glad?" he repeated, "that is hardly the word. I don't know how others may feel at a time like this, but it seems to me that I have only just begun to live. Glad? If the surrender of my own breath would bring back the lives that are lost—if my own blood would efface from the country the stain of that which was shed last week—it is little to say that I would gladly give them; but as it is—Grace, you know my heart; to you I have confessed what it has been to me never to know my parents; can you think what it must be to me to have found in my country a mother at last?"

He smiled, while a light, half fierce, half tender, shone in his eyes. His fervour struck an answering spark in Grace, even while she felt a momentary pang of womanly jealousy of the patriotic enthusiasm that rose above and beyond even the thought of her.

"And you must do your part," he said, kissing her; but she remained silent. "Grace, can you be brave—for yourself and others?"

ANNIE FOWLER ROTHWELL

"I will try," she said; but as she spoke she clung closer to his arm.

"Now," he resumed after a pause, "let us think of others; there is much to say and my time is short. How is Annis?"

"Very ill. Her grandfather is going to send her here with me for advice, attendance and care."

"He is going to do something sensible at last? Grace— was it that business with Norman Wright that has made Annis so much worse?"

"I am sure of it. She was very fond of him, and never being strong the worry and grief overcame her."

"Tell me, Grace, how was it?"

"There's little to tell. You know Norman was—well, not quite steady; not much amiss, but still—and uncle spoke to him—seriously—and he took it in bad part. He wanted Annis to promise him, but she took her grandfather's advice — and the end was that Norman got very angry—he would listen to nothing, and at last he broke it off and went away. We don't know where he is now."

"Grace, he is here now—with me."

"Paul, you don't mean it!"

"I do. He's sorry enough he ever left. I met him in L—— and proposed to him to come and he jumped at the chance of going as substitute for one of my men who met with an accident. He was too likely a fellow and too well drilled to be refused. I'll look after him."

"How will Annis bear to have him go?"

"She must bear it as others do, sweetheart. He is at all events more worthy of her now than ever before, and maybe her grandfather will think so too, when we get back."

"And we must stay here—and do nothing—while you are fighting!" said Grace, sadly.

"You'll have plenty to do, dearest. You have Annis to care for, and me to think of and write to. And—who knows?—there may be no fighting after all. Some people laugh at the thought."

But Grace drew no comfort from this. She saw he did not think so.

"Now I must go," he said, gently disengaging her clinging hand. "Thanks, dear, for what you have not said; you are my own brave girl. Take care of the weaker one for poor Norman's sake. We go on Friday, and I will see you again if I can, but if I can't—you will trust me, Grace?"

She looked at him with brimming eyes. It would be scarcely fair to listen to their last good-bye.

II.

This short tale, is in one sense, not history. Abler pens have already recorded those events which made the spring of 1885 a landmark of our time, and this is but the simple chronicle of the way in which they moulded and affected a few unimportant lives. But events do not constitute the whole of history; it is also written in the lives of those who make it; and as the industry or sloth of each individual unit adds to or takes from the material of prosperity of a nation, so is her inner life reflected in the discipline, joy or sorrow of each separate soul.

Among those who awoke to a new existence was Grace Thorpe. Never selfish, in the whirl of emotion and sensations never hitherto dreamed of, her own grief was almost lost sight of. Those who remember that Good Friday, remember also the snow that late as the season was, fell in blinding masses, blocking traffic, and detaining the troops concentrated at Rexborough till the icy Easter dawn. Grace never confessed it, but in the dusk of that Friday she took her way, wrapped from recognition, past the crowded barrack square where the men were exchanging farewells and anticipations of return, and over the deserted bridge where the snow lay piled unbroken. Her one hasty glance past the pacing sentry and through the gate was her farewell to Paul, her last weakness and self-indulgence. With the next day she returned to the duties that took her out of self; and in the removal to the city of the invalid girl who filled to her the place of sister, and in tendance of her and the querulous old man who wished neither to go nor stay, she found enough to occupy her heart and her time.

ANNIE FOWLER ROTHWELL

Then there came a harder trial, the waiting for news; the hardest indeed, of all trials, as those who have borne it know well.

Alternating between the quiet of the sick room and the scarcely less quiet of her daily walk Grace's life yet held much busy thought. She heard from Paul—short accounts, written where and how he could, of tiresome marches, unaccustomed duties, and conjectured movements to a doubtful end—letters which in their spirit of loyalty and honor made her heart glow. Through him also Annis heard of Norman, (who, under stress of duty and renewed hope was bearing himself as a soldier should) and the girl brightened visibly; so much so as to sensibly lighten the remorse of the grandfather who in his over-care of his fragile darling and denial of what seemed to her hurt, had brought about the very mischief he had striven all her tender life to avoid. There was no question of denial now; and when in Paul's letter at last came a few lines which Annis read with a happy blush and hid upon her heart before she slept, the doctor on his next visit marvelled what had wrought so sudden a change for the better in his patient. Grace knew—she had her own heart-medicine of the same description—but she held her peace.

Then came a day when all thought of peace was ended, and the dream of those who had preached it was rudely broken; when the crack of the rifle on the far Saskatchewan was echoed in the hearts that throbbed by the St. Lawrence, and the news came that a fresh harvest of young lives had been cut down like the grass; when the beautiful old city was stirred as never before in the memory of living man; when in street, and home, and market, there was but one cry—for news; when the bulletin was besieged and amusement forsaken; and when people coming even from the house of God thought less of the holy words still sounding in their ears than those of the yet wet "extras" that met them at the door.

On Grace and Annis the tidings of the skirmish of that eventful 26th of April wrought very differently, though neither found the loved name in the lists that brought grief to so many. To the one, lifted above self by an agony of sympathy, not the least strange sensation was that of the unreality of surrounding things, the triviality which seemed suddenly to invest the items that made up the sum of daily life, and the feeling by which the distant and unknown became the essence of existence. That life should go on as usual and all the pageantry of Nature remain unchanged—that roses should bloom and birds nest and sing while blood was flowing, groans were drawn, and hearts were aching—seemed to Grace an unpermissible anomaly; that business cares should engage and youthful gaieties be indulged in while pain, danger, privation and death were the lot of companion, comrade and friend, appeared unfathomable in its depth of pettiness; and the consciousness of a double self, of the contrast between the outward contact with the world of sense and the inner life that pulsed and throbbed with unspoken and unshared emotions, remains with Grace as the most ineffaceable memory of that never-to-be-forgotten time.

The interest of Annis on the contrary was but a kind of sublimated selfishness. "It toucheth thee and thou faintest," are words not applicable to Job alone. To the sick girl, prostrated anew by the fresh excitement, and shut in upon herself and from all outward intercourse, the North West Force soon came to mean Norman Wright alone, and every incident of the struggle, success or failure, shame or triumph, to be only thought of as it regarded him. Annis had known that sorrow was the common lot, but when brought face to face with the truth in her own experience she found it harder than she could endure. No doubt the Dispenser of causes has known how to apportion each to the work it is to perform, and if to the mother or mistress the welfare of son or lover outweigh the obliteration of battalions we are bound to believe that that force was needed to preserve the balance of creation; but to eyes that have opened on a wider horizon it looks incredible that others should have less range of vision—that personal joy or pains should engross the mind is wonderful to the soul touched and awakened by patriotic fire.

ANNIE FOWLER ROTHWELL

Grace was sadly ignorant; she knew nothing of that noble art of the politician by which the interests and sufferings of others are made the means of self-aggrandizement, and to her the accusations and recriminations which form the missiles of the wordy war of faction were worse than idle sounds. Many times was her indignation roused by the squabbles of opposing cliques and the endeavor of angry parties to fasten on each other blame which neither was willing to bear, during those succeeding weeks of anxious waiting when so few could guess what the immediate future was to bring—when intelligence false, if not falsified, and rumours contradicted as soon as circulated made life a fever of expectation and suspense. In the light of later knowledge we can wonder, and almost smile, at the darkness that then enveloped places and events; but then we learned that it is not what we know but what we fear that is hardest to be borne.

Then on the morning of the 10th of May, a wild tempestuous Sunday, suspense came to an end. It might not be well to inquire how many of those who worshipped that day in Rexborough, with the knowledge of what was at that moment passing at Batoche's Crossing filling their thoughts, profited greatly by their devotional exercises; we remember but the rapid emptying of the churches, the crowding of the people to the newspaper offices, the eager watching through the windy afternoons for the tardy news, the demand for the "extras" which when news did arrive were seized upon faster than the presses could give them out, the thrill that struck us when we knew that the end was come; but not yet the end of the end. We remember the days that followed, with their watching, their doubt and dread, their scanty, untrustworthy tidings, the wavering balance of victory or defeat, the angry mourning for those gone, the anguish of anxiety for those whose turn it might be next to go—all this Grace remembers and will never forget.

And all this Annis knew, and the knowledge wrought her to fever, which, fading, left a weakness from which there was no rally. Letters of course, there were none; the message of life or death must be looked for in the public prints, whose terse phrases added bitterness to their bitter tidings; but to Grace and Annis came no tidings, either of pain or consolation. Never did days appear so long as that 11th and 12th of May; never did Grace find it so difficult to utter the words of hope and cheer her heart denied; and never was relief greater or thanksgiving deeper than when the wires flashed the message that, whatever might be the individual loss, victory had declared itself on the side of authority, and that further strife was stayed.

That individual loss! oh, how it tarnished the satisfaction given by the triumph of law! What eagerness of search of the dreadful lists! What heart-break were they right, what terror lest they should be wrong!

For two days Grace searched those lists with shrinking eyes, but met no sorrow, and was fain to hope that they were spared. But on the Wednesday afternoon, a warm, still shining day, that seemed made for life and joy, she came upon her hostess with a newspaper spread before her and tears dropping on the page. She gathered up her courage and scanned the lines, and this was what she read, in letters that seemed to turn to fire. "Wounded; Severely: Private Norman Wright." And Grace laid her head down upon her arms, and wept as in all her life she had never wept before.

After that her hands and heart were full. She could scarcely be glad of her own immunity in face of the sick girl's agony and swift decay, and Paul's safety seemed a blessing to which she had no right while others mourned. She hardly heeded the public interest of the events which followed, in the knowledge that no peace now could bring back to young limbs or happiness to young hearts again: that page was folded down.

Then the victorious troops went on their further march to the north, and began the long, weary search for the retreating Indians; invalided men began to return with their heart-stirring tales, and rejoicing friends to welcome them; but to the two women in the quiet room in Rexborough life consisted only in watching and waiting—

ANNIE FOWLER ROTHWELL

for tidings from the woods and swamps of Saskatchewan and bulletins from the hospital at Saskatoon.

It was the 6th of June. Long weeks of anxious suspense and uncertainty had succeeded the fever of expectation and the excited reception of startling news. Those whose friends had disappeared into an unknown northern wilderness, whence tidings could scarcely come, felt that they had changed little for the better from the knowledge of risk and privation to conjecture of greater evils still; too often the words "Wires down" took the place of the news looked for more eagerly each day, and it was difficult, in the face of the doubtful future to find as much satisfaction as before in the work already accomplished, the honour already won.

Grace was growing very weary. The strain of the constant care of the invalid, the ceaseless anxiety as to the effect upon her of the daily news from the north, and the worse result of no news at all, the thought of poor Norman which could scarcely be called suspense when hope there was none, the endless fretting of the old man over what he had deemed he had brought about and what was yet to come, all this had so wrought upon her that she no longer dared to let her mind dwell upon her own troubles, or strive to penetrate the darkness that now hung over the wanderings of the soldiers—for with her Paul was not all. She tried to concentrate her thoughts upon the present, to lighten as she best could the burdens of others, and not yet face the dread that she might have to share it with them later on.

On this evening she was especially overwrought. The announcement "Wires down" had thrown Annis into an excitement only allayed as darkness fell. She had sunk into a troubled sleep, then Grace felt the jarring of her own nerves. The silence oppressed her, and when the clock tolled eight and she realized how long the night would yet be she dreaded lest her own strength might fail when needed. She left the old man on watch and wrapping a shawl around her went out alone under the trees of the path that bordered the river.

The June night was moonless and cool. The air was damp with a promise of rain, and heavy with the scent of lilac blossoms that tossed aloft their purple plumes. Grace leaned over the water, looked at the lights reflected in the dark stream and at the grey walls of the fort on the other bank whence came a faint bugle call, and listened to a man's deep voice singing near by. Then for a short season she allowed her thoughts to stray.

"A pretty town of about forty houses, arranged in a square." She recalled thus the only description she had then seen of Saskatoon, that place where so many thoughts were then centred, for which so many prayers went up, and tried to picture to herself how it must look. There rose before her a vision of the wide plain, the rapid rolling river, the starlit northern sky. She felt the fall of the dew, the sigh of the breeze. Fancy played her part only too well; as the dusk deepened Grace forgot her actual surroundings, and her mind, straying from the sick-bed she had left and mingling remembrance with imagination, was filled with confused images of dimly lighted rooms, of silence broken only by whispers and soft tread, of pallid, pain-drawn faces, languid limbs, faint, fluttering breathings, powerless hands, and weary eyes. She could hear the checked groan and muttered exclamation as the wrench of agony wrung the strong man's frame, she imagined the gentle voices that spoke hope and courage and the fierce hopelessness that rejected comfort. All the suffering and the sorrow, all the vain longing for the sound of a home-tone or the touch of a loved hand by those who would never again know or feel them, all the present misery and the future dread seemed to take bodily shape and weight and to crush her heart. Her very ignorance of the reality intensified the imaginary picture, and she put her hands before her eyes to shut it out.

Only a woman's foolish fancies, altogether wide of the truth? Maybe: but the fancies of those days stung deep and sore. They have left some scars that will never be effaced— some wounds that will never be healed.

Grace recovered herself with a start of self-reproach. In the silence the clock tolled nine, and the bugle rang out

ANNIE FOWLER ROTHWELL

its call from the hill. With a sudden impulse she turned and looked upward to the North-western heavens; Corona hung trembling in the blue vault, and with her eyes Grace's thoughts rose, and the words came to her mind, "Now they do it to obtain a corruptible crown, but we—" she shivered a little, as though a breath from another world had chilled her, and returned to her watch.

Her uncle was waiting for her at the door.

"She was awake, Grace, and better, I do believe; her eyes are so bright and her voice so strong. She must have been dreaming, for she laughed in her sleep, and woke calling out "Wait! I am ready!" Grace made no answer, but went to Annis with a fresh and sudden fear. She did not like the news.

"I've had a lovely dream," Annis said, as Grace stooped over her. A kiss was the only reply—no need to ask the subject of the dream.

"Isn't it a good sign, Gracie? May I take it to mean that I shall live to see him come back?"

"I—hope so—darling—"

"I—don't want more than that—now. I did once—then—I was going to leave a message for him with you, but now—if I can just see him—and tell him I never mistrusted him, and hear him speak—and leave him safe with you—"

"Hush, dear, you must not talk," said Grace, as the groan the old man could not stifle came to her ears. She did not dare to tell him what she feared; but her heart was very heavy as she watched the sleeping girl through the long night. She longed for tidings, but this unearthly communion disquieted her; and the next day was Sunday when no news could come.

The weary Sunday dragged itself out, spent by Annis in a lethargic patience; perhaps the memory of her dream stood as a shield between her and the worst—that dream which to Grace, with the recollection of her own vision at the same hour was only a haunting presage of ill. The long warm still hours were laden with suspense, and fear and anxiety were as the breath Grace drew.

The morning brought neither letter nor telegram; there was nothing to do but wait for the public news of the afternoon. When her uncle went to obtain it, Grace concealed his departure from Annis, and waited during a time that seemed both leaden-footed and to fly with wings. Annis appeared asleep when the returning footstep sounded, and Grace went down feeling that the worst that could be told would be a release compared with the tension of a moment such as this.

The old man's hand trembled as he held a paper towards her. "No letter," he said, hoarsely, "but there may be something here—"

Grace took it and scanned the lines over which so many hearts had sunk, so many tears had fallen. If for one moment her eyes went to that spot where news of Paul might be looked for, let it be forgiven her; she resolutely averted her attention to that quarter where she must learn what was now alas! an oft-told tale. The search was short; her uncle, watching her, saw a little start; then she held the paper out to him without a word. He followed where she pointed, and read the form familiar enough in its terseness, but charged for each who sought it with new and keen-edged meaning. "Clarke's Crossing, June 7th. Private Norman Wright, wounded at Batoche's, died last night in the hospital at Saskatoon."

That was all. Of the young vigorous life gone out—of hopes quenched and promise blighted—of the long vain struggle with pain and death—that was all the world would ever know. Nor the world only. Of the self-sacrifice that had concealed the suffering of the fever-flush of hope and the gloom of the dark valley—of the yearnings never to be satisfied—of the last thoughts and prayers of the heart whose faint final throb had fluttered into silence alone in the far-off desert—there could come no whisper to the hearts that craved it; the voice had passed "where beyond these voices there is peace."

"One more gone for honour's sake
    Where so many go,"

And those few words, over which few eyes would glance with more than indifference, or at least a half-careless pity, his only record and reward—too often the soldier's sentence, epitaph, and eulogy, all in one.

"Who shall tell her?" whispered Grace with white lips, and without a tear. Then she covered up her face as the old man held up a shaking finger and left the room.

It was over—over. If words were needed they had been spoken—if tears had fallen they were dried. The majesty of death might reign here, but the monarch had laid aside his frown. The glory of the sunset streamed through the open window, shed a halo round the head of the dying girl, and fell on the joined hands laid lovingly on the grey head bowed upon her knees; outside the leaves rustled softly, and a bird carolled its even song; the scent of flowers hung on the air like incense; the stillness was as deep as the hush of prayer; and the smile on the lips of Annis "filled the silence like a speech."

Grace hesitated on the threshold; the place seemed to her holy ground. But Annis saw her, and at a look she came and knelt beside her.

"I need leave no message with you now," said Annis, softly.

Grace kissed the slender hands—they were quite steady—but she could not speak.

"I am very selfish, Gracie. I am so glad for myself that I cannot be sorry for him—or you."

Grace glanced at the old man; but he did not seem to hear, and did not move.

"It shocked me—for a minute—to think he could be—dead—he was so strong—but now—it would be hard to live on—and think so—and I am so glad to know that he will never—have to—miss me." She drew a little fluttering sigh. Grace leant her head on the heart whose faint beat she could hear in the stillness, and her tears fell unchecked and uncontrolled.

"Don't cry Gracie. Do you think I am worthy of him now? 'Greater love hath no man—' you know—"

"Who can ever be worthy—" began Grace.

"And yet—will you say that verse for me—about being faithful over a few things? I can't quite—remember—"

With a mighty effort Grace steadied her voice. "Well done, good and faithful—"

But the verse was never finished to mortal ears. There was a trembling of the hand Grace held, then the two were clasped together and flung upward, and there rang out a joyful agonized cry—"Wait for me Norman! I am ready!" Grace started up with a scream—to see the strained eyes close softly, the pale lips quiver into silence, and the head fall back.

"Oh my God! she has fainted!" cried the old man, even now refusing to accept the truth.

But Grace knew better. She knew that in that last—or first—glimpse of recognition the eyes had seen no mortal vision; that in that parting cry of passionate appeal the lips had uttered their last words on earth.

EPILOGUE

The past history of Canada is already recorded in many places in her monuments and the homes of her dead; but there is a fair city towards the sun-setting where the prophecy of her future may be read by those who have eyes and hearts. Paul and Grace Thorold believe they have so read it; in the sculptured stone above the flower-wreathed graves of those who laid down their lives at her call is the assurance that lasting as marble shall be the unity they died to save; in the weed-grown resting-place, by which the utmost that the heart can do is to pity and endeavour to forgive, lies the shadowing forth of their success, who, like him who lies below, are troublers of their country's peace.

∽
The Week (12 May 1893), 560–564.

Lily Dougall (1858–1923)

THRIFT (1895)

A writer of fiction and religious philosophical works, Lily
Dougall was born 16 April 1858 in Montreal. She was the
daughter of John Dougall—a prosperous Scottish immigrant and founder of the religious paper *Montreal Witness*—
and Elizabeth Redpath, the daughter of another prosperous
Scottish immigrant. After 1880, when she moved temporarily to Scotland to act as companion to an aunt, Dougall
moved back and forth between Canada and Great Britain.
In 1900 she settled permanently in Great Britain, but continued to spend extended periods in Canada. In 1911 she
moved to Cumnor, near Oxford, where she made her home
a centre for discussion of theological and philosophical subjects. Dougall died in Cumnor on 9 October 1923.

Dougall published ten novels and eight religious
philosophical works, and contributed essays to several collections on moral and religious topics, which were the out-
come of the discussion groups that met at her Cumnor
home. From 1889 her short fiction had appeared variously
in *Temple Bar*, *Atlantic Monthly*, *Longmans Magazine*, and
Chambers Journal. Her earlier stories were published anonymously or pseudonymously, but following the great success
of her first novel, *Beggars All*, in 1892, she published under
her own name, with the exception of "A Freak of Cupid,"
which appeared anonymously in *Temple Bar* (October
and November 1896), and her theological works, which
appeared anonymously until 1916. In 1897 twelve of her
stories appeared under the title *A Dozen Ways of Love*. The
earlier stories were considerably revised for republication.

In both fiction and non-fiction, Dougall deals with
serious moral concerns. Her novels are characterized by
unusual plots and intriguing and original characters. There
is a serious intellectual quality to her writing and often an
unconventional—one might say controversial—interpretation

of morality. While she admired Jane Austen and Samuel Richardson and learned from both of them, in her intellectual quality and her concern with the importance of everyday actions, she resembles George Eliot.

One of Dougall's main tenets, spelled out clearly in her first theological work, *Pro Christo et Ecclesia* (1900), is that Christ did not choose as his friends the leaders of the Church of His day, the Pharisees and Sadducees; in fact, his criticism of them was marked. In her novels, Dougall shows that the Church as an institution today, as in Christ's day, fails to express God's love; it is not concerned, as it should be, with poverty, hunger, injustice. It lacks compassion and concern for the individual.

In "Thrift," which consists largely of a dying woman's story, the same ideas surface. What the priest first notes about the elderly woman is her strength, not of body, but of mind and spirit. Her story reveals the truth of this observation, as it ironically reverses the young priest's—and the reader's—expectations. The priest assumes that he has been called to hear the woman's confession of her sins and repentance for them. On the contrary, her story is designed to show him the sinfulness of the Church itself. Mrs. O'Brien's experience is a forceful example of the possible consequences of obedience to the Church's insistent demand that a woman's duty is to marry and "fill the new land with good Cath'lics." That a woman can argue so convincingly for murder as a positive act—an act for which the Church itself is ultimately responsible—and can demonstrate the value of her action through its beneficial effect on her children, is certainly a contradiction of conventional wisdom and conventional morality. In "Thrift" the Catholic Church—as are other denominations elsewhere—is shown to be dogmatic, lacking in compassion, and blind to the individual. Perhaps the conclusion is designed to hint at some hope for change within Church hierarchy; the elderly Father M'Leod is shown as a man who does have the compassion for others that was lacking in those other representatives of the Church whom Mrs. O'Brien had known. The narrator stands aside, allowing the woman to tell her own story, taking no sides, making no judgment, leaving the reader to ponder what has been said and to form her own opinion.

"Thrift" first appeared in *Atlantic Monthly* in August 1895 and was republished in *A Dozen Ways of Love*. It did not appear in *Young Love* (1904), a selection of six of the stories from *A Dozen Ways of Love*. Revisions of the story for publication in *A Dozen Ways of Love* consisted in minor changes in syntax and punctuation, and some tightening by cutting words and phrases, which improve expression. The revised version of the story appears here.

~

Suggested Reading:
Dougall, Lily. *What Necessity Knows*. 1893. Reprint, Ottawa: Tecumseh Press, 1992, with an introduction by Victoria Walker.
McMullen, Lorraine. "The Canadian Vision of Lily Dougall." In *Amazing Space*, ed. Shirley Neuman and Smaro Kamboureli. Edmonton: Longspoon/Newest Press, 1986.

THRIFT

Lily Dougall

The end of March had come. The firm Canadian snow roads had suddenly changed their surface and become a chain of miniature rivers, lakes interspersed by islands of ice, and half-frozen bogs.

A young priest had started out of the city of Montreal to walk to the suburb of Point St. Charles. He was in great haste, so he kilted up his long black petticoats and hopped and skipped at a good pace. The hard problems of life had not as yet assailed him; he had that set of the shoulders that belongs to a good conscience and an easy mind; his face was rosy-cheeked and serene.

Behind him lay the hill-side city, with its grey towers and spires and snow-clad mountain. All along his way budding maple trees swayed their branches overhead; on the twigs of some there was the scarlet moss of opening flowers, some were tipped with red buds and some were grey. The March wind was surging through them; the March clouds were flying above them,—light grey clouds with no rain in them,—veil above veil of mist, and each filmy web travelling at a different pace. The road began as a street, crossed railway tracks and a canal, ran between fields, and again entered between houses. The houses were of brick or stone, poor and ugly; the snow in the fields was sodden with water; the road—

'I wish that the holy prophet Elijah would come to this Jordan with his mantle,' thought the priest to himself.

This was a pious thought, and he splashed and waded along conscientiously. He had been sent on an errand, and had to return to discharge a more important duty in the same afternoon.

The suburb consisted chiefly of workmen's houses and factories, but there were some ambitious-looking terraces. The priest stopped at a brick dwelling of fair size. It had an aspect of flaunting respectability; lintel and casements were shining with varnish; cheap starched curtains decked every window. When the priest had rung a bell which jingled inside, the door was opened by a young woman. She was not a servant, her dress was furbelowed and her hair was most elaborately arranged. She was, moreover, evidently Protestant; she held the door and surveyed the visitor with an air that was meant to show easy independence of manner, but was, in fact, insolent.

The priest had a slip of paper in his hand and referred to it. 'Mrs. O'Brien?' he asked.

'I'm not Mrs. O'Brien,' said the young woman, looking at something which interested her in the street.

A shrill voice belonging, as it seemed, to a middle-aged woman, made itself heard. 'Louisy, if it's a Cath'lic priest, take him right in to your gran'ma; it's him she's expecting.'

A moment's stare of surprise and contempt, and the young woman led the way through a gay and cheaply furnished parlour, past the door of a best bedroom which stood open to shew the frills on the pillows, into a room in the back wing. She opened the door with a jerk and stared again as the priest passed her. She was a handsome girl; the young priest did not like to be despised; within his heart he sighed and said a short prayer for patience.

He entered a room that did not share the attempt at elegance of the front part of the house; plain as a cottage kitchen, it was warm and comfortable withal. The large bed with patchwork quilt stood in a corner; in the middle was an iron stove in which logs crackled and sparkled. The air was hot and dry, but the priest, being accustomed to the atmosphere of stoves, took no notice, in fact, he noticed nothing but the room's one inmate, who from the first moment compelled his whole attention.

In a wooden arm-chair, dressed in a black petticoat and a scarlet bedgown, sat a strong old woman. Weakness was there as well as strength, certainly, for she could not leave her chair, and the palsy of excitement was shaking her head, but the one idea conveyed by every wrinkle of the aged face and hands, by every line of the bowed figure, was strength. One brown toil-worn hand held the head of a thick walking-stick which she rested on the floor well in front of her, as if she were about to rise and walk forward. Her brown face—nose and chin strongly defined—was stretched forward as the visitor entered; her eyes, black and commanding, carried with them something of that authoritative spell that is commonly attributed to a commanding mind. Great physical size or power this woman apparently had never had, but she looked the very embodiment of a superior strength.

'Shut the door! shut the door behind ye!' These were the first words that the youthful confessor heard, and then, as he advanced, 'You're young,' she said, peering into his face. Without a moment's intermission further orders were given him: 'Be seated; be seated! Take a chair by the fire and put up your wet feet. It is from Father M'Leod of St. Patrick's Church that ye've come?'

The young man, whose boots were well soaked with ice-water, was not loth to put them up on the edge of the stove. It was not at all his idea of a priestly visit to a woman who had represented herself as dying, but it is a large part of wisdom to take things as they come until it is necessary to interfere.

'You wrote, I think, to Father M'Leod, saying that as the priests of this parish are French and you speak English—'

Some current of excitement hustled her soul into the midst of what she had to say.

''Twas Father Maloney, him that had St. Patrick's before Father M'Leod, who married me; so I just thought

Lily Dougall

before I died I'd let one of ye know a thing concerning that marriage that I've never told to mortal soul. Sit ye still and keep your feet to the fire; there's no need for a young man like you to be taking your death with the wet because I've a thing to say to ye.'

'You are not a Catholic now,' said he, raising his eyebrows with intelligence as he glanced at a Bible and hymnbook that lay on the floor beside her.

He was not unaccustomed to meeting perverts; it was impossible to have any strong emotion about so frequent an occurrence. He had had a long walk and the hot air of the room made him somewhat sleepy; if it had not been for the fever and excitement of her mind he might not have picked up more than the main facts of all she said. As it was, his attention wandered for some minutes from the words that came from her palsied lips. It did not wander from her; he was thinking who she might be, and whether she was really about to die or not, and whether he had not better ask Father M'Leod to come and see her himself. This last thought indicated that she impressed him as a person of more importance and interest than had been supposed when he had been sent to hear her confession.

All this time, fired by a resolution to tell a tale for the first and last time, the old woman, steadying as much as she might her shaking head, and leaning forward to look at the priest with bleared yet flashing eyes, was pouring out words whose articulation was often indistinct. Her hand upon her staff was constantly moving, as if she were about to rise and walk; her body seemed about to spring forward with the impulse of her thoughts, the very folds of the scarlet bedgown were instinct with excitement.

The priest's attention returned to her words.

'Yes, marry and marry and marry—that's what you priests in my young days were for ever preaching to us poor folk. It was our duty to multiply and fill the new land with good Cath'lics. Father Maloney, that was his doctrine, and me a young girl just come out from the old country with my parents, and six children younger than me. Hadn't I had enough of young children to nurse, and me wanting to begin life in a new place respectable, and get up a bit in the world? Oh, yes! but Father Maloney he was on the look-out for a wife for Terry O'Brien. He was a widow man with five little helpless things, and drunk most of the time was Terry, and with no spirit in him to do better. Oh! but what did that matter to Father Maloney when it was the good of the Church he was looking for, wanting O'Brien's family looked after? O'Brien was a good, kind fellow, so Father Maloney said, and you'll never hear me say a word against that. So Father Maloney got round my mother and my father and me, and married me to O'Brien, and the first year I had a baby, and the second year I had another, so on and so on, and there's not a soul in this world can say but that I did well by the five that were in the house when I came to it.

'Oh! "house"!——d'ye think it was one house he kept over our heads? No, but we moved from one room to another, not paying the rent. Well, and what sort of a training could the children get? Father Maloney he talked fine about bringing them up for the Church. Did he come in and wash them when I was a-bed? Did he put clothes on their backs? No, and fine and angry he was when I told him that that was what he ought to have done! Oh! but Father Maloney and I went at it up and down many a day, for when I was wore out with the anger inside me, I'd go and tell him what I thought of the marriage he'd made, and in a passion he'd get at a poor thing like me teaching him duty.

'Not that I ever was more than half sorry for the marriage myself, because of O'Brien's children, poor things, that he had before I came to them. Likely young ones they were too, and handsome, what would they have done if I hadn't been there to put them out of the way when O'Brien was drunk, and knocking them round, or to put a bit of stuff together to keep them from nakedness?'

'"Well," said Father Maloney to me, "why isn't it to O'Brien that you speak with your scolding tongue?" Faix! and what good was it to spake to O'Brien, I'd like to know? Did you ever try to cut water with a knife, or to hurt a feather-bed by striking at it with your fist? A nice good-natured man was Terry O'Brien—I'll never say that he wasn't that,—except when he was drunk, which was most of the time—but he'd no more backbone to him than a worm. That was the sort of husband Father Maloney married me to.

'The children kept a-coming till we'd nine of them, that's with the five I found ready to hand; and the elder ones getting up and needing to be set out in the world, and what prospect was there for them? What could I do for them? Me always with an infant in my arms! Yet 'twas me and no other that gave them the bit and sup they had, for I went out to work; but how could I save anything to fit decent clothes on them, and it wasn't much work I could do, what with the babies always coming, and sick and ailing they were half the time. The Sisters would come from the convent to give me charity. 'Twas precious little they gave, and lectured me too for not being more submiss'! And I didn't want their charity; I wanted to get up in the world. I'd wanted that before I was married, and now I wanted it for the children. Likely girls the two eldest were, and the boy just beginning to go the way of his father.'

She came to a sudden stop and breathed hard; the strong old face was still stretched out to the priest in her eagerness; the staff was swaying to and fro beneath the tremulous hand. She had poured out her words so quickly that there was in his chest a feeling of answering breathlessness, yet he still sat regarding her placidly with the serenity of healthy youth.

She did not give him long rest. 'What did I see around me?' she demanded. 'I saw people that had begun life no better than myself getting up and getting up, having a shop maybe, or sending their children to the "Model" School to learn to be teachers, or getting them into this business or that, and mine with never so much as knowing how to read, for they hadn't the shoes to put on——

'And I had it in me to better them and myself. I knew I'd be strong if it wasn't for the babies, and I knew, too, that I'd do a kinder thing for each child I had, to strangle it at it's birth than to bring it on to know nothing and be nothing but a poor wretched thing like Terry O'Brien himself——'

At the word 'strangle' the young priest took his feet from the ledge in front of the fire and changed his easy attitude, sitting up straight and looking more serious.

'It's not that I blamed O'Brien over much, he'd just had the same sort of bringing up himself and his father before him, and when he was sober a very nice man he was; it was spiritiness he lacked; but if he'd had more spiritiness he'd have been a wickeder man, for what is there to give a man sense in a rearing like that? If he'd been a wickeder man I'd have had more fear to do with him the thing I did. But he was just a good sort of creature without sense enough to keep steady, or to know what the children were wanting; not a notion he hadn't but that they'd got all they needed, and I had it in me to better them. Will ye dare to say that I hadn't?

'After Terry O'Brien went I had them all set out in the world, married or put to work with the best, and they've got ahead. All but O'Brien's eldest son, every one of them have got ahead of things. I couldn't put the spirit into *him* as I could into the littler ones and into the girls. Well, but he's the only black sheep of the seven, for two of them died. All that's living but him are doing well, doing well' (she nodded her head in triumph), 'and their children doing better than them, as ought to be. Some of them ladies and gentlemen, real quality. Oh! ye needn't think I don't know the difference' (some thought expressed in his face had evidently made its way with speed to her brain)—'my daughter that lives here is all well enough, and her girl handsome and able to make her way, but I tell you there's some of my grandchildren that's as much above her in the world as she is above poor Terry O'Brien—young people that speak soft when they come to see their poor old grannie and read books, oh! I know the difference; oh! I know very well—not but what my daughter here is well-to-do, and there's not one of them all but has a respect for me.' She nodded again triumphantly, and her eyes flashed. 'They know, they know very well how I set them out in the world. And they come back for advice to me, old as I am, and see that I want for nothing. I've been a *good* mother to them, and a good mother makes good children and grandchildren too.'

There was another pause in which she breathed hard; the priest grasped the point of the story; he asked—

'What became of O'Brien?'

'I drowned him.'

The priest stood up in a rigid and clerical attitude.

'I tell ye I drowned him.' She had changed her attitude to suit his; and with the supreme excitement of telling what she had never told, there seemed to come to her the power to sit erect. Her eagerness was not that of self-vindication; it was the feverish exaltation with which old age glories over bygone achievement.

'I'd never have thought of it if it hadn't been O'Brien himself that put it into my head. But the children had a dog, 'twas little enough they had to play with, and the beast was useful in his way too, for he could mind the baby at times; but he took to ailing—like enough it was from want of food, and I was for nursing him up a bit and bringing him round, but O'Brien said that he'd put him into the canal. 'Twas one Sunday that he was at home sober—for when he was drunk I could handle him so that he couldn't do much harm. So says I, "And why is he to be put in the canal?"

'Says he, "Because he's doing no good here."

'So says I, "Let the poor beast live, for he does no harm."

'Then says he, "But it's harm he does taking the children's meat and their place by the fire."

'And says I, "Are ye not afraid to hurry an innocent creature into the next world?" for the dog had that sense he was like one of the children to me.

'Then said Terry O'Brien, for he had a wit of his own, "And if he's an innocent creature he'll fare well where he goes."

'Then said I, "He's done his sins, like the rest of us, no doubt."

'Then says he, "The sooner he's put where he can do no more the better."

'So with that he put a string round the poor thing's neck and took him away to where there was holes in the ice of the canal, just as there is to-day, for it was the same season of the year, and the children all cried; and thinks I to myself, "If it was the dog that was going to put their father into the water they would cry less." For he had a peevish temper in drink, which was most of the time.

'So then, I knew what I would do. 'Twas for the sake of the children that were crying about me that I did it, and I looked up to the sky and I said to God and the holy saints that for Terry O'Brien and his children 'twas the best deed I could do; and the words that we said about the poor beast rang in my head, for they fitted to O'Brien himself, every one of them.

'So you see it was just the time when the ice was still thick on the water, six inches thick maybe, but where anything had happened to break it the edges were melting into large holes. And the next night when it was late and dark I went and waited outside the tavern, the way O'Brien would be coming home.

'He was just in that state that he could walk, but he hadn't the sense of a child, and we came by the canal, for there's a road along it all winter long, but there were places where if you went off the road you fell in, and there were placards up saying to take care. But Terry O'Brien hadn't the sense to remember them. I led him to the edge of a hole, and then I came on without him. He was too drunk to feel the pain of the gasping. So I went home.

'There wasn't a creature lived near for a mile then, and in the morning I gave out that I was afraid he'd got drowned, so they broke the ice and took him up. And there was just one person that grieved for Terry O'Brien. Many's the day I grieved for him, for I was accustomed to have him about me, and I missed him like, and I said in my heart, "Terry, wherever ye may be, I have done the best deed for you and your children, for if you were innocent you have gone to a better place, and if it were sin to live as you did, the less of it you have on your soul the better for you; and as for the children, poor lambs, I can give them a start in the world now I am rid of you!" That's what I said in my heart to O'Brien at first—when I grieved for him; and then the years passed, and I worked too hard to be thinking of him.

'And now, when I sit here facing the death for myself, I can look out of my windows there back and see the canal, and I say to Terry again, as if I was coming face to face with him, that I did the best deed I could do for him and his. I broke with the Cath'lic Church long ago, for I couldn't go to confess; and many's the year that I never thought of religion. But now that I am going to die I try to read the books my daughter's minister gives me, and I look to God and say that I've sins on my soul, but the drowning of O'Brien, as far as I know right from wrong, isn't one of them.'

The young priest had an idea that the occasion demanded some strong form of speech. 'Woman,' he said, 'what have you told me this for?'

The strength of her excitement was subsiding. In its wane the afflictions of her age seemed to be let loose upon her again. Her words came more thickly, her gaunt frame trembled the more, but not for one moment did her eye flinch before his youthful severity.

'I hear that you priests are at it yet. "Marry and marry and marry," that's what ye teach the poor folks that will do your bidding, "in order that the new country may be filled with Cath'lics," and I thought before I died I'd just let ye know how one such marriage turned; and as he didn't come himself you may go home and tell Father M'Leod that, God helping me, I have told you the truth.'

The next day an elderly priest approached the door of the same house. His hair was grey, his shoulders bent, his face was furrowed with those benign lines which tell that the pain which has graven them is that sympathy which accepts as its own the sorrows of others. Father M'Leod had come far because he had a word to say, a word of pity and of sympathy, which he hoped might yet touch an impenitent heart, a word that he felt was due from the Church he represented to this wandering soul, whether repentance should be the result or not.

When he rang the bell it was not the young girl but her mother who answered the door; her face, which spoke of ordinary comfort and good cheer, bore marks of recent tears.

'Do you know,' asked the Father curiously, 'what statement it was that your mother communicated to my friend who was here yesterday?'

'No, sir, I do not.'

'Your mother was yesterday in her usual health and sound mind?' he interrogated gently.

'She was indeed, sir,' and she wiped a tear.

'I would like to see your mother,' persisted he.

'She had a stroke in the night, sir; she's lying easy now, but she knows no one, and the doctor says she'll never hear or see or speak again.'

The old man sighed deeply.

'If I may make so bold, sir, will you tell me what business it was my mother had with the young man yesterday or with yourself?'

'It is not well that I should tell you,' he replied, and he went away.

༺ঞ

Atlantic Monthly 76 (August 1895), 217–223; revised and included in *A Dozen Ways of Love* (London: Adam and Charles Black, 1897), 59–75.

Maud Ogilvy (fl. 1890s)

A DANGEROUS EXPERIMENT (1895)

Ellen Maud Ogilvy was born in Montreal about 1870, the daughter of well-to-do Montrealer John Ogilvy and his wife Ellen Grassett Powell. Maud was one of two sons and two daughters of the couple; one brother, John Ogilvy, died while in military service in the South African War. Maud Ogilvy inherited her literary interests to some degree: her maternal great-grandmother, the wife of Toronto Chief Justice William Dummer Powell, was a lively diarist of early Upper Canada.

For her part, Maud Ogilvy published poems and novels, as well as a biographical study of Canadian Pacific Railway magnate Donald Smith. She was also a feminist. Her observations on the women of Montreal appeared in the January 1891 issue of *Wives and Daughters* (London, Ontario), one of whose editors was Ethelwyn Wetherald (see page 15). Maud Ogilvy supported education and work outside the home for women, and felt that women workers should form trade unions. She maintained ". . . most emphatically, that no hindrance should be put in the path of women who desire education in any branch whatsoever to enable them to earn a livelihood for themselves. 'Knowledge is power.'"

Maud Ogilvy's two novels, *Marie Gourdon* (1890) and *The Keeper of the Bic Light House* (1891), are both set on the shores of the lower St. Lawrence, a locale familiar to Ogilvy from summer sojourns there. *Marie Gourdon* draws on the history of the region, fictionalizing the descendants of Scots who settled in the area around Rimouski after the Battle of Culloden and the resultant interaction of Scottish and French cultures. The novel blends Scottish and Quebec settings, and presents the heroic figure of the female artist in the person of Marie Gourdon, who chooses love over wealth and status after a successful operatic career. *The Keeper of the Bic Light House*, another love story, set in the lower

St. Lawrence, Ottawa, and Montreal, also has an intrepid female hero, Julie Lafleur, and some satire of the social pretensions of Montreal and viceregal Ottawa.

"A Dangerous Experiment" takes place in the Adirondacks of upper New York State—a fashionable holiday destination in the 1890s for Eastern Canadians. The plot—a lurid story within a story—draws on the interest in hypnotism, spiritualism and the paranormal that were strong at the period thanks in part to the spiritual insecurities of the post-Darwinian age, and which peaked during World War I, with its horrendous casualty lists and scores of bereaved families. Sinister Continental Europeans and dark doings at English manor houses were staples of the popular magazine fiction of the period.

∽

Suggested Reading:
Ogilvy, Maud. *The Keeper of Bic Light House: A Canadian Story of Today*. Montreal: Renouf, 1891.
_____. *Marie Gourdon: A Romance of the Lower St. Lawrence*. Montreal: Lovell, 1890.
_____. "Progress of Women in Montreal." In *Wives and Daughters*, 7. London, Ontario: January 1891.
_____. "Two Christmas Eves." In *The Land We Live In*, 7–9. Sherbrooke: January 1892.

~

A Dangerous Experiment
Maud Ogilvy

I was one of a merry house-party given by a fashionable
society woman at her country residence, among the piney
Adirondacks. The party was composed chiefly of young
people; but one guest, old Dr. Peers, was the life and soul of
the house, and his many tales of travel and adventure were a
source of unfailing entertainment to us. We had had beautiful weather all the week, but this particular Saturday morning, of which I write, was very unpleasant, and the rain was
pouring down as if the clouds meant to thoroughly empty
themselves before they stopped. Suddenly one of the group
of merry girls approached the Doctor who was on the piazza
perusing a dry leading article on the Income tax.

"Dr. Peers," she said, "we want to have some hypnotism. You have just come back from Vienna, and know all
about it. Put someone to sleep—do!"

"Excuse me," he replied hurriedly, "I shall never try
that again."

"Why not?" the girl questioned, wondering at the
gravity of his tone.

The rest of the party came crowding round the Doctor
eager for a story. "Why not Doctor?" queried more than
one feminine voice.

"Well ladies," the old gentleman replied, "I will com-
ply with your second request, if you will pardon my refusal
of your first."

"Several years ago," he went on, "I was much interested in this very subject, and with one or two scientific friends, studied it extensively both in Paris and Vienna, where it is much used in medical practice. Some time after this, during a brief summer holiday, I went to England as the guest of a gentleman I had met at the American Legation in Vienna. I had then struck up a most agreeable acquaintance with him. His name was Harry Stanley, and he was many years my junior. He was a typical Britisher, flaxen-haired, blue-eyed, and athletic, and possessing the true English phlegm and doggedness.

"At the time he wrote to invite me to visit him, he had just come into a comfortable fortune, and had been married about three months. He gave me an enthusiastic description of his bride, who was the daughter of a widowed Italian countess, whom he had met in Paris the previous winter.

"It was a lovely evening in early June, when I arrived at the little country station of Woodville, and Harry was there in his dog-cart to meet me. He greeted me warmly, and we had a delightful drive home through the verdant English lanes, balmy with dog-roses, sweet-briar, and all the thousand perfumes of a summer night.

"Harry's estate and house passed my expectations, for it was a spacious old manor with extensive grounds, gardens, coverts, and outlying farms. I confess I was anxious to see the newly-made mistress of this demesne, though I did not expect she would come up to my friend's rapturous description.

"When I had dressed for dinner, I went to the drawing-room, which was empty, but presently I heard the *frou-frou* of silken skirts, and Harry's voice following closely. On the entrance of my friend and his wife I started in amazement, and he gave an amused laugh, as much as to say, 'I told you so.'

"For Mrs. Stanley was a magnificent woman, no mere girl, but a woman in the zenith of her charms. Strange for an Italian, her hair was of pale gold color, but her eyes were dark, deep, and unfathomable. Her figure was superb, rounded gracefully, and more fully developed than is usual in English or American women of six-and-twenty, which was her age. Her manner, too, was that of an accomplished woman of the world, and my first thought was, 'How came she to marry my stolid English friend?' She ought to have been the wife of an ambassador at least.

"A moment before dinner was announced a tall, dark young man entered. Mrs. Stanley introduced him to me as her cousin, Signor da Vega, and she herself called him Luigi. He did not talk much during the meal, but my hostess did all in her power to please and entertain me. She certainly succeeded in dazzling me, though that night when alone and pondering over the occurrences of the evening, I had a vague feeling of distrust mingled with my admiration of the fair Italian, she seemed so utterly out of place in that peaceful English manor.

"Next morning Harry and I went out for a long day's fishing, a sport of which we were both extremely fond. Luigi did not accompany us.

"'He is a queer fellow,' my host explained, 'and I must confess I don't fancy him much, but he is the nearest relation my wife has, and they were brought up together, and are like brother and sister. Luigi has always got some political scheme on hand, and hob-nobs with all the diplomatic swells abroad.'

"Time went on uneventfully at the manor for about a week, and I found Mrs. Stanley always charming, quite devoted to her husband, and giving no ground for my incomprehensible distrust, except on one or two occasions, when I came upon her and Luigi speaking Italian excitedly, and immediately changing to English on seeing me. The second Monday after my arrival, a dinner party was given in my honor. At it were present the vicar, his wife and two daughters, bread and butter misses, and two or three neighboring squires with their consorts. It was altogether a most commonplace assembly. After dinner, when the two young ladies had played their little pieces, and, in spite of our hostess' vivacity, animation seemed to flag, some one suggested trying mesmerism, hypnotism, thought-reading, or something of the sort. I was drawn into the discussion, and told several of my medical experiences, showing them also a recently published work I had on the subject.

"'But I don't believe you could hypnotize Harry, Dr. Peers,' Mrs. Stanley said, after the company had gone away, and we were alone, Harry and her cousin having gone to see the ladies to their carriages.

"'You put me on my mettle,' I said.

"Just then Harry returned with Luigi.

"'Will you let me hypnotize you?' I asked the former.

"'Willingly, old man,' he replied, 'if you can.'

"He leant back in the arm-chair, and I soon put him to sleep.

"'Now, Mrs. Stanley, what is he to do?'

"She had been turning over the leaves of my book slowly, and now pointed to a page.

"'Here,' she said, 'is an account of an experiment tried in Germany,' and she read, 'It consisted of suggesting to a subject a predetermined act to be performed at a fixed hour.'

"'This was successfully tried with a harmless object which the subject believed to be a dagger, and with which he was supposed to kill himself. Shall we try this, doctor?'

"'By all means,' I answered.

"She handed me a dainty, fragile, carved ivory paper-knife, which was lying on the table beside her. I took it and turned to my sleeping friend. 'See this dagger,' I said, holding the paper-knife towards him, 'I will put it here on the table. To-morrow, at two o'clock, when the gong sounds for luncheon, you will take this dagger and kill yourself.'

"I then woke him up. He laughed heartily, and remembered nothing of what had occurred during his sleep. He was in good spirits, and begged his wife to sing him one more song before we said good-night. She sang several in her rich, deep contralto, which brought tears to the eyes of the listeners. Then Luigi joined her with his exquisite tenor, and they gave us several charming duets, so that it was long past midnight ere we retired.

"'As good as the opera, listening to those two,' said Harry, as he bade me good-night.

"Next morning we were all late for breakfast, except Harry, who had gone to see the manager of one of his outlying farms, on a little matter of business. Mrs. Stanley, Luigi, and I were sitting lazily on the verandah, discussing the latest novel. Presently Harry returned, kissed his wife and wished us all good-morning in his usual hearty fashion; he then began to tell us of his morning's work. When the first note of the luncheon-gong sounded, his face suddenly changed, he raised his head quickly, and then with a rapid step entered the house. I glanced at Mrs. Stanley, she had become deathly pale, and trembled from head to foot. Luigi retained his usual imperturbable calm.

"Come quickly," I said to her.

"She did not move: 'What is the use?' she said. 'I see you have succeeded; he has gone.'

"I rushed to the drawing-room, but at the threshold I stopped aghast. There lay Harry, stretched out on the floor—dead—a dagger through his heart."

∽

"Was it a real dagger, doctor," asked one of the young ladies.

"Yes," said the doctor, "a real dagger," and he added, "I afterwards looked on the table, and the paper knife was not there."

After a few moments he said slowly, "Mrs. Stanley, in less than a year, married her cousin Luigi. All Harry's property had been willed to her."

∽

Canadian Magazine 6 (November 1895), 38–40.

Catherine E. Simpson Hayes (1865–1945)

AN EPISODE AT CLARKE'S CROSSING (1895)

Journalist, poet, short-story writer, dramatist, local historian, and active feminist, "Kate" Hayes made her reputation as an early writer of the Northwest Territories.

Hayes, daughter of Patrick Hayes, was born at Dalhousie, New Brunswick in 1856. She first became a teacher, then moved in 1879 to Prince Albert, Northwest Territories. She married Ontarian C. Bowman Simpson in 1882, but they separated in 1885 and she moved with her two children to Regina, where she wrote for the *Regina Leader* and became librarian to the Territorial Legislature. There she met Nicholas Flood Davin, founder and editor of the *Leader*, with whom she developed a long-standing relationship, and who encouraged her writing career. Born in Ireland in 1840, Davin had come to Canada in 1872 and to Regina in 1882. A successful writer and journalist, admired for his wit and ingenuity as well as his polished prose style and skill as a speaker, Davin was the first Member of Parliament for Assiniboia West and played an important part in the cultural life of the Northwest. He was the father of two of Hayes' children, a boy born in 1889 and a girl in 1891. Although she obtained a legal separation from her husband in 1889, Hayes never attained a divorce. Her daughter was placed in an orphanage, no doubt because of the complexity of Hayes' personal situation, married to one man, the mistress of another, and involved in her own career. In 1895 Davin married an Ottawa woman, Elizabeth Jane Reid. As a result of Hayes' strong support for women's suffrage, Davin introduced a motion in its favour in the House of Commons on 8 May 1895. Hayes died at Vancouver on 15 January 1945.

In 1895 Hayes was co-founder with Kit Coleman of the Canadian Women's Press Club. Under the pseudonyms

"Mary Markwell" and "Yukon Bill," as well as "Kate Simpson Hayes" (reversing her birth and married names), Hayes wrote fiction, non-fiction, and poetry for the *Globe* and *The Week*, and for such periodicals as *Pacific Monthly* and *Rod and Gun in Canada*. The raucous poems of *Derby Days in the Yukon and Other Poems of the Northland* are suitably ascribed to Yukon Bill.

Hayes' *Prairie Potpourri* (1895) was the first work of fiction published by a Northwest Territories press. It was praised by critic-anthologist W.D. Lighthall: "Its place is one of real honour in literature." *The Week* recommended the book to "anyone interested in Canadian literature and good short stories" (26 July 1895: 833). The book is indeed a "potpourri." It includes three short stories, a novelette, a play for children, and several poems.

"There is an inexpressible pathos in the passing of the Red Man," Hayes wrote later in the "Author's Note" to *The Legend of the West* (1908), a brief, prose-like lament for the end of the Indian people. The painful story of the dilemma of the aboriginal peoples with the coming of the first white men, traders and missionaries, is at the heart of "Clarke's Crossing," one of the short stories in *Prairie Potpourri*. Through the elderly Sioux, Daddy Pete, and his granddaughter Tannis, Hayes strongly criticizes the effect on Indian culture of the growing white presence on the prairie. The narrator obliquely and ironically reveals the blindness and lack of true Christian love of the Christian missionaries. A young missionary's blindness includes, for example, his judgment that Daddy Pete's delight in the simple trinkets for his granddaughter for which he trades his valuable pelt is materialistic, while he is seemingly oblivious to the greed and materialism of the Hudson's Bay trader in this exchange. The most worldly person of all proves to be the missionary himself, who betrays his Indian fiancée to return to a life of wealth and pleasure in England. The true "Christian" is Daddy Pete, who never wavers in his devotion to his grandchild. Hayes' criticism, through the clergyman, of the Church's lack of compassion and concern for the individual is reminiscent of Lily Dougall's criticism implicit in her story "Thrift" (see page 188).

"How the End Came" is equally sympathetic to the Indian cause in its description of the life of an Indian woman married to a drunken and abusive white man. On a different note, the longer story in *Prairie Potpourri*, "The La-de-dah from London," is an amusing account of the adjustment to life in the pioneering West of a highborn Englishman, D.G. Periwinkle Brown, whose ancestry goes back to William the Conqueror. Brown learns that in this new land neither money nor name will bring success. His initiation is a difficult one. Even with much assistance from practical Canadian friends and neighbours, Brown loses the considerable sum he brought with him. As a result, however, he becomes a man: having fallen in love with the educated daughter of a neighbour, he goes to work for a friend, rather than giving up and returning to England. In this way he comes to understand farming, which he failed to do when he had the funds to hire others to do everything for him. Hayes portrays the difficulties of pioneer life with realistic detail and the misadventures of the neophyte with much humour.

❧

Suggested Reading:

Besner, Neil K. "Nicholas Flood Davin." In *Dictionary of Literary Biography*, vol. 99, 87-91.

Hayes, Kate Simpson [Mary Markwell, pseud.]. *Prairie Potpourri*. Winnipeg: Stovel Printers, 1895.

_____. *The Legend of the West*. Victoria, 1900.

An Episode at Clarke's Crossing

Catherine E. Simpson Hayes

Old Peter Larue was indisputably the caliphate of the plains; an authority on any subject that might be introduced in any of the four languages; English (broken), French, Sioux and Cree (which he would seldom use).

Daddy Pete, as he was called, had but one grandchild, the only daughter of his son Modèste, and the old man doted on his human flower with a love and devotion almost beyond belief.

Daddy Pete was the sole link between the early days, when no footfall save that of the moccasined hunter trod the prairie, and the buffalo swept across the plains in droves, like black clouds, and fast encroaching civilization with its noisy railways, its awkward river ferries, its improvements that came creeping on like an incoming tide, wiping away all the old landmarks, sweeping away old-time associations, and making a new era in the West. With the innovations Daddy Pete (being an aristocrat by nature) would have nothing to do. When the half-picturesque half-squalid splendour of life began to be lost, when "the Company" began to cater to new settlers, then Daddy Pete drew his blanket about him and scornfully moved further West. He would go to the Company's no more. Barter in peltries and other native riches were solemnly conducted by Modèste, and for company's sake he sometimes took his black-eyed daughter

CATHERINE E. SIMPSON HAYES

along, the gay-striped blankets and colored beads filling Tannis' young mind with longings new to the prairie maid.

Daddy Pete's proud boast was that he "never see no railway," and he threatened many times to move camp when the advent of some Missionary gave signs of encroaching influence. To such Modèste gave a warm welcome, for the black-eyed daughter had with her savage ways interested His Lordship greatly, when in those annual trips he saw her. His Lordship pitied her ignorance, and admired her beauty, and calling Modèste aside explained to him his great responsibility, the magnificent opportunity, with the help of this child, for doing something towards the grand work of salvation. He should educate her, prepare her, not for the wandering life of the camp, but for home and motherhood. All this sounded vague to Modèste but he understood it to mean that 'his gal' was different to other women of the camp, and the Bishop's fair daughter had taken Tannis kindly by the hand and led her to the drawing-room filled with beautiful things, sowing in this way the first seeds of Christianity—and discontent—in the Indian girl's mind.

To Clarke's Crossing then came Mr. Penrhyn, his boyish face full of youthful enthusiasm, came to do his Master's work—the work of salvation. He went out on the chase with Modèste, and after one particular day the latter announced to Daddy Pete that Tannis was to be sent away to the white man's school. To Daddy Pete this came as a death blow. Who would help him prepare the bait for the traps? Who would seek out the rabbit lairs? Who would make the snares and tan the skins, and who would sight the game—for Daddy Pete's eye were growing dim like long-burned candles. To all those questions Modèste answered nothing. He squatted by the camp fire with his pipe the while the old man argued, then after a long silence he spoke:—"Newitcha will come to the camp. Newitcha is strong; Newitcha will trap the beaver, snare the rabbit, prepare the bait, Newitcha is strong." Daddy Pete stood up, his blanket trailing about him, and his words were full of anger:

"Bring a Cree woman to camp? A Cree woman take the place of his lit'le gal! No! ten times no! Had he not stalked the game and hunted buffalo for sixty-nine years? Had he not followed in the chase and trapped the silver-fox? Had he not worked, saved, *starved* for his lit'le gal—and now bring Newitcha, a Cree woman to fill her place? No! Ten times no!

That night the old man sat by the river many long hours smoking his pipe of kinnikinic, thoughtful, sad, fearing much; and when the next evening came, Newitcha, brass ringed, her face daubed with yellow paint, followed Modèste into camp trudging under the burden of skins—her marriage portion—as befitted the wife of the bravest trapper along the banks of the Saskatchewan, Daddy Pete sighed.

Between the old man and the Cree wife there was unspoken enmity. Newitcha was strong; she was up before dawn laboring and carrying all day; she tanned the pelts and gathered the campa-berry to make pemmican; she built the strong willow stands whereon hung the bear meat drying in the sun. Truly she was strong, but she hated Tannis and she hated the old man.

It was summer then and Daddy Pete with his "lit'le gal" could roam over the plain all day long. At night the air was soft, the grass was kind and the sky watched over them as they sometimes slept under the cottonwood trees. With delight the old man would snare a prairie chicken, and by the river he and his chattering grand-child would build a fire in a little hollow scooped out of the ground, line it with hot coals placing therein the fowl in all its feathers, heaping the savoury bit with red coals, until the tender flesh was done; then upon a table of nature's own laying they would feast in innocent happiness and delight, whispering to each other loving words, and look guardedly over your shoulders when they breathed Newitcha's name.

Then came a day when word from the Bishop, good man, who had arranged with Madam ——— at Montreal, to take the prairie maid and educate her—that Tannis was to go. Daddy Pete, after a long day's fasting among the

212

cottonwoods, fought out the battle with his own heart, and won just because his only desire was to do whatever was best for "lit'le gal;" but Daddy Pete must himself see her off on the first stage of the long, long journey, he would go as far as the Company's with his "lit'le gal."

The Red River carts were got ready for the overland trip which must be made a paying one. Modèste would bring back freight for the Company, and away from the Crossing one June day went the creaking carts one after the other along the trail leading to the Company's Post. There final preparations were completed for the trip to Winnipeg; there good-by's were said, speechless ones on the part of Daddy Pete, joyous on the part of the dusky maid perched on the rear of the last cart rattling along the grass-grown trail, swinging her stout legs encased in newly-beaded leggings, her tawny tresses a lovely tangle about her bright face, her bare and sun-burned arms waving good-bye while she shouted: "Goo'by——e Daddy; dun fergit t' feed mi' whi' rabbit, an' min' dun' let Newi'cha smash d' palin's behin' de ol' shad, feer de fox'll——git——awa—y—y, goo'by——Dad—d——y——y!"

A bend in the road and she was lost to view. Then over the dust-stirred trail, and above the rattle of the crasy wheels came to Daddy Pete's ears the cry of the wild plover—this being the well-known signal between them ever since she began to follow him about on the chase, when she made the discovery of a new rabbit burrow, or another nest of duck eggs along the sloughs in the deep grass fringing the water.

Daddy Pete tried to answer that cry with the old familiar call, to answer as he had done all the long happy years, but something like a pine knot forged itself into his throat, he threw up his arms, raised his eyes to the Great Spirit and then the tears fell, the first tears since he wept over his darling, a motherless babe thirteen years before. He turned around to pick up his staff to go back, but the Rev. Mr. Penrhyn was standing there too. Daddy Pete could have struck him down where he stood, but Daddy Pete must be excused a great deal; he was a heathenish old man who had been so long upon the plains that he had outgrown whatever goodness he had known, and he was unwilling that civilization should overtake him.

"Ah!" the clergyman said, walking by the side of the old man, "I am too late, I see; I would have liked to have seen Tannis, to have spoken with her, impressing upon her mind the *very great* advantages His Lordship has——secured for her. "You see, Peter," went on the young divine, "She will eventually be of great use to——to us in out work; of great use——to have a native woman whose sympathies will be in touch with—the Indian mind"——Mr. Penrhyn stopped. The face of the old man turned now towards him, was distorted by passion; some inner emotion forced itself to the surface of his thought; he opened his shrunken lips to say something, but the words were left unsaid, his head, whitened by the many hard winters, and crowned by this new grief bowed itself, and moving voiceless lips he trudged on.

There was little opportunity for Mr. Penrhyn to exercise his sacred office here; the old man was beyond all human influences; there was but one thing the clergyman could do—he did that fervently, devoutly; he prayed that the dull old man might see in this the over-guiding Hand.

All this had happened eight years before. Daddy Pete was eight years older, and eight times eight years lonelier and sadder; and in all the long weary months no word from Tannis, save through the occasional visits of Mr. Penrhyn, when on his mission he came to the Crossing. At such times Daddy Pete always went off on the hunt; it seemed as if the minister's coming was the signal for the old man to go away to his wild haunts and away to the traps and snares he would go. All this Mr. Penrhyn saw and grieved for; grieved that no good seed would take root in this old man's hardened heart; for surely it was very offensive and wrong in an old man tottering upon the verge of the grave, not to give heed to Christ's message.

Mr. Penrhyn had been fully ordained a minister; he was an enthusiastic worker in the Vineyard, and he excited the admiration of the Bishop, whose eyes began to look

CATHERINE E. SIMPSON HAYES

upon him as one worthy to take up the divine work, when he, now an old man, should be called; and sometimes—outside of prayer time—the Bishop looked at his lovely daughter, and thought——

Over study and hardships attendant on the missionary life had impaired Mr. Penrhyn's health. His Lordship thought a sea voyage might be beneficial, but something in the thought of going back to London made the clergyman tremble; an apprehensive glance, half timid, half despairing, he gave His Lordship, who, perhaps, suddenly remembering something, moved restlessly across the room, and, placing a hand kindly upon the young man's head, murmured:—

"*He that cometh to Me shall never hunger, and he that believeth on Me shall never thirst.*"

The temptations beyond the sea must not be risked; the witchery of London life contrasted with the deprivations of missionary labor might——what might it not do?

Just at this time of doubt, the mail, which came by slow and circuitous route, reached His Lordship, and with it came the announcement of Madam ——— that Tannis Larue had completed her studies. Madam, in her own words, was sending her back "accomplished in person, amiable in mind," and Madam "hoped the care and attention lavished upon this wild child of the plains would repay His Lordship" (Madam might have more truthfully said "Daddy Pete," for the wealth of peltries that went to balance the expenses were provided by many a long day's chase) "for the cost of her education." You see, the phraseology was more delicate, but, after all, that was what was really meant.

So, word having to be sent to Modèste, it was decided that Mr. Penrhyn's holidays should be spent at the Crossing. A summer there would build up his strength; the dangers of the city must be avoided. "*In due season we shall reap if we faint not,*" said the good Bishop. And to carry word to Modèste went the young clergyman.

Once more were the shaky old carts strung out upon the trail, so teased by travel and traffic that the grass had lost its habit of creeping boldly over the roadway, and now shrank timidly back. Upon the front cart come the young minister with Modèste, and behind them Daddy Pete, his withered old face shining with a joy that seemed brighter than earth. He had come thus far, to where, eight years ago, he had said good-by to his "lit'le gal."

"Hoh, boy!" said the old man, turning to the minister and forgetting his eight years' enmity, as Modèste drove away along the trail, "my Modes he cum plenty soon—two, five, twenty, 'leven days, hoh!"

Mr. Penrhyn was glad to find Daddy Pete in a friendly frame of mind once more, and he walked back along the way, patiently listening to the garrulous old heathen, who was expressing his delight in exultant chuckles, rubbing his claw-like yellow fingers together and repeating over and over again: "My lit'le gal cum some more plenty soon; plenty rabbit, plenty duck, plenty berry, hoh!"

At the Company's, whither Daddy Pete carried his load of peltries, the clergyman waited, while an exchange was made for powder and shot in generous quantities, tea and tobacco in considerable supply, and, his dim old eyes illumined by genuine love-light, he demanded: "Hoh! fixin's f'r gals?"

This being out of the usual line of demands at the Company's, the puzzled attendant began a voluble jargon of Sioux, but Mr. Penrhyn, divining the old man's thoughts, explained that Modèste's daughter was coming home from the East, and, doubtless, it was some gew-gaws Daddy Pete wanted.

A gorgeous array of green, yellow and red blankets was produced, a selection made by the old man, whose skinny fingers fumbled critically over texture and size. Then bright print stuffs, gilt pins, brass bells, rings, and bright beads in goodly supply were taken, against which tawdry lot many a valuable pelt was piled by the Company; and the minister looked on, noted, with pain, the simple delight of the silly old man, and he sadly thought how all the years devoted to teaching the beautiful story of the Gospel were barren of results, and it grieved him to think that this old man, over whom the shadow of death hung, should place his mind on things that perish, and the minister sighed.

That evening beside the camp fire Daddy Pete, mumbling and smiling, spread out the purchases that were to be his offerings, his gifts—gifts that would make glad the heart of his "little gal"! This crimson ribbon to weave in her black hair; these glittering beads to close about her throat; these shining bands her bared arms to clasp. He mumbled and laughed as he had not done for years—Newitcha was not there with her sharp tongue to reprove him for his silliness, and in one—two days, his "lit'le gal" would come!

The clergyman spoke solemnly to old Pete, earnestly remonstrating with him on the sin of setting his failing mind upon the vanity of earthly joys; reminding him of eternal glories that fade not—that were to be had without money and without price!

The old man listened, and shook his head with many a scornful "hoh!" intimating broadly that what "the Company" had was "plenty good for ol' Pete," and that his "lit'le gal" would have "the best the Company kept!"

Each evening Mr. Penrhyn passed some hours by the camp fire with Daddy Pete, speaking words of divine promise to the old man who sometimes listened, sometimes slept, and ever and always kept busy fingers among the trumpery gifts, his eyes blinking with childish delight, his shrunken lips whispering "my lit'le gal!"

Each day he added to his gifts, and after spreading them out, and mumbling over them with childish delight, he would trudge over the prairie to the bend in the trail and there with worn shaking hands shading his sight, peer across the waste of green for signs of the carts.

At last the long line, like motes, appeared in the distance, connected, and then became a snake that crept slowly on, slowly nearer; the serpentine coil-like thing breaking again into fragments, and just as the sun, big-eyed and wondering, cast a last look over the prairie trail, came the carts around the bend, the peculiar music of the wheels like shrieks of tortured souls suffering purgatorial pains.

And where was daddy's "lit'le gal?" Daddy Pete wiped the mist from his sight and stared. He winked hard and stared again; something like a fluttering bird rose from his heart and like that same thing, wounded, beat helplessly a broken wing.

"How do you do, grandpa? Oh, it *is* Mr. Penrhyn! how good of you both to meet me here!" A small muffled hand sought Daddy Pete's palsied palm, and something, he thought like a closely woven snare, barred the meeting of their lips. Mr. Penrhyn stared at this vision too, stared with unbelieving eyes—eyes that spoke their amazement. Where was the little wild child of the plains? Where was Daddy's "lit'le gal?"

These the questions that rose in the minds of the two men standing there in silent wonder; the confusion of the moment was broken by awful roars of "haw!" "gee!" from Modèste as the stolid oxen, foaming at the mouth, and panting after the heavy march, switching their stumpy tails at the horde of sand flies following the carts, passed along the trail, the shouts sounding like profanity amid the serene stillness.

They walked on down the trail, the clergyman and the young girl side by side, the old man, dull of eye and trembling in limb, following after, in the fashion of his race. Was that his little gal—that tall creature arrayed as was His Lordship's daughter, the same grace of manner, the same sweet voice, that walk—his little gal? Tears of disappointment welled up in the eyes of the old man; welled up and overflowed their banks, and in his mind but one wish: to see her turn round once, to hear her call him "Daddy," in the old-time tender way; hoh! he'd give the best season's lot of silver-fox pelts to hear her call him "Daddy Pete" once again; to hear the cry of the wild plover as she gave it that day she called out "Goo'-bye, Daddy!" Ah! that was so long ago, so long ago, and he had come between them since then.

"You see," Mr. Penrhyn was saying, "what we need is schools; now you can understand that we—that Eastern people are not—cannot be in sympathy with the—well, with the Indian mind; now my idea—in fact His Lordship's idea—

when we asked your father—to—to send you to be educated," he hesitated, "—was to—to—to secure that which your people—the Indians, you know, lack—sympathy."

"I understand," she answered, "I am to"———

"To teach," said Mr. Penrhyn, "there is a great work—a noble work, Miss"———

"Oh! call me Tannis, Mr. Penrhyn," she said, turning to him and smiling. "Do you believe," breaking into a little laugh, "that I did not know my own family name until I went to Madam ———'s. It was exactly like being a princess of the blood, not hearing one's real name, wasn't it?" and a laugh of real merriment rang out from her lips.

"Hoh!" The shout made them turn suddenly; there was the old man rubbing his hands and gasping with delight, tears of joy rolling down his shrivelled cheeks; that laugh took him back eight years, but the next moment it was gone.

"How grandpa has altered!" she said.

"He is quite childish," replied Mr. Penrhyn. And while the two walked on, talking and smiling, Daddy Pete, leaning more heavily upon his staff, followed, his heart sinking lower and lower until in one great sob it swamped with his hope, leaving nothing but a dumb despair.

They went to the new brick hotel. It was there Daddy Pete was stopping, but he knew now that the smoke-grimed tent would never do. At the brick hotel a room for "Modèste's gal" was ordered, and having settled her comfortably there, away went the old man, back to where the tent was pitched against the Company's. He went sadly back upon the old trail, the fag-end of his happiness hanging by the slenderest thread to his sore heart; he would get out the "fixin's;" ah, yes, he had made a mistake in going to meet her without them; "hoh! the bright things would bring him nearer to his lit'le gal!"

He remembered well one trip made in the long ago when he brought home to her a string of blue beads—remembered the shout of joy and how she clung about his neck; how he fastened them on her baby throat; he would go to her now with brighter, better ones; a double row, and larger than those of long ago. He gathered up his offerings with eager hands that shook until the gew-gaws rattled again and again, and he laughed aloud, anticipating her delight. Then he started out acknowledging for the first time in his life that "things mou't a bin diff'rent bim-bye" if he had "ever see a railway."

He was taken to the room where Modèste's gal was, but she said she was "dressing for dinner," which really meant she was changing the dusty travelling gown for a fresher one, but some way the message, given through a narrow opening in the door, gave to her a more embarrassing splendour; the old man hugging his offerings, felt a chill rise up in his heart, but still he hung about, unwilling to believe it was not the same "lit'le gal" he had loved and tended with so much devotion and care.

By and bye she came out looking lovelier and fresher than before; the dainty grey frock with its crimson velvet bodice showing the outlines of a lithe form, her step, a natural grace of movement blending with the English training in something captivating and complete. Mr. Penrhyn was standing by the window and if questioned could doubtless truthfully declare that this descendant of a Sioux mother was to him, nothing more than "that most promising person." Daddy Pete was waiting too squatted upon the floor, and at her feet like some devout worshipper he laid with trembling hands his offerings.

He saw the hot tide of shame rise from throat to chin and from chin to forehead, and the last slender thread of his hope snapped within, when, raising her hands with a motion of horror she said:—

"For me? oh, grandpa! I could never wear——such things——now!"

The old man looked at his "lit'le gal" just one little moment, then without a word gathered up the gifts again and trudged back to the tent where he found the oxen and carts forming a barricade. Modèste was there, unusually silent, smoking his pipe of kinnikinic and watching the red blaze, over which the iron pot hung on a tripod of poplar.

CATHERINE E. SIMPSON HAYES

⁓

"I dun'no, boy," Daddy Pete was saying one evening returning from the chase, "I b'leve lit'le gal's sick."

His son's answer was to draw deeper puffs of his kinnikinnic. "Ol' Pete got plenty—hoh, boy—by'm-bye die putty soon,—plenty beaver, plenty silver fox—all for lit'le gal—better go back school some more plenty—hoh, boy!"

In truth the prairie maid grew weary and wan because the long happy holiday was over; the young minister must go back to Emanuel College; he would go back and tell his lordship that he would wed the Sioux maid; he would ask to be sent to some remote northern station, where, among the wilds, together with his wild prairie flower, he might bear the glad tidings.

When Daddy Pete learned of this arrangement he gave such a shout of joy that a startled covey of ducks were sent a-wing. "Hoh!" he shouted in his cracked voice, "Ol' Pete got plenty buffalo, plenty fox, plenty beaver!" He laughed so long and so often that Newitcha scowled more darkly each day. He smoothed down his lit'le gal's dark locks tenderly and said "hoh!" with such explosive earnestness that Newitcha muttered in her Cree tongue savagely and often, with many shakings of the head.

Then the day came when Mr. Penrhyn said good-bye to his friends of the camp; he would come back in two months. At Clarke's Crossing Modèste would meet him; he would come to be with his prairie flower, never more to part, their hearts were young and strong and hopeful and he went his way alone.

Soon the poplar trees sent their shivering leaves hither and thither; the evenings grew chill and longer and drearier; the summer was gone and the winter set in early. It would be a long hard winter. Daddy Pete said so, and hadn't he learned it from the beavers and the gophers, who know such things?

He had not come, there was no such thing as mail delivery beyond the Company's in those days, but surely he would come. Had he not said so?

One day an old Indian, passing along the trail towards Fort-à-la Corne, stopped at Pete's camp. He hung about the lodge all day, and after supping he loosened his belt, and from inner rags that covered his wretched body, stolidly and soberly produced a letter; he explained that he had been asked to give it to the "moonias squaw." It proved to be for Tannis, and it was from Luke Penrhyn, dated months before, asking her to come down with her father to see him before he left for England. The Bishop having suddenly decided on sending over to London one of the clergy to secure funds for opening new missions in the far North,— would she go to him to say good-bye?

The letter was written in October, and it was April now; the Indian had got it when he was at the Company's last; he had been on the hunt and was now going back to his band.

Tannis did not leave the little poplar bluff all the next day; she sat there white of face, reading over and over again his words, and suffering as no tongue can tell.

She told Daddy Pete the contents of the letter in her own words, and the old man smiled contentedly at thought of having his darling his own, longer. May came and with it another letter, this time from across the sea and through the agency of the Company; it was written but a few weeks before, and with it came hope thrice renewed. It said that he would leave for Canada in six weeks; the work had been almost completed; great interest had been taken in the new land and he had secured funds for missions in the far North; there he "would make his home with his sweet prairie flower." And she believed!

Once more she sang in the old happy way. Once more she set snares with Daddy Pete, hunted for wild duck eggs along the thatch-grown lakelets, and scurried across the hillocky grass for wild-birds' nests.

Daddy Pete grew feeble; he did not go on the hunt always now; Newitcha watched under her black brows, and many little brown faces hunted among the grass for the kammass root all day, and at sundown gathered with noisy arrogance about the knee of Modèste, claiming full share of his attention, and the half-sister, with the strange dress, crept in silent sorrowing supplication to Daddy Pete's side, where she found refuge and sympathy as when a child.

June came with flower and bursting bud and Modèste was going to the Company's. The lark was not so early nor so blithe of song as Tannis, now. All day long she played with the smaller witch-like brown brothers and sisters, sang and watched the trail. Four days passed and then Modèste came back—alone.

Tannis sang no more. The snares were neglected; Daddy Pete dozed nearly all day now, and the son had double work to perform, and another moss-bag hung upon the poplar tree beside the tepee; Newitcha followed Modèste on the chase and to Tannis was left the care and the work of the camp.

One day Daddy Pete came suddenly upon her below the camp where the poplars trembled and shivered, and where awe-whisperings of the winds were heard. She was lying prostrate upon the ground, beating the grass, her fingers reached out, moaning the hurt that had so long been held in bounds within her breaking heart. One moment the old man stood transfixed; he knew nothing of emotion, but his dull mind could understand one thing; his "lit'le gal" was suffering. He caught the straggling white hairs that hung down about his bewildered head and cried out; he gathered her up in his trembling arms as he had done many a time in her childish griefs, and crooned over her in his Sioux tongue: *O! O! Nicante pi kin magaqu iyecaca ateyapi pa kin akan, hinphaya qa wicakican!*[1]

This was harder to bear than cruel words; she had hated the camp; had despised her tribe; had longed to leave the one kind creature whose only thought had ever been her comfort, her enjoyment, and now she was without all. "O! Daddy! Daddy!!"

---

1. "O! O! Let the heart's rain fall upon the head of thy father, he will weep for thee!" [Author's note]

That cry at last! she was clinging to him, and folded to his heart in the old, old way! At last Daddy Pete had found his lit'le gal! He understood it all now; understood it as if he had been learned and clever, and not the silly old heathen he was.

"Hoh! don't cry plenty much; boy come back! Ol' Pete make walk Company; ol' Pete fin' boy! hoh! Lit'le gal make plenty laugh some more; hoh!" And the next morning, before dawn, afoot and feeble, away went Daddy Pete, his knife sheathed and hanging from his belt, upon his bent shoulders the pack of furs, his heart full of a great sorrow, his troubled mind strong in one determination—his "lit'le gal's" happiness to find.

When Tannis awoke the next morning, Daddy Pete was many miles on his journey. At first she thought he had gone to look at the snares or lingered along the sloughs, but as the day grew and then died out, and he did not come, she knew that he had gone. Daddy would bring———he would bring word; he *might* bring a letter, a letter that would explain everything—or, oh, joy of joys! would he bring her lover?

The third day after this she was sitting by the tent door drying roots. She saw coming up the trail a figure. It was a white man, and she knew the dress to be that of a missionary. She was unable to rise, for a faintness and trembling of the limbs overcame her, but, when the blur had passed from her sight and he came nearer, she saw it was a stranger. He spoke to her in Cree.

She explained that her father was absent, and, learning that the stranger had lost his way, she offered him the hospitality of the camp, making supper and attending to the brown babies that peeped from curious corners at the newcomer.

Tannis now wore the ordinary dress of the Indian women; her hair, neatly braided, hung down her back, and nothing, save her language when she spoke in the English tongue, would betray her better training. She spoke to the children in the Cree tongue, as the stranger had, in that language, first addressed her.

　　　　　　　　　　CATHERINE E. SIMPSON HAYES

During the preparation for the meal the stranger told Tannis that he was on his way to a new mission field. His Lordship, the Bishop, had received large funds from England; the work of carrying the Gospel to the far north was opening and he was now on his way to take the post destined for Mr. Penrhyn.

The clergyman did not observe the wild look fixed upon him; he did not note the clenching of the fingers, nor did he see the blood drip from the palms of those shaking hands.

"And Mr. ———— Penrhyn?"

"Ah, you knew him then? Yes, I believe his route was along this way. Oh, Penrhyn? poor fellow!" The speaker shook his head solemnly, and then gave his attention to the venison before him.

"Is——he——dead?"

She gasped this with so much eagerness that the stranger looked up, but the face, though white and tired looking, was void of expression.

"It's rather a sad story," the gentleman said, "but, as you knew him————. You see," he went on, suddenly, "His Lordship thought a good deal of Penrhyn—rather favored him we used to think, but out here somewhere he met an Indian girl; she had some sort of education I believe, and—well, I guess he fell in love with her—compromised himself by some sort of promise I believe, and of course, His Lordship was obliged to——send him away."

"Ah! then it was the Bishop—sent him—away?"

"Yes, you see Penrhyn was the second son of Lord Gathness. He was a gentleman, and he couldn't——oh, well, you understand————."

"And this Mr. Pen————?" her voice failed, but her face betrayed nothing.

"Penrhyn," said the visitor, as if he suddenly recollected the subject—"well, you see, after His Lordship got him out of the way, and over in London, it appears Penrhyn's father died quite suddenly, just as he was about to sail, in fact, and the elder brother, who at the time was in the south of France, coming home in haste, his yacht was lost in a gale crossing the Channel, and my friend Penrhyn, came in for the whole thing, estate and title."

Tannis neither moved nor spoke. She felt a wave of something like fear coming over her; something sharp like a little stab seemed to enter her heart—it was his letter, the last letter, which she kept close to her flesh—that last sweet false message to "his prairie flower!"

"It was a great disappointment—a great blow to His Lordship"—

"A blow to His Lordship? it was His Lordship sent him away, was it not?"

"Ah, yes—but you see before Penrhyn—who was, you understand, a younger son—left England the lady Agatha Glyde, to whom he was engaged, threw him over for his brother Audrey—what shocked His Lordship, who knew the story—was that Penrhyn should throw up his missionary work, for you know his brother's death left him heir to everything, and he married Lady Agatha when"—

The speaker saw the girl sway, but she seemed to recover herself, and put up her hand in a bewildered way, pressing the other above her breast, as though something hindered her breathing.

"You are Peter Larue's grand-daughter?" said the stranger, and he held out pitying hands. But the girl-woman tottered by him, passed from the tent, and was seen no more.

Daddy Pete came back from his trip more feeble than ever. He did not seem to realize the absence of his grand-daughter. Sometimes he would ask pettishly 'had she come in yet?' and Modèste who grieved in silence, would look at Newitcha, and that black-eyed wife awed into silence would whisper *"wendigo"*! and gather her brown brood about her knee.

Sometimes the old man would rouse up and say he must go and find her; he would gather his pack of furs and then sitting down to rest, would doze off, and waking, forget the intention.

226   CATHERINE E. SIMPSON HAYES

One evening Modèste whispered to the old man: "She was at the Crossing yesterday; she asked them to put her across—the ferryman went up to his shack, and when he came back she was gone."

Daddy Pete cried out on hearing this. He would go now; this very night; he would be there when she came again; his lit'le gal, he had the beads all ready for her. He took the gew-gaw things from his bosom where he hid them the day she refused them so scornfully; he drew them through his fingers, and the sparkle was reflected in his dim old eyes. He looked at them and laughed, thinking of her joy when he would place them on her throat, and he said "hoh!" a great many times and wiped his eyes.

They went away to the Crossing, not telling Newitcha where they were going. Modèste carried the pack, and waited patiently while Daddy Pete sat by the wayside and rested while he slept. Thus they reached the crossing.

It was moonlight, bright opaline moonlight, and across the river fell a broad shaft of light that sparkled and shone and broadened until it seemed to the foolish old man to be a road leading somewhere.

That must be the road the *Sinsapa* talked about; the road leading to that beautiful hunting grounds; *he* said it sparkled with jewels; gates of pearl? hoh! he could see them; could see the jewels glistening and sparkling over there; it led right over the river; *he* had said it was a river. If *he* went that road, then Daddy's lit'le gal would follow after! Hoh! it was but a step. Daddy Pete tottered to the very edge of the river and looked across. Something was over there. Was it Daddy's little gal waiting?

Upon the river a shadow fell, swift rose a winged form, and the dead stillness was broken by that plaintive far-reaching call, the cry of the wild plover. A cry of joy—one instant a bent figure was outlined against the sky, its arms outreached; then the answering note rang out, waking Modèste from a fatigued sleep; a loud splash that broke the jewel-like surface of the silver bar upon the water, and then silence.

Along the bank of the river ran the trapper Modèste. The lustrous flood of light across the river fascinated his eyes. He called; he went up and down peering, watching; but no sign of the old man. He surely slept somewhere in the long grass. He was old and weary.

At dawn some half-breeds came to the ferry with their traps and tents; they found a distracted man there, old Peter Larue's son, stone deaf to words and wringing his hands. By-and-by the ferryman came down, and they began the toilsome pull across. Part way over Modèste, who had been staring into the water with wild eyes, gave a shout and pointed down. There was great commotion then. One dived into deep water and came up holding some dark thing. Outstretched hands took up Daddy Pete's still form dripping with jewel drops of water. He had passed through the pearly gates! Ah, yes, Daddy Pete had surely found his "lit'le gal" at last. Within his shrivelled old hands, tightly clasped, the double row of shining beads, his face calm, smiling, child-like; the deep sleep of death had blotted out all the lonely sorrow-fed thoughts; Daddy Pete had gone to his "lit'le gal," gone at her call, and, simple old man he, taken his offerings, his gifts.

∽

At the same hour the doors of a fashionable club in fashionable London opened; gay laughter and badinage passed from lip to lip of the throng of noble lords just leaving the fascinations of the card table.

"I say, Gathness! before we go tell us about that tawny beauty of yours out West?" drawled one.

A handsome man of the *beau monde* flushes to the temples, as he laughs carelessly and says: "Oh! you mean that little episode at Clarke's Crossing?"

∽

Prairie Potpourri (Winnipeg: Stovel, 1895), 43–59.

Catherine E. Simpson Hayes

Sarah Anne Curzon (1833–1898)

THE ILL EFFECTS OF A MORNING WALK (1896)

Sarah Anne Curzon, poet and journalist, was a pioneering
Canadian feminist who did much to give Canadians a sense
of their own history from the perspective of an ardent
proponent of Imperial Federation and of the heroic myth of
the United Empire Loyalists—a myth her popular closet
drama *Laura Secord* (1887) helped to popularize.

Sarah Anne Curzon was born in or near Birmingham,
England, in 1833, the daughter of glass manufacturer George
Philips Vincent and Mary Amelia Jackson. She enjoyed a
comfortable and cultured upbringing, being privately
tutored in music and other subjects as well as attending a
Birmingham girls' school—possibly one source of the
setting of "The Ill Effects of a Morning Walk." Curzon had
published short fiction in English periodicals before her
marriage in 1858 to Robert Curzon of Norfolk and their
emigration to Canada four years later.

Curzon quickly became active in journalism, history
and Canadian feminism. As assistant editor of the *Canada
Citizen* (Toronto), she spoke out for women's rights, including suffrage, and women's right to attend university and to
enter the professions, especially medicine. (Fittingly, a
daughter was to graduate from the University of Toronto.)
Her blank verse comedy *The Sweet Girl Graduate* was
published in the satirical magazine *Grip* in 1882. Written
at a time when women were barred from much higher
education, the comedy features a cross-dressing heroine
who obtains top honours at university, subverting male
pretensions to intellectual superiority. Curzon's feminism
was clear in an 1890 letter to *Dominion Illustrated*, which
she wrote as secretary of the Woman's Enfranchisement
Association of Canada:

> . . . I trust that the time is not far distant when our men, laying aside their selfishness, jealousy and prejudice, may say to woman, "Come over and help us," [in government] not only in making pure and righteous homes, but in making our nation.

Curzon was active in the writing of Canadian history, valorizing in prose and poetry the loyalism of the War of 1812 and the Rebellion of 1837, the latter depicted in a serial novel for *Dominion Illustrated* in 1889–1890 called *In the Thick of It*. In her best known work, *Laura Secord*, Curzon's female hero is both an intrepid woman and a valiant patriot, a dramatic figure conceived out of both Curzon's feminism and her patriotism. When Mrs. Secord sets out on a dangerous journey to warn the British, leaving her injured husband at home, she says:

> Then will you taste a woman's common lot
> In times of strait, while I essay man's role
> Of fierce activity. We will compare
> When I return.

The Loyalist servant Betty in Curzon's story "Betty's Choice," published in 1888, is a similar creation: a woman who chooses to come to Canada and endure material hardship rather than marry her suitor and remain in the United States.

In 1895, Sarah Curzon was elected first president of the Women's Canadian Historical Society of Toronto, and corresponded with such fellow antiquarians as William Kirby, Sir James MacPherson Le Moine and William Douw Lighthall who dubbed her "the loyalist Poetess." For women's causes, she worked closely with pioneer female physician Emily Stowe and writer Mary Agnes Fitzgibbon. When Curzon encountered financial difficulties in 1889, writer Louisa Murray (see page 123) helped to spearhead a public appeal for funds. Sarah Curzon died in Toronto on 6 November 1898.

"The Ill Effects of a Morning Walk" draws on Curzon's memories of an English girls' school. The imagery of the story is of particular interest, counterpointing as it does the pseudomilitary regimentation of a girls' boarding school in its attempt to mould them into repressed and restrained "ladies" against the pastoral and free imagery of the morning walk. Playing on the word *reform*, the story asks whether the ranks and conformist regimen "reform" as well as "re-form" school girls. The first-person narrator wins a moral victory but suffers a worldly defeat as her attempt to nurture "girls' hearts and souls" comes up against shallow and coercive "boarding school regulations."

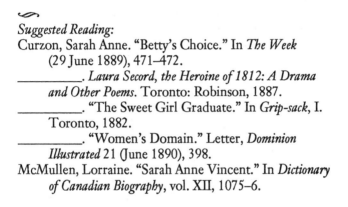

Suggested Reading:
Curzon, Sarah Anne. "Betty's Choice." In *The Week* (29 June 1889), 471–472.

_____. *Laura Secord, the Heroine of 1812: A Drama and Other Poems*. Toronto: Robinson, 1887.

_____. "The Sweet Girl Graduate." In *Grip-sack*, I. Toronto, 1882.

_____. "Women's Domain." Letter, *Dominion Illustrated* 21 (June 1890), 398.

McMullen, Lorraine. "Sarah Anne Vincent." In *Dictionary of Canadian Biography*, vol. XII, 1075–6.

THE ILL EFFECTS OF A MORNING WALK

Sarah Anne Curzon

It was my first experience of the responsibility of taking the girls out for their daily walk. Miss Rose, the second governess, usually performed that duty, an elder girl on either side of her to act as orderly or *aide-de-camp*. But Miss Rose was ill and so I got the order.

The day was lovely, the month was May, and I had not been out in broad daylight, save to church, for a fortnight, my duties as first governess and music mistress allowing me very few spare moments any day in the week, so that on this occasion I looked forward with some pleasure to filling my stuffed lungs with the sweet fresh air, and enjoying once more that buoyancy of spirit that in youth is inseparable from sunshine and a companion.

My companion on this occasion—I was satisfied with one *aide*—was Helen Tudor, the life of the school.

There were twenty-two girls, of all ages between seven and nineteen. Seven was Emmie Jones, an orphan, with blue eyes, and black hair which fell in great clusters all over her little white shoulders, and nineteen was Helen Tudor, a Juno in face and figure, and the anxiety of principal and teachers alike, both in church and out, so much were the young men of the place prone to ogling and giving the housemaids surreptitious sixpences along with bouquets of roses, lilies, or any other flower that might be in season.

I had no experience in walking out with young ladies in procession, never having been at a boarding school myself, but I had seen such processions and knew that the proper thing was to keep in rank and not go too fast. Trusting to the force of habit with the girls, I presumed that my ignorance was not likely to be betrayed on the hum-drum streets of a little country town; and certainly all went well until we had defiled through the main street, through the grounds of a Hall whose owners were liberal-minded, and out upon the high road to B———, a large town about ten miles south of us. Here I was at a loss, not being acquainted with the neighbourhood, though none but Helen Tudor knew that.

To go back the way we had come struck me as an unmitigated folly, besides, my feet were cold, the slow march proper to school processions affected the blood but little, and I felt, as Helen Tudor expressed it, "as dull as ditch water."

"Why there isn't even a proper person to wink at, Miss Pearson," she remarked to me quite gravely.

"My dear Helen!" I exclaimed, in a most reproving tone, which, however, did not seem to impress her.

Feeling that something was wrong the procession had slowed up until it absolutely stood still, and some of the bigger girls turned round to receive orders.

"I really do not know which would be the better way home," I weakly remarked.

Instantly half a dozen voices cried "O let us go by the canal, *please* Miss Pearson, ah, do!" Helen said nothing nor did it occur to me to ask her; our relative positions put such an idea quite beyond consideration. Knowing no better way out of the difficulty and supposing that the girls knew that route at any rate, I replied: "Yes, we will return by the canal." But oh, fatal error! if I had but known!

In a trice we were in motion again, and before one could say Jack Robinson the whole procession had turned in at a field-gate and were crossing a big meadow. Out of this we emerged into a narrow lane bordered by a brook; the grass on either side was studded with daisies; bluebells nodded from beneath the hedges; and buttercups and harebells brushed our feet. Before I knew it I had broken rank and was gathering flowers; and in less time than I tell it the twenty-two girls little and big had broken rank too, and were gathering flowers. It was like an overturned hive, only the air was musical with little laughs, bits of song, exclamations of delight, accentuated by an exclamation or two as here and there an adventurous spirit slipped into the brook in efforts to reach across for a flower. O, how delightful it all was! the delicious breezes, the soft sunshine, the velvety grass, the music of lark and linnet, the pretty ripple of the brook into which many white hands dipped for a drink, and above all, the freedom! I felt so refreshed and happy myself that I had even begun to congratulate myself on the ease with which lessons would be done by pupil and teacher alike during the coming week—for it was Saturday—when Helen, good girl, whispered to me, "Don't you think we had better get on, Miss Pearson, it must be nearly twelve." "Twelve!" I exclaimed, "why no!" But my watch said ten minutes to twelve, and I did not know how far we were from Magnolia House, where dinner was always on the table punctually at noon.

The word to re-form was therefore passed, but the procession was broken at frequent intervals by one or another of the dear children running back with the choice of her posy for my acceptance; and dear little Emmie, with a colour like a rose, eyes like diamonds, and curls in "most admired confusion," begged to be allowed to walk by my side the rest of the way. At the end of the lane the canal came into view. Not one of your triumphs of engineering, all stone and locks and works, but a broad, placid, deep stream, up and down which only barges and canal boats, drawn by horses and a tow-rope, ever travelled. Its margin was fringed with flowers, chiefly the lovely blue forget-me-not; and the water-vale plunged into its depths, as the whole twenty-three of us ran lightly down the bank that bordered the towing-path, both a little muddy.

SARAH ANNE CURZON

"O!" "O!" "O!" "O!" burst from every throat as the gems of the British flora caught the eye of my happy girls, and there was another stop. "O! *pray do* let us get a few, Miss Pearson, and we will take home a lovely bouquet of them for poor Miss Rose, and another for Mrs. Rhys." "Oh, yeth, pleathe do!" cried pet Emmie at my side.

"Well, young ladies"—"girls" was a word tabooed in the parlours of Magnolia House—"Well, young ladies, we are late for dinner already, I fear, but if you will just get two or three each as quickly as possible and then step home as fast as may be, I will give you leave; but I am afraid you are getting me into trouble."

That I was getting *them* into trouble never occurred to me.

Ten minutes later a crowd of happy girls, with rosy cheeks, bright eyes, tossed hair, dirty boots, and sad to relate, in many instances, mud-besprent frocks, filed into the front hall of Magnolia House, to encounter a very Cerberus in Jane, the housekeeper, who stood at the dining-room door, waiting.

Thinking no harm, I laid a posy on her folded hands saying, "There, Jane! that's for you, isn't it sweet?" "Dinner's bin on table this half an hour," she replied with an ineffable scorn of me and my pretensions as a teacher in a well-regulated ladies' school.

Running up stairs to my den of a room I threw my bonnet and cape on my bed, washed my hands, patted my hair smooth, and ran down again to the dining room. The girls were nearly all there, and all looked uncomfortable. Innocent I could not understand it, for a prettier crowd one seldom sees, the alchemy of fresh air, sunshine, and natural exercise had done so much for them. Mrs. Rhys was at the head of the table as usual, and a junior teacher, who had not been out, occupied Miss Rose's seat, and looked daggers at me, while Mrs. Rhys did not speak a word. I was puzzled. When the meal was over and grace had been said, Mrs. Rhys ordered "all the young ladies who had been out with Miss Pearson to go to the cloakroom." This was a room where the day-boarders hang their things, and the house-boarders always left their rubbers and clogs. Before I had reached the schoolroom the housemaid brought me a message that Mrs. Rhys desired to see me in the cloakroom, "an' oh! Miss Pearson," she added, "there be sich a rumpus about them dirty boots an' frocks, an' Miss Wilson she's torn hern." And truly there was "a rumpus"! It had never occurred to me before that dirty boots, and frocks that needed brushing or washing were a grave offence; but truly I knew little about boarding schools!

When I entered the cloakroom Mrs. Rhys, a tall, heavy woman of solemn aspect, was standing near the window; before her stood poor little Emmie Jones, her eyes full of tears, a drooping posy in her sash, and a pair of muddy boots in her hand on which Mrs. Rhys was making severe remarks. All the other girls were ranged round the room, holding each her boots for inspection, and on my entrance I was somewhat peremptorily ordered to enter the name of each in my note book and place before it ten bad marks for dirty boots only, and twenty for boots and a soiled dress. Every mark meant ten lines written out ten times, so that the poor girls' punishments were indeed heavy. Then I saw the mischief I had done by thinking more of the demands of my poor girls' hearts and souls than of boarding-school regulations.

I grew hot and indignant. I tried to remonstrate, but Mrs. Rhys would not allow me to speak. "What you may have to say, Miss Pearson, I will listen to in the blue parlour presently."

Two or three sobs among the smaller girls almost broke me down, and at last I could bear it no longer, and facing Mrs. Rhys, my notebook behind my back, I said: "I beg your pardon, Mrs. Rhys, but if there is anyone to blame for muddy boots and soiled frocks it is me; I gave the young ladies leave to gather flowers, and to run about in the lane. No one was hurt or annoyed, and I thought only of the young ladies' happiness and refreshment. I am sorry I did not know your rules better, but I beg you will allow me to

SARAH ANNE CURZON

apologize for such as I have broken, and to take such punishment as you may see fit to inflict, letting the young ladies go free."

A scoffing laugh greeted my proposition. Not one word did the woman deign in reply, but turning to Helen Tudor she said: "*You*, Miss Tudor, will see that the frocks are brushed clean before any of you leave this room. Miss Pearson will retire."

I retired. When I reached my room my pretty flowers had been put into water, and set in my window. A bunch of clover pinks out of the kitchen garden stood upon my dressing table, and my dirty boots were nowhere to be seen. In these pretty attentions I recognized the hand of Eliza the kind-hearted housemaid whose sympathy was not with her employer, evidently.

Saturday afternoons were always devoted to the bath, the hairdresser, and stocking-darning, the girls always doing this latter for themselves under the superintendence of Miss Rose. One by one the poor children came straggling into the schoolroom bearing each her usual complement of stocking; Amy Wilson with the addition of her torn frock. I took it from her to mend myself; but somebody was sharp, and I was sent for to the music-room to select some "pieces" and attend to other matters. I was very anxious lest the poor girls should not do their tasks properly and I should be called upon to inflict further impositions. Tea-time, however, reassured me, no word of fault-finding broke the peace and I concluded wise Helen Tudor had used her influence with the restive. Glowering looks bent upon me by the head of the table, and supercilious ones from the junior teacher made the hour unhappy, yet the weight of their disgrace no longer seemed to burden the girls, and before bed-time most of the impositions were placed in my hands ready for Monday morning.

At nine o'clock each night lights were out in all the bedrooms, and the teachers and two or three of the elder girls—parlour-boarders—were expected to spend the rest of the evening, that is until the great clock in the hall struck ten, with Mrs. Rhys in the blue parlour, where we sang, or played simple games. Thither, therefore, I went, not intending by any means to play the culprit, but I was "sent to Coventry" very decidedly. That was to be my punishment in part, but I bore it good-humouredly as if I expected it, and made my profoundest courtesy to Mrs. Rhys on leaving the room and I saw the lady blush.

Sunday passed in the usual duties of church-going and Bible study. I wished to spend an hour with poor Miss Rose, but she excused herself "with her love." Something unusual was afloat; I could feel that; so I spent the evening with myself in my room. Lights, however, were scarcely out when there was a gentle tap at my door, and Helen Tudor crept in.

"Do you know what all the fuss is about, Miss Pearson? Miss De Retske's maid saw us coming in yesterday, and told her mistress that such a lot of hoydens as Mrs. Rhys' young ladies were, running through the streets as if lions were after them, she never did see, and Miss De Retske sent one of the teachers over to ask if anything had happened to Mrs. Rhys' young ladies while they were out on Saturday, and how sorry she was."

Miss De Retske kept the very highest-toned establishment for young ladies within fifty miles. Fancy the blackness of my sin!

While I was dressing on Monday morning a paper was pushed under my door. It proved to be a round-robin. Within a circle in the centre was written:

Dear
Miss Pear-
son, Never Mind;
We all Love
You.

Twenty-two names between rays neatly ruled out surrounded the document. What could it mean? But how happy it made me! Twenty-two young loves! Who can deserve such a treasure?

238   SARAH ANNE CURZON

Very expectant eyes were mine at the breakfast table, and if ever eyes looked love to eyes again, ours did.

By the side of my plate lay another paper, a note. I begged pardon and opened it: it was my dismissal from Magnolia House, on the ground of incapability and insubordination. I certainly was surprised; never having dreamed what, to me, appeared so slight a matter, should be taken so seriously; evidently the De Retske poison was working. But I had my innings. The dismissal was not in the form of a notice, but absolute, yet I felt morally certain that I was expected to stay until the end of the quarter. I did nothing of the kind, but ate my dinner with my mother and sister at home that evening.

↶

The Week (12 May 1896), 688–690.

Joanna E. Wood (1867–1927)

A MOTHER (1896)

Joanna Wood's powerful and sometimes lurid fiction brought her some attention in American and Canadian literary reviews in the 1890s—a taste of fame that gave way to years of obscurity at the end of her career.

Joanna Ellen Wood was born in Lesmahagow, Lanarkshire, Scotland, the youngest of six surviving children of Agnes Todd and Robert Wood. When she was a small child, her family emigrated to a farm in the Queenston Heights (Niagara) area of southern Ontario, a setting readily recognizable in this story. Joanna was educated at St. Catharines Collegiate Institute, and went to New York in the late 1880s, where her brother was a successful insurance executive. Wood's early publications appeared in American periodicals. Her pseudonyms included "Jean d'Arc," and she won several short story contests.

According to Carole Gerson, Wood mastered a variety of forms of popular fiction, but she seems to have had an affinity for grim, rural stories of iron-willed and unfortunate women, particularly mothers. There is a strong naturalistic strain in her work, which displays something of the cynicism of Maupassant, or the brooding sense of sin in Hawthorne. Her first novel, *The Untempered Wind* (1894), tells the story of the persecution and endurance of a single mother in a harsh and censorious small town. As in "The Mother," maternal feeling is powerful but it is accompanied by the death of the child. Wood's unsympathetic portrayal of conventional religion is found in both story and novel. Her second novel, *Judith Moore, or, Fashioning a Pipe* (1898), is, by contrast, a romance that employs the figure of the woman artist who intrigued nineteenth-century female writers, perhaps as an alter ego. Here Judith Moore leaves her opera career for a happy marriage with her northern lover. Wood's melodramatic third novel, *A Daughter of*

Witches, was serialized in *Canadian Magazine*, a measure of her success. Another novel is *Farden Ha'* (1902), a tragic romance set in a Scotland full of doom and portent.

According to Carrie MacMillan, Wood's success in the 1890s enabled her to travel extensively. Her publicity photographs, for example in Morgan's *Types of Canadian Women* (1909), show a handsome, dramatic and flamboyantly dressed woman. Her cosmopolitan lifestyle included presentation at court and an acquaintanceship with Swinburne, a lock of whose hair, pressed in a gold locket, was found among her effects after her death. Wood's interest in the dark side of life and in sensuality was perhaps another token from Swinburne. By 1910, Wood's career had faltered and she had settled with her widowed mother in Niagara-on-the-Lake, where she became friendly with historian Janet Carnochan and gave occasional lectures on her travels and the like. The last years of her life were spent living with siblings in New York and Detroit, where she died on 1 May 1927. Her obituary in the *Niagara Falls Review* spoke of a nervous breakdown, which had added to the obscurity of this intense woman writer.

"The Mother" shows Joanna Wood's grimly ironic use of natural beauty to counterpoint fruitless maternal devotion. Another story, "Malhalla's Revenge," presents a paralysed old woman who lives on for decades to spite her farmer husband and his mistress/housekeeper; as is the case in "The Mother," all the characters are grotesque. In "The Mother," the border setting of what is probably the Niagara River enables Wood to introduce the theme of the smuggling of illegal Chinese immigrants into the United States to serve as exploited labour, a practice prevalent at the period.

☙

Suggested Reading:
Gerson, Carole. "Joanna E. Wood." In *Dictionary of Literary Biography*, vol. 92, 388–390.

MacMillan, Carrie. "Incendiary Women: The Novels of
    Joanna E. Wood." In *Silenced Sextet*, ed. Lorraine
    McMullen. Montreal: McGill-Queen's University
    Press, 1993.
Wood, Joanna. *A Daughter of Witches*. Toronto: Gage, 1900.
_____. "Malhalla's Revenge." In *New England
    Magazine* 18 (April 1895), 184–187.
_____. *The Untempered Wind*. New York: Tait, 1894.

A Mother

Joanna E. Wood

"For scarcely for a righteous man will one die; yet peradventure for a good man some would even dare to die.—Holy Writ.

She lived in a country village, on a river between Canada and the United States. She was unlovely of feature, rubicund of visage, blind of one eye, and lame. Her ordinary attire was a 'Dutch blue' print dress and a checked gingham apron, one corner of which was usually tucked up diagonally in its belt.

She was a washerwoman—and had the pleasing task of supporting a drunken husband and an equally worthless son. The latter was handsome and useless, his character being a bad combination the ingredients of which were dare devil-try, moral weakness, indolence and conceit.

He had been in gaol many times, and at each trial, his mother, her thin lips quivering piteously, her face crimsoned and shining from many tears, her one eye bloodshot and swollen, her toil-stiffened old hands clasping and unclasping nervously, her bonnet perched on the very back of her head and holding on precariously by its stringy ribbons, had plead for him—and to such purpose that his sentences were always light. But each time her task was harder—judge and jury sterner. Nevertheless, she always found some extenuating circumstance for him.

"He was just up to it for fun, being full of the divil," or "He was that reckless! he'd no thought of harm, poor lad," or, darkly, "There was others had a bigger hand in them doin's than poor Bob"—and if all these excuses were untenable, then, simply and unanswerably, "The drink was in him."

She was pious enough in her own way, and thanked God familiarly and sociably for any extra washing or a windfall of old clothes. But she was not right in her theology; she inclined too much to the "doctrine of works." This beam in the spiritual eye led her to regard Mrs. Bethney, who, to say the truth, did not trouble much about her soul, as a far better christian than Mrs. Ward, for the former bestowed upon Mrs. Reddy many a bundle of half-worn clothes, whilst the latter never gave her anything but two tracts, one entitled "The Sins of Luxury," and the other "The Perils of Wealth."

Mrs. Reddy had once, in the far-off days of her youth, separated from her now by oceans of soap suds, lived in her own house and helped to till her own little farm. But with the death of her first husband she had fallen upon evil days, and when she married her second husband, tall, good-looking, and "in the millingtary," she effectually shut herself out from the places of Hope. Yet she went withal cheerily on her way. But, as time after time, Bob was mixed up with disgraceful affairs, or escaped the effects of some mad escapade narrowly, "as by the skin of his teeth," her smiles grew fewer and her gossip less light-hearted.

She was day after day oppressed by an increasing nervousness. There were strange whisperings hissing about the village. She acquired the habit of suddenly arresting herself in the midst of work or speech to listen apprehensively—for what? She did not know.

Mysterious waggons came to the sheds of the one hotel, canvas-covered waggons such as those from which rural butchers peddle their meat. Their tired horses certainly had need of refreshment, but rumor had it that the hotel keeper took out tea and bread and boiled rice in covered baskets to his barn. Now, surely the horses did not eat this? The horses and waggons always went away after nightfall, and long ere dawn noiseless boats stole out from the silent shore of the boundary river.

At this time, too, Bob Reddy had money and to spare. He tippled continuously, and treated the village loafers to many a keg of smuggled beer. He swaggered about, singing derisively, and with idle hands jingled the money in his pockets. At last people began to say that at this point Chinamen were being smuggled across the river into Uncle Sam's domains, and when the villagers and farmers spoke of this they added with a significant *addendum* of nods that the hotel man and Bob Reddy "knew more'n they'd tell about this Chinee business——"

So matters stood one bitter night in earliest spring, when the river's swift current bore an unruly burden of broken ice from the great lakes. Mrs. Reddy had early retired to rest—she had been washing all day, the cold was intense, and she had no fire. Her husband snored in a drunken sleep before the kitchen fire. The air was full of the mysterious complaints and murmurs which the night evokes from an old house. Bob was abroad.

A loud knock echoed from the door. She gave a sigh of relief. "Bob," she said to herself, so she called without stirring:

"What is it? Come in, Bob."

"Is Bob in, Mrs. Reddy?" asked the voice of the village constable.

"No," she answered. For Heaven's sake, what do you want him for?"

"Do you know where he is?" asked the man outside.

"No; I've no notion at all," she said, hopelessly.

"Are you sure?"

"Yes, sir, I'm quite sure. No good ever came o'lying. What's he 'cused of now?"

But the man outside moved away. Another man's voice came to her faintly. There were two of them evidently. Then she heard their voices clearly. They had stepped to the lea of the house, and directly outside her window paused to arrange their route.

JOANNA E. WOOD

"Well—where is he then?" said the constable's voice, irascibly.

"I'm tellin' ye as fast's I kin," said the other, doggedly. "I knowed it were no use comin' here; he's down in the 'cave' at the fishin' machine, and he's settin' em up for the boys like a new elected council man."

"Well, I suppose we'll have to go by the river edge. They'd see the light."

"Supposin' they do? The path is covered in ice. It would be crazy for a sober man to try it to-night. I'll be bound they're too full by this time to notice half-a-dozen lights, let alone one. Gosh! How bitter, bitin' cold it is."

"Well, come on. You're going to get a square half of the reward, so you needn't kick. This Chinee business—"

Their steps crunched off on the frozen snow; their voices failed in the distance. She heard no more, but it was enough. All the holy mother instinct, so divine in its self-abnegation, so unerring in its divination, was alive in her. She rose, and taking by habit her old silk bonnet, tied it on. Her apron she assumed instinctively. It is the washer-woman's insignia. Her other clothes she had not removed. It is truly deplorable that the poor continue to prefer heat to hygiene.

She opened the door and went out.

She heeded neither the cold, which was paralyzing, nor the wind, whose breath congealed her own. The atmosphere was rarefied by the intense frost, her quivering lips parted with each inhalation, but she heeded not.

She had but one thought. If she could go diagonally up through the cedars, then down the cliff path, she could warn Bob before the constable and the informer could reach the cave by the more circuitous river path.

She toiled up the steep ascent and her thoughts fled before her. Already she had warned Bob; they had retraced their steps up the cliff together to the road; he had kissed her, called her a 'brave old gal,' damned himself for a brute and a beast (as he did after each of his trials) and started upon his six miles walk to the town, from whence, in early morning, he could conveniently cross the river and be safe with hospitable Uncle Sam.

"If he dassn't come back I'll mend up his cloes and Jim Baine will take 'em to him. He's owin' me, Jim Baine is, for tendin' Kit when she was took. Bob'll soon git work—a likely young fellar like him—poor Bob."

She fell.

The hill was a mass of ice, and she was not certain where the descent of the cliff path began. She rose and struggled on, and presently she found she had gone too far up the road. She turned with nervous haste and once more fell. She hit her head this time, and cut it, and though she knew it not was some time in rising.

But she struggled up again. Her hands instinctively tucked up the corner of her apron in its belt; it was thus she girded her loins to attack a hard day's work. Once more she started on her search for the leaning tree, which marked the beginning of the descent. A rain, colder than snow, keener than frost, was falling, and was being instantly converted into a sheathing of ice upon everything. She was growing confused, uncertain, when she fell again.

"I must have a pane of glass put in that window," she murmured, "there's a draught— — —poor Bob."

The rain still continued, congealing as it fell. The wind still blew, freezing with its breath. But she did not rise.

෴

Some hundreds of feet below, a choice selection of boon companions were enjoying beer and tobacco. The beer had been put on tap by Bob Reddy, and he was the hero of the hour.

The banqueting place was unique and warm. In the bank of the river was a deep cleft, widening into a narrow ravine at the summit, narrowing to an angle of a few feet at the base, extending between rocky walls into the bank. Some genius had put a plank flooring from side to side, and roofed it with logs covered with fir branches and sods. The result was a long cavern-like room, wider at the roof than at the floor, with no windows, and closed by one heavy door. It was completely sheltered from storms, and had witnessed many a drunken orgie.

Upon this occasion it was illumined by many lanterns, whose lights strove with the tobacco smoke. The men were seated on empty boxes or short segments of tree trunks. Bob Reddy astride of the cask was a beery Bacchus. The men were talking loudly and boastfully. Vulgar and brutal egotism paraded, naked and not ashamed.

One of them stepped to the door to see what manner of atmospheric visitor it was. A gleam of light, thrown on the river from the shore, caught his eyes. He called the attention of the others to it. They elbowed each other about the door, watching it with interest; now it glowed broadly on the water, then shaded off to an uncertain glimmer again. It drew nearer, nearer. Presently they heard a well known voice shout,

"Which of these two turns do we take?"

All, or nearly all, the men in the cave knew from personal experience the unpleasant authority behind that voice. Each asked of himself, "Is the summons for me?" But as they had given Bob Reddy the chief seat in their synagogue all evening, they felt the ingratitude of depriving him of the leading role now. With one accord they rushed to the barrel of beer, and secreted it in a place cunningly contrived beneath the flooring; then they turned to Bob.

"He's after you," said one, and the rest assented with superfluous oaths.

"Then I'll git out," said Bob, with drunken nonchalance.

"Which way kin ye slope? Its a pity the cables is no use."

"Who says they're no good?" demanded Bob surlily. "Yez all know I can cross them if I want to."

"Git out! Not in this weather," said the man who had first seen the light. "Try the cliff."

"I'm goin' by the cables," said Bob, with emphasis, "and I'm goin' now."

The men looked at each other. The light, wavering upon the water in consonance with the winding of the path, drew even nearer. They were anxious to be rid of Reddy, who was muddled with drink and decidedly indifferent as to whether he fell or not.

So with an unsteady gait Bob Reddy went along the fifty feet up the river bank to where, from low stone piers, the old cables of the blown-down suspension bridge swayed in the wind. Stretching, like filaments in the gigantic spider's web, across the river to the United States, they were lost to the eye in the night's dusky distance ere half their length.

As he went those fifty paces the keen air brought back all his bravado. "Not cross!" he muttered to himself, "I've crawled across afore now, and I'll just show them fellars what I *kin* do."——

He seized the cable with his hands—and hand over hand made his way along the few feet they stretched over *terra firma*. It was the madness of a drunken brain. As soon as his feet dangled clear of the bank he realized his madness, but did not turn back. He thought only of the terrible gulf before, and beneath him; he forgot the short return journey to safety. Hand over hand he went, already he could feel the cable oscillate as his hands clutched it.

Hand over hand—away from the over-hanging branches of the trees. The rain had coated the cable with ice. It was now a question of seconds.

At that moment, the moon, obscured before by rain and wind clouds, shone out effulgently. It showed alike to the watchers at the mouth of the "cave" and to the two men creeping up the uncertain pathway, a black figure, clutching in desperate silence, hand over hand at the icy cable. A shout of horror and of warning broke from the men. At that moment the figure shot downward. It struck the water flat, and for an appreciable instant floated stationary in the hopeless outspread fashion of a fly when it falls into boiling liquid. The next moment the current had it—and the moon was hid.

Next morning the sun rose serenely to smile upon the awakened world. It shone upon the village roof trees, upon the river hurrying by with its burden of ice, on the great boulders beside the river path, on the old cables athwart the water. It shone far up the hill on the leaning tree which marks the descent of the cliff path and upon a grotesque heap at the tree's foot. The heap was awkward, stiff, coated with ice. From it there protruded a frozen corner of blue gingham, and upon this perch a snow bird sat singing—revelling in the sunshine, its throat feathers ruffled as its crystal flutings floated out upon the still morning air. And the same sun which shone on the grotesque heap at the tree's foot and waked the snow birds joyous thrilling, shone also far down the river, where the silent grey gulls, wheeled in ever varying circles above a black *something* caught in the embrance of the current and the ice, and hurrying with them to the wider waters and oblivion.

∽

Canadian Magazine 7 (October 1896), 558–561.

Margaret Marshall Saunders (1861–1947)

POOR JERSEY CITY (1896)

Marshall Saunders became famous with her best-selling
story *Beautiful Joe* (1893), and in her life and writings gave
much time to nurturing animals and fighting for their
rights. Animal stories like *Beautiful Joe* and Anna Sewell's
American classic *Black Beauty* (1877) were in vogue at the
turn of the century in tandem with a growing public interest
in the issues of conservation and animal rights—issues
reflected in the work of writers like Saunders and Adeline
Teskey. The work of such Canadian women writers tended
to show more anthropomorphism and overt didacticism
than the Darwinian animal stories of their male contemporaries such as Charles G.D. Roberts and Ernest Thompson
Seton. Saunders in particular addressed primarily juvenile
readers, with works calculated to arouse sympathy for animals at the mercy of the human world, and reached a large
audience for much of her career.

Margaret Marshall Saunders was born in Milton,
Nova Scotia, one of seven children of the Baptist clergyman
Edward Manning and Maria Freeman. In 1867 the family
moved to Halifax, where the Saunders were active in social
causes amid urban problems of the port city. Maggie
Saunders studied with her father, and soon preferred Latin
to sewing. Animals were already part of her world in this
close-knit family, and she had various pets. At fifteen, she
spent a year at a girls' school in Edinburgh and then learned
French in Orléans—an experience plagued by homesickness,
especially for her mother. The study abroad later prompted
her favourite novel, *Esther de Warren: The Story of a Mid-
Victorian Maiden* (1927).

Upon her return to Halifax in 1878, Saunders
taught for several years, but found her métier in writing.
Her romantic first novel, *My Spanish Sailor* (1889), was soon
overshadowed by the phenomenally successful *Beautiful Joe*

(1893). Modelled on the story of a friend's dog that was maltreated as a puppy, the novel won a $200 prize from the American Humane Society. Henceforth many of Saunders's publications and much of her time were devoted to animal and child welfare causes, and she was as known for her menageries of pets—particularly dogs and birds. She described her Halifax aviary in *My Pets: Real Happenings in My Aviary* (1908). In 1895, she moved to Boston for two years, then to California for another two years, travelling widely the while. With her sister and companion, Grace, she spent the last three decades of her life in Toronto, giving lecture tours and talks on her animals and her career, before being restricted by age and financial problems. She died in Toronto on 15 February 1947. While Saunders is now known only for *Beautiful Joe*, some of her other novels, such as the Acadian romance *Rose à Charlitte* (1898) and *The Girl From Vermont* (1910), are of interest.

"Poor Jersey City" is found in a volume of juvenile stories, *For the Other Boy's Sake, and Other Stories*, published in 1896, which was designed by its publisher to capitalize on the success of *Beautiful Joe* three years earlier. "Poor Jersey City," with its two whimsical animal characters, the runaway circus dog of the title and the cow Mooley, has a charm which encloses its indictment of the treatment of animals by circuses. The story is designed to interest and affect children. The Nova Scotian setting is sparely but effectively presented, and Jersey City the dog not only finds a haven himself but learns to respect other creatures—notably Mooley the cow. Jersey City initially approaches Mooley the Nova Scotian in a slick and cynical fashion, much like his famous human forebearer, Thomas Haliburton's Sam Slick. Like Bliss Carman, another literary Maritimer famous at that day for his "Vagabondia" poems, the two animals discuss Bohemia. Other stories in the Saunders volume deal with the degradation of native life by contact with white society ("The Two Kaloosas") and with children's need for both positive nurturing and sound character development. Like L.M. Montgomery and Nellie McClung a decade later, Saunders was an important source of values for young Canadians.

ᔕ

Suggested Reading:

Conrad, Margaret, Toni Laidlaw and Donna Smyth, eds. *No Place Like Home: Diaries and Letters of Nova Scotia Women, 1771–1938*. Halifax: Formac, 1988.

Gerson, Carole. "Margaret Marshall Saunders." In *Dictionary of Literary Biography*, vol. 92, 327–330.

McMullen, Lorraine. "Marshall Saunders' mid-Victorian Cinderella; or, the mating game in Victorian Scotland." In *Canadian Children's Literature* 34 (1984), 31–40.

Saunders, Marshall. *Beautiful Joe: The Autobiography of a Dog*. Philadelphia: Banes, 1893.

Waterston, Elizabeth. "Saunders, Margaret Marshall: A Voice for the Silent." In *Silenced Sextet*. Montreal: McGill-Queen's University Press, 1993.

POOR JERSEY CITY

Margaret Marshall Saunders

Near the city of Halifax, Nova Scotia, is a beautiful place called Prince's Lodge; so named because the father of Queen Victoria of England once had a country house there. The house is in ruins now and the garden has grown wild, but the old road still winds up from the city past the quiet spot and leads on to the town of Bedford, situated at the head of the Basin—the sheet of water on the shores of which the house was built.

Walking along this road one hot day a few summers ago was a waggish-looking dog of the breed known as bull terrier. He was going slowly and he acted as if he was very tired. Presently with a heavy sigh he dropped down on a patch of grass under some spreading trees.

A red cow, munching clover on the opposite side of the road, lifted her head and looked fixedly at him.

"How do you do, madame?" he said.

The cow said nothing but continued to stare at him.

"In my country we speak when we are spoken to," said the dog wearily yet mischievously.

The cow switched her tail and lowered her head still more.

"A cow that shakes her tail when there aren't any flies on her and a horse that shakes his when you touch him with the whip, are two things that I haven't much use for," said the dog with a curl of his lip. "But don't distress yourself, madame, I have no intention of running at you. Lie down and have a talk with me; I am dying to hear the sound of my own voice."

The red cow scanned him all over for the space of a few minutes, then she doubled her legs under her and began to chew her cud.

"You have beautiful eyes, madame," said the dog politely. "I wish I had such eyes, they would have made my fortune."

"Who are you?" asked the cow.

The dog threw back his head and laughed. "You Nova Scotian animals beat everything—so English, you know—you never enter into conversation with strangers till you learn their whole pedigree. What would you suppose had been my business, madame, to look at me?"

"You are not a tramp dog," said the cow, "because you have on a silver collar."

"Well put, madame; but I may cheat you yet in spite of that silver collar. Don't put too much faith in a bit of metal."

"Have you run away from home?" inquired the cow with some curiosity.

"I have never had a home, madame."

The cow forgot to chew her cud and let her lower jaw hang down as she stared at him.

"Shut your mouth, madame, you don't look pretty with it open," said the dog slyly.

"You have not told me what your business is," replied the cow in some vexation.

Without speaking the weary dog rose from the grass and proceeded to stand on his head, dance on his hind legs, turn somersaults, and perform a number of other curious tricks.

Half in fear and half in astonishment the cow stumbled to her legs and watched him from behind the tree.

"Frightened, madame?" said the dog throwing himself again on the grass and bursting into laughter. "Why you could kill me with one of those horns of yours. I suppose you have never seen an exhibition of this kind before. I'll give you lots of them, for love too—no tickets required—if you'll do me the trifling favor of telling me of a quiet place where I can spend a few days."

The cow would not come out from behind the tree. "Who are you?" she said shortly.

"Oh, I'm a clown dog in a show," said the terrier impatiently. "Bankston & Sons' Great Traveling Exhibition of Trained Animals—have you never heard of them? They're in Halifax now and I've cut them."

"Cut them," repeated the cow slowly.

"Yes; got tired of them, bored to death—run away, skedaddled."

"And are you not going back?"

"No, madame, I am not."

"What is to become of you?"

"I don't know and don't care as long as I never see that old show again."

"I have never met any animals like you," said the cow nervously; "I think I will go home."

The dog got up and made her a low bow. "Thank you, madame; my originality has always been my drawing card, and your suspicions do you credit. You are exactly like all the other cows that I have met. Permit me to say that the slightest taint of Bohemianism would spoil you."

"What is Bohemianism?" asked the cow with some curiosity.

The dog smiled. "Bohemianism—what is it? I don't know. Taking no thought for the morrow will perhaps best express it to you."

"I don't like the sound of it," said the cow.

"I dare say not, madame. You probably like to look ahead and think of your comfortable stall and good food and pleasant home, don't you?"

"Yes," said the cow.

"You would not like to live on the road as I am doing, not knowing what minute you may be pounced upon and run back to town and——"

"Well," said the cow, "what were you going to say?"

Margaret Marshall Saunders

"I was about to tell you what would happen to me if I am caught."

"What would happen?"

"Did you ever go to a circus, madame?"

"No."

"Or to any kind of a performance where animals were made to do tricks?"

"I have seen animals in cages going by on the trains."

"And they looked happy, didn't they?"

The cow shuddered. "Oh no, no; there was a dreadful look in their eyes."

"But you should see them on the stage," said the dog ironically. "A goat rolling a barrel is a charming sight, and a pig wheeling a barrow is another. The people scream with delight at dancing monkeys and leaping dogs. I guess if they knew——"

"Knew what?"

"Knew everything," exclaimed the dog bitterly, as he paced back and forth on a narrow strip of grass. "The public see the sugar—an animal gets through a pretty trick and he runs to his trainer for a lump. They don't notice the long whip in the background. I tell you I have felt that whip many a time, and I am accounted a smart dog."

"I hate to be run along the road, or have boys throw stones at me," said the cow mildly. "It makes me feel bad and poisons my milk."

"I never heard of a cow doing tricks," said the dog, stopping in his walk—, "by-the-way, what's your name?"

"Mooley."

"Mooley, is it? And mine is "Jersey City." Jersey City, the clown dog in Bankston & Sons' Big Show, and in just about one hour you'll see Bankston's trainer on his bicycle spinning around the curve in this road looking for me."

"How do you know that?" asked the cow.

"Well, you see I ran away this morning. There aren't many ways to leave the city down yonder. Old Jimson will know that I have too much sense to jump into the Atlantic Ocean. I wouldn't be likely to cross the harbor in a ferry boat. He'll guess that I've taken this road along which we came in the train, so that I can make for Boston."

"Do you belong to Boston?"

"No, I don't belong anywhere. I wasn't stolen from a lovely home like the dogs in the story books. I was born and brought up in the show; but I'm tired and sick of it now, and my bones ache, and I'd rather die than go back. Good-bye, I'll just crawl off here in the woods till I feel like looking for something to eat. You'll not say anything about having seen me?"

"No, I will not," said the cow slowly. "I'm sorry for you, and I'll do what I can to help you. If you will follow me, I'll show you an old fox hole where you can hide till dark. Then if you will come up to my stable I'll put you in the way of getting something to eat."

"Thank you," said the dog gruffly. Then he muttered under his breath, "I wasn't such a fool after all to trust the old softie. She'll not give me away," and he walked painfully after her up a green and shady path leading to a thick wood.

∽

"I never felt such a good bed in my life," murmured Jersey City rapturously.

It was one week later and in the middle of a hot July day. He lay stretched out on a patch of thick fern moss. Above him on a bank grew lovely purple violets and the trailing green linnæa studded with pink bells. The air was full of the delicate perfume of the flowers, and the sunlight filtering through the treetops lay in wavering patches on the moss, the flowers, and Jersey City's dark body.

"You look like a happy dog," said the cow, who had just come walking up a path and stood knee deep in ferns.

"I am happy, thanks to you, Mooley," said Jersey City. "I never had such a good time in my life. Oh, this is delicious," and he buried his muzzle in the moss.

The cow surveyed him in placid satisfaction. "Why do you not stay here instead of going to Boston, as you plan to do?"

"Well, you see, Mooley, I am a marked character here. As soon as I show myself I'll be spotted. You've lots of English bull terriers about here, but not any like me. I'm what is called a Boston terrier, and I'd better get back to the place where I can mingle with a number of other dogs resembling myself."

"The search is over now," said Mooley kindly. "A milkman's cow who was driven out from the city yesterday, told me that Bankston & Sons' Big Show had gone away. I don't think that you are in any danger."

"Perhaps not," said Jersey City thoughtfully, "and I don't know how to leave this lovely place. Oh, Mooley, what a change for a weary dog from the heat and noise and dust of theatres and halls and railway trains. I should like to stay here forever."

"Do you not get lonely?" asked Mooley.

Jersey hesitated an instant. "You have been very good to me, Mooley, and I hope you won't think me ungrateful if I say I could stay in this wood forever if I only had one thing."

"What is that?" inquired the cow.

"Some human being to be with me."

"I understand that," said Mooley.

"You see," went on the dog, "we four-legged animals were made to serve the two-legged ones, and we can't be happy without them. I am ashamed to say that tears come in my eyes when I think of cross old Jimson, and the Bankstons, who weren't much better. It is such a bitter feeling not to be with the people who have had me since I was a little puppy, that sometimes I feel as if I must run back to them."

"Don't you do it," said the cow hastily.

"No, I won't; I just think what a whipping I should get, and that stops my paws when I want to run."

"You have never told me what your life was like," said Mooley, lying down near him and drawing some of the ferns into her mouth.

"In season time—that is when we were traveling—it was the train nearly all day, and performances nearly every night. You see it is an enormous expense to take car loads of animals from one city to another, and it must be done as quickly as possible. How my legs used to pain me from standing all day, for the dog car was usually so crowded that we could not lie down. Then as soon as we arrived in a town we were herded together like sheep, and the trainer drove us to the place where we were to give our performance. We waited our turns to go on the stage. I always wore a Toby collar made of deep lace, and my role was to make people laugh."

"To make them laugh," said the cow. "I don't understand."

"I was like the clown in a circus. Whenever an animal did a smart trick I had to follow him and turn a somersault, or fail in some way in trying to do it, though I knew well how it should be done. Then I faced the audience and laughed like this," and Jersey City, turning back his lips, grinned dismally at the cow.

"I don't see anything funny in that," said Mooley.

"The people used to," said Jersey City dryly. "They would go off in roars of laughter; and often I would listen to them with a sore heart. I'm very fond of human beings, but I don't altogether understand them. They cry about things that you'd think they'd laugh about, and they laugh about things that you'd think they would cry about. Now I never used to see anything in our cage trick but a cruel trap."

"What is a cage trick?" asked Mooley.

"There's a big revolving thing in the middle of the stage, and dogs climb up on it and hang by their paws—then it is whirled round. I have seen little dogs clinging to the top with a look of mortal terror on their faces, for they knew if they were to fall they would break their legs—and yet the people laughed. Only occasionally a little child would cry."

"I wonder how the men and women would feel if they were hanging there?" said Mooley half angrily.

"Yes, I wonder; if any one asked me to go to see men and women and children running about on their hands and feet, I'd say 'What a silly performance; they weren't made to go in that way,' and yet they flock to see us going on two legs, which is just as unnatural."

"Perhaps they don't think," said Mooley.

"Perhaps so," said Jersey City. "There is one thing that they do think of, and that is having a good time and making money. That's what most human beings live for, Mooley."

"My mistress doesn't," said Mooley.

"By the way, who is your mistress?" asked the dog.

"A poor old widow who lives here. She is such a good woman and she takes fine care of me. I wish you would come and live with her."

"I wish I could," said Jersey City wistfully. "Do you think she would take me in?"

"She is kind to everything that is in trouble," said Mooley. "I know that she would let you lie by the fire when the cold weather comes."

"This is a very retired place," said Jersey City; "that is, there aren't many people about."

"There are only two houses near here besides the Widow May's," said the cow; "then three miles away is the village."

"That will just suit me for a while," said Jersey City. "I can't bear to leave this lovely place; and I don't believe that these families have heard that there is a reward offered for me."

Mooley chuckled quietly.

"What are you laughing at?" the dog asked.

"Let me ask you a question in my turn," said the cow; "why did you trust me with your story that day on the road?"

Jersey City hesitated for a short time.

"Come, now, tell the truth," said the cow.

"Well, Mooley, I thought you looked honest."

"And stupid," added the cow. "I know you did; but you clever traveled animals must remember that the stay-at-home ones aren't always so stupid as they seem. I did you a good turn that day; for as soon as I brought you to this wood I returned to the village. I knew that the man looking for you would stop there."

"And did he?" asked Jersey City breathlessly.

"Yes, he asked at the post office about you. Nobody paid much attention to him; then he tacked a piece of paper on a tree and jumped on his bicycle and rode away."

"That was Jimson," said Jersey City bitterly.

"What do you think I did to the paper?" asked Mooley.

"I don't know—what did you?"

"Ate it," said the cow, her great brown eyes full of merriment; "tore it in strips from the tree and chewed it finer then my finest cud."

"Mooley," exclaimed Jersey City in delight, "you ought to have been a dog."

"Thank you, my friend, I prefer to remain an animal that cannot be taught tricks. But you must hear the rest of my tale. After I tore down the paper I had to go home, lest the widow should think I had wandered away; but I met my brother, who is an ox and lives farther up the Basin road, and I told him that if he saw any of those bits of paper on trees he was to tear them off. He will pass the word to the other oxen who are in the woods, and I think you need have no fear of remaining here."

Jersey City sprang up and affectionately touched his nose to the cow's head. "You good old Mooley, I shall keep an eye on you as you go to and from your pasture, and if any boys chase you, I will bite their heels."

⌒

Jersey City took the advice of his friend the cow, and one day went to lie under the apple trees in the Widow May's orchard. She saw him there and spoke kindly to him, and the next day he took up a position under the window.

She noticed that he was very thin—for not being used to provide for himself, he had considerable difficulty in finding enough to eat—and preparing a plate of bread and milk she put it on the doorstep.

264   MARGARET MARSHALL SAUNDERS

This he ate with so much gratitude and with such a pleading look in his dark eyes, that the widow invited him into her house, and there by the time autumn came he was snugly and contentedly domiciled.

One day when the first snowflakes of the season were flying through the air, Jersey City sprang up on a chair by the window and looked out.

"I wonder whether Mooley is snug and warm," he said to himself. Then he ran out to the Widow May's small stable.

Yes, Mooley was comfortable for the night, and lay on her bed of straw with a sleepy look in her eyes.

"Where is our mistress, Jersey City?" she asked.

"Gone to the village to buy meal and molasses. She has very little money left," said Jersey City soberly, "and human beings are helpless without that."

Mooley looked uneasily at him. "I hope that she will not have to sell me. If she does, I shall be terribly unhappy and my milk will be spoiled. I wish that her son would send her some more money."

"Her son is a sailor, you told me, didn't you?" said Jersey City.

"Yes; a fine young man. He goes to the West Indies. I hope that his ship is not lost."

"I try to eat as little as I can," said Jersey City, "but this is such a wholesome place that I am hungry all the time."

"You have got quite fat and sleek since you came here," said Mooley, looking at him with satisfaction. "You are the handsomest dog that I ever saw."

"Thank you for the compliment," said Jersey City laughing; "you remember I told you the first time we ever met that you had beautiful eyes."

"You were rather saucy to me that day," said Mooley smiling, "but you were tired and unhappy. You never feel in that way now, do you?"

"Never, except when I am thinking of other dogs."

"What dogs?"

"Why, Bankston's dogs, the ones that were brought up with me. When I am lying by the fire so warm and comfortable they come into my mind, but I try to put them right out, for it seems as if I would go crazy thinking of their doing those dreadful tricks over and over again and being cold at night and half fed."

"Run away to meet the widow," said Mooley; "it is time for her to come and it is getting dark."

Jersey hurried from the stable and down the frozen road. Soon he espied a little bent figure in a black dress, and jumping and springing with delight about her and carrying a fold of her dress in his mouth, he escorted her to the house door.

Half an hour later the Widow May sat down to her scanty tea of bread and molasses. Jersey City lay on a small mat before a wood fire in the kitchen stove and gazed lovingly at her.

Presently there was a knock at the door. Jersey City got up and stood before the widow till he saw one of the neighbors entering, then he slunk behind the chairs in the small bedroom.

"Good evening, Mrs. May," said a young man in a cheery voice, "I've just stepped in to see how you are— what's that, a cat?"

"No, a dog," said Mrs. May, "a poor stray thing that came to me in the summer. I think he must have been stolen from some nice family, for he had on an expensive collar."

"You call him Rover, do you," said the young man absently.

"Yes—come here, good dog," and she rose and went to the door. "I should like you to see him. He is such a handsome dog, but he is shy. He always hides when any one comes, and I can never get him to go to the village with me."

"Does he do any tricks?" asked the young man, with a far-a-way look in his eyes, for he was not thinking of the dog at all, but of a certain newspaper in his pocket.

"No, he is the most stupid dog I ever saw, but he is very loving and I shall never turn him away."

"How long is it since you have heard from your son?" asked the young man suddenly.

MARGARET MARSHALL SAUNDERS

"Three months," said the widow, turning her quiet gray eyes toward him.

"Does he usually go so long without writing," asked the young man.

"Yes, sometimes—not often. Why, have you heard anything about him?"

"It is a dangerous calling to follow the sea," stammered her visitor, "and there are a good many gales in the fall."

"You know something," said the widow, "tell me——"

The young man looked hesitatingly round the kitchen. "It mayn't be true, Mrs. May, but father said I'd best prepare you——" and he pulled the newspaper from his pocket.

"Read it to me," said the widow, "I can't see," and she covered her face with one hand, while the young man hurriedly read a paragraph which reported a vessel called the "Swallow" to have been lost with all her crew.

"But it may be only a rumor," he said comfortingly. "Don't give up hope, Mrs. May."

"No, I won't," she said; "the Lord knows what is best. If he has taken my son from me, I know that I shall soon go to join him."

The young man was misled by her calmness. With an air of great relief he rose. "I am glad to see that you don't take it too hard, Mrs. May. I am going to town, and I'll make inquiries. Mother and Lucy will be over to see you tomorrow. Good-night," and after warmly shaking her hand he left her.

As soon as the door closed behind him, Jersey City left his hiding-place and ran to look anxiously in his mistress' face. He was frightened by what he saw. Better than the young man he could read her expression, and he knew that her heart was breaking. Slowly she went into her little room and lay down on the bed. Hour after hour passed and she did not move. Jersey City sat uneasily watching her.

She had not cleared away the tea dishes and she had forgotten to put out the lamp. It was not like her to waste anything.

After a time he sprang up on the bed. Her face and hands were quite cold, and when he licked them to make them warm she moaned feebly. Jersey City lay down close beside her, so that she would get some warmth from his sleek body.

He did not close his eyes that night, and by the time the morning came he was nearly frantic. The gray streaks of dawn stealing in at the window showed him that his dear mistress was insensible. In vain he tried to rouse her.

"She will die if I do not bring some one to her," he said. "I will go and speak to Mooley."

He could easily unfasten the latch of the back door by pressing his paw upon it, and he hurried out to the stable.

"Mooley," he cried, "the widow is very ill, what shall we do?"

Mooley stumbled to her feet and looked at him uncertainly.

"One of us must go to the neighbors," went on Jersey City.

"What can a cow do?" asked Mooley feebly. "Oh, my poor mistress," and she leaned against the side of her stall.

"You can go to Jones' and stand by their gate and low," said Jersey City. "Then they will know that there is something the matter and will follow you home."

Mooley's legs bent under her, and with a moan she lay down.

"What is the matter, are you ill too?" asked Jersey City.

"Oh, yes I am," said the cow, "what a fool I have been."

"What have you done?"

"I drank some fish oil last evening. I didn't know what it was," said Mooley dismally; "it was standing by the grocer's and I was thirsty."

"You old simpleton," said Jersey City sharply. Then he added more kindly, "That was not like you, Mooley."

"I am just like old Mr. May, the widow's husband, who is now dead," said the cow with a sigh. "He had a great thirst and was always drinking something he shouldn't."

"Well, it can't be helped," said Jersey City; "put your head down and go to sleep; I see you can't walk. I'll go to Jones'."

"But some one may recognize you," said Mooley; "be careful what you do. Oh, I shall never forgive myself if it is found out that you are a runaway dog."

"Don't worry," said Jersey City; but as he trotted down the lane he muttered to himself: "I am afraid they will. This is a most unfortunate affair. I wish I had been born a cur and not such a remarkable looking dog."

Ten minutes later he was looking desperately up at the Jones' window. "Oh, what stupid people. I have barked and scratched and clawed at the door, but they won't come out. I'll have to go to the village. What sleepy heads they must be; they ought to have been up long ago; however I must lose no time. What should I do if my kind mistress were to die?"

At this thought he raced off at full speed to the village.

The grocer, who was an early riser, was just taking down his shutters. Jersey City, who had scarcely any breath left, rushed up to the shop and dropped panting on the doorstep.

The grocer looked at him. "Get out of this, you impudent dog. Get out, I say," and he kicked him aside as he went into the shop.

Jersey City came back and stood behind him as he bent over to kindle a fire in his stove. "Not gone yet," said the grocer, looking over his shoulder and throwing a piece of wood at him. "Ugh, I hate dogs."

Jersey City rushed out, his heart beating almost to suffocation. There pinned against a row of canned vegetables he had seen a placard bearing a large picture of himself and offering a reward of one hundred dollars for his recovery.

Jimson was a clever man—he had not given him up. What an unobserving man the grocer was not to have recognized him. He had better hurry away before he did so. He ran several paces then he stopped.

"I love the widow," he thought, "and she has been very good to me. Can I let her die alone?"

"No, no," something seemed to say inside him. "But if I make myself known to this cross grocer he will give me up to Jimson. How can I go back to that life?" reflected poor Jersey City in deep misery.

He lifted his eyes to the blue sky. "It is so pleasant here in this open country. If I go back to the show I shall die. Never mind, I must do my duty or I shall despise myself," and without hesitating an instant longer, he hurried back to the grocer.

A few tumbles on the floor and a sad little waltz on his hind legs around some empty boxes brought the attention of the amazed man upon him.

With his mouth wide open and holding up his sooty hands, the grocer looked from the performing dog to the placard on the wall.

"The circus dog, as sure as I live," he muttered. "That's one hundred dollars in somebody's pocket; I wonder if I can catch him."

He snatched up a piece of rope and went cautiously after Jersey City, who had danced out through the door and into the road. Jersey City was careful not to let him catch up with him, and the grocer, half laughing, half angry, followed what he supposed was a crazy dog till he got near the widow's cottage.

Then Jersey City gave up his antics and ran to the house as fast as he could go. The grocer ran after him, exclaiming, "Soho, this is where you have found a hiding-place, is it?" Then he stopped short and threw up his hands, for on the bed lay a poor old woman, who looked as if she was dead.

⁓

It was a beautiful winter day. The sun was shining gloriously on white fields of snow and on the blue waters of the Basin. Everything in the landscape was calm and cheerful except two distressed figures of animals that stood on a high bank overlooking the water.

One could tell that they were unhappy just to look at them. The cow stood with a drooping head, and there was a

Margaret Marshall Saunders

sad expression in her beautiful eyes. The dog's tail hung limp, his ears were not pricked; there was a desperate, hunted expression on his face.

"I wish you would give me a toss with your horns and send me over that bank, Mooley," he said mournfully.

The cow turned slowly toward him, "What, down on those rocks? It would hurt you, Jersey City."

"If you were to break a leg for me, Jimson would not take me away," said her companion. "I would be spoiled for a trick dog if I only had something the matter with me."

"I don't think it would be right," said the cow soberly; "the widow says that we mustn't do a bad thing in order to bring about a good one."

"I daresay that is so; but oh, Mooley, I am so unhappy," and Jersey City turned away his head to hide the tears in his eyes.

"It seems very hard," observed the cow, "that just as the widow has recovered and her son has come home with some money, and we are all so happy, that that miserable Jimson should come for you."

"He will be here in an hour," said Jersey City with a shudder, "and I shall have to go back to that old show with him. A week hence, Mooley, you may think of me jumping and rolling on a stage covered with sawdust; my poor tricks drawing shrieks of laughter from a crowded house, and my heart like to break when I think of this peaceful home. I shall not live long, that is one consolation."

"Jersey City, don't," said Mooley, and with a quick, ungainly trot she started for her stable.

Jersey City ran beside her. "I will say good-bye to you now, Mooley, for Jimson will allow no time for leave-taking, and I must spend my last minutes with my mistress."

Mooley stopped short and Jersey City went on, "Good-bye, good-bye, dear old Mooley. You have been a kind friend to me. Some people say that animals do not love each other, but we know that that is not true."

The cow bent her head till it almost touched the ground. It seemed to her that she could never lift it up again, and Jersey City, who hated to see her suffer, hurried away.

The widow sat by the fire talking to her son, who was a fine, strapping young man with red cheeks and curly hair.

Jersey City sprang into his lap, for the sailor had petted him even more than the widow.

"Good dog," said the sailor, playing with the dog's velvety ears.

"Here is the man now," exclaimed old Mrs. May, as a sleigh containing the grocer and Jimson drove up to the door. "Oh, dear, dear."

A terrible feeling came over Jersey City. He crept under the stove and tried to make himself as small as possible.

He was a brave dog and had planned to put a bold face on the matter, but the ordeal was too trying for him, and he felt like a timid young pup.

"Come in," said the sailor, when Jimson had knocked at the door.

"Ah, good afternoon," said a little, thin, wiry man who entered. "You have property of mine here, I think."

"Yes, sir," returned the sailor, "and not stolen property either. This dog came here of his own free will."

"I daresay, I daresay," replied Jimson politely. "Ah, there you are, Jersey City; come out from under the stove."

It seemed to Jersey City that the bitterness of death was upon him. With a hunted look in his eyes he rushed across the room and crouched tremblingly at the sailor's feet.

The young man laughed sarcastically. "Your dog does not seem to be very glad to see you, sir," he said, addressing Jimson.

"Do you call him Jersey City?" asked the widow; "what a strange name."

"Yes, it is peculiar," said Jimson; "he was born in Jersey City, that's why we named him so. Come, my little clown," and drawing a handsome steel chain from his pocket, he walked toward the dog.

"Stop," exclaimed the sailor, "you don't touch that dog, sir, till you prove to us that he is willing to go with you."

"Willing to go ——" repeated Jimson, with a black look, "why, he's our own dog; and I can tell you, a dog that costs us a trip from New York to Canada in the dead of winter isn't one we're going to have anybody dictate to us about,"

"Come, now, that's an old-fashioned doctrine," said the sailor. "Formerly a man's horse or cow or dog or any other animal was his to do with as he liked. Now the law says if a man owns a dumb beast he's got to be merciful to it or he'll be punished."

"I'd like to have any one prove that we have been cruel to this dog, or to any other animal we own," said Jimson sneeringly.

"Prove—ah, yes, that's where you have the advantage," said the sailor. "I've voyaged a bit, and I know as well as you that the cruelty that goes on in dark and hidden places is the worst to get at. Look at that dog licking my feet and begging as plainly as a human being could that we will save him from you. I can't prove that you've ever beaten him, but I know by his actions that you've done it, and I know that you're going to do it again if you get a chance."

"Oh, shut up," said Jimson disdainfully, "and get out of my way. I've got to take the train in thirty minutes."

Mrs. May opened her arms and took in the trembling form of her pet. "My son is right," she said firmly to Jimson. "Poor Rover is unhappy; you shall not have him."

Jimson fell into a terrible rage. "I never saw such fools in my life," he said in a low, furious voice. "That dog is worth five hundred dollars to us. Do you suppose we are going to give him up for such trumpery notions as these?"

"Sit down, sit down, sir," said the sailor, "and take things coolly. You don't understand us yet. I'll just explain to you. Here's a dog that ran away from you; probably you treated him so well that he felt embarrassed. He came to my mother. She petted him, and when she fell ill he brought some one to her and saved her life. The man that helped her does the dog a bad turn by letting you know that he is here. You come, and if the dog had jumped on you and licked your hands as he licks mine, I'd have let you take him. But what does he do ——"

"Do," repeated Jimson sullenly, "it's none of your business what he does. He hasn't seen me for six months, and I'm going to have him, so you just hold up."

"Does a dog ever forget a good master?" asked the sailor warmly. "Never—not so long as he has breath. That dog fears you with all the power he has, and I tell you you're not going to have him to-day, so the sooner you make up your mind to that the better. I'm only a poor man, and you can get the law on me if you choose. I'll go to court and the judge can see for himself how the dog acts. Then if the law gives him to you, I'll follow you wherever you're going, and if there's any kind of society that'll watch you, I'll set them to work, and if I'm spared, I'll be with you wherever you are, and I'll take the liberty of telling the kind ladies and gentlemen, who are probably your patrons, this little story about your clown dog."

Jimson looked speechlessly at the young man.

"I'm not down on shows in general," pursued the sailor; "I daresay there may be some where dumb animals are well treated, but I claim that there's many a cruel one, and I believe yours is one of them. Perhaps if you take your own clown dog and have me trailing around after you explaining why he doesn't put much heart in his tricks, you'll wish that you had listened to me."

The sailor was a very resolute looking young man and Jimson stared at him, wondering if he would do what he said.

"I brought home a little money to my mother," said the sailor. "I'll give you fifty dollars of it if you like."

Fifty dollars—Jimson glared wrathfully at him. Fifty dollars, and he had said that the dog was worth five hundred dollars. However it was better than nothing. "Put your money aside," he said in a choking voice, "and you'll hear from me." Then he rushed from the room. He saw plainly that he couldn't get the dog that afternoon and he would have to consult his employers before doing anything further.

"Don't you ever come sneaking around here to steal him," called the sailor as he stood in the doorway and watched Jimson get into the sleigh. "I'm going to stay home now and work the farm, and I'm fond of the dog and he is fond of me, so he'll never be more than two feet away from me. Try to be a little kinder to your other animals or they'll be running away too."

Jimson sprang into the sleigh and drove away as fast as he could.

"I wonder what he'll do," said Mrs. May thoughtfully as she and her son re-entered the house.

"I don't know," said the young sailor; "but I have made up my mind, mother, that he's got to have a struggle if he wants to get our little brother here away from us," and he laughingly surrendered one ear to Jersey City, who in a transport of gratitude had sprung on his knees and was trying to lick his face.

"So, so, good dog—that will do—we're going to have a long life together I hope," said the young man.

Jersey City leaped on the floor, ran round and round the room a dozen times as if he were crazy, then dashed out to the stable to tell the joyful news to Mooley.

The cow was almost beside herself with joy. She could not speak for a long time and looked as if she had been struck dumb. At last she said solemnly: "Jersey City, do you think that bad man will ever come back?"

"No, no," said the dog wildly; "I understand Jimson better than the sailor does. It would never do for him to get into the papers. It would ruin his business. The Bankstons will be very angry, but they won't dare to molest the sailor, for the people who go to their show are good people and if they thought the animals were cruelly treated they would make a fuss and the Bankstons would be ruined. They will send for the fifty dollars and let me stay. Oh, oh, I am so happy. I cannot keep my paws still—I must go for a run in the orchard."

"Can't you do some tricks here?" said the cow; "that standing on the head is a beautiful one."

"I will do it to please you, Mooley, but after that I shall never do any more tricks," said Jersey City. "They make my muscles ache and the blood rush to my head. Here goes for the last trick of Bankston and Sons' clown dog." And he walked all around the stable on his fore legs, then rushed out into the open air where for an hour and more the cow saw him careering over the snowy ground.

Jersey City was right. Jimson never returned, but he sent for the fifty dollars; and at this day the famous five hundred dollar clown dog of Bankston and Sons' Great Show is living contentedly and happily with the widow and her son on the shores of the beautiful Bedford Basin of Halifax harbor, Nova Scotia.

⌒

For the Other Boy's Sake and Other Stories (Philadelphia: Banes, 1896), 49–76.

MARGARET MARSHALL SAUNDERS

Ella S. Atkinson ("Madge Merton") (1867–1931)

THE WIDOWED STRANGER (1897)

Ella Atkinson, like her contemporary Marjory MacMurchy, was a gifted journalist who wrote successful short fiction; both also married other prominent Canadian journalists, colleagues whom they met in the course of their work.

Elmina (Ella) S. Atkinson was born in Oakville, Ontario, on 20 July 1867, the daughter of Elizabeth Culham and James Elliott. She attended Oakville High School in what was then a pastoral village on the shores of Lake Ontario, a setting that she was to draw on for many of her stories.

Her desire to write flowered early: she was one of the contributors to the weekly *Saturday Night* at its founding in 1887, under the nom de plume "Frances Burton Clare." She joined the staff as a regular columnist on fashion and women's interests in August 1889, and gained a following as "Clip Carew." In the spring of 1891 she joined the Toronto *Globe*, filling a position vacated earlier by Sara Jeannette Duncan, and gaining a following there as "Madge Merton," the name under which she also published much of her fiction. In 1892, she married her *Globe* colleague Joseph E. Atkinson (1865–1946), later editor and publisher of the Toronto *Star*, and had two children. She left the *Globe* to edit the women's page of the Montreal *Herald* and later wrote a popular page for the Toronto *Star* as "Azdera." In 1915, the London *Bookman* awarded her a prize for best original lyric for her poem "Grey Gauntlet."

She died in Oakville on 22 October 1931. In her obituary, *Saturday Night* praised her as a pioneer, noting that "Mrs. Atkinson laid down her pen long ago, but those who recall her professional years have always honoured her not only for her skill but for the loveable personal character that was reflected in her writings."

The best of Ella Atkinson's stories are clever and humorous. Their depiction of small-town life anticipates Adeline Teskey's *Where the Sugar Maple Grows* (1901) and Stephen Leacock's *Sunshine Sketches of a Little Town* (1912). In "The Widowed Stranger," Atkinson creates a realistic narrator and subverts the stereotype of the devout widow—in reality a confidence artist bilking the naïve and the devout of a village congregation. Like the works by Leacock and Teskey, the story is part of a cycle. Atkinson's story cycle, centred around a village and its Protestant church, is called "The Pillars of the Old Meeting House," and was published in *Canadian Magazine* in 1897. The six stories deal with small-town characters—the doctor, the MP, and a local churchwoman—and examine small-town life with affectionate irony. Unfortunately, the cycle seems never to have been published in book form.

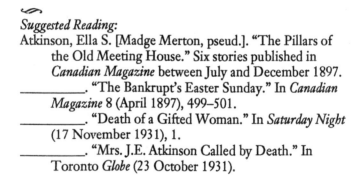

Suggested Reading:

Atkinson, Ella S. [Madge Merton, pseud.]. "The Pillars of the Old Meeting House." Six stories published in *Canadian Magazine* between July and December 1897.
_____. "The Bankrupt's Easter Sunday." In *Canadian Magazine* 8 (April 1897), 499–501.
_____. "Death of a Gifted Woman." In *Saturday Night* (17 November 1931), 1.
_____. "Mrs. J.E. Atkinson Called by Death." In Toronto *Globe* (23 October 1931).

~~~

THE WIDOWED STRANGER

Ella S. Atkinson ("Madge Merton")

I t was a warm July morning when the strange widow came
to meeting and was shown into Dr. Jordan's pew, for Bro.
Silas Smith knew the Doctor wouldn't come that morning.
Poor old Hetty Brown was dying, and the Doctor was staying with her boy Zeke till it was over. Zeke is half-witted,
and he couldn't sense it, and didn't know what to do.

As soon as the widow came up the aisle all the congregation fastened their eyes on her, and she couldn't complain
of that, for she was dressed in what we considered a "loud"
way. I always maintain that when widows and others get
themselves up into mourning that is obtrusive, they must
expect to be stared at. If their reason for wearing mourning
is to shrink away from people's gaze, they've gone the
wrong way about it.

This widow, whose name was Mrs. Miller, which we
all found out as quickly as we could, was dressed in the
height of style, and her things were all new. Her veil was not
so heavy as we were accustomed to see, and she wore those
white fixings wherever they could be put. That was the reason we all stared so hard; but a reason's no excuse. She was
boarding at the hotel then, and next week she brought her
little girl out and rented the Bates cottage, and the Bateses
went to live in the barn.

She sent her card to the minister, and when he called
she explained that she wanted to get right into church
work—she hadn't anything in the world left to live for, and

would he give her something to do—teaching in Sunday School, or visiting the sick, or collecting for the missionaries, or anything. She hadn't any money, but such as she had she would freely give, and the minister was delighted. He put her on the visiting list and gave her a missionary book, and introduced her to the Ladies' Aid, and she was right in the swim of church goings-on in no time.

And she was a clever woman—could get up and make a speech better than many a man, and write fine letters, and bills and posters for tea-meetings, and advertisements in the paper, and do secretary work lovely, and keep treasurer's books so they'd balance, and pray—oh, how she came by it I don't know, but she could pray most beautifully, with never a sob or a gasp, which spoils some women's praying, to my mind. Naturally such a woman was a treasure, and we all tried to overlook her giddy way of wearing widow's clothes, and just to profit by what she had in her that was good. Not but what there were some that were bitter against her. Mrs. Alice Graham, who had worn deep mourning for her husband for twenty years—all clear, heavy black, with just the white frill in her bonnet—she did have a lot to say about the white ties and cuffs and collars our new widow wore. And Mrs. Larkins, the President of the Ladies' Aid, tried to smooth her down by saying Mrs. Miller was younger, but that didn't help it a bit, and we all considered it a lack of tact on Mrs. Larkins' part.

Mrs. Miller had plenty of new ideas about how to raise money, and we needed them, for there was a heavy debt on the church even after fifteen years of begging and tea-meetings. It was natural enough that most of the heavy givers were drawing off, and we had to think of new ways of coaxing out the dollars, and doing it so carefully they wouldn't know it, or at least think they were getting something for it, which generally isn't so, as far as church goings-on are concerned. But then nobody is really deceived, so there is no real harm I hope.

Mrs. Miller told us how to get up pink teas, and lemon socials and green luncheons, and we had a married men's

ELLA S. ATKINSON

supper, and she started five o'clock Aid teas for the members. They came early to each other's houses, and brought the cake and sandwiches, and the hostess made the tea and chocolate. Each of the members paid ten cents, and then the husbands came at six and paid a quarter, and they said it wasn't worth it, but we made lots of money. Once Mrs. Miller suggested a widows' tea, but there were only four widows in the congregation, and they wouldn't work with her. Somebody did say she set it down to their jealousy, because they thought she'd look nicer than them; but that could not have been the reason, for they all said she looked "such a fright."

We were quite gay that summer with all our teas and socials, and our apron bazaar in September was a grand success. Mrs. Miller was treasurer, and the way she counted and counted the money, and told us how it was growing in the bank book, was just wonderful. She was enthusiastic and no mistake. People came to look to her for everything, and the minister praised her before her face and behind her back, and said, "See what one energetic woman can do." It seemed as if he was reproving us, and we felt as if perhaps we hadn't been pushing enough, so we worked doubly hard, and everything went on splendidly.

Along in September the barn got too cold for the Bateses, and they said they'd have to have their house. Mrs. Miller didn't seem to know what to do. She said she couldn't bear to leave the church just now, for she had set her heart on getting up an autograph quilt for it. A friend of hers in Winnipeg had sent her word that one their church had made brought them over five hundred dollars, and she thought it would be so nice if we could start one.

We all said couldn't she board, and she got red in the face and said she couldn't afford to, unless she could rent her city house, and her daughter would have to go to school next week, and schooling cost so much. Then Mrs. Moore spoke up—she's a good-natured woman, with a large family and none too much money to come and go on; but she was born with generosity, and she's let it get strong with being used.

"You come right home with me," she said. "I've got a big spare room and you're welcome to it; and you can pay me for what you eat, if you feel like it; and it won't cost much."

So the matter was settled. The little girl went to school and Mrs. Miller went to board with Mrs. Moore.

Then the autograph quilt was begun. We made it good and big, twenty blocks by twenty, and twelve names to a block. We worked them small, but, as Mrs. Miller said, if folks wanted their names to set out they ought to pay more than ten cents; and of course some did. Each of us furnished our own silk—at least Mrs. Miller bought it from a wholesale friend of hers, and we paid three cents a block for the cashmere, and it would all help along. Mrs. Miller wrote the names on tissue paper and basted them on, and the way she worked was a caution—nothing was too much trouble for her to do.

We got names from all parts of the country, and how we did work and pester our friends, and beg of acquaintances and strangers alike. If it wasn't for a good cause it would have been shameful, and sometimes when I think of it, all to myself, I am not so sure that it wasn't shameful anyway. But I may be wrong.

After a while it was finished, all pieced and lined and bound and tufted down, and it was a beauty, all yellow and white. Mrs. Miller suggested that we should have a yellow social the night it was sold and have everything yellow—custard pies and pumpkin ones, and peach tarts and orange cakes and yellow icings, and yellow flowers and yellow on the lamps, and we agreed, and we all worked at yellow things till we almost had the jaundice. Then the day before the social Mrs. Miller told us that old Timothy Barton was going to buy the quilt for two hundred dollars, and she thought it would be a fine idea to get him to pay the money and then draw what we had in the bank, and get it all in gold, and put it up in yellow sateen sacks tied up with yellow ribbons, and let the president of the Ladies' Aid give it over to the chairman of the trust board with an

ELLA S. ATKINSON

address. The names on the quilt had made near five hundred dollars, and two made seven, and we had nearly four hundred in the bank, so we could put a hundred dollars in each sack and have ten of them. It was a fancy sort of a plan, and it took the young people mightily. Polly Marsden said she could see those little fat yellow bags every time she shut her eyes. Some of the older women thought a cheque would be better, but gold was yellow, and it was a yellow social, and Mrs. Miller had her way. Granny Kyle said it wasn't safe to have so much money about, and Mrs. Miller just smiled and said, "Poor old thing! I suppose she is not accustomed to handling money, and it seems a large amount to her."

We joined with Mrs. Miller, but it seemed a large amount to us, too—a whole thousand dollars. Why, it would be a sight to see, and ought to draw a crowd, even if the quilt and the social didn't.

Timothy Barton paid down his money. No one but Mrs. Miller could have persuaded him to buy the quilt, let alone pay for it, before he got his hands on it, but he had taken to acting real foolish about her, gone eighty as he is.

That night was a splendid night for socials, fine and clear and moonlight, and the school-room looked very pretty all fixed up with yellow. We had tied oranges on Mrs. Hastie's rubber plant and Mrs. Currie's oleander, and they set off the platform well. About six, Mrs. Miller came with all the sacks. They were in a box, and we all peeped at them and admired them. They were the crowning glory of the evening. Mrs. Miller was worried about them. "It's such a responsibility," she said, "and I feel as if I mustn't let it out of my sight till it's given over to the trustees," which was quite natural.

Timothy Barton had come very early and sat in a front seat admiring his quilt, which was hung up at the back of the platform. The crowds were wonderful. The quarters just clanked down on the plate at the door, and it kept Mrs. Miller busy running around getting bills, because the silver was so heavy and so bulky.

After all the refreshments had been served, we women, who were all hot and tired with our much serving, came into the front row to see the quilt given to its owner and the little chunky bags delivered up. Mrs. Miller said she'd just run into the church for a fan, but we all got so interested in Timothy we never thought of fans.

We all thought that for an old man he acted real boyish. He must have his new quilt right down on the seat beside him, and he patted it and held it up to his face till the boys were in roars of laughter. But then, I suppose he ought to get the worth of his money out of it somehow, and he really could not get it out of the quilt itself.

Then it was time for the bags, and Mrs. Larkin read an address and the chairman replied, and we all leaned back and sighed, and the trustees beamed on us, and we were very proud.

After it was all over Timothy Barton wanted to see the money, and Martin Thompson, the treasurer, undid one of the yellow ribbons, and then he gasped. Every one crowded around, and he lifted up the pretty sack and tumbled out a little pile of yellow and brown and white stones and never a cent of money.

"A little joke, I presume," said the minister, with a smile that had more teeth than cheerfulness in it; but no one answered. Most of us were white and had chills, and brother Thompson went on solemnly emptying those stones out on the table. The commotion was something fearful. Three or four started off to look for Mrs. Miller. Timothy was crying because his two hundred dollars was gone, and he was mussing up the quilt with his hands and declaring we would have to take it back. The minister's wife whispered that the missionary money was not handed in as it should have been at the first of the year. Mrs. Moore said Mrs. Miller had promised to pay her board the next day, and she was looking to it to help with her grocer's bill. She had never paid a cent.

"I thought something was wrong," drawled the banker's son, "when she wanted every cent out, and said she'd rather have it in bills than gold anyway, after we'd got up some gold especially for you."

"She's a fine pillar," snapped out Mrs. Graham, and the talk got sharp, so the minister raised his hand and said: "Let us pray for the poor broken pillar," and when he had finished you could have heard a pin drop, and I believe we all felt sorrier about her than about the money.

Of course they hunted for her; but she got off and we never heard a word of her from that day to this. So we had almost a year's hard work for nothing, and it wasn't long before we got a bill for the white cashmere and the yellow silk in that tiresome quilt. Mrs. Miller had never paid a cent on it and—well, we all had.

᭞

Canadian Magazine 9 (October 1897), 464–467.

Jessie Kerr Lawson (1838–1917)

LOVE ME, LOVE MY DOG (1898)

Jessie Kerr Lawson was an exceptional woman. A prolific
novelist and journalist, she supported her husband, who was
invalided five years after their marriage, and educated their
ten children, all but two of whom went on to post-secondary
education and all of whom became very successful. One son,
James Kerr-Lawson, a painter, was responsible for two
murals in the Senate Chamber of the Parliament Buildings
in Ottawa. Another son was an eminent geologist at the
University of California, and another a foremost botanist at
the University of Sydney, Australia.

    Janet (Jessie) Kerr was born in Edinburgh, Scotland,
on 18 May 1838, daughter of Janet Kerr and Andrew
Cowper. She was brought up by her maternal grandfather,
James Kerr, and aunt, Jessie Kerr, at St. Monans, Fifeshire.
She taught briefly, then married William Lawson, a carpen-
ter, on 1 June 1860. Lawson developed a heart condition in
1865, which limited his ability to work and forced his
complete retirement in 1873. In 1866, the family emigrated
to Hamilton, Upper Canada. By this time they had four
children between one and five years of age.

    Jessie Lawson published essays and stories in *The
Week*, *Saturday Night*, and the satirical magazine *Grip*, as
well as in the Dundee, Scotland, *People's Friend* and the
Glasgow Herald. She made frequent extended trips to
Scotland, sending travel sketches from there to *The Week*.
Lawson used a number of pseudonyms, including Jay
Kayelle and Mona Fife, whose givens included plays on her
name and birthplace. In *Grip* she wrote as the Irish Barney
O'Hea, the Scottish Hugh Airlie, and the black Washington
White, as well as J.K.L. and J.K. Lawson, sometimes
contributing two or three items to the same issue under
various pseudonyms. Lawson enjoyed good health to the

end of her life, dying at her Toronto home as the result of an accident on 30 July 1917 at the age of seventy-nine.

Among Lawson's novels, *The Epistles of Hugh Airlie* (1888) is a collection of amusing letters by a Scottish immigrant to Canada, originally written for *Grip*. *A Vain Sacrifice* (1892), set in Scotland, while somewhat melodramatic, contains interesting characterization and social observation. *The Curse That Came Home* (1894), also set in Scotland, is a more psychological study of greed and envy; *The Harvest of Moloch* (1908) is an admonitory temperance novel. Lawson, a staunch Presbyterian, reportedly broke with her church over the temperance issue. One Sunday in 1882, her pastor in Toronto announced to church-goers, "It is possible for a saloon-keeper to be a Christian; aye, and a good Christian"; she walked out and never returned.

Lawson's one volume of poetry, *Lays and Lyrics* (1918), includes primarily meditative and philosophic poems, with a section of "poems in the Scottish dialect." The first poem, "The Evolution of Woman," is a revisionist version of Genesis. Eve, an angel who kissed Adam to comfort him, lost her wings, and was required to remain with him, "Not lost, but strayed/ From Heaven's estate"; henceforth, God decides, "Truth, Grace, Wisdom . . . shall feminine be."

"Love Me, Love My Dog" appeared in the 1898 Christmas issue of *Saturday Night*. The setting is divided between Glasgow and the Canadian Northwest, beginning with a Dickensian description of Christmas Eve shoppers in Glasgow and shifting to a grimly realistic tale of a Canadian winter wilderness adventure, and returning to Glasgow for the happy resolution of the love triangle that has developed. A thirty-two-year-old spinster is portrayed as neither bitter nor frustrated nor unattractive, but, on the contrary, still possessing the charm to captivate her bachelor friends.

∽

Suggested Reading:

Lawson, Jessie K. *The Epistles of Hugh Airlie*. Toronto: Grip, 1888.

Vaughan, Frances E. *Andrew Lawson, Scientist, Teacher, Philosopher*. Glendale, California: The Arthur H. Clark Company, 1970.

LOVE ME, LOVE MY DOG

Jessie Kerr Lawson

Rain, rain, rain. It had rained all last night, it had rained all day, it was drizzling still. But through the gray discomfort the long roar of the city traffic held on; on the slippery, glistening streets the clank, clank, clank of horse hoofs rang incessantly; the omnibuses were crowded within and without as the thick night closed in, and the lamps began to wink, and the shop windows lit up, illuminating the long vista of Argyle street. These windows, always attractive by their varied display of color, were to-night many-hued and brilliant as an Eastern bazaar. And despite the showering overhead and the damp underfoot the streets were crowded with citizens well-to-do, and citizens not well-to-do at all; citizens in comfortable overcoats and rubbered feet, citizens with second-hand coats buttoned sparsely over the shivering chest, and with shoes that pumped water in and out at every step; citizenesses with stout commonsense boots, and reliable waterproof cloaks and umbrellas; citizenesses with shawl-shrouded heads and, alas! alas! bare feet, washed white with the cold, cold rain.

But, well-off or ill-off, all like night-moths around a lamp, kept up a continuous hovering buzz around the shop windows to-night, some considering how much they could buy, some how little; some looking on grimly, trying to make themselves believe the grapes were sour—the grapes that ripen at Christmas tide, full of the wine of goodwill to all; the grapes that sad circumstances forbade them either to taste themselves or give to others, as fain they would.

The shops appeared to be doing a rushing business, for in and out, in and out, still poured the customers, going in purse in hand whispering together, and coming out with hands full of parcels—mysterious parcels—which they preferred to carry instead of having them sent; parcels to be consigned to the keeping of Santa Claus, to be brought by him along the aerial dreamland route, down many and many a sooty perpendicular tunnel. To be sure it was a moonless and slippery night for reindeer hoofs to be clattering around chimney tops, but being sure-footed as the love of little children could make them, the parcels always arrived safe, as dawn proved to bright and early waking eyes.

Now, among the well-to-do citizens gazing in at the mimic world in a toy-shop's window, were a group of three, two men and a woman—John Milne, his wife, and his brother Tom, the latter just returned from a many years' sojourn in Canada. Presently they moved into the shop and were served, and were about to pass out again when Tom's eye caught sight of a comical-looking toy dog.

"Show me that dog, will you," he said to the saleswoman.

"Oh, Tom, you have spent enough on the children already," protested his sister-in-law.

"All the same, I'm going to invest in this dog. It won't break me," he answered, smiling to himself, and in the ear of his wife John murmured, not displeased:

"Better let Tom have his own way, Mary. He always did, ever since I could remember."

Tom heard, and, turning to his brother with an appreciative wink, echoed:

"You bet," and bore off the dog in triumph.

That evening, after the children had gone to bed, a few friends dropped in on their way home from shopping.

"Why, what have you got here—a dog?" cried Kate Wyn.

"Yes, Miss Wyn, that's my dog; that's Jim Mackenzie's Twinkle to a T. I bought that because it was the dead spit of Twinkle."

"Twinkle? Jim Mackenzie?" breathed Kate, with a sort of gasp, but in another moment she quietly sat down and said "Oh."

Kate was a friend of the family, a woman over thirty-two now, but still blooming and still strikingly fine-looking. Why she had never married was a mystery to all who knew how much she was admired by the men of her acquaintance; but, somehow, she had a knack of keeping acquaintances of the masculine order as acquaintances; and not the most Platonic of friendships had she ever contracted with any of the opposite sex. There had been at one time a whisper of some love disappointment, but that had been long ago, before her father had moved from Irvine into Glasgow to become one of its most respected citizens. Over this love affair Kate's curved lips were sealed. If she had an unhealed wound in her inner consciousness she made no moan over it, not even to her most intimate women friends. When they rallied her on not being married she laughed and said she would marry when the right man came along.

The present company were too merry, and themselves too much taken up laughing at Tom's toy dog, to observe Kate's momentary agitation and the sudden paling of her clear complexion at the mention of Jim Mackenzie and the dog Twinkle.

"Is that the Mackenzie you wrote about, Tom?" enquired his brother, with some interest, "the man that wouldn't let you eat his dog when you were all starving."

"That was Jim. He had just got an appointment to one of the Hudson Bay stations and was on his way there, him and me and the half-breed. You know one of the chief doctrines of the Hudson Bay Company is that the only men to be trusted in the employ up there are Scotchmen. No other need apply. This doctrine had been evolved from long experience of other nationalities, the thistle coming out purple crown on top every time."

"You might tell us how you got through that time, Tom. Your letter was most unsatisfactory. You seemed to be more taken up with the fact that you had been saved, than the way it came about."

"Well, rather!" snorted Tom. "If you'd been traveling as we had been, on snow-shoes for weeks, through a country that was one group of lakes; a couple of miles or so on snow, then across a lake, then tramp it again, then another lake on ice, till all unexpectedly the air got unseasonably warm, and when you came to a lake as we did and found the ice all broken up and floating about, and your grub nearly out, and your powder flask about empty, nothing but miles on miles of slush, and the nearest Indian village thirty miles away across the lake and no canoe to reach it, by ginger! Them's the kind of experiences you want to forget immediately, if not sooner. You don't want to be going over the agony on paper right away, I tell you. However, that's more than seven years ago. The distance smooths things considerably, so I don't mind if I tell you how I wanted to kill and eat Jim's dog. That there is his livin' picture, only of course Twinkle was a big dog, a collie, and Jim thought no end of that brute. Of course, I am glad now he fought me for his life, but when a man's blue with despair and hunger makes a ravening wolf of him, the old beast of prey wakes in him, and life, life, life is the only thought he is capable of."

The friends assembled looked their interest in Tom's story. "Let us hear it, Tom; you must have been pretty well screwed when you wanted to eat a collie," said one of them with a laugh.

Kate Wyn lay back in the easy-chair, and with her elbow on the table, shaded her face with her hand.

"Do tell us, Mr. Milne. Tell us all about it. I should like very much indeed to hear your adventure," she said in a calm, incisive voice, and Tom began:

"As I was sayin', we were traveling, the three of us, Jim Mackenzie, myself and the half-breed, and not at all unpleasant traveling it was on snow-shoes until we came to this lake and found the ice broken up, our food and powder given out, the Indian reserve thirty miles off and no canoe to cross the lake in. Jim looked at the ice floating and swaying about; he looked at the black woods and the long wastes of slush between—slush, mind you; sheer slush, for the air had been soft for some days, and the sun shone out unseasonably strong, and then Jim looked at me. I said nothing; no more did the half-breed. There were some fallen trees covered with the melting snow. We brushed them bare and sat down and thought hard. You see, Jim being one of the Hudson Bay Company's officers had been sent up to this Indian post, right across Crooked Pine Lake, in order to trace up some of the Company's goods which had gone astray; and myself and Michel Noyes going with him, we thought we might as well do some trapping by the way. Of course we never dreamed of the ice breaking up a clear three weeks before the usual time; never dreamed but what all we had to do was to step on to the lake and continue our tramp on the ice clear across. As it was, there we were, trapped ourselves, and, unless the lake froze over again, with a strong probability of starvation staring us in the face. For, you understand, we were traveling over a country which was literally honey-combed with lakes—a vast net-work of lakes; and to attempt to go around on land would mean tramping hundreds of miles without food, without ammunition to bring down game of any kind—an utter impossibility. There was nothing for it but to camp here upon Brule Portage and see what Providence had in store for us.

"We were all dead tired, used up, and this shock just finished us. We had no heart to speak. Every one of us knew just exactly how much grub was left, and everyone was privately calculating how long these two days' provisions could be made to last. Dear knows how long we might have sat there glooming, but all at once Jim's dog, Twinkle, got up and begged, standing on his hind legs and looking right into his eyes. It was a dog some friend in the Old Country had given him, and he had taught him all sorts of tricks. Twinkle was hungry and was begging for something to eat.

JESSIE KERR LAWSON

"'All right, Twinkle,' says he, jumping up. 'I guess it won't help things sitting mooning here. Let's go and snare some rabbits.'"

Twinkle barked and gamboled around him and off the two went to set snares. Michel Noyes and me got out string and went to set snares too, and about sunset we all returned to the portage. Jim looked anxiously at the sunset—it was too red for his taste. A clear, hard strip of cold pea-green along the north would have suited him better, and would have meant cold, and possibly frost throughout the night, and frost meant our salvation. As it was, the air was warm and balmy, and brought the scent, the spring scent of pine to us.

"'Do you think we could do without supper to-night?' Jim asked. 'We are more likely to be hungry to-morrow, and if we roll in our rabbit-skin blankets and go to sleep now, we won't miss it so much.'

"Michel shrugged his shoulders, which signified that he was agreeable under protest, and as for myself, though I never can sleep on an empty stomach, I let on to be delighted.

"'After breakfast we'll go hunting partridge,' said Jim quite hopefully. 'I saw some tracks in the snow up there.'

"It was a good hope to sleep on, so we began to cut down spruce and balsam branches and made fine springy mattresses over a foot thick. On these we lay down, rolled in our rabbit-skin blankets, before the roaring fire we had made."

"Under the open sky? Weren't you cold?" said Mrs. Milne.

"Cold? No, only ravenously hungry. You can't feel cold wrapped in a rabbit-skin blanket. They are warm and waterproof. No fellow can be cold wrapped in one of these blankets."

Mrs. Milne shrugged her shoulders with a smiling shiver. Evidently the idea of sleeping under the stars on a spruce mattress laid on the snow, did not commend itself to her. Kate slid her hand from her face and looked at Tom with unmistakable sympathy. His eye caught hers and he resumed:

"Next morning we ate very sparingly indeed, and after making a sort of wigwam with poles crossed and covered with flat spruce branches, we set out to see what luck we could get. Not a rabbit to be seen; the snares set just as we left them. Jim looked at the powder and shot and remarked that we would have to make pretty sure of our aim before letting fly at any partridge we might scare up. We could not afford to waste any shot. All that day we got nothing; same story next day, and the next. We saw tracks of partridge in the snow, but never a bird; they had been scared out by our arrival there. Things were looking pretty blue, I tell you. The grub finally gave out, and for a whole day and a night we had nothing to eat. Then Jim wakened us all with a joyful whoop one morning. The lake had frozen over in the night. Instead of the ice floating about, it was all welded together. We started up, got our traps together, bound on our snow-shoes, and forgetting our faintness and hunger in the hope of getting across the lake, we set out once more. Ah, poor wretches! We hadn't gone far before we discovered that the freezing was only in patches. Where the ice had drifted asunder, leaving long strips of clear water, only a thin coating of treacherous sheet ice had formed. It creaked and crackled under our feet, bent and gave way when we attempted to cross.

"'It's no use,' said Jim. 'Let's get back before the sun gets warm.'

"I tell you we were three blue men as we trudged back over them blocks of ice, looking so firm all along the shore. Our spirits sank into our boots, the hunger and the faintness got worse and worse. Michel lay down on his belly upon the spruce, saying never a word. Jim's dog had begged and begged till he had given it up for a bad job, and now he sat down on the snow and, lifting his nose in the air, let out one long despairing howl. I looked at the dog. He'd got mighty little to eat since coming here. Like ourselves, he had had nothing for two days.

"'He's mighty thin,' I remarked to Jim.

"'Yes, poor fellow; come here, Twink', and he put out his hand and hauled the beast to him and hugged him as you might hug a baby.

"'There isn't much flesh on his bones,' I remarked again.

"'No, no more than there is on your own, Tom,' he says quietly.

"'Yes,' says I, 'but a man's a man, and a dog's a dog.'

"Well, do you know, Jim twigged me at once.

"'Yes,' says he, as sharp as you please, 'and the dog's so much better than the man that I don't suppose it has ever entered into his head to eat you. And he could throttle you as easy as winkin' when you are lying asleep there.'

"By ginger! I felt ashamed of myself, and the dog was really more of a man than I was, for he was a strong, powerful fellow, and might have had my blood any night, had he felt like it.

"That day we caught a rabbit in one of the snares, and hungry though we were, Twink' got his share of it. Then a cold snap set in and we kept the fire roaring night and day, and to our joy we saw the lakes again freezing over. If the cold wind would only last a couple of days more the ice would be safe to cross, and we could get to our destination and be relieved. The frost held and on the third night we decided to try again.

"Our powder and shot was entirely out, we had tasted nothing for the last two days but a sort of tea made from stewing dead leaves, and now when we made up our minds to try again, Michel, the half-breed, gave out altogether. He rose from the spruce bed, but staggered and fell back upon it, unable to stand. We determined to go without him, and when we reached the Indian village to send him food and help. We two were feeling pretty shaky. Jim as gaunt as a wolf, and I suppose I looked quite as bad. I felt bad enough I know. However, we set out, Jim and myself and Twinkle, Twinkle keeping close to Jim. The ice was pretty good for over a mile or so, and hope kept our spirits up, but all of a sudden Jim stopped and shading his eyes with his hands looked away ahead. Seeing him—I looked too—and all I could say was, 'God, have mercy on us!'

"There, away some couple of miles off, was a blue and shiny streak cutting clear through the whiteness of the ice, and that meant water—a belt of clear water many miles long.

"'Water, Tom,' says he.

"'Yes,' says I, and without another word we turned back once more, weary, discouraged and scarcely able to crawl.

"When we got back again to the portage, Michel was lying where we left him, and Jim threw himself on his bed with his face downward and his arm around the dog. I went out looking for rabbits, but there was none to be seen. The sun shone out hot and fierce, the snow thawed everywhere, in a few hours the ice again began to move and float about in detached pieces. A light, warm breeze had sprung up, and had we not returned as promptly as we did we should have been at the bottom of Crooked Pine Lake. But I had no heart to go back to camp—the sight of these two big fellows lying there, dead broke, made me feel like caving in myself; I was bound to find something to eat or—bust.

"Well, I did find something. I came upon the trail of a partridge and I followed it up to some bush in a copse some distance up. I was going to get that partridge or die in the attempt. I had no gun, but I could bring him down with a good hard snowball once I started him, and I knew by the feet marks in the snow he was not far off. So I ate some of the snow and made a couple of balls and crept around the copse—around and around, winding in and out among the bush—then all of a sudden I threw up my hands and grew deathly sick for sheer joy."

"You found the partridge!" exclaimed Kate, eagerly.

"Partridge? no!—better than that—I found a canoe. It was like this, you see. When the frost sets in in the fall, if an Indian or a white man lands anywhere with his canoe he makes a cache; that is, a sort of small roof made by propping

JESSIE KERR LAWSON

up poles in a slanting position against a tree and then covering these over with plentiful layers of spruce branches and any other brush lying about handy. Over this the snow falls thick and freezes, and in this shelter the canoe lies secure until the next spring.

"So, when in pursuit of the partridge I came upon this cache, I knew a canoe was there and that we were saved. You'd scarcely believe what I tell you, but when I went to the portage and told Jim the way that the half-breed jumped up was a caution. He rose, staggered about a bit, and then the way we all three made a bee line for that canoe was a sight to see."

"Thank God you were saved," murmured Kate, and Tom noted that her eyes were wet.

"Ah! but—hold on!; we weren't out of our troubles yet, by any means. In the first place we were very weak, and though we stewed leaves and drank the tea, it was all we could do to paddle, taking turns. As I told you, the breeze sprung up, which we were thankful for, seeing it cleared the water, but we had so much circumnavigating to do, steering clear of the floes, that we seemed to make no progress. Then night came on, and though the wind went down a little with the sun, still there was enough to keep the ice bobbing and knocking about. There were plenty of stars but no moon, and there we were, in that frail canoe, steering here and steering there in the clear places, trying to avoid being jammed in and smashed to smithereens—by ginger! Weren't we glad when the morning broke, and we saw that we had paddled straighter than we knew, and that another hour or two would land us on the Indian reserve. Michel had given out once more—there isn't half the endurance in a half-breed as in a healthy white man—and when we got to the shore the Indians had to lift him out of the canoe and carry him up into a wigwam, where they had to doctor him up for a fortnight, before he was any good. We had nothing to brag of ourselves, indeed, for both Jim and me and the dog were laid up for three days; and when we got on our pins again you couldn't tell which was the weaker. But all the time Jim lay there, that fellow Twinkle never budged from his side, and half the time he lay with his nose across Jim's breast. He has that old dog yet."

"He has!" said Kate, speaking slowly. "He appears to be very fond of him."

"Fond is no name for it. He says that is the one thing he can never forgive me—wanting to eat him when we were so hard up at Crooked Pine Lake."

Tom had the supreme felicity of seeing Miss Wyn home that night. In walking along with her under an umbrella, he felt he had not been a hero in vain. She seemed never to tire of asking him questions about the life they had led out in these boreal quarters of the Hudson's Bay Company. The story of Jim and his dog interested her immensely.

"Is Mr. Mackenzie a married man?" she asked, when he called on her next day.

"Mackenzie married? What an idea! Why, no! I never in all my experience of him knew him to go sparking the girls like the other fellows. No! Give him his pipe and his book, and the others may take the girls. That's Jim."

"You would think he might like to come back to his native land, as you have done, Mr. Milne?"

"Yes, you'd think so; but he don't seem to want to. I asked him once if he didn't think of going back to old Scotland, but he said no; said he had nothing to come for, and so had no desire to."

Kate lapsed into silence for some minutes; but presently, with an effort, set herself to entertain her visitor. So agreeable did she make herself that Tom came back again; not once, but many times, growing more shy and more reserved as the spring wore on and the time for his return to Canada drew nigh. The truth must be confessed— Tom was in love; not for the first time, it is true, but none the less very genuinely and in solemn earnest. He had had one or two *affaires de cœur* with girls, young, bright, laughing girls, whose smiles had made him for the time being deliriously happy; whose frowns had overwhelmed him with despair, bringing visions of romantic suicide and the rest of it. But out of all these experiences he had ever emerged right side up and very little the worse for wear.

This was a different, a more serious affair. This was no smiling girl, but a sweet and womanly woman, strong and self-reliant; and with that in her which somehow inspired others to be strong and self-reliant also.

Tom found himself confiding all his history, his present plans, his future prospects to her; and he had got so accustomed to this friendship that the thought of it coming to an end and leaving him just where he was when he returned from Canada, was far from agreeable. He could not be the same man after knowing her; he had developed and softened and sweetened since enjoying her conversation and society. In his inmost soul he recognized the fact that he loved her as he could never love another woman. But what of her? That was the problem he could not solve for the life of him. For she was always so frankly kind, so considerate, so sweet. But then she was that to everyone.

In his perplexity he confided his case to his sister-in-law, who assured him that the only way to find out whether he had any chance was to ask Kate herself. Did he expect her to offer herself to him? Oh, these men!

Tom, thus prompted, set out one evening to test his fate, and it so happened that Miss Wyn met him at the door. She was dressed to go out, but turned back with him. Tom protested, but she declared that she had only dressed to go out from sheer weariness. She was so glad he had come. She hung her hat and cloak on the rack as they passed in, and at once relieved him of all embarrassment filling his soul with joy.

"Do you know, Mr. Milne, if you hadn't come to-night I should have sent you a note to-morrow morning. I have been hesitating and deliberating on a certain step ever since you told us that story of the lake with the Indian name. Now I have come to a decision in the matter."

Here a soft color crept over her face, quite bewitching poor Tom. She was not given to blushing, but now she blushed divinely. What was she going to say? It was leap year; could it be possible? Ah!

"We have been very good friends, Mr. Milne; almost what you Canadians would call chums, these three months, haven't we?"

Here she blushed again and Tom reflected it as he answered:

"We have, and I'm sure I shall feel very lonely when I go away. In fact, to-day I felt——"

Tom paused, feeling he hadn't started out right.

"And I am certain you would do me a service, a very particular favor, if you could," continued Kate.

"Well, rather. Just try me and see. How could you ask me such a question when you must know that——"

He was about to utter, "I love you," when Kate broke in impulsively:

"Then I will confide in you. You are his friend now, as well as mine. Mr. Milne, will you take this letter from me to Mr. Mackenzie—Jim, as you call him?" As she spoke she produced from her pocket a letter addressed to "James Mackenzie, Esq., care of Hudson's Bay Company, North-West Territory, Canada."

Keeping her eye on the letter, she explained:

"Mr. Mackenzie and I were at one time engaged to be married, and I loved him as he loved me, but I was young and thoughtless, and I was jealous—jealous, as I now know, without a cause. We quarreled and parted. He went to Canada, saying in a note to me that when I wrote and asked him to come back, he would come. This letter is to ask him to come back. I was wrong; he was right. If I had known where to write to, I would have written years ago. I gave him Twinkle when it was a little puppy. I didn't know until I heard your story that he had ever taken the dog with him. You may judge what I felt when you told me about him. Now, will you give him that letter from me?" she begged.

Tom's eyes were upon the letter she held in her hand. He did not reply immediately; except by nodding his head and clearing his throat. She was quite satisfied with the nod, however. She understood him to be affected by her love story. So he was—very much so.

He took out a memorandum book, carefully deposited the letter in the pocket thereof, and rising to his feet, again hemmed repeatedly. She looked somewhat surprised when he took out his watch and said quietly:

"I must ask you to excuse me this evening—I forgot. An engagement—I have to see John at eight o'clock."

Which, of course, was an unmitigated fib, but—poor Tom.

Kate Wyn thought he acted queer—very queer; but how was she to know? She was still more puzzled when she heard that he had gone off next morning without warning.

Once a glimmer of light dawned on her when Mrs. Milne, in a tone of friendly reproach, asked her why she had given Tom his *conge* so sharply.

"Me! You must be dreaming, Mrs. Milne. Tom never said a word of the kind to me."

"He didn't?"

"He did not, I solemnly assure you."

Then there was another sorely puzzled woman, for Kate kept her own counsel about the letter she had commissioned Tom to deliver. But the truth had dawned upon her now, and it grew in the light of many little memories of Tom's sayings and doings, till she understood.

"If I had known, I couldn't have given him that letter," she said to herself. "However, it's too late now."

It was too late. Tom was on the Atlantic, grinning and bearing it as best he could; and before the new moon was a month old, the letter had reached its destination, and the Hudson Bay Company had granted their respected employee the usual one year's leave of absence to visit the land of his birth, as they put it. When he arrived at Mavis Bank Quay, Twinkle was the first to leap ashore.

ᗌ

Saturday Night (Christmas issue, 1898), 41–45.

Agnes Laut (1871–1936)

KOOT AND THE BOB-CAT (1903)

Agnes Laut is a true representative of Western Canada.
Born in Stanley Township, Ontario, on 11 February
1871, she was two years of age when her family moved to
Winnipeg, then a frontier town and gateway to the West.
After graduating from normal school, she taught briefly,
then attended the University of Manitoba. When ill health
forced her to withdraw after her second year and spend the
summer in the Selkirk and Rocky Mountains, she conceived
a love for the wilderness and for wilderness travel, which
remained with her throughout her life. She turned to
journalism as an editorial writer for the *Manitoba Free Press*
from 1895 to 1897, and submitted articles to Canadian,
American, and British publications.

In a letter to Dr. Lorne Pierce, publisher of
Ryerson Press, Laut dates her enthusiasm for Canada's past
back to her childhood:

> Canadian history was to me a horror in those
> days. We had to commit governors' and battle
> names and dates to memory without the faintest
> idea of what they meant; and even when age
> eleven, passing old Ft. Garry Gate, I knew
> Canadian history must be crammed with
> romance and adventure; for we saw the dog
> trains coming in with fur packs, went to school
> with the sons and daughters of old H.B.C. and
> North West heroes, who used to tell us folk lore
> stories of the recent past, like the Loup-Garou,
> or the Phantom Horseman of White Horse
> plains, or the massacre of Semple and the awful
> fate of the Gardapees and Deschamps in that

murder, who were themselves all "shot up" at
Fort Union on the Missouri.[1]

Later in the same letter, Laut concludes: "In fact, I
know now, it was those old unconscious childhood contacts,
made me resolve some day to make Western history a <u>living
true life thing</u>, not a dead skeleton of dates, which I can reel
off to this day."

A special admiration for the wilderness travellers
who opened up Canada's North and West and the American
West led Laut to write historical novels. *Lords of the North*
(1900) and *Heralds of Empire* (1902), which celebrate the
courage, daring, and initiative of the early traders of the
Hudson's Bay and North West trading companies, and
recount their rivalries in stories of fast-paced action, launched
Laut's successful writing career. Laut prided herself on her
historical accuracy, as she celebrated heroes who she felt
were comparable to the daring robber barons of the Middle
Ages. *The Story of the Trapper* (1902) collects separate stories
published originally in *Outing* magazine. While Laut's
earlier novels focussed on the leaders of the fur-trading
companies, these stories merge fact with fiction, folklore
with wilderness tales of individual experience. Laut based
the stories on personal interviews with trappers, manuscript
material from the Hudson Bay Archives, and her own
experiences. The result is far different than, for example,
Gilbert Parker's *Pierre and His People* (1892), a melodramatic account set in a North the author had never seen.
Laut mixes genres much as Ernest Thompson Seton does in
his animal stories, which, while fictional, are based on fact.

Her life, too, echoes Seton's. Like him, she alternated between life in the wilderness she loved, gathering
material and taking photographs, and life in her civilization
base, negotiating with publishers and searching through the
Hudson Bay archives. In the early part of the century, Laut

---

1. Agnes Laut. Typescript, letter dated 7 October 1926, from
Wassaic, New York. Lorne Pierce papers, Box 3, Queen's
University Archives.

made her home in the Sandy Hill district of Ottawa, moving in 1904 to Wassaic, a country estate in northern New York state, which was to be her home for the rest of her life and where she died on 15 November 1936. Laut was the first person given permission to use material from the Hudson Bay Company archives, such as diaries and photographs, for her works. A successful popularizer of historical and wilderness lore, her closest counterpart today in popularizing the history and adventure of Canada's past is Pierre Berton.

While women do not play a large part in most of Laut's writing, which directs its attention to a largely male world, those women who do appear are intelligent and independent-minded. Coming from civilized surroundings, they nevertheless relate positively to the natural world. Later, Laut wrote a series of articles for *Outing* under the title *Pioneer Women of the West*, including in the series such subjects as "Daughters of the Vikings" and "The Heroines of Spirit Lake."

"Koot and the Bob-Cat" gives a realistic description of one winter in a trapper's life. Koot is a Métis who combines the skills of Indian lore with the knowledge learned from the white men at the post. Praying at the Catholic mission when at the trading post and calling on the Indian Great Spirit when in danger in the wilderness, Koot moves easily between the two worlds. As the narrator explains, the snow is a white page on which he reads the animal tracks that reveal the life of the wilderness.

Laut begins her story by noting the combination of instinct and intelligence that guarantees that the hunter never gets lost, then proves it with Koot, who, despite becoming snow blind, is able to find his way back to the post. With simplicity and directness, and in cadenced prose, Laut echoes in style the tone and character of her story. She captures the urgency of the hunter's situation in the latter part of the story with the urgency of her prose.

First published in *Outing*, "Koot and the Bob-Cat" appeared later in *The Story of the Trapper* (1907). In revising the story for the book, Laut added some introductory and connecting material suitable to the new format. The story appears here as it was first published in *Outing*.

∽

Suggested Reading:

Buchanan, Harriette Cutting. *American Women Writers*, ed. Lina Maineiro. New York: Unger, 1980, 522–524.

Gerson, Carole. "Agnes Christina Laut." In *Dictionary of Literary Biography*, vol. 92, 181–183.

Laut, Agnes C. *Lords of the North*. 1900.

_____. *The Story of the Trapper*. 1907.

_____. *Heralds of Empire*. 1902.

_____. "Pioneer Women of the West." In *Outing*, vols. 51–52 (March–July 1908).

~~

KOOT AND THE BOB-CAT

Agnes Laut

I.

Old whaling ships, that tumble round the world and back again from coast to coast over strange seas, hardly ever suffer any of the terrible disasters that are always overtaking the proud men-of-war and swift liners equipped with all that science can do for them against misfortune. Ask an old salt why this is, and he will probably tell you that he *feels* his way forward or else that he steers by the same chart as *that*—jerking his thumb sideways from the wheel toward some sea-gull careening over the billows. A something, that is akin to the instinct of wild creatures warning them when to go north for the summer, when to go south for the winter, when to scud for shelter from coming storm, guides the old whaler across chartless seas.

So it is with the trapper. He may be caught in one of his great steel traps, and perish on the prairie. He may run short of water, and die of thirst on the desert. He may get his packhorses tangled up in a valley where there is no game, and be reduced to the alternative of destroying what will carry him back to safety or starving with a horse still under him, before he can get over the mountains into another valley—but the true trapper will literally never lose himself.

II.

When the midwinter lull falls on the hunt, there is little use in the trapper going far afield. Moose have "yarded up"; bear have "holed up"; and the beaver are housed till dwindling stores compel them to come out from their snow-hidden domes. There are no longer any buffalo for the trapper to hunt during the lull; but what buffalo formerly were to the hunter, rabbits are to-day. Shields and tepee covers, moccasins, caps and coats, thongs and meat, the buffalo used to supply. These are now supplied by "wahboos—little white chap"; which is the Indian name for rabbit.

So when the lull fell on the hunt, and the mink-trapping was well over, and marten had not yet begun, Koot gathered up his traps, and, getting a supply of provisions at the fur post, crossed the white wastes of prairie to lonely swamp ground, where dwarf-alder and willow and cotton-wood and poplar and pine grew in a tangle. A few old logs, dove-tailed into a square, made the walls of a cabin. Over these he stretched the canvas of his tepee for a roof at a sharp enough angle to let the heavy snowfall slide off from its own weight. Moss chinked up the logs. Snow banked out the wind. Pine boughs made the floor; two logs with pine boughs a bed. An odd-shaped stump served as chair or table; and on the logs of the inner walls hung wedge-shaped slabs of cedar to stretch the skins. A caribou curtain or bear skin across the entrance completed Koot's quarters for the rabbit hunt.

Koot's genealogy was as vague as that of all old trappers hanging round fur posts. Part of him—that part which served best when he was on the hunting field—was Ojibway. The other part, which made him improvise logs into chair and table and bed, was white man; and that served him best when he came to bargain with the chief factor over the pelts. At the fur post he attended the Catholic mission. On the hunting field, when suddenly menaced by some great danger, he would cry out in the Indian tongue words that meant "O Great Spirit!" And it is altogether probable that at the

AGNES LAUT

mission and on the hunting field Koot was worshiping the same Being. When he swore—strange commentary on civilization—he always used whiteman's oaths, French patois or straight English.

The snow is a white page on which the wild creatures write their daily record for those who can read. All over the white swamp were little deep tracks; here, holes as if the runner had sunk; there, padded marks as from the bound—bound—bound of something soft; then, again, where the thicket was like a hedge, with only one breach through, the footprints had beaten a little, hard rut, walled by the soft snow. Koot's dog might have detected a motionless form under the thicket of spiney shrubs, a form that was gray almost to whiteness and scarcely to be distinguished from the snowy underbrush but for the blink of a prism light—the rabbit's eye. If the dog did catch that one tell-tale glimpse of an eye, which a cunning rabbit would have shut, true to the training of his trapper master he would give no sign of discovery except, perhaps, the pricking forward of both ears. Koot, himself, preserved as stolid a countenance as the rabbit playing dead, or simulating a block of wood. Where the footprints ran through the breached hedge, Koot stooped down and planted little sticks across the runway till there was barely room for a weasel to pass. Across the open he suspended a looped string, hung from a twig bent so that the slightest weight in the loop would send it up with a death-jerk for anything caught in the tightening twine.

All day long Koot goes from hedge to hedge, from runway to runway, choosing always the places where natural barriers compel the rabbit to take this path and no other, travelling, if he can, in a circle from his cabin, so that the last snare set will bring him back with many a zigzag to the first snare made. If rabbits were plentiful—as they always were in the fur country of the North, except during one year in seven when an epidemic spared the land from a rabbit pest—Koot's circuit of snares would run for miles through the swamp. Traps for large game would be set out so that the circuit would require many a day; but, where rabbits are numerous, the foragers that prey—wolf and wolverine and lynx and bob-cat—will be numerous, too, and the trapper will not set out more snares than he can visit twice a day.

Finding tracks about the shack, when he came back for his noonday meal, Koot shouted sundry instructions into the mongrel's ears, emphasized them with a moccasin kick, picked up the sack in which he carried bait, twine, and traps, and set out in the evening to make the round of his snares, unaccompanied by the dog. Rabbit after rabbit he found, gray and white, hanging stiff and stark, dead from their own weight, strangled in the twine snares. Snares were set anew, the game strung over his shoulder, and Koot was walking through the gray gloaming for the cabin when that strange sense of *feel* told him that he was being followed. What was it? Could it be the dog?

Koot turned sharply—and whistled—and called his dog. There wasn't a sound. Later, when the frost began to tighten, sap-frosted twigs would snap. The ice of the swamp, frozen like rock, would by and by crackle with the loud echo of a pistol shot—crackle—and strike—and break as if artillery were firing a fusillade and infantry shooters answering sharp. By and by moon and stars and northern lights would set the shadows dancing; and the wail of the cougar would be echoed by the lifting scream of its mate. But now was not a sound, not a motion, not a shadow, only the noiseless stillness, the shadowless quiet, and the *feel*, the *feel* of something back where the darkness was gathering like a curtain in the bush.

It might, of course, be only a silly long-ears loping under cover parallel to the man, looking with rabbit curiosity at this strange newcomer to the swamp home of the animal world. Koot's sense of *feel* told him that it wasn't a rabbit, but he tried to persuade himself that it was, the way a timid listener persuades herself that creaking floors are burglars. Thinking of his many snares, Koot smiled and walked on. Then it came again, that *feel* of something coursing behind the underbrush in the gloom of the gathering darkness. Koot stopped short—and listened—and listened—

listened to a snow-muffled silence, to a desolating solitude that pressed in on the lonely hunter like the waves of a limitless sea round a drowning man.

The sense of *feel* that is akin to brute instinct gave him the impression of a presence. Reason that is man's, told him what it might be and what to do. Was he not carrying the snared rabbits over his shoulder? Some hungry flesh-eater, more bloodthirsty than courageous, was still-hunting him for the food on his back, and only lacked the courage to attack. Koot drew a steel trap from his bag. He did not wish to waste a rabbit skin, so he baited the spring with a piece of fat bacon, smeared the trap, the snow, everything that he had touched, with a rabbit skin, and walked home through the deepening dark to the little log cabin, where a sharp "woof-woof" of welcome awaited him.

That night, in addition to the skins across the doorway, Koot jammed logs athwart, "to keep the cold out," he told himself. Then he kindled a fire on the rough stone hearth built at one end of the cabin, and, with the little clay pipe between his teeth, sat down on the stump chair to broil rabbit. The waste of the rabbit he had placed in traps outside the lodge. Once his dog sprang alert with pricked ears. Man and dog heard the sniff—sniff—sniff of some creature attracted to the cabin by the smell of broiling meat, and now rummaging at its own risk among the traps. And once when Koot was stretched out on a bear skin before the fire puffing at his pipe-stem, drying his moccasins, and listening to the fusillade of frost-rending ice and earth, a long, low, piercing wail rose and fell and died away. Instantly from the forest of the swamp came the answering scream—a lifting, tumbling eldritch shriek.

"I should have set two traps," said Koot. "They are out in pairs."

III.

Black is the flag of danger to the rabbit world. The antlered shadows of the naked poplar or the tossing arms of the restless pines, the rabbit knows to be harmless shadows unless their dapple of sun and shade conceals a brindled cat. But a shadow that walks and runs means to a rabbit a foe; so the wary trapper prefers to visit his snares at the hour of the short shadow.

It did not surprise the trapper, after he had heard the lifting wail from the swamp woods the night before, that the bacon in the trap lay untouched. The still-hunter that had crawled through the underbrush lured by the dead rabbits over Koot's shoulder wanted rabbit, not bacon. But at the nearest rabbit snare, where a poor dead prisoner had been torn from the twine, were queer padded prints in the snow, not of the rabbit's making. Koot stood looking at the tell-tale mark. The dog's ears were all a-prick. So was Koot's sense of *feel*; but he couldn't make this thing out. There was no trail of approach or retreat. The padded print of the thief was in the snow, as if the animal had dropped from the sky and gone back to the sky.

Koot measured off ten strides from the rifled snare, and made a complete circuit round it. The rabbit runway cut athwart the snow circle, but no mark like that shuffling padded print.

"It isn't a wolverine, and it isn't a fisher, and it isn't a coyote," Koot told himself.

The dog emitted stupid little sharp barks, looking everywhere and nowhere, as if he felt what he could neither see nor hear. Koot measured off ten strides more from this circuit, and again walked completely round the snare. Not even the rabbit runways cut this circle.

The white man grows indignant when baffled, the Indian, superstitious. The part that was white man in Koot sent him back to the scene in quick, jerky steps, to scatter poisoned rabbit meat over the snow, and set a trap in which he readily sacrificed a full-grown bunny. The part that was Indian set a world of old memories echoing, memories that were as much Koot's nature as the swarth of his skin, memories that Koot's mother and his mother's ancestors held of the fabulous man-eating wolf called the loup-garou and the great white beaver, father of all beavers and all Indians, that glided through the swamp mists at night like a ghost, and the monster grizzly that stalked with uncouth gambols through the dark, devouring benighted hunters.

This time when the mongrel uttered his sharp bark-ings that said as plainly as a dog could speak: "Something's somewhere! Be careful there—oh!—I'll be *on* to you in just one minute!"—Koot kicked the dog hard with plain anger; and his anger was at himself because his eyes and his ears failed to localize, to *real*-ize, to visualize what those little pricks and shivers tingling down to his finger tips meant. Then the civilized man came uppermost in Koot, and he marched off very matter of fact to the next snare.

But if Koot's vision had been as acute as his sense of *feel*, and he had glanced up to the topmost spreading bough of a pine just above the snare, he might have detected, lying in a dapple of sun and shade, something with large owl eyes, something whose penciled ear-tufts caught the first crisp of the man's moccasins over the snow-crust. Then the ear-tufts were laid flat back against a furry form hardly differing from the dapple of sun and shade. The big owl eyes closed to a tiny blinking slit that let out never a ray of tell-tale light. The big round body, mottled gray and white like the snowy tree, widened—stretched—flattened till it was almost a part of the tossing pine bough. Only when the man and dog below the tree had passed far beyond did the penciled ears blink forward and the owl eyes open and the big body bunch out like a cat with elevated haunches ready to spring.

But by and by the man's snares began to tell on the rabbits. They grew scarce and timid. And the thing that had rifled the rabbit snares grew hunger-bold. One day when Koot and the dog were skimming across the billowy drifts, something black far ahead bounced up, caught a bunting on the wing, and with another bounce disappeared among the trees.

Koot said one word—"Cat!"—and the dog was off full cry.

Ever since he had heard that wailing call from the swamp woods, he had known that there were rival hunters, the keenest of all still-hunters, among the rabbits. Every day he came upon the trail of their ravages, rifled snares, dead squirrels, torn feathers, even the remains of a fox or a coon. And some times he could tell from the printings on the white page that the still-hunter had been hunted full cry by coyote or timber wolf. Against these wolfish foes, the cat had one sure refuge always—a tree. The hungry coyote might try to starve the bobcat into surrender; but just as often the bob-cat could starve the coyote into retreat; for, if a foolish rabbit darted past, what hungry coyote could help giving chase? The tree had even defeated both dog and man that first week when Koot could not find the cat. But a dog in full chase could follow the trail to a tree; and a man could shoot into the tree.

As the rabbits decreased, Koot set out many traps for the bob-cats, now reckless with hunger, steel traps and dead falls and pits, and log pens with live grouse clucking inside. The midwinter lull was a busy season for Koot.

Toward March, the sun glare had produced a crust on the snow that was almost like glass. For Koot on his snow-shoes, this had no danger; but for the mongrel that was to draw the pelts back to the fort, the snow-crust was more troublesome than glass. Where the crust was thick, with Koot leading the way, snowshoes and dog and toboggan glided over the drifts as if on steel runners. But in midday, the crust became very soft, and the dog went floundering through as if on thin ice, the sharp edge cutting his feet. Koot tied little buckskin sacks round the dog's feet and made a few more rounds of the swamp; but the crust was a sign that warned him it was time to prepare for the marten hunt.

To leave his furs at the fort, he must cross the prairie while it was yet good traveling for the dog. Dismantling the little cabin, Koot packed the pelts on the sled, roped all tightly so there could be no spill from an upset, and putting the mongrel in the traces, led the way for the fort one night when the snow-crust was hard as ice.

IV.

The moon came over the white fields in a great silver disk. Between the running man and the silver moon moved black skulking forms—the foragers on their night hunt. Some times a fox loped over a drift, or a coyote rose from the snow, or timber wolves dashed from wooded ravines and stopped to look, till Koot fired a shot that sent them galloping. In the dark that precedes daylight, Koot camped beside a grove of poplars—that is, he fed the dog a fish, and whittled chips to make a fire and boil some tea for himself; then digging a hole in the drift with his snowshoe, he laid the sleigh to windward, and cuddled down between bear skins with the dog across his feet.

Daylight came in a blinding glare of sunshine and white snow. The way was untrodden. Koot led at an ambling run, followed by the dog at a fast trot, so that the trees were presently left far on the offing, and the runners were out on the bare white prairie with never a mark, tree, or shrub to break the dazzling reaches of sunshine and snow from horizon to horizon. A man who is breaking the way must keep his eyes on the ground; and the ground was so blindingly bright that Koot began to see purple and yellow and red patches dancing wherever he looked on the snow. He drew his capote over his face to shade his eyes; but the pace and the sun grew so hot that he was soon running again with a face unprotected from the blistering light.

Toward the afternoon, Koot knew that something had gone wrong. Some distance ahead, he saw a black object against the snow. On the unbroken white, it looked almost as big as a barrel, and seemed at least a mile away; lowering his eyes, Koot let out a spurt of speed, and the next thing he knew, he had tripped his snowshoe and tumbled. Scrambling up, he saw that a stick had caught the web of his snowshoe; but where was the barrel for which he had been steering? There wasn't any barrel at all—the barrel was this black stick—which hadn't been fifty yards away. Koot rubbed his eyes and noticed that black and red and purple patches were all over the snow. The drifts were heaving and racing after each other like waves on an angry sea. He did not go much farther that day; for every glint of snow scorched his eyes like a hot iron. He camped at the first bluff and made a poultice of cold tea leaves, which he laid across his blistered face for the night.

Any one who knows the tortures of snow-blindness will understand why Koot did not sleep that night. It was a long night to the trapper, such a very long night that the sun had been up for two hours before its heat burned through the layers of his capote into his eyes, and roused him from sheer pain. Then he sprang up, put out an ungauntleted hand, and knew from the heat of the sun that it was broad day. But when he took the bandage off his eyes, all he saw was a black curtain one moment, rockets and wheels and dancing patches of purple fire the next.

Koot was no fool to become panicky and feeble from sudden peril. He knew that he was snow-blind on a pathless prairie at least two days away from the fort. To wait until the snow-blindness had healed would risk the few provisions that he had and perhaps expose him to a blizzard. The one rule of the trapper's life is to go ahead, let the going cost what it may; and drawing his capote over his face Koot went on.

The heat of the sun told him the directions; and when the sun went down the crooning west wind, bringing thaw and snow-crust, was his compass. And when the wind fell, the tufts of shrub-growth, sticking through the snow, pointed to the warm south. Now he tied himself to his dog; and when he camped beside trees, into which he had gone full crash before he knew they were there, he laid his gun beside the dog and sleigh. Going out the full length of his cord he whittled the chips for the fire and found his way back by the cord.

On the second day of his blindness no sun came up, nor could he guide himself by the feel of the air, for there was no wind. It was one of the dull, dead, gray days that precedes storm. How would he get his directions to set out?

Memory of last night's travel might only lead him on the endless circling of the lost. Koot dug his snowshoe to the base of a tree, found moss, felt it growing on only one side of the tree, knew that side must be the shady, cold side, and so took his bearings from what he thought was the north.

Koot said the only time that he knew any fear was on the evening of the last day. The atmosphere boded storm. The fort lay in a valley. Somewhere between Koot and that valley ran a trail. What if he had crossed the trail? What if the storm came and wiped out the trail before he could reach the fort? All day whisky-jack and snow-bunting and fox scurried from his presence; but this night, in the dusk, when he felt forward on his hands and knees for the expected trail, the wild creatures seemed to grow bolder. He imagined that he felt the coyotes closer than on the other nights. And then the fearful thought came that he might have passed the trail unheeding. Should he turn back and look for it the other way?

Afraid to go forward or back, Koot sank on the ground, unhooded his face, and tried to force his eyes to see. The pain brought biting, salty tears. It was quite useless. Either the night was very dark or the eyes were very blind.

And then, white man or Indian—who shall say which came uppermost?—Koot cried out to the Great Spirit. In mockery back came the saucy scold of a jay.

But that was enough for Koot—it was prompt answer to his prayer, for where do the jays quarrel and fight and flutter but on the trail? Running eagerly forward the trapper felt the ground. The rutted marks of a "jumper" sleigh cut the hard crust. With a shout Koot headed down the sloping path to the valley where lay the fur post, the low hanging smoke of whose chimneys his eager nostrils had already caught.

☙

Outing 42 (April 1903), 32–38; revised and included in *The Story of the Trapper* (1907).

Frances Elizabeth Herring (1851–1916)

Nan: A Tale of Crossing the Plains to California in the Rush of '49 (1913)

Frances Elizabeth (Clarke) Herring, journalist, travel writer, author of fiction, was born at King's Lynn, Norfolk, England, and educated there and at Reading, Berkshire. In 1874, she married druggist Arthur May Herring of New Westminster, B.C., and became a chronicler of British Columbia history. Writing for the Toronto *Globe*, the New Westminster *Commonwealth*, and other periodicals, she made the history of this most recently settled part of Canada come alive. She also made history herself, becoming the first woman to pass the British Columbia examinations for a class-A teacher's certificate. Herring bore eight children, of whom four survived. She was an active worker for women's rights. She died in 1916.

At the time of Frances Herring's marriage, New Westminster had a population of 1650. Situated fifteen miles from the mouth of the Fraser River, it was the entry point to the interior of British Columbia. Many of Herring's sketches and stories are concerned with the influx of immigrants into British Columbia in the latter half of the nineteenth century. Among her books are *Canadian Camp Life* (1900), an entertaining, at times fictionalized account of a camping group on the British Columbia coast, and *Among the People of British Columbia: Red, White, Yellow, and Brown* (1903), non-fiction sketches of northern Indians and Indian missions, Japanese and Chinese immigrants, and fisherfolk. *In the Pathless West with Soldiers, Pioneers, Miners, and Savages* (1914), tells the story of the Royal Engineers who sailed from England in 1858 to assist British Columbia Governor Douglas to cope with the vast influx of 60,000 miners into an area hitherto inhabited by Indians, and a few Hudson Bay traders and missionaries. Herring begins with the Engineers' lengthy voyage around Cape Horn and up the Fraser River to Fort Langley, and continues with a series of episodes involving miners, soldiers, wives, and children.

Nan, and Other Pioneer Women of the West is a collection of stories based on historical realities. Although published in 1913, the stories have their origin many years earlier, as the preface explains: ". . . these sketches date back forty and even fifty years, and are the result of many reminiscences of which careful note has been kept by the writer for at least thirty years." The stories realistically portray women's lives in the British Columbia interior during the days of the gold rush, the Canadian Pacific Railway surveys, and the building of the railway. All classes are described: good women and bad; intelligent and ignorant; wives, spinsters, and widows; educated and uneducated; naïve and worldly wise; old, middle-aged, and young; in relation to husbands, children, parents, neighbours; women coping and women failing to cope. Some are happy stories, some sad, some romantic and some humorous; all are characterized by their vivid portrayal of a frontier land, of everyday life and of simple pleasures in a society with few women. A frequent theme of the stories is the shortage of women, which allows any woman of any age or class to choose among the many bachelors in the region. "Miss Phoebe's Courtship," for example, tells of a woman nearing forty who comes to live with a married sister in a town of 400 in the interior of British Columbia. Despite being well past the usual marriageable age, she can have her pick of any man between eighteen and sixty. Through a series of humorous incidents contrived by her adolescent niece and nephew, she is happily married to the most eligible backwoodsman in the district.

The title story, "Nan," is the harshest in the collection. As a child, Nan journeys with her family across America in a tragedy-beset caravan. The story follows the family up the coast and into the interior of British Columbia. With a lazy father and brutal mother, Nan, a willing worker, is from early childhood a slave to her parents. Her attempt to escape

FRANCES ELIZABETH HERRING

at seventeen leads her to an even grimmer life with an abusive husband. Nan's sole source of affection is a young half-breed girl. Ironically, the true survivor in this story of pioneer life is Nan's mother, an unfeeling, ruthless, hardworking woman, who takes advantage not only of her daughter but of the kindly neighbouring Indians who offer help. The story is told in simple, understated prose that adds to its bleakness, which a more emotional telling would not.

∾

Suggested Reading:

Herring, Frances E. *Nan and Other Pioneer Women of the West.* London: Frances Griffiths, 1913.
_____. *In the Pathless West with Soldiers, Pioneers, and Savages.* London: T. Fisher Unwin, 1914.

⁓

Nan: A Tale of Crossing the Plains to California in the Rush of '49

Frances E. Herring

CHAPTER I

Among the nondescript element that lent itself readily to the reckless stampede for the California Gold Fields, was a family named Lickmore. Luke, the father, Tryphosa, the mother, with Polly and Nan, their hopeful progeny.

No one seemed to know whence this family came, or how they travelled, only that they had joined a western bound caravan, somewhere on the great plains. Trailing into camp one night after sunset, without asking anyone's leave, they out-spanned and cooked their evening meal. Next morning their ox cart fell into line behind the more pretentious bullock wagons, (prairie schooners), with their white covers, and the mule teams. The strangers evidently wished to cast in their lot with the rest, and with them brave the dangers of the unknown trail, a country swarming with hostile Indians, and all the uncertain elements of nature.

Tryphosa, or as her husband called her Try-phosy, with a long accent on the first syllable and a pause after it, had a sharp tongue of her own, but she had learned in the school of adversity that 'silence is golden.' Like the cat, watching her opportunity, that comes quietly in and takes the warmest corner by the fireside, without disturbing anyone, she is allowed to remain because unnoticed; whilst the dog, which snarls for his place, is promptly driven out; so Mrs. Lickmore worked her way, dragging her good natured but helpless husband in with her.

Several companies of men had joined this same caravan, but, finding it over-burdened with women and children, they had left what provisions they could spare from their own outfits and hastened on, some of them falling into the hands of marauding savages, as relics they came across showed; others passing carelessly on to the diggings, and different fates; while this hen-and-chicken-gang, as they were dubbed, went scatheless. They raised their voices night and morning in prayer, praise, and exhortation, under their leader; the sound travelling far and near, but never a Redskin did they see. In these services the Lickmores joined, Try-phosy from policy, Luke because he loved the music, and the little girls because their mother took them.

This being the only instruction, religious or secular, they had ever known or ever did know, the girls, especially Nan, looked back upon it in after life, and still marvelled at the power of these people to sing lustily, talk long and loudly, and pray without ceasing. Thus they journeyed.

Their leader was a good man, and an upright, but he had never been over the trail before, and was indulgent with his flock. A day in camp was allowed when a little soul arrived among them, to give the mother a chance before she travelled on again in her bullock-wagon-home. Or he camped an hour or two ahead of time to give some unfortunate member of the party, who had succumbed to the hardships of the weary way, decent burial, with prayers, psalms, and exhortations over the remains, so soon to be left in their lonely grave.

Few horses or mules remained with them, and the man who had been hired as guide, sneaked off one night with the owners of those remaining, and left the caravan to its fate.

He had frequently warned the leader of the risk he ran of being caught in the mountains by the winter storms, if they did not make better progress. The bullock wagons were slow enough without these delays.

But time was no object, they argued, so long as the 'grub' held out; and they dawdled on their sunny way, killing their oxen for meat as their dunnage grew lighter, feeling that the summer never would pass, and that they were journeying not only to 'a land flowing with milk and honey,' as their leader daily reminded them, but to a country where gold could be picked up without the trouble of working for it. So they took things easy, careless of the mountain difficulties which lay between them and their 'land of Canaan.'

The mountains had looked so beautiful in the distance, furnishing many a poetical allusion to their leader, that the party had no apprehensions as they commenced the upward trail, but with fewer oxen they found it necessary to throw away everything that could be spared from their outfit, and the ascent became slower and more arduous every day, till one morning the camp awoke to find itself buried in snow, and the storm still sweeping around in dark and blinding eddies.

Several of the more hardy advised to push on, but those who knew anything of mountain travel refused point-blank, for as yet the summit had not been reached. Those who were strong enough followed the daring few, and were soon lost to view in the snow clouds.

The leader counselled that they try to find a cave large enough to shelter them and their animals, and that they make themselves as comfortable as possible till the storm had passed, saying in conclusion, that a week or ten days' rest would do none of them any harm, he thought, except it might be the animals; and for them their owners must 'get out and hustle.'

One of their number had noticed such a cave, somewhere off the beaten track, and volunteered to find it.

FRANCES E. HERRING

While he was gone camp was struck, and all made ready for moving, so when he returned with a favourable report, they eagerly followed him.

They found the cave both large and well sheltered, and the wanderers soon made themselves at home. Part of the men and boys attended to the animals, others brought in and stored the supplies, whilst strong arms swung heavy axes and brought in fuel.

Soon fires blazed cheerily, bacon frizzled, pan-bread stood baking over the coals, and the bean-pots of the night before were put to heat.

Here they enjoyed the rest for one, even two weeks, but the snow continued to fall, and it was impossible to get food of any kind for the oxen, so they had to be killed to save them from dying.

There was natural cold storage to have kept the meat good for months, but those who owned the cattle ate to the full, and sold to their neighbours at big prices all they chose to spare, with neither thought nor care for the future.

The leader, who, as we said before, was a good man, honest in his convictions, was scarcely a fit person to rule over the others; he lacked the strength of purpose, the firmness of will and the power of initiative, which go to make the ruler of men. He had prayer meetings both morning and night, with lengthy exhortations and much singing of hymns and psalms.

This kept the minds of the people occupied and saved much bickering and quarrelling, whilst the remainder of the waking hours was spent by the men in digging themselves out for the wood supply, and by the women in cooking and gossiping, washing and mending. For some sixty persons require a great deal of looking after to keep up the general comfort.

The children of course were happy so long as their natural protectors were by, and the pinch of hunger as yet unfelt.

A month passed thus, then the elders began to look at the weather very gravely, and at the fast diminishing supplies.

It was agreed to lump all the provisions, and allow them to be rationed three times a day, then morning and night, then once a day. But they all clamoured for more than their proper allowance, and contentment was at an end as soon as the rations fell below the satisfying point.

The people murmured, threatened and quarrelled, berating their leader for having lingered by the way, and laying all disasters at his door.

Many refused to join in the long services, but they could not help hearing those who did, and thus their minds were somewhat diverted for the time being from their calamities.

The weaker members died and were buried away back in the caves, that being the only unfrozen ground available.

Looking for a burial place, they came across a rippling spring flowing into a self-made basin, thus they were saved from the ills of snow water.

Then there came the fateful morning when the last bean was served out, and starvation stared them gauntly in the face.

For five days they had nothing but water, and they sat huddling over the fires, there was little strength to keep up.

More deaths occurred; and as they looked at the stiffening bodies, the thought occurred to some, 'If they were only cattle.' Surreptitiously the bodies were taken, cooked and eaten in the far recesses of the mountain caves.

The leader sat with his head between his hands, feeling powerless to restrain, but he prayed and exhorted, being too weak to sing. All to no purpose, when the pangs of hunger again passed reason, and no one died, they demanded that one be killed for the day's supply.

Shuddering with horror: for this leader, grotesque as were some of his methods, had the courage of the old martyrs, and would have sat with his followers praying and awaiting release by merciful death, glorying in the providence that took him and them on a nearer road to Heaven. He refused to consent, and actually put them off till next day. Then, insane with hunger, and ignoring him, they cast lots, and the lot fell upon a woman.

328   FRANCES E. HERRING

With wolfish, pitiless eyes, they stood by while she was blindfolded, killed and divided by weight among them.

One of those present (from whom this narrative was obtained), saw the daughter of the unfortunate woman, ravenously devouring a part of her mother's heart, and he 'wondered what her feelings must be!'

The leader formed the next repast, he fell forward while engaged in lonely prayer, and his soul returned to its Maker. Starvation itself could not force him to break the laws of nature.

For a week longer they subsisted in this ghastly manner, each one eyeing the other suspiciously, and speculating as to who would be to-morrow's victim.

Then, as one of the men, almost a skeleton, was weakly trying to get more fuel, he was hailed by two men in a sleigh, drawn by a pair of horses.

Getting the strangers to give him something to eat first, he guided them to the starving community, who, in their madness or hunger, would surely have eaten them, had they not been provided with both weapons and supplies. While one dealt out what they had, the other stood with a loaded gun, and made the community pass one by one and receive its small allowance.

The two men drove away with only one horse, leaving the other for food. It was easy to see the regret with which they parted from the animal, but to these starvelings, who had daily been called upon to sacrifice one of their number for the subsistence of the rest, the slaughter of the horse was an easy matter, and not even a drop of blood was allowed to go to waste.

Some days later when mule teams arrived with provisions, they found the unfortunates of the cave, chewing the hide of the horse, and clamouring for lots to be again cast. So easy is it for poor humanity to descend even below the level of the 'beasts which perish.'

Those who brought the supplies had taken the precaution to cache the greater part of them at different places on the way.

Again the rescuers had to stand behind their guns to keep off the starving crowd, now reduced to some thirty people, make them take only their own share, and not steal from each other the necessarily small allowance made. As they followed their rescuers, though some dropped by the way and were buried, the insanity of hunger died out from their wolfish eyes, and they were themselves again.

Their benefactors were a religious body which had established itself in a neighbouring valley, and thither they took the survivors of the caravan, but needless to say the members dispersed as soon as possible, none caring to come in contact with others of the party who had known of their fearful experiences.

CHAPTER II

Having passed through such scenes of horror, Tryphosa was scarcely likely to be filled with the milk of human kindness, and her naturally hard character grew harder and more grasping.

Now her husband, poor Luke Lickmore, had been born with an incurable disease. It permeated his bones, went untiringly through his circulation, and his very flesh was under its potent sway. He would look up sadly from his usual occupation of sedulously doing nothing, and say mournfully, "I comed of a consumpted fambly, and taint no use'n you goin' on Tryphosy. I was borned 'ith a"—when Tryphosa would break in with "Yis, yis, I'n got good cause ter know as yu's borned 'ith a bad enough disease, an' thet's nothin' but laziness! bone laziness!! durned laziness!!!" her voice growing shriller at each repetition of the word "laziness."

Seeing him about to open his mouth she would raise her hands, and, knowing from experience, that anything it might contain, from a hot teapot to a bucket of cold water, would come flying his way if he continued his plaint, he generally made discretion the better part of valor, and contented himself by pretending to choke back a cough.

330   FRANCES E. HERRING

"Durned laziness that's what yu's borned 'ith, an' yer gels is es bad es yu be."

From the same cause Luke never worked more than a day in any man's mine or camp, and Tryphosa had to wash and mend, bake bread and cake for the miners, and get along as best she could,—but never for a moment allowing her lord and master to forget that he depended on her efforts for every mouthful he ate. His dress cost him nothing, for he was not in any way proud, and would wear whatever old clothes the miners chose to throw his way; consequently, though a tall and rather well made man, he usually looked like a scare-crow.

There had been several stampedes to fresh diggings in the mountains of Nevada, and the good woman became tired of following up her work, so she made the best of her way to 'Frisco only to find herself and her 'fambly' more out of place than ever.

People were now coming North to British Columbia, in steamers, barges, sailing vessels, sloops, and even row-boats and canoes, for they could follow up the coast all the way, the only danger being that sometimes they went up the Columbia river, or Puget Sound, instead of the Fraser river, the latter being the entrance to the Cariboo country, where the placer mining had been struck, this being the mining where any man could stake his own claim, and wash out the gold for himself, needing no other machinery than a hand rocker and a shovel.

Tryphosa shipped herself on a good size schooner as cook, her man as deck hand, and the two little girls were readily taken by the good-natured captain as super-cargo.

They carried as many passengers as could crowd in, and lie under tarpaulin on the deck at night.

Tryphosa was a happy woman, for her hands were full of good supplies, and she cooked all day, and would have kept on all night if necessary. Thus she brought her 'fambly' to Victoria, then called.

Here the Captain decided to go on to Port Douglas, then the head of navigation for the Cariboo diggings, for to that port he could get eight cents per pound for all the freight he could stow, and ten dollars per head for each passenger. He was anxious to keep so thrifty a woman as Tryphosa on board, and actually went so far as to suggest "it would be better to chuck that freckless Luke overboard," figuratively speaking, of course, and "take up with him," for he was fond of the little girls, and would make her a good man.

Tryphosa spurned his offer, although she continued to make use of him. She had plans of her own, and 'sending herself to the dogs' was not one of them. She had married her man before the priest knowing what he was, and she meant to stand by him, in her own way, of course.

Passing on up the wide and beautiful Fraser, whose virgin forests of splendid pine and maple reached the water's edge, she kept a lookout for some deserted cabin, on land which had been taken up and abandoned, such as she had heard some of the passengers talking about, who had been up that way before.

Just such a place she saw a few miles below the mouth of the Harrison River. Here she made the reluctant captain put them ashore with her few belongings, and all the groceries she had brought with her or had confiscated from the liberal supply on board the sloop. These consisted of tea and coffee, a sack or two of potatoes, a little sugar and molasses, a sack of beans, vegetable seeds, nails, blankets, and so on.

When Tryphosa reached the cabin, she found four good walls of logs, but no roof, no floor and no fireplace.

Nothing daunted, she made Luke cut wood to keep a fire of logs going outside, while she and the girls raised a couple of blankets for shelter inside.

What mattered it that there was no roof? It was May, and all the country was green and fresh, only a little snow here and there in the thick forest and up the mountain sides.

Much against his will, Luke had to cross-cut some fallen cedar trees; 'shake' lengths (4 ft.), and split them for roofing.

Frances E. Herring

Nan held one end of the saw, and helped to split the cedar with an instrument called a 'frou,' while Polly and her mother constructed a 'Miner's oven,' and baked some pan-bread over the ashes of the camp fire.

Any one might have noticed when Tryphosa landed, she had been very particular about the safety of a certain barrel; this was with a view to her miner's oven, and many a savory meal she cooked in it.

The usual construction of a miner's oven was in this way:—You secure good clay and build it up about two feet high, and four feet square. Wood of equal length is then laid upon it, and finished with an arch of supple cedar or vine maples placed close together; this again, is covered with clay, and plastered neatly over. Then you fire the wood inside and burn away the arch, which leaves an oven of clay. You heat the oven by burning wood or sticks inside till it is sufficiently hot, then you remove the ashes, and bake whatever you require, and your oven lasts a long time.

It may be that fresh air, out-door exercise and hunger furnish a better sauce than one finds in the confines of civilization, but let any one try a sockeye salmon just drawn from the Fraser, and baked in one of these ovens, and he will see for himself how good it is.

Tryphosa, not knowing what wood might be obtainable in a new country, had therefore brought this two hundred pound sugar barrel along, for with that she had been sure of making a good job of her oven, and one of the ends could be nailed together to form a door, which otherwise would have to be cut from some good sized hard wood tree, and she knew, though Luke would relish what was cooked, he would grumble at a 'consumpted' man having to cross-cut an oven door of hard wood.

It was not long before some of the Cheam tribe of Indians came over to see who was in the white man's cabin.

This greatly delighted Tryphosa, who had no fear of these people, for she had been brought up near them on the plains of the United States, being a soldier's daughter; and Luke, for all his slovenly appearance, had drilled and marched with the army. It was the fact of his desertion therefrom, which made them say so little of their antecedents, and at the same time accounted for their sudden appearance among the ill-fated caravan. Tryphosa knew better than to truckle to the Indians, she felt safe, too, for she had taken the precaution to 'cache' or hide, her provisions.

With such a river flowing by, Tryphosa thought there ought to be plenty of fish, so she made the Indians understand she was hungry, that she had no canoe, and she wanted them to go and catch fish for her.

Off they paddled, and up a small stream or slough running into the main river. There they waited, spear in hand, for salmon are never taken by hook and line in the Fraser. The big spring salmon, weighing from forty to sixty pounds were running, and soon one of these gladdened the eyes of Tryphosa.

She sent the Squaw to clean the salmon in the river, and the Buck for fuel. Soon the savages were squatting on their heels gravely watching the mysteries of a miner's oven, and patiently waiting the course of events.

Tryphosa had made a huge tin of tea, that is, she boiled a small quantity of tea in a large pot of water.

When all was ready, she seated everybody on the ground, and served each of them with a bountiful supply of fish on a clean piece of bark. Sweetening her tea plentifully with molasses, she handed it round in large tin pannicans, and with copious draughts of this decoction, they washed down the delicious fish and the soggy bread; the Indians burning their throats in their eagerness for the sweetened delicacy.

"Whether you be consumpted, or whether you be not, Luke Lickmore, you kin allest eat a good square meal, when it is set afore you," remarked Tryphosa, to her better half, as a kind of indispensable sauce to the repast.

Wiping the grease of the salmon from his mouth on the back of his hand, Luke slowly remarked, "It's allest good when you cook it, Tryphosy." Which compliment so astonished the good woman, that she forgot what she had intended to say.

Luke, who could see his way to some help worth having from the stalwart savage, took him off, and Tryphosa muttered to herself, "Well, he hes got some sense arter all," for she caught his idea.

Beckoning the squaw, she followed the men. Ordering Luke on the roof, she kept the buck splitting shakes, the girls handing up nails, (which her foresight had provided from the cargo of the sloop) while she and the squaw kept Luke supplied with shakes.

That night they had a good tight roof on their cabin, and next day a chimney, the lower part of stones plastered together with mud, the upper of green wood, was added.

When others of the tribe paid visits, Luke tried to get them to help him to dig ground for potatoes, beans and corn, but the noble savages were afflicted with Luke's own disease, perhaps even to a greater extent, for in those days they could still make their squaws work for and wait on them; so he got the squaws to help, and then only by the bribe of some garment or other from the general stock, which, needless to say, was small.

Tryphosa went over to the ranch-a-rie, or Indian village, at the foot of the mountain, and found she could exchange some of her clothes for chickens and a young sow in pig. Also that a buxom squaw would give her a young heifer for the dress she wore. So Tryphosa promptly closed the bargain, and returned to her cabin minus her outer garment, for she knew the mind of woman, especially savage woman, is apt to change, and this bargain was too good to tamper with.

Then poor Luke had to dig and delve with Tryphosy on the spade beside him, and he found it really hard work to keep up with her, for she was as the Indians called her, 'hyas skookum, tecoup kloothman' (big, strong, white woman).

Thus they worked for several years, till Tryphosy had butter, eggs, chickens, vegetables, and sometimes a whole pig or calf to sell to the steamboats as they passed.

They began to be what they considered, 'very well off,' especially when you come to think that butter was fifty or sixty cents per pound, according to the season; eggs, from fifty cents to a dollar per dozen, and all the other articles in proportion.

Tryphosa had found that the original squatter had never proved up on his claim, and so she took advantage of the fact, counted his improvements in with her own, and obtained her Crown Grant, perhaps all the easier that she was a woman, and a comely dame at that.

Here the girls grew in stature and in ignorance, for Tryphosa's one idea was to hustle everybody, and the girls never saw the inside of a school or a church, but were kept incessantly at work, and few beyond the inhabitants of the ranch-a-rie, knew of their existence.

Some ten miles above them was a cord wood camp, run by two white men. They cut trees from the forest, floated them to a rude landing they had made, cross-cut them in four-foot lengths, split and piled them close to the water's edge, and here the steamboats put in for their supply of fuel, as they were all fitted to burn wood, it being before the discovery of the vast deposits of coal at Nanaimo, on Vancouver Island.

One of these men, the elder, had taken to himself a maid of the forest, without banns or license, named Kehala, whom he called Kitty, and for some years she had patiently borne his blows and vagaries of temper, had toiled to raise potatoes, catch and cure fish and keep together some kind of a home according to her lights, leaving him the greater part of his hard-earned money to spend in saloon and dance-house orgies when he went to town.

The second man was younger, of large stature and great strength. He had set his mind on a good-looking half-breed girl, and was doing his best to get her to come and live with him, as poor Kitty had done with his 'pard.'

But Juanita had come under the influence of the Roman Catholic Mission, which had been established among her people, and refused utterly to have anything to do with him, unless he put upon her finger a plain gold ring,

FRANCES E. HERRING

"same as white woman," she said, and that with the blessing of her own Mission Priest.

This angered the insolent bully. On his return from one of these unsuccessful expeditions, he came across Nan Lickmore, hunting her cows through the woods, and struck up an acquaintance with her.

He drove home the cattle and tried to make himself agreeable to her mother, but that thrifty personage could see in that transaction only the loss of Nan's services, and little profit in a son-in-law like Long Ned. She ordered him roughly off the premises, and threatened Nan with vengeance if she dared to meet him anywhere else.

This was unfortunate for the poor girl, because, if she had had a chance to see more of him, his utter wickedness, and his shameless disregard for all the decencies of life, even as she knew them, would most likely have disgusted her, for she would have seen him as he was, not as her inexperienced fancy pictured him.

Her whole being longed for love and sympathy. She was of a gentle, yielding disposition, as guileless as a fawn, and therefore an easy prey.

She frequently met Long Ned now, when she was hunting the cows, and he had several times proposed that she should come with him and look after his cabin, promising her plenty of new dresses, that she should go to town whenever she had a mind to, and anything else he thought likely to tempt a young girl.

One thing Tryphosa had done beside make the girls work. She had impressed upon them the necessity of rectitude with regard to themselves, and we have seen her pass through 'much tribulation,' but with her good name unsullied. This, she had taught her girls, and Nan had remained true to herself, and would only consent to go with Ned upon condition, that they went first to town, and got a 'passon' to marry them.

Town was a city of wonders to this shy girl of nature. She had only been there twice with her mother, and its few wooden stores were like enchanted palaces to her: she had never thought so many fine clothes, and such imposing supplies of groceries, hardware, boots and shoes, crockery and so on, were to be found in the world.

The girl's clear skin, blue eyes and auburn hair, which hung fluffily about her face, received many an admiring glance on the second visit, and thrifty Tryphosa determined to "keep her away from that," for Nan was her best worker, Polly being as lazy as her father, who had now the real excuse of rheumatism, which he had contracted by lying down on the damp earth and going to sleep when sent after the cows, so as not to be on hand for any 'chores' before milking time.

Tryphosa would say to him, "Yous aint consumpted wuth a cent, Luke Lickmore. Ef yu hed, I cud a gotten a better man, an' now yu hev ben an' got the rheumatis, an' I guess yer mean ter hang on, whether ur no."

The cabin had been enlarged by the addition of two shake rooms, one on either side; they had board floors now instead of earth, an iron cook stove stood in the original cabin, which was parlor, dining-room, and kitchen. Here were brought a sickly calf, a neglected pigling, or an early brood of chickens, so the place had an odour all its own, but it was home, and Tryphosa was content, for had she not succeeded? What more does any one want?

Some klis-klis, or Indian mats, made from the dried tooley, a kind of rush, which grows in swampy places, were on the floor. These the squaws usually wove in squares of different sizes, the main portion being in the natural colour of dry straw, with bars and borders of brown strips of smooth cedar-bark.

The rough cedar table was covered with an oil cloth. There were two rocking chairs of wood, several smaller chairs, shelves upon the walls, on which were arranged cups, plates, and dishes of earthenware, with which the battered tin had been replaced, curtains and flowers in the one window, and a cheerful fire, showing through the open front of the cook stove, which shed a general air of comfort over all.

Tryphosa's mornings were busy in making butter, dressing turkeys, chickens or ducks for the steamboat; her afternoons in sewing, patching and knitting, or by way of pleasure, she allowed herself time for sewing carpet rags and 'hooking' these laboriously into mats and rugs.

Long Ned had met Nan a few days before, and set a limit to his time of probation. Nan must leave her cabin home and go with him to the 'passon,' or he would take Juanita to the priest.

The day had arrived, but Nan was still undecided. One kind word from her mother would have been enough, but it had been drive, drive, drive, since daylight that morning, and the girl was weary and heartsick.

"Nan set that theer bread. Run, Nan, hookey's in them cabbages. Ef on'y yer pare'd stir his stumps and nail up that fence. Nan dig taters fer dinner. Nan start on thet theer wash. Wheer is thet good-fur-nothin' Polly?"

Never a word of approval, nay even a continued dissatisfaction with her efforts. Some flour was spilt as she kneaded the bread. She used too much soap and too little water for the wash. She had picked on the smallest 'taters' to dig, and so on, while Polly, after chopping some wood, had made excuse to go and hunt a stray pig or two, which she knew were in the barn, and was herself taking things easy on the sunny side of that structure.

Dinner over, and the precious cups, saucers, and plates of thick white ware washed and returned to their shelves, Polly and her father had gone to cut wood at their leisure, and Nan had put together her best clothes, wondering to herself if she would go with Ned if he came for her, sometimes longing for him to come, then hoping he would stay away and take the half-breed girl.

Now it was "Nan! Nan! Them cows be waitin' in the barn. They'll jest be most eat up 'ith the meskeeters. What kin the gel be a doin'? Fixin' up some of her clos, I guess. She's dead stuck on thet theer Long Ned, but he's no good, no good."

Mrs. Lickmore got up from her carpet rags, and went to the girls' room. "Yes. I jest thought so. Fixing' up, aint yer goin' tu milk tuday? Yer father fetched them cows inter the barn half an hour or more sence, an' they'll be most tu wild ter milk, 'ith them skeeters an' flies."

"Mare," said the girl, as she turned her pretty, youthful face pleadingly to her mother, "Do you ever think anything of us gels 'ceptin' the work we kin git through?" Without heeding look or tone, with only the milkin' on her mind, the mother replied unfeelingly, "Yer kin bet I think er yer, when I'ver gotten shews an' clos, an' wittals to pay fer, an' taint much work as any on yer does to pay fer it. Ef yer hed'nt got me ter look arter things yer'd starve, thet yer would, an' I don't know es the world'ed be much the wuss off ef yer did."

These outbreaks were not at all unusual on the part of Tryphosa, but Nan's pretty blue eyes hardened as she took up an old jacket and put it on over the cheap, clean cotton dress she wore. Her auburn hair lay in curls on her forehead, hidden by an old hat of her father's.

"You be'nt goin' inter the barn wi' them best boots on, be yer? An' yer be comin' right back arter the milkin'?" asked Tryphosa, suspiciously.

"Wheer else shud I be goin'?" asked the girl, tears of defiance now in her eyes.

"Oh, I dunno, yuse fixin' up so much, I 'lowed you might be goin' off tu suthin' or other wi' that feller they call Long Ned; an' ef yer du, don't yu be acomin' round heer no more, thet's all; for yu'll be no gel o' mine ef yer du, mind thet now. Jest let me ketch him anywheres round heer, thet's all. He's arter no good, an' I tell yer so."

She shook her fist in the girl's face, and went off satisfied that she had done her duty, and warned her daughter. At the same time, Nan knew that the die once cast, and her lot thrown in with Ned, that, as she expressed it, her mother would "have no more use for her." "I shan't disgrace yer, Mare, niver you fear," called out the girl.

Then she hurriedly put out her best boots, hat and jacket through the one pane of glass, which served as a window in the girls' room, and passed out with a great show of dirty boots, and clatter of milk buckets. The mother, for all the hard experiences of her life, must have had a soft place left in her composition, for she sighed as she looked after her and repeated, "Niver disgrace me, I ain't 'feared o' thet, but I be afeard yu'd git hard usage 'ith thet great hulks of a feller, thet's all my gel. All the same, ef yer go, yer stay."

But the girl passed on to her doom, all unconscious of this latent kindness, and fully convinced that her mother was as hard as she seemed.

"Oh, is thet yu, Ned?" and the start the girl gave was not feigned.

"Skeered to see me, be'nt yer? Didn't expect me, did yer?" Then catching the slim figure in his arms, he kissed her repeatedly, a liberty, callous as he was, he had never dared to take before.

As she struggled unavailingly to free herself, he said, "Why don't yer yell, call the old woman. She'll soon turn me out."

"Why couldn't we be married right from hum, like other people," she found breath enough to say. "I don't like sneakin' off like this, and Pare away, tu."

"You won't niver want him, when yu've got me. Come on, I'll take yer fixin's."

"Polly," called Mrs. Lickmore, "what be talkin' 'bout in the barn? let Nan git thru 'ith her milkin'."

"Hear that?" he whispered. "The old woman'll come herself presently, an' then there'll be a rumpus."

Nan stood undecided. She half wished her mother would come. Ned saw this, he made a dash for the 'fixin's,' picked up the girl and deposited them and her in a rowboat, jumped in and began to pull up river, under cover of the overhanging bush.

Nan had been looking wistfully, but fearfully up the path, and did not at first notice this.

"What be goin' up fer?" she asked.

"To camp, where else?"

Nan stood up, and seizing the branch of a tree, stopped the boat.

"Well, what be doin' now?" he asked slyly.

"Goin' back. I ain't goin' to no camp, 'cept I go to passon fust."

"Allright," he returned with assumed carelessness. "It's all the same to me." Then seeing Nan was not satisfied, he added, "I thought you might want ter fix up a bit, and the steamer stops at our place." This the steamboat did not do on her down trip, and that Nan knew very well. He turned the boat, crossed the river which is very wide here, and rowed down to the point where a steamer was sure to stop, and Nan turned her attention to her own personal appearance, and dressed for her wedding, as she sat in the rickety old boat.

⟋

"Long time milkin'," grumbled Tryphosa, as she sat sewing on her carpet rags, in the shade of the cabin.

Another half hour passed. "She aint brought none in yit, wonder what she's at." Then seeing Polly, she called, "Go an' see ef Nan aint done milkin' yet, I dunno what's keepin' her so long."

"I aint a goin' to help her, I'm dead beat out," returned Polly, as she reluctantly went to the barn. But forgetting her assumed tiredness, when she reached the barn, and running back breathless, she panted, "Nan aint theer, an' no milkin' ben done."

Together they returned. There lay the old hat, they found the worn jacket by the river, with the marks of a man's footsteps, and a dent in the clay where a boat had pushed in. They raised their voices and called, "Nan! Nan!" till river and forest rang with the name. No answer. Nan was steaming away down river, her heart sinking, and wishing herself back among the mosquitoes, milking in the barn.

The passengers seemed to understand the situation. Women stood away from her, while men plied Ned with whiskey, and 'chaffed' him coarsely on his matrimonial venture.

"Ef on'y your Pare was to hum," said Tryphosa, turning to a broken reed for support, as for once in her life she felt powerless to act.

"Theer's no boat an' no horse anywheres round heer," returned Polly, "an' if theer was, they've got the steamer fer town more'n an hour ago. I seen her pass when I was at the p'int."

"Do you think they've gone to town?" questioned the mother fearfully.

"Niver yu feer, they've gone theer, sure enough. Our Nan aint the gel to go any wheer's else."

"Did yu's know es they was goin' then?"

"No, I didn't know, but I 'lowed es much from the things she said in her sleep. Suthin' 'bout nary a body carin' 'bout her heer, an' work, work the hull time. Then tellin' Ned to marry her frum hum like any one else."

"Thet he niver would," exclaimed Tryphosa with decision.

"No, I 'lowed not, an' thet's why they're gone off like this."

"Well, she stays off, an' ef yuse go anigh her, yu kin stay off tu, an' so kin Pare."

CHAPTER III

Nearly a year had passed and Nan had never left the lonely cord wood camp by the river, with the big mountain towering behind, and shutting off the afternoon sun early, from the soppy low-lying land, between it and the river.

The high water of the spring freshet had carried off her chicken house, and she had not been able to replace it, and Ned would not trouble; that was her business.

"Why don't yer fix up a gardin, an' hev some taters an' truck growin', like Juanity, an' some o' them other wimmen.

All yer du fum mornin' till night, is ayther to set an' cry, or else spile good flour makin' bad bread. It's a nice thing fer a man tu keep a wife an' hev ter cook his own grub an' hearn tu. Here! Fetch in some water an' wood, yer ———. Ef I'd on'y hed sense enough tu marry Juanity, 'stead a lettin' thet loafen half-breed get her, I'd a ben alright. I hed to go to passon wi' yu, an' thet's all she wanted. Ef I hedn't a bin fule enough to du thet, yu could a gone home ef they'd a tuk yer, or any wheers else, an' good riddance tu bad rubbage." She took up a kettle and dragged herself to the river to fill it, thinking sadly, "ef he on'y hed a took Juanity, ef he on'y hed," but she dared not answer him, for it was plain he had gotten liquor off the passing boat, and was just far enough gone to be brutal. As she set the kettle on the rickety old stove, she looked up at him, trembling, for fear of a kick or a blow, for poor young thing she was drawing nigh to motherhood, and longed for some woman's presence, especially her mother. Taking her courage in both hands, she asked, "Don't yer think, Ned, Mare'd come, ef yer went an' told her what was the matter, I du feel powerful bad."

"Yer Mare," he shouted with an oath. "She aint goin' ter set fut in this shebang. I've hed enough o' one o' the fambly, I don't want no more on 'em. Ef any o' them crowd come around, I'll chuck 'em in the river, an' thet'll be one better'n the old woman, orderin' me off'n the place like a dawg."

Nan began to cry.

"Yes cry. It's all yu iver du or iver hev done, sense yer come heer. I haint no patience wi' it all."

He gave her a push as he spoke, which sent her full length on the floor, over a broken chair. He was astonished at the effect of his blow, for it must be remembered that he was very strong, and Nan very weak.

She screamed in mortal agony, for there, lying where the blow of her husband had sent her, a babe arrived in this world of calamity.

"What kin I du. Tell me what to du. I didn't mean to hurt ye like thet."

"Fetch Kitty," she said faintly.

Glad to have something to do, he ran down to his partner's shack. Kitty was sitting in a canoe, away out in the river, patiently fishing. Even after she heard him and comprehended that she was wanted, it took some time for her to paddle in.

She returned with him. Nan was lying, very faint and weak, where she had been left.

Kitty lifted her upon the bunk, gave her some tea sweetened with coarse sugar, and made her as comfortable as she could.

Nan drank the tea eagerly, and presently feeling somewhat revived, asked, "Kitty, wheer's the baby?"

"Mamalushe (dead)," said Kitty, laconically.

"Let me see it."

The girl mother stroked it tenderly, kissed the lips, through which the breath of this life had never passed, and said, "He can't hurt you, my poor little feller," apparently relieved to think it was beyond his power.

Kitty went out and buried it.

After lying quiet for awhile, Nan asked again, "Shall I die, Kitty?"

"Halo!" (no).

"Oh, how I wish I would," she sighed wearily. "I be'nt twenty yit by two year, what shall I du? Life is orful long. Mare was hard on me, or I'd a niver took up wi' Ned. Polly allest made me du my work an' hearn, but Pare was good to me, when the others didn't know it." Kitty nodded comprehendingly, she understood very well what was said, but like most of her people, would never speak English if she could help it.

Nan seldom waited for her to answer, but rambled on, as she had gotten into the way of doing, from being whole days and weeks alone, with only Kitty to come, in her bare feet, silently up the muddy path from the river, often bringing Nan a basket of berries, a string of fish, or a loaf of her own bread. Sometimes Kitty's bread was very good, just as it happened; at others, the yeast had gone bad, and Kitty had taken the chance of making good bread with bad yeast. The art of making yeast with potatoes and hops, being a process which needed careful calculation. She usually made biscuits with baking powder, thus saving herself trouble, and being less likely to raise the ire of her lordly white man.

Kitty would sit silently around on her heels for hours at a time, and Nan was very glad to have her.

Occasionally she had a fit of industry on, and would make a batch of bread, clean up the shack, wash some clothes, and do other things around. She even suggested to Nan that she would help her to dig up a patch of ground to plant potatoes in; but poor Nan seemed to have no energy for anything. Hope was dead within, and her young life a burden too heavy to be borne.

This was all very well till Ned came home one day, the worse for drink, and found his partner, who had come to look for Kitty, there. A fight ensued, and Ned threw both Kitty and her man out of the shanty, and gave Nan a good beating for having them there.

"Nice kind o' company yu keep," he sneered, "don't yer?" "I aint got no other," she replied, with her ragged apron to her eyes. "What decent white woman'd come wheer sech as yu be?"

"Look out," he growled, and raised his hand to strike her again. For once, Nan did not flinch, and like the coward that he was, the blow was stayed.

"I aint fit fer decent folk to come anigh. Look at me! An' niver another rag to my back, 'ceptin' what I'm got on."

"Well, heer's some money," and he threw down ungraciously a ten dollar bill, "Go an' git yerself suthin."

Ned earned plenty of money with his cordwood. The steamboats were regular customers and good pay. He spent it freely enough in town, on the same unworthy objects as his partner did, but he seemed to think that if he kept the shack supplied with tea, sugar and flour, his duty as provider ended there. If Nan wanted anything more, she could "raise chicken and garden truck," and supply herself.

Nan dragged on a miserable existence for a few months longer, then another little soul threatened to find its way into misery.

She could bear her isolated existence no longer, and without saying anything to Ned, she thought she would go and see if her mother would not be friends with her, and come and help her out, or perhaps let Polly come.

She pulled herself to the landing, from which she had eloped only two years before with Ned.

Any one who had seen her then, would not have recognised her now. She had sent Kitty to buy her some boots and a piece of woollen goods, with which she had made herself a dress. She wore the same hat and jacket in which she had left.

Having moored the boat, and stepped heavily out, she made her way to the old cabin home.

It was a palace to the place she had left it for. She went in and sat wearily down on the home-made settee. A brood of chickens occupied the floor, a weak pigling grunted comfortably from his straw in an Indian basket near the brightly burning stove, and she thought to herself, how much better cared for they were than she was.

The general air of comfort went to the poor exile's heart.

"Lord Nan! is thet you, I'lowed it were yer ghost come back," exclaimed Polly as she entered.

"I wish it was my ghost," said Nan sorrowfully, as she gazed upon the plump, strong girl before her.

"It's good fer yu, as Mare and Pare be gone to town. She's gone tu get suthin' fer his rheumatis, he kearnt du nothin' now.

"But I wanted ter see 'em so powerful bad. Kearnt yo say a good word fer me Polly! Yu kin see fer yerself, I'm most dead wi' hard treatment."

"I dunno. I hearn her say to Pare, when he wanted to go an' fetch yer hum, ef yu put fut inside heer she'd chuck yer in the river, an' be done of yer."

Nan began to cry, partly because her father had pleaded for her, and partly because of the hopelessness of it all.

Polly continued. "Don't yer know es folks heer been talkin' 'bout yer an' Kitty's man?"

Nan started up to speak, but Polly would have her say.

"They du be sayin' es how Ned ketched him to your place, an' most killed yer both. That was when Pare wanted ter get yer fetched away."

"Oh, Pare is good to me, he allest was. But thet's nothin fer Ned tu du. Kitty's man on'y come theer fer her; theer wasn't no harm in thet."

"Well, folks say es theer was, an' thet gels es is in sech a hurry to git married, an'll run off wi' one feller, aint perticeller 'bout another. Pare, he stuck up fer yer, but Mare said es she'd done wi' yer fer good an' all, an' yu ougther know Pare kearnt say much when Mare sets on, special now he kearnt du nothin' ef he would."

Nan got up without a word, and went back to her boat, her husband's camp and her old life. Only now the hope that her people might some day make up with her, was gone, and she had hoped, even more than she knew of, for a reconciliation.

If her mother had only seen her, she must have had some pity, for we know that there was more kindness in her composition than she owned up to; but everything had gone wrong with poor Nan, since her one misguided step, and she had neither the courage nor the strength to right herself; she could only suffer dumbly, and await she knew not what.

Polly, from purely selfish motives, never said that she (Nan) had been home, for she thought if Nan was allowed to come home again, there would naturally be less for her, and she had been out more, had more dress and less work since Nan went. Tryphosa had had to pay the Indians or half-breeds to dig plant and sow since her husband had become helpless, and a half-breed boy, whom she had adopted, paid dearly for his keep.

But Polly had still another motive. She had now a beau of her own, who was allowed to visit at the cabin. This young man brought very ill news of Ned, and spoke slightingly of Nan, for he had an eye to the future, and thought that a whole farm with Tryphosa's improvements, would be better than half.

"Wheer hev yu bin?" asked Ned angrily, as Nan came up from the boat.

"Down to hum."

"An' they turned yer out," he sneered.

"No they didn't. On'y Polly was theer, an' I come out myself."

"What fer?"

"Polly said I was no good; an' yer know, Ned, whativer mistake I made goin' off wi' yu, I niver did no wrong."

"I dunno anything 'bout it. Folks'll talk any way, 'specially when a gel is in sech a hurry to git married es tu run away wi' a feller."

"But it was yu over-persuaded me," she pleaded piteously, quite astonished that he should take the same stand as Polly had done.

"Yu didn't tek much persuadin'. Oh, yes, cry; I hate the sight o' yu, an' yer everlastin' cryin'." Nan turned and walked deliberately down to the water, intending to jump into the river, but Kitty met her there and told her that her man had gone to town, and she was coming to stay with her if Ned was not there.

"Never mind him, Kitty, I want yu, I'm sick. Come an' help me. You're the only one hes bin good to me"; and to Kitty's astonishment, the girl kissed her.

Ned remembered the last time, and without a word, went off and left the two women in possession.

Kitty brought in wood and water, made hot tea, and sat silently round for hours. Before morning a puny mite of a girl was born, and Nan hugged it to her with all her little strength, she was so heart-hungry for love.

"Oh, ef yu on'y grow up, I'll be so good tu yer, so good."

The squaw, squatting on her heels by the stove, shook her head as she heard these words, for she knew it would never grow up. Kitty stayed with Nan till her man came and fetched her away. Three whole days, the happiest in Nan's married life.

She lay in weakness, cuddling the almost inanimate babe to her breast, and drank deep draughts of that mother-love, which is the deepest and holiest of mortal passions opening up a world of possibilities to the woman who is content to rule only through her husband and children.

Women's rights outside that are only a need created by fallen manhood, which is apt to run to sensuality, and so to abuse the 'weaker vessel.' When manhood has learned self-control, there will be no necessity for any 'protection' for women; but, when that time arrives, the millenium will be at our door.

Kitty, the savage, left everything as handy for Nan as she could, although she puzzled herself greatly over the weakness of her white sister.

Had it been herself, she would have gone as she had done, into forest when her time came, prepared with a suffi-ciency of bandages, for the new arrival, and a papoose bas-ket. Could we have followed her, we should have seen her rest by a flowing brook or stream; then after she had washed the papoose in ice cold water, bandaged it to the resem-blance of a mummy, with nothing movable, but its large fawn-like eyes, she would strap the stiff little figure in its papoose basket, prop it up by some tree, and throw over it the woollen shawl, which all squaws wear over their heads and shoulders at any season of the year. Her only other gar-ment would likely be a short skirt. Out of this she would step, take a bath herself, resume the skirt, (and perhaps a kind of loose jacket besides), sling the papoose basket over her shoulders, keeping it in place by the prettily woven band of coloured grasses placed across her forehead, throw the shawl over her own head, thus enveloping the papoose, and swing back at a jog trot to her man's shack, in time to pre-pare his supper.

FRANCES E. HERRING

The only refreshment she would need, might be a hearty draught of the cold mountain water, and if she could get it, a pipe of tobacco between her teeth.

But why this tenas tecoup klootchman, (little white young woman), was as helpless as her babe Kitty could not understand.

Now began Nan's troubles. For two days no one came near her, and she had to get up and help herself. A fire was out of the question, she drank a little water, and ate a small piece of bread, which had been left, but she grew too weak to rise even for that.

When Ned came home on the third day, she was lying across the bed, where she had fallen after the last attempt.

"Well, you're a lazy varmint, sure!" was his greeting, "'stead o' gittin' up an' makin' suthin' tu eat an' drink. I'm a mind tu jest leave yer theer, till yer du git up."

His words fell upon unhearing ears. Before going away again, he went over to look at her, there was something in the silence, which struck even his dull sense.

"Looks mighty bad," he said to himself, and taking a flask from his pocket, he mixed some of its contents in a cup, and poured it down her throat.

Next day Kitty came, and stayed this time for a week. Poor Nan brightened up, and could get around with her weakly little baby by that time.

She was so cross and puling, Ned said he couldn't stay where it was. One night he came home in his usual condition, and as it cried and cried, every time Nan laid it down, to try and get him some supper, Ned gave it a smart slap, which almost sent it into convulsions. Nan caught up the sobbing babe, and running out into the bush, hid till morning.

Ned thought she had done down to Kitty's, and went after her, intending to show his authority; but, when Nan walked in next morning, saturated by the heavy dew, he could see she had been in the forest all night.

That day the baby died. Nan always thought it was from the effects of the blow, but Ned accused her of killing it, by taking it out into the bush.

Which ever way it was, Nan developed a terrible cough, and wasted almost to a skeleton.

Ned said, "Ef she wasn't coughin', she was cryin'; an' ef she wasn't cryin' she was coughin'." So he stayed home less than ever, and, but for Kitty, Nan would have starved.

"Git up an' git the breakfus yerself this mornin', Nan," he said roughly. "I'm done it offen enough."

"Theer's no wood an' no water," she said, between coughs, "an' it du rain powerful hard."

"Let her rain. You git up. I kearnt git no rest wi' thet infernal cough o' yourn, an' I aint goin' ter git up."

Nan went to the river for water, and was wet through when she returned. Trying to bring in wood she fell almost fainting.

She dragged herself back again, and laid down on the bed. "I kearnt do it, Ned," she said piteously, "Ef yer kill me, I kearnt."

With an oath, he sprang out of bed, saying, "You'll git yer own, you bet, or else, stay athout."

As he was going out of the door, Nan said feebly, "Send Kitty to me," but whether he heard or not, he took no notice, and no Kitty came.

There, alone, in weakness and misery, she lay all day, unable to help herself.

Towards evening her head began to wander, and when Kitty came in, she thought it was her father.

The squaw lighted a fire, gave her some tea, made her as comfortable as circumstances would permit, and then paddled off at her utmost speed to Nan's old home.

They were sitting down to supper as Kitty noiselessly opened and closed the door, only making her presence known by the gust of wind and rain which entered with her.

Luke looking up saw her first. "Nan!" he exclaimed, rising as quickly as his rheumatism would permit.

Kitty nodded.

"Papoose?" asked Tryphosa coolly.

Kitty nodded again, and said with a long, sadly drawn accent on the word, "Mam-a-lushe" (dead).

"Nan mam-a-lushe?" they all asked with a start.

"By and bye," returned Kitty. "Papoose mam-a-lushe."

"Is Nan dyin'?" gasped Luke.

Kitty nodded again.

He got his hat and an old military overcoat, and said decisively, "Come on, Mare."

"You kin go back 'ith Kitty. I'll git some things together. I dessay she'll git on alright 'ith Kitty. Polly an' me'll come arter. Them young pigs hes got ter come in to-night, or mebbe the sow'll eat 'em," and she proceeded leisurely with her supper.

Luke hobbled out into the pouring rain, followed by Kitty; and in her canoe, they quickly made their way back.

Nan knew him as he entered, and brightened right up.

"Yu'll git better my little gel," he said reassured. But she shook her head.

"What does the doctor say, my lad," he enquired, turning to Ned, who had come during Kitty's absence.

"Aint had no doctor, Boss," he returned sullenly.

"Best fetch en quick then, lad."

Ned slunk out, wishing he had stayed away; for this wife of his would 'stick' him for another forty or fifty dollars.

He paddled down with the swift current to town, went to a doctor, who was moving into the upper country by the morning's steamboat, and told something of Nan's case. The doctor promised to go ashore at the cordwood camp, if the boat would wait for him, and see what was the matter with Nan.

Luke made as if he would get up when the doctor arrived, some half-hour before the end, but she clung to his twisted fingers, with her poor emaciated hands, and he sat down again.

The doctor looked her over, and made short work of his diagnosis.

"Galloping consumption. Nothing can be done. Fifty dollars." And he was gone to catch his steamer.

Nan beckoned Kitty to kiss her; clung to her father for a moment, and became unconscious.

Her mother and Polly came in time to lay her out.

Looking scornfully at Ned, Tryphosa remarked, "I niver thought a gel o' mine'd live and die in a hole like this. Well I warned her. I warned her afore it was tu late."

They carried Nan's light form out and laid it in the general burying ground of the few white people and many Indians across the river, with its broken down fence, where the pigs from a neighbouring ranch disported themselves, and rooted to their heart's content, giving special attention to any newly-made grave.

But Nan was resting in peace with her children, who had gone before, with nothing to come between her and her mother-love.

Her time of trial had been short and sharp, but she had lived even beyond her lights. Her probation was over.

Happy Nan.

∽

Nan and Other Pioneer Women of the West (London: Frances Griffiths, 1913), 9–45.

FRANCES E. HERRING

The Canadian Short Story Library, Series 2

The revitalized Canadian Short Story Library undertakes to publish fiction of importance to a fuller appreciation of Canadian literary history and the developing Canadian tradition. Work by major writers that has fallen into obscurity will be restored to canonical significance, and short stories by writers of lapsed renown will be gathered in collections or appropriate anthologies.

John Moss
General Editor

New Women: Short Stories by Canadian Women, 1900–1920
Edited by Sandra Campbell and Lorraine McMullen

Voyages: Short Narratives of Susanna Moodie
Edited by John Thurston

Aspiring Women: Short Stories by Canadian Women, 1880–1900
Lorraine McMullen and Sandra Campbell

Pioneering Women: Short Stories by Canadian Women, Beginnings to 1880
Lorraine McMullen and Sandra Campbell

Le papier utilisé pour cette publication satisfait aux exigences minimales contenues
dans la norme American National Standard for Information Sciences -
Permanence of Paper for Printed Library Materials, ANSI Z39.48-1992.

Printed by
Ateliers Graphiques Marc Veilleux Inc.
Cap-Saint-Ignace (Québec)
in September 1993